DATE		

HER
FATHER'S
DAUGHTER

Other books by William J. Coughlin

No More Dreams
The Stalking Man
Day of Wrath
The Twelve Apostles

HER FATHER'S DAUGHTER

William J. Coughlin

G.P. Putnam's Sons
New York

G. P. Putnam's Sons
Publishers Since 1838
200 Madison Avenue
New York, NY 10016

Library of Congress Cataloging-in-Publication Data

Coughlin, William Jeremiah, date.
Her father's daughter.

I. Title.
PS3553.O78H4   1986   813'.54   85-25654
ISBN 0-399-13128-0

Printed in the United States of America
1 2 3 4 5 6 7 8 9 10

To my father

PART
ONE

PART
ONE

1

The restaurant was full, the tables occupied by the rich and those who hoped to become rich. It was a quiet place where conversations were private and laughter muted. A network anchorman dined one table away from a male movie star whose career was enjoying new life since he had become the lead in a nighttime soap opera. Both were in deep discussions with their respective agents. The waiters moved like shadows among the tables. It was a place for polite negotiations and the construction of deals.

"I think you can assume that we're interested." His was a typical banker's smile, wide and all teeth, but his eyes remained cold. "We need to know more about your security in order to protect our investment."

"It's not an investment, it's a loan."

His eyes seemed to lock with hers. But she was accustomed to dealing with bankers. She stared back, unintimidated.

He chuckled humorlessly. "Technically it is a loan, of course. But it really amounts to an investment. We'll be putting up the lion's share of the money. We'll make a profit if you do. And if you fail, we stand to lose at least that much of our cash that's unsecured. So, as you can see, it's not entirely remote from investing."

She glanced around the small, elegant restaurant. He was well known at Le Cirque, where he was provided his own table, one of the so-called power tables, a testament to his standing in the status-conscious New York community. He was relaxed and at home in the pale peach and mauve surroundings. Allowing him to choose the restaurant had been a tactical error. It tended to give him the upper hand.

Out on East Sixty-fifth Street the cold spring rain was still falling. The restaurant was warm and comfortable, but the weather outside nevertheless seemed to cast a depressing winter mood.

"Your proposed rate of interest is hardly designed to bankrupt you people," she said.

"We compute interest in proportion to the risk."

"So does the Mafia."

His irritating chuckle sounded again. "We tend to think we're better at it. Smoother, in a manner of speaking." His steely eyes boldly appraised her. He liked what he saw, a dark-haired young woman, fashionably and elegantly dressed, with a model's beauty and confident poise.

"I can get the money elsewhere."

He shrugged. "Perhaps, although I rather doubt it. If you could, I'm sure you wouldn't have gone to all this trouble. You're the one who brought all the participating banks together for this transaction. If you had another source I don't think you would have wasted all that effort."

She was aware that other diners were staring at her. Le Cirque was a restaurant patronized by presidents and royalty. But she was the main attraction today. Victoria Van Horn had purposely made herself a celebrity, the result of a careful and well-planned campaign. She didn't really enjoy the attendant public attention, but it was all part of the price of success. No important businessman or banker would have paid serious respect to her ideas otherwise. She would have been just another thirty-three-year-old woman—albeit damned attractive, but with no credentials, except those as the daughter of a famous and powerful man.

"We will provide the usual mortgage agreements and assignments of interest to protect you," she said. "This new development will be the most ambitious private project ever envisioned for the Hudson River. Apartment towers, office buildings, shops and a river mall. It will be stunning."

"I'm sure it will," he said without enthusiasm.

"Mortgages will protect your banks."

"We will need more," he replied quietly.

"You seem to know what you want, so name it."

His eyes appeared to narrow just slightly. "We will want a mortgage on your successful East Port project."

Victoria felt a chill, as if death itself had suddenly brushed her cheek. The East Port project had been the most important thing in her life.

She fought to control her fear, forcing herself to make a calm, measured reply. "There's a mortgage on it now. The Chase made the loan, as I'm sure you know."

He nodded. He was a handsome man in his early sixties, his dusty brown hair beginning to turn silver. Hours of tennis and golf in the sun had given his skin the texture of fine leather. "We know about the Chase. There's only a small amount owing. Nothing even approaching the overall value of that project of yours."

"You call sixty million small?"

He smiled. "Your East Port project is worth, we estimate, somewhere in the area of three hundred million. We'll pay off the Chase people and you can give us a mortgage to cover the money you wish to borrow for this new adventure."

She managed to conceal her panic. "I have poured my very life into that development. I'm not about to put it at risk."

"If I were in your position, Victoria, I wouldn't either." His smile was now almost conspiratorial. "You have accomplished miracles, my dear. And you have done it, I am led to understand, without one bit of help from your famous father. That makes your achievement all the more splendid. If I were you, I'd abandon this new plan of yours and enjoy life a little. God knows, you've certainly earned it."

She glimpsed her reflection in a distant wall mirror. She had selected the dark mauve Galanos suit, the cream-colored silk shirt and the Hermès scarf to make a statement, a visible declaration that she was a successful, capable and mature woman. But despite the exquisite clothes and the scant but artful application of makeup, she thought she still looked too young. Her youthful appearance had always been a definite liability. Men, important men, particularly her father, were reluctant to admit that an exquisite face could have anything of substance behind it. But she had shown them. She had shown him. And she was determined to continue to prove herself.

"If I do agree to mortgage East Port, what then?"

"We will need a personal assignment from you, putting up all your assets as collateral."

"My God, you don't want much, just everything I own!"

"And we will need the same from your business associates."

She again felt the sudden grip of panic, but she forced herself to respond calmly. "I can only bind myself. I have the support of some very substantial people; I doubt they would want to risk everything on this proposal, or on any single business venture, for that matter."

"Why do you need them?" he asked quietly.

"The more influential the people who will come in and participate, the greater the confidence and support from the business community. That was my secret in putting together the winning combination to build East Port. I needed them."

"That's right, you did need them. No one would have backed your idea if it hadn't been for your, ah, partners. But this is entirely different. You don't need anyone now. You have firmly established yourself, Victoria. You have built a formidable reputation very quickly. We would still provide the necessary financing if you decided to go it alone." He smiled. "I don't expect an answer right away. Think about it and get back to me tomorrow."

"That's very little time."

"Money is only profitable if it's working. It's absolutely worthless just lying around. We must invest it or loan it in order to make more money, Victoria. We are holding up certain commitments to see what you may choose to do. But we can't hold them forever. I speak for all the participating banks. We must have a decision quickly."

"I'll let you know by tomorrow afternoon."

"If you decide against it, we will certainly understand." Suddenly his professional smile faded. "I wonder if you'd mind a word of advice?"

"Go on." Her voice turned steely.

"Abandon this idea. You are very young, you have earned a massive fortune, and now, considerable fame. You're the envy of every woman in New York. You'll be risking everything. Even if you succeed at this new venture, it can hardly matter. You have more than sufficient money now. And if you don't succeed, if you lose, well, you will lose everything."

"Do you know how I got this fortune you speak of?"

"I read the *New York Times*, and the magazines." There was a mocking quality in his voice. "You're a lawyer who has had enormous success as a commercial developer. Hard work and persistence, or so the articles report."

She was enraged at his pompous and patronizing attitude. She spoke calmly, but her words were sharp and cold. "I have everything because I am willing to take a risk."

He sighed and signaled the waiter. "Check, please, Henri." He then turned to her. "You make up your own mind, my dear," he said softly. "But remember, Victoria, even the best gambler can roll those dice once too often."

Policemen saluted his black limousine as it passed. Ira Larson was secretary of transportation, a cabinet officer, and the citizens of Washington, D.C., were always careful to show respect for high-ranking officials. A cardinal, as a prince of the church, when in Vatican City was treated accordingly. Larson, not unlike a cardinal, was a prince of the government and in the nation's capital was elevated to something approaching royal status, a circumstance he very much enjoyed.

They drove past rows of huge limestone buildings, squat and fortresslike, where hordes of federal employees toiled at a variety of tasks, trying to keep the vast federal government functioning.

At the White House the guards were deferential. They knew him, and his arrival was scheduled. They merely glanced into the limousine, then saluted as they motioned the big car through the gate.

Larson was greeted by a young assistant who escorted him into the White House executive offices. This was the heart of the government, the hub of all power, and Larson had never been quite comfortable here. No one here was impressed by a cabinet officer. In these rooms he was merely another federal employee.

He was guided into the office of Roy Barclay, the White House chief of staff. Barclay was on the telephone and motioned Larson to sit down. Larson, who had been a governor of a western state before joining the cabinet, did not like Barclay. To him Barclay was a typical Easterner, smooth, cold, with a ruthlessness barely concealed beneath a thin veneer of Boston-bred and accentuated politeness.

Barclay seemed to avoid eye contact as he grunted responses into the telephone. Roy Barclay was tall, angular and just forty, though his thinning hair made him appear older. He was coatless, his shirt sleeves rolled up, his collar open and his tie loose.

Ira Larson thought his manner of dress inappropriate. As White House chief of staff, Barclay directed the full force of presidential power. He looked more like a harassed real estate salesman than the man who ran the highest-level operation of the vast federal system.

The office was as unimpressive as its occupant. Papers were stacked in messy bundles. Books, magazines and newspapers added to the overall impression of careless clutter. One picture, of Barclay and the President, hung on the wall. The only other decoration was a calendar.

Barclay snapped a curt command into the telephone and then hung up. He swung around to face his visitor. "You're looking well, Ira."

Larson shrugged. "I feel fine. I work out. I jog. I try to stay in shape."

Barclay nodded. "No more problems with the heart?"

"Roy, that was five years ago. It's past history. I'm in the best of health." He paused. "I'm sure you didn't call me all the way over here just to inquire about my health. What's up?"

Larson found Barclay's unexpressive face irritating. He could never tell what the man was thinking. Barclay smiled infrequently, and Larson had never seen him laugh.

Barclay reached into a file perched on top of a pile of reports. He extracted a paper and handed it to Larson. "Do you remember this? It's a copy of the original."

Larson glanced at it. "Sure. It's my undated letter of resignation. Every cabinet officer signed one. Why?"

"Take a closer look. It's been dated."

"What!" Larson looked at the upper right corner of the letter. The next day's date had been typed in. "What the hell is this?"

Barclay picked up a well-chewed pipe. He no longer smoked, but he used the pipe as a convenient prop, something to occupy his hands. He pointed it at Larson. "You have two options, Ira. You can leave government entirely, that's one choice. However, the President likes you and he wants to name you ambassador to Portugal. That's your other option. There is a vacancy."

Larson's features reddened in anger. "What the hell are you telling me, Roy? That I'm out as secretary of transportation? Just like that? Well, you can't do it. I won't stand for it!"

Barclay's bland expression never changed. "You have resigned, Ira. If you don't believe me, there's your letter. Look, I'm busy this morning. If you want the Portugal thing, we'll nominate you and keep you on as transportation secretary until the Senate clears you for appointment. Understand, however, that it will be in name only. You won't be running the department anymore."

Ira Larson had been a politician most of his adult life. He had been a lawyer in the West who had clawed his way to the governorship. The cabinet job had been even more difficult to obtain. He was a fighter, but he was also a practical man.

"What the hell have I done?" he asked quietly. "If there's some kind of scandal brewing, I don't know of it. Look, if I've fucked up, then you're correct to throw me out. But I've been doing my job, and pretty damn well too. People say I'm one of the best transportation secretaries in years."

"Not everyone," Barclay replied, idly tapping the pipe stem against his teeth.

"Everybody is bound to make a few enemies, Roy, especially if they do their job right. You can't please everyone."

"I asked you not to withhold that road money from New York, didn't I?" Barclay spoke quietly. "It was a direct order to you. Do you remember? I made the call myself."

Larson shifted uncomfortably in his chair. "Is that what this is all about? Good God, I was just using that money to force New York City into complying with our regulations. The sons of bitches have been absolutely unreasonable."

"Unreasonable or not, you disregarded a direct order from the White House."

"Hey, I have to have some freedom to run my own department."

Barclay slowly shook his head. "Not this time. That order was important, Ira. Anyway, the matter is no longer open to debate. The President says you're through. Do you want the ambassadorship or not?"

"This whole thing is crazy. I want to talk to the man himself."

"You know how he hates confrontations. He's at Camp David. These things are part of my job. You've made a mistake, Ira, a beaut. Now what about it, do you want to go to Portugal?"

Larson felt a trickle of sweat roll down his back. "You don't give me a hell of a lot of choice. If that's the only way, Jesus, I'll go to Portugal."

Barclay nodded. "Good. It's a delightful country. Balmy climate, you'll love it. In the meantime you'll retain your title, salary and office, but no power. Frank Cook, your deputy, will run the Transportation Department until the Senate clears you. I'm busy this morning, Ira, so I'll have to ask you to leave."

Larson could feel himself shaking but managed to control his rage. "This really stinks, Roy, but I'm sure you already know that."

Barclay looked up. "You brought it on yourself, Ira. You stepped on the wrong toes."

"Whose toes, for Chrisakes! Whose goddamned toes are so big they can get a cabinet member fired just like that?" His angry words echoed throughout the cluttered office.

"The Vault," Barclay replied softly.

"What the hell is the Vault?" Larson shouted.

Barclay pulled out another file, as if dismissing Larson. He looked up again. "It's not a 'what,' Ira. The proper question is who."

"All right then, who is the Vault?"

Barclay studied the file before him. "Ira, I'm busy. Like the old Irish bartender used to say, don't let the door hit you in the ass on your way out." Barclay buzzed for a secretary. "And don't worry about the public relations stuff, Ira. We'll handle all that." He gently tapped the pipe against the side of his cheek. "You'll love Portugal, Ira."

Lucas Shaw was forty years old and in robust health. He played squash and swam on a regular schedule, but like many New Yorkers, walking was the exercise he most enjoyed.

And despite the well-proclaimed dangers, walking was the most convenient mode of transport in Manhattan. The subways were too dangerous, at least at times. Taxis, buses and all other forms of ground transport seemed forever caught up and jammed together in horn-blaring frustration. And walking provided the opportunity to see the people of New York, a rich mixture of all races, classes and types, a moving blend of humankind imparting a vital and throbbing sense of life.

In addition, walking was good exercise. Manhattan women, in Luke Shaw's opinion, had a just claim to having the best legs in the world.

But there were some areas where a pedestrian was considered easy prey. New Yorkers knew these dangerous grounds and avoided them. Only tourists, or people willing to take enormous chances to obtain illicit forms of pleasure or profit, risked penetrating those sinister zones.

Shaw waited for the light to change, then crossed to the other side of Fifth Avenue, moving in a throng of marching people headed toward an equally compressed throng coming from the opposite curb, looking like two armies about to clash. As if by magic, not unlike cards shuffled in a deck, the two converging masses passed through each other with a minimum of bodily contact.

There were techniques to walking in Manhattan. Shaw, like everyone else, avoided direct eye contact. Looking directly into another person's eyes could be interpreted as an invitation to anything from a sexual advance to permission to beg. All real Manhattanites, unless looking for sex or a handout, moved at a brisk clip, striding purposefully, even if they had no purpose, their eyes everywhere except on other eyes. Muggers, bums and bag ladies considered a quickly moving man or woman a poor target—a stroller was much easier. Therefore, a brisk stride was protection, a barrier to any personal contact in an impersonal city.

The last of the rush-hour crush was beginning to ebb, the crowds dispersing somewhat, the street traffic beginning to make a slow kind of progress to the accompaniment of a cacophony of multitoned horns.

Shaw strode along Fifth Avenue, then turned right on Fifty-seventh Street. He enjoyed the sights, sounds and smells of the city as he passed art galleries, boutiques and restaurants. Although it was officially springtime, winter refused to give up, sending a chill damp wind swirling down the concrete canyons.

Shaw nodded to the doorman at the Oseola Club as he bounded up the stairs to the ornately carved wooden doors of the entrance. One of the oldest men's clubs in the city, the Oseola was a relic, a ghost from the age of gaslights and horse-drawn carriages. The club's townhouse quarters seemed almost hidden amid the elegant restaurants and chic European shops. Only a small, polished brass plate alongside the door proclaimed the club's existence.

Martin, known to all only by that name, waited to greet him. The elderly black man wore spotless white gloves. His uniform hung loosely on his thin form. He smiled, almost gently, as though the expression might tire him.

"Mr. Shaw"—Martin was always precise and formal—"your father is waiting for you in the main lounge."

Luke Shaw slipped out of his topcoat. Martin received it solemnly, as though it were a rare and ancient vestment that needed to be carefully handled and guarded.

When possible, Luke Shaw had dinner with his father once a week. It was always at the Oseola, his father's club and permanent home. Shaw passed by the tall brass artillery shell inscribed with the names of the club members who had volunteered in the Spanish-American War. The names were all familiar, a roll call of New York's finest families. A similar but far more pretentious memorial, celebrating the members' contributions in the Civil War, had a place of honor in the club's main meeting room. Later wars were similarly noted, but, reflecting the passage of time, the names were fewer. There was nothing to note the Vietnam War, no salute to men, like himself, who had served there. It was as if it were too recent to be acknowledged. The membership had aged over the years and had thinned; the sons, for the most part, showed no special interest in maintaining a membership. The Oseola was no place for youth. The Oseola Club looked more like a theatrical set for a Victorian play than a place where busy gentlemen might meet to discuss the affairs of the day. The club was no longer a place for busy men.

Luke Shaw nodded to a very elderly gentleman who hobbled by on a worn cane. The man's family had once commanded a commercial seagoing fleet, but their name was no longer associated with active commerce.

Shaw passed by the huge oil painting of New York as seen from the Statue of Liberty. It was a gaudy oil, depicting the city before the glittering skyscrapers took over. It was a winter scene, the city teeming with life, the Hudson busy with steamboat traffic.

He glanced at himself in the full-length mirror near the wide mahogany staircase. A touch over six feet, and heavily muscled, he looked lean in his carefully tailored clothing. His hair was thick and dark. He wasn't handsome, not in the classic sense, but he had strong features and a rugged look more associated with life outdoors than with his position as the chief executive of one of America's largest construction engineering firms. His face testified to years spent as a working engineer, his skin toughened—baked or frozen—according to the demands of various jobs and climates.

Shaw climbed the stairs quickly and easily. His father was seated in a large, deep leather armchair, engrossed in reading a book. He sensed movement near him and looked up.

"Well, Luke, how are you?" His father closed the book and slowly stood up. He was almost as tall as his son, but much thinner and stooped. Forty years and, in some ways, a great deal more separated them.

"You're looking well, father," Luke replied. It was a gentle lie. His father, like an old photograph, seemed to be progressively fading. There was nothing physically wrong, not as far as Luke knew, but each time they met, somehow his father seemed smaller, older, more shrunken.

"Ready for dinner, Luke, or would you like a drink?" the older man asked.

"I have a meeting later. If you don't mind, let's have a drink at the table."

His father chuckled. "I don't mind. You seem to have become much busier since your elevation to membership in the Vault."

Both men knew what being a member of the Vault meant. It apparently was a sore point with his father. Despite his superb education and privileged background, his father had never achieved anything of note in his life, and thus hadn't even been considered for Vault membership. From the beginning, Preston Shaw, who had enough money to live comfortably, had chosen to spend his life among the shadows of the past. Luke Shaw hoped that his being chosen for membership in the Vault hadn't made his father regret that choice which had effectively denied himself the chance.

Luke knew the club's familiar menu routine. Monday was veal. The club's menu never varied. As usual, his father selected the veal. Luke ordered bourbon, his father asked for a sherry.

Their waiter, also black and almost as old as Martin, moved slowly away as if on painful legs.

"You're fast becoming my only contact with the outside world, Luke. In addition to the evening television news, of course, and the *Times*.

What's happening in our fair city? Or, I should say, your fair city. You people in the Vault run the damn place." He tapped a finger against the table. "And lately you've been doing a rather poor job of it."

Luke laughed. "I've only been a member of the Vault for a few months, father. Just since Uncle Cy died. You can't blame everything on me. At least not for a while."

His father snorted. "Your mother's brother was an old pog, but I'm sure you know that."

They had been over this ground often before. "Cyrus Alger was a homosexual," Luke replied quietly. "But his sexual preference certainly didn't interfere with his effectiveness. He built the family business into a national giant."

His father slowly nodded. "He was a tough customer, your uncle. He accomplished a great deal, I'll admit, but I never liked him. He was the maverick of your mother's family. And I don't mean just his faggotry—if there is such a word—he was always so driving, so intense. He was never a gentleman, never in the true sense of that word, anyway."

Luke was about to reply, but his father held up a thin hand. "Enough about dead people," he said. "Now tell me about the Vault." Preston Shaw smiled. "What's going on there, or do you people swear some blood oath of secrecy?"

His son laughed. "There's no oath. To hear you tell it, we're a sinister committee not only running the world but setting subway fares and collecting city taxes. The Vault has no hand in running this city, at least in no direct way."

Preston Shaw scowled. "Oh no? God knows I've tried to educate you, Lucas. I may have failed, but at least I made the attempt."

Luke took the bourbon from the waiter and waited until his father was served. "Good health," he said, raising his glass.

His father's blue eyes were nearly translucent, his most remarkable feature in an otherwise rather ordinary face. "At my age, good health could turn out to be a curse. I shouldn't wish to live forever." Preston Shaw sipped his sherry. "I would hate to end my days in some hotsy-totsy nursing home, gulping tapioca and having my damn diapers changed. I'm not ready for that just yet, although that is indeed the fate that has befallen several of my acquaintances. The choice isn't mine; suicide is for poor people. I can only hope to expire from something quick, painless and, if I'm lucky, elegant."

"Let's not get into morbid subjects at dinner," his son interjected.

"That old faggot, your uncle, went out in style. Slipped on the ice, broke a hip, and pneumonia carried him off to wherever fairies go when they die. Quick and efficient, so like him, really."

"Cyrus was almost ninety."

"And in good health, right to the last. Anyway, if genes really do count for anything, you should enjoy a long and active life."

Luke laughed. "Uncle Cy was a fine man. You just refuse to admit it."

His father merely arched an eyebrow in reply. "By the way, have you heard from Barbara?"

He knew his father would bring her up, he always did. "It's the same as always. She calls about twice a month from Boston to let me know how Jason is coming along. We're friendly, as you know." There was a guarded shade of wariness in his voice.

"If you were such good friends, why did you get divorced?"

Luke knew his father liked and approved of his ex-wife. "For starters, Barbara fell in love with another man. That's usually sufficient reason for divorce, isn't it?"

Preston Shaw sipped again at his sherry. "Not in my day, son. Those affairs only last for a couple of months. Barbara's family is as distinguished as our own. You could have looked the other way for a while."

"I was away for months in Saudi Arabia on company business. I was seldom home. She wanted a divorce. We just drifted apart. It really didn't bother me when she filed, as you're well aware."

His father sighed. "Society is breaking down, I'm afraid. Soon we'll be nothing but howling savages. The old rules were there for a purpose."

"I know, father. Anyway, it's over and done with. There's no calling it back, so let's drop it, shall we?"

"Please don't think this indelicate, Lucas, but do you have a girlfriend presently?"

Luke sighed. "The same one as last week," he answered, smiling.

"That Foster girl? Amy Foster's grandchild?"

"The very same."

"The Fosters are good people. I knew Amy quite well, she was a close friend of your mother's. Are you planning to get married?"

Luke shook his head. He had been asked the same question the previous week. "No, there are no marriage plans. She has a demanding career, as do I. At the moment it's not convenient for either of us. We're really not serious about each other anyway."

His father seemed to become slightly agitated. "Luke," he said, in a tone of voice that had subtly changed. "It's most urgent that you make a good marriage now."

His sudden urgency was startling.

"Why, father?"

"You're a member of the Vault now. For almost two centuries the members of the Vault have looked after this town, and the interests of the founding families. You are one of eight men who actually run this city and protect all of us, our businesses, our interests, and even our charities."

"No one mentioned marriage to me as a criterion for membership. I rather doubt that anyone at the Vault really attaches much importance to my being married or not." Luke sounded decidedly defensive.

"After your mother's death, your uncle saw to your early schooling. I should have, I suppose, but he did a very good job, so I saw no reason to interfere. You chose engineering, and that dismal little midwestern college. But after you joined the family business, Cyrus brought you along and trained you to take over. And, again, he did a good job. Unfortunately, I really have had little input into your life, Lucas."

"More than you know."

"No. You regard me as some kind of wizened old ancestor-worshipper, existing only to kowtow to the ghosts of the past, to perpetuate a sense of meaningless history. Don't deny it. We both know, of course, that you're absolutely right. I am all of those things. I am a creature of my class, in some ways, a captive. The point is, Lucas, so are you. You will need a son to someday take your place on the Vault."

"I have Jason."

The old man slowly shook his head. "Nice boy, but he's hardly yours. Blood, yes, but that's about all. He is being brought up in Boston by some middle-class college professor."

"Harvard."

"I don't care if it's Oxford, Cambridge or the Sorbonne. You should be the one overseeing Jason's development. He should be carefully brought along, as you were, to take command one day. And not only of the business. The seat on the Vault goes to one of our family members, unless, of course, the line has died out or there is no suitable successor. To be brutally realistic, Jason is fated to be a nice middle-class lad in a middle-class world. He will have no comprehension of our situation or responsibilities. Since Jason is not being groomed to take over, you need to start a new line. You need an heir, not only for the business but especially for the Vault."

"You attach too much importance to the Vault, father."

"And you attach too little." His father paused for a moment before continuing. "You fail to realize, Luke, that the Vault keeps us all from being devoured by the raging tides of social change. It always has. You eight stand as our guardians."

"Come now, father, it's hardly more than an elite social club, like the Oseola."

Preston Shaw frowned. "It's much more than that."

"I rather doubt that."

"Luke, social considerations can shape history. Cities have had groups like the Vault since the beginning of time. I've made a study of them, from the ancient city-states of Italy to modern London. The past teaches us that a city, no matter how large, is only as good as the people who lead it. And I mean the real leaders, not just the ceremonial frontmen. You, Lucas, as a member of the Vault, are one of New York's real leaders. And it is vital that you eventually prepare someone to take your place."

Luke smiled wryly. "I rather doubt that the mayor would agree with that assessment."

His father's eyes narrowed slightly. "What do you suppose would happen if right now you called the mayor's office?"

Luke shrugged. "I'd probably get switched to a secretary or some young assistant, why?"

Preston Shaw shook his head in disagreement. "No. The mayor and his key people know exactly who you are, and what you are. The mayor himself would be on the telephone instantly as soon as you had been identified. You have enormous power, my son. How very odd that you're not even aware of it."

The waiter unobtrusively served their meal. His father merely picked at his food, then asked the waiter for another glass of sherry. He seemed tense, almost agitated. "I really can't blame you for being skeptical. You've endured my theories and abstract lectures for years. I suppose you can't be expected to believe that what I'm telling you now is not merely abstract but quite real, and I might add, quite serious."

Luke only shrugged in response.

His father's blue eyes flickered with intensity. "Hunter Van Horn is head of the Vault, correct?"

Luke nodded.

"I know his opinion would carry great weight with you. Sit down with Hunter. Ask some questions. He'll be candid, I'm sure. You may just discover that you are privy to a whole new world."

"Hunter is a very busy man."

"I know all about Hunter Van Horn," his father replied, a slightly withering tone creeping in. "As I said, I do read the *Times*. And I not only read about him, but about that pushy daughter of his, too. She seems to be in the newspapers almost every other day. I imagine she's quite an embarrassment to him."

"If she is, he doesn't show it."

"Too bad she wasn't born a male. A lawyer, a successful real estate developer. Do you know her?"

"I met her once, at a United Nations reception. Quite a good-looking lady."

"Her mother was a Magnusson. Bad strain in that family, at least in the women."

Luke was amused. "How so?"

His father's agitation seemed to fade. The history of New York's families was safer and more familiar ground. "Passionate lot, the Magnusson women. General Dan Sickles, that old fraud, had an affair with one of them."

"That was during the Civil War. Sickles was a Union general."

"Before the war, actually. Sickles was a great ladies' man, so they say. One of the Magnusson women made quite a fool of herself. Runs in the family. No discretion when it comes to men."

"Father, for God's sake, that was well over a hundred years ago."

"Makes no difference. Blood is blood. Otherwise, a very fine family, good connections. I believe Hunter divorced the girl's mother, correct?"

"Hunter Van Horn has been married several times, at least as far as I know."

"Strange, isn't it, how blood will tell? I suppose someone should have warned Hunter about the Magnusson women." His father paused as if lost in thought, then continued. "You know, that reminds me of a similar strain in the women of the royal line of Serbia. Did I ever tell you about them? Interesting people, every damn one of them."

Luke folded his napkin and placed it on the table. "Father, I hate to eat and run, but I do have an important meeting this evening. Perhaps another time?"

His father nodded. "How was your meal? I swear this veal becomes increasingly more tasteless. Of course, the chef is getting old. Perhaps that's the explanation." His eyes followed his son as Luke stood up. "Will I see you next week?"

"Of course, father."

His father remained seated but extended his hand. "Remember what I said. Talk to Hunter Van Horn." Then he smiled. "But watch out for that daughter of his. She's a Magnusson. She could prove to be quite a handful."

Luke laughed. "I think you're trying to get me interested. Anyway, I really have to go. I'll see you next week."

Luke left the oak-paneled dining room and hurried down the wide staircase. He genuinely liked and respected his father but felt Preston Shaw was mistaken about the Vault. He considered his own membership as nothing more than just another community duty. But should he take the time to talk to Hunter Van Horn? He instantly dismissed the thought as ridiculous. No group had the kind of power his father attributed to the Vault.

He retrieved his coat from Martin then hurried out onto Fifty-seventh Street to look for a taxi.

2

It had been a long day and Hunter Van Horn, Jr., was glad to be home. His wife glared up at him as he walked into the living room of their apartment.

"Your bitch of a sister has her picture in another magazine." She snapped at him as if somehow that was his fault.

"Oh?"

"She'll end up as a centerfold yet, mark my words. She's publicity-mad. One of these days the whole country will be treated to a view of her crotch, wait and see!"

He sighed. He considered his sister and his wife very much alike. They even looked alike. They were about the same age. Both were beautiful, both aggressive. But his sister had a knack for making money, while his wife had a definite knack for spending it. From the beginning, his wife had always disliked Victoria.

"Which magazine?" he asked.

"*People,*" his wife said sharply. "Last week she was in *Newsweek.*"

"I remember," he said, lightly kissing her lips. He detected a slight odor of alcohol. She knew he disapproved of her drinking.

"Junior, something has to be done about her. She's disgracing the Van Horn family."

A large framed photograph of his father seemed to stare down at him from above the mantle. Although people called him "Junior," he knew that he looked nothing like his famous father. In school there had even been cruel jokes. And as time had gone on, he had found himself to be much different from his father in many other ways. He wondered if there might be some truth to the giggles. Perhaps he was another man's son.

The maid served his tea. He always took tea before dinner; it was as close to a cocktail as he cared to get. His wife continued to glare at him.

"Our friends are laughing at us, I hope you realize that. The entire Van Horn family has to bear the shame of that damned sister of yours."

He sipped his tea. It was just the way he liked it, not too hot.

"No one is laughing," he replied quietly. "My sister Victoria may be a trifle flamboyant in business, but she has made quite a success of herself. Believe me, Cecelia, no one laughs at success."

"Your father should do something about this."

"My father, I would imagine, is secretly delighted by what she has accomplished. I think he's always hoped I'd do something similar."

"Why don't you?"

He looked directly at his wife. "I don't have to, Cecelia. It's as simple as that. I am president of Demas Industries, one of father's subsidiary companies. I bear his name, and in due course, I expect to take his place."

"Suppose you don't?"

"Don't what?"

"Take his place."

He smiled slowly. "My only rival is my lovely younger sister. She hasn't spoken to father in years. They are actually very much alike, the two of them, but they just can't get along. Which is fortunate for me. I merely have to avoid scandal, make sure my company doesn't lose too much money and wait."

"Maybe you'll wait too long."

He sighed again. She was exceptionally beautiful, at least on the surface. Beneath, there was basically nothing, no real substance. She had only one main interest in life, herself. And lately that had seemed to have become her full-time job. As soon as the children had grown old enough, she had packed them off to school. She no longer had to keep up a front as dutiful mother, a role that had always been strange to her. She was free now to focus all her attention solely upon herself.

"Victoria will be in the news for years to come," he said. "You might as well get used to it, Cecelia. I have long ago."

"You make it sound as though you two were close. You don't talk to her either."

"She is much younger than I. We never really had much in common. She was just a brat who always seemed to get in the way when we were growing up. Rather ugly then, as I recall. I suppose it's a tribute to the Van Horn genes that she has blossomed into such an attractive woman."

"I think you have the hots for her." She snorted. "Your own sister! No wonder you're strange."

Evidently she had had more to drink than he had first suspected. It usually took a healthy amount of alcohol to loosen her tongue to the point where she would refer to the sexual tension that existed between them.

"Incest has never been one of my weaknesses," he said quietly. "As a matter of fact, I have always found Victoria to be a bit repulsive. I think she's a bit too much like my beloved father." He mockingly raised his teacup in a salute to the picture above the mantle.

"They say she's fucked everybody in town."

His wife's language always deteriorated in direct proportion to the amount of liquor she had consumed. He looked at her, seeing her objectively. The beauty was still there, but soon all the expensive creams and ointments in the world wouldn't protect her skin against her mania for following the sun. The hint of severe lines showed at the corners of her lips and eyes. She would eventually be a hard-looking woman; her face was already beginning to reflect the sourness within her.

"Anyone who's in the public eye has to expect rumors like that," he said.

"Well, if she is laying everyone in town, she's more like your father than . . ."

"Than myself?"

She looked away.

Their early married life had been exuberantly sexual. But that had quickly ebbed, and now he found himself without any sexual drive. Surprisingly, his almost neuter condition seemed to him to be pleasantly peaceful. She had taken lovers, he knew that. As long as she was discreet, he didn't really care. But she apparently was still bitter that he no longer desired her. They occupied separate bedrooms in their luxury apartment. It was an arrangement he preferred.

"My father has always been a ladies' man," he said evenly. "I understand, despite his age, he still is. My mother knew all about it. She tolerated it for as long as she could before leaving him." He looked up at the picture. "He's quite handsome, you must admit, even now. That, plus his enormous fortune, seems to make him quite irresistible to women. I am led to believe he's always taken full advantage of it."

"And now your sister is doing the same thing."

His laugh was without humor. "I honestly don't give a damn what she does or doesn't do. She is as far removed from me as a Tibetan monk. We may both reside in New York, but we live in entirely different worlds."

"Your world seems different from everyone else's."

He picked up the television remote-control device. "Let's not argue any further, Cecelia," he said evenly. "You're no different than I. You're waiting too. You'd divorce me in a second if it weren't for that. One day I will inherit my father's kingdom and ascend to his corporate throne. I shall become a member of the Vault. And I will reign for many happy years. You want to be my queen, and you're willing to pay almost any price to obtain that. So, you see, we are both waiting, only I seem to be the more patient."

He snapped the television set to life, and the face of a newscaster came into view.

She stood up. "Well, tonight you can wait alone. I've been invited to a party."

He turned up the audio. The newsman was earnestly reporting on some minor occurrence in central Asia.

"Have a good time, Cecelia," he said.

She glared at him. "Go fuck yourself," she snapped as she flounced out of the room.

———————————

The shuttle flight from Washington was like a short bus ride. Randolph Johnson glanced out of the window as they started the approach into La Guardia. The aircraft was flying a few hundred feet over seemingly endless acres of cemeteries.

"If I were you, Barry, I wouldn't vote on that tax bill. Shit, no matter which way you go, it'll be wrong. Fuck 'em. Take a trip when the thing comes up for a vote. Set up a subcommittee hearing, anything, only be sure you're out of town. Don't get your ass recorded on that issue, or you'll pay for it next year if you do run for the Senate."

Congressman Barry Lytle looked over at his seatmate. They were both congressmen. Lytle represented a so-called silk stocking district just outside the city, while Randolph Johnson had been elected from a very tough area of the Bronx. They were, on the surface, as different as two people could be. Lytle was white, Harvard-educated, Republican, wealthy and physically slight. Johnson was black, a Democrat, working hard at becoming wealthy, and extremely large—both in height and weight. Yet, despite their differences, they had become fast friends, sharing a preference for reckless living, good-looking women and expensive liquor. Both men enjoyed Congress, both relished the deferential status bestowed upon them by the paid personnel of Capitol Hill.

Lytle grinned. "Do you think I'd duck an important roll call merely for political reasons?"

Johnson chuckled, a sound not unlike distant rumbling thunder. "You bet your ass you would. Your daddy's money might have gotten you into office, but your own smarts is what has kept you there. Hell, you may be a candy-assed aristocrat, but you're just as fast on your feet as any of us poor boys."

The airplane flew lower, now over open water, seeking the airport's landing apron that jutted out into the bay.

"Can you deliver your district if I run for Senate?"

The chuckle turned into a throaty laugh. "Shit, ain't none of my people goin' to vote for a honky like you. We had a Republican in my part of the Bronx once, but he moved. So don't go lookin' for any positive help from me, Barry. I'll be right there in the front line attacking your Republican ass, and you know it."

"I need help, not political suicide."

"Look, if you get nominated, and if it looks like you got half a chance, I can pass the word that you're the lesser of two evils. Some of my people, especially my financial people," he winked, "will get the word."

"Money really isn't what I need."

"Goddamn it, Barry, don't I know that? You got unlimited funds. Fuck, you need money the way a drowning man needs water. But I'll tell you who will need money, and lots of it."

"Who?"

"Don't play with me. Any one of those Democratic assholes who are going to run against you. They'll need every dime they can raise just to stay in the game with you. I can choke off most of the help coming out of my district. It ain't much, not in the general scheme of things maybe. But, for what it's worth, I can keep your opponent, whoever it is, from getting any black bucks, in a manner of speaking."

"And what will you want for all this negative assistance?"

The chuckle returned, this time more quiet, sounding almost sinister. "We'll talk if you get nominated. Hell, we were both trained in Congress. If we can't bargain, no one can. I'll think of something. You can count on it."

Their aircraft rolled toward the landing gate.

"Barry, no offense, but I got some of the brothers from one of the churches in my district meeting the plane." His wide, shiny face split into a grin. "We'll get off separate, if you don't mind. It wouldn't look good to my brethren if I was seen hobnobbing with a candy-ass honky. Especially one whose father is a member of the Vault."

"How do you, ah, happen to know about the Vault?"

"Are you surprised that an old nigger like me knows about your secret organization? Hell, for centuries we figured there was a group of white men somewhere fuckin' us over. We know all about the Vault now. Your old man and his friends run things here." He stood up, then smiled down at Lytle. "But don't get me wrong. I don't bear no grudges. Listen, I don't give a shit what they do, just as long as I get mine. Dig?"

Lytle laughed.

"Take it easy, Barry. Watch out for them strange sexual diseases. I'll see you back on the Hill on Monday."

Lytle kept his seat as he watched Congressman Johnson struggle forward with the other passengers. Lytle usually waited until everyone was out anyway. He detested having to push and shove through crowds. And there was no hurry, no one would be waiting for him. His father had offered to send the limousine, but he had declined, saying a taxi would be more convenient. It wasn't more convenient, but he wanted minimal contact with his father, and somehow that seemed to extend even to the family car and driver.

A lifetime battle to escape the dominance of his father had accomplished nothing, ironically, except to draw him even closer to the power of his famous and distinguished parent.

In the line waiting for cabs several women eyed him admiringly. Always dapper and stylish, Barry Lytle had been told that he was considered handsome and sexually attractive. He was aware that he had a easy boyish charm that seemed devastating to women of every age. He smiled back and was delighted at the women's obvious flush of pleasure.

He waited in line with the others until it was his turn. The seemingly endless procession of waiting taxis moved up, and Lytle climbed into one.

"The Von Kalt Bank and Trust Building," he said to the driver. A Hispanic face stared back at him from the photo attached to the license that hung over the glove compartment. "That's just off Wall Street at . . ."

"Hey, do I tell you your business?" The driver turned and glared at him. The mustache was thicker than in the photo, and although he had Hispanic features, the harshness and inflection of his voice was pure, native New Yorker. "The tunnel or the bridge?"

"The tunnel."

"Good choice." The driver tried to make conversation as they drove, but Lytle's grunts signaled that he wanted to be left alone. He focused on the skyline of Manhattan as they sped along the expressway toward the city.

His father, Stewart Lytle, had controlled his life, carefully choosing his schools from nursery to Harvard law. Only when he was in the Navy, serving as a supply officer in Japan during the Korean War, did Barry Lytle feel really free of his father. He found out later that the supply post too had been carefully arranged.

The family business, dating all the way back to their original ancestors, had become the powerful investment banking firm of Perry Stanley. And although his father had served for a short time as ambassador to Spain, otherwise he had been in charge of the family's firm for most of his adult life. Surprisingly, the elder Lytle had not objected to his son's desire to stay out of banking, even endorsing his decision to enter politics. It wasn't until his second term in the House of Representatives that Barry Lytle realized his father was carefully chartering a course for him that would eventually lead to the White House itself. And once again he found himself completely dependent upon his father's will and determination.

Private polls showed that Congressman Lytle had a good chance to be elected to the Senate. It wouldn't be easy, it would take a major effort with all the stops pulled out. But it would be done. His father wanted it, and Barry Lytle knew he couldn't withdraw even if he wanted to.

The cab pulled up to the mass of cars thronged and waiting for admittance to the tunnel under the East River. In a few minutes they would be on their way to Wall Street.

As they approached Manhattan, old feelings of resentment seemed to rise like ghosts. Barry was tired of being a plaything. But a life of his own seemed impossible. His father had even approved his selection for marriage. But now that he had determined that his son's wife might prove to be a political liability, a friendly and quiet divorce had been arranged and was in progress. Both Barry and his wife were glad the marriage was ending, but it still had been his father's decision. Sometimes it seemed to

Barry that he was merely some kind of life-sized toy that existed only for the amusement of his father.

And it was all happening again. Ambassador Stewart Lytle, one of the world's most powerful bankers, was quietly gathering support for his son's candidacy, busily lining up commitments from key power brokers. He had been summoned from Washington to have lunch with his father and Hunter Van Horn, the industrialist, but more importantly, the head of the Vault. If the members of the Vault decided it was in their best interest that Barry Lytle serve in the Senate, it was the same as done.

But he didn't want to be a senator, not if that office would only serve to bring him even more deeply under his father's domination. Nor even President, not under those terms.

Lytle began to feel the onset of that special tension, a feeling he knew well and hated. He thought it was over, but it was back. It came when he had to face his father. He began to feel the tremors. He held out his hands; they were shaking slightly.

He feared what he felt he would have to do to bring an end to the unbearable tension. He hated it, but there never seemed to be any other way that worked.

"Those fuckin' Yankees," the driver said as they raced downtown toward Wall Street. "It's going to be the same as last year. They got everything money can buy, except victories. Shit, what kind of a world is it if you can't buy your way? It just ain't American, you know?"

Barry Lytle chose to say nothing. He held his hands close to his body to keep the tremors from showing.

Unknown to Barry Lytle, a small private jet high above him was lining up in a landing pattern for La Guardia, coming in over the tip of Manhattan.

Hunter Van Horn looked down at New York. The awe-inspiring sight of the World Trade Center towers, the Empire State, and the cluster of other giant buildings thrusting up at the sky always thrilled him. It was the place of his birth, the city of his father, grandfather, and a number of generations before them. Van Horn owned houses in California, Texas, London and even Paris, but New York was his home. He regarded the city as something essentially personal, like an arm or leg, an important part of his being.

He was concentrating on the view and barely heard his secretary as she spoke. "That still leaves the problem with the Entertainment Group."

He turned and looked at her. Joyce Spitz, in her mid-thirties, was devoted to her job and even more to him, but not in a sexual way. She seemed to take pains to make herself plain and unattractive, which he considered just as well, since there were far too many women in his life anyway. She seemed to exist for the sole purpose of being efficient, and succeeded at that superbly. As a result, although her title was simply secretary, she was paid the salary of a senior executive.

"Have Herb Beekman report to me tomorrow." Beekman was vice-president in charge of the Entertainment Group, an unctuous, pretentious man whom Van Horn disliked.

"You have a full schedule. I could never fit him in."

"Juggle things," he snapped. "I'll need at least a half hour with Beekman. It's important."

"Will you need anyone from legal or accounting there?" It was a shrewd question. Rumors were circulating that Beekman was stealing from the company.

Van Horn shook his head. "No. Not this time."

Van Horn's whole empire appeared to be in trouble. He had built the family business into one of the world's largest conglomerates. Now, section by section, the entire structure threatened to shake apart. He knew he would have to perform drastic surgery to save it. That meant reorganization and replacing losers with winners, or at least with people he hoped would prove winners.

"I'll want you there when I talk to Beekman," he said. "It promises to be a most unpleasant meeting. I'll need a witness. I'm going to order Beekman to fire Conrad Barnaby. The goddamned movie studio is losing buckets of money again. That idiot Barnaby has no more idea of how to run a movie company than he does about screwing an elephant."

Joyce gave no sign that she might be offended by his vulgarity. "Barnaby is Beekman's man," she said. "He brought him into the company."

"Then it's only fair that he do the firing. He has to clean up his own messes. I want Adam Robins promoted to run the studio. He may not be a genius, but he's better than what we've got now."

"Beekman's not going to like that."

Hunter Van Horn snorted. "If he raises any strenuous objection, I'll fire him too. Jesus, this isn't some little Bronx chicken business. We're running one of the largest companies in the world here. It's about time Beekman appreciates the fact that no one is sacred or irreplaceable in this organization, not even him."

She half smiled. "No one?"

"Well, no one except me. Remember, I used to own this whole damn thing until I was forced to go public. I still control a lot of stock, so as far as people in this company are concerned, I'm as close to God as anything they'll ever know on this earth."

"What about Chilton Vance?" Vance was the executive vice-president and generally considered to be Van Horn's right hand.

"What about him?"

"There's been some talk floating around the company lately that he's planning a palace coup d'état. I'm not saying that's true, but it is a rumor."

He studied her for a moment. She was serious, almost solemn. "If it's true, Vance would be risking everything. He knows I'd nail his hide to the wall if he tried anything like that. Frankly, I don't think he's got the guts."

She flushed. "As I said, it's only idle chatter."

He knew it was more than that. It was her way of warning him. He wondered if Vance really was up to something, and how far he might have progressed. The company was in trouble and a fight for control could get sticky now, with everything coming apart.

"By the way, your daughter is in *People* again. The issue just hit the stands today."

He laughed. "Showing her legs again, or God knows what else?"

She extracted the magazine from her briefcase and handed it to him, neatly folded back to the article about Victoria.

Her completed East Port project with its new buildings and fancy restaurants provided the background for the photograph. She had an uncanny ability to generate publicity about herself and her ventures. As usual, his daughter photographed well. Her expression was determined, challenging. He thought the picture captured a sense of inner strength, as well as her obvious beauty. The article prattled on about another new project she was planning for Manhattan. He looked again at the photo; there was definitely a tough quality underneath those stunning good looks.

She was so different from her brother.

He had failed to recognize her intelligence and determination. He recalled his attitude when she had enrolled in law school—he thought it was a lark and that she would never finish. But she had, and with honors. Four years had passed since their screaming, shouting confrontation at Christmastime. She had inherited his quick temper. Four years was a relatively short time, but in that period Victoria had gone from a rich man's pampered daughter to a major business force in her own right. A dynamic person who had scored enormous success, she had proved herself to be a power to be reckoned with. He reluctantly had to admit to himself that he missed her.

He remembered that Christmas vividly. Victoria had talked to him privately during the family Christmas party at his apartment. She resembled her mother physically, but not emotionally. Even as a child Victoria never whined or made excuses for herself. After the divorce he saw little of her, usually briefly at holidays. She had grown into a beauty, had obtained a liberal arts degree but disdained the volunteer work and arty jobs usually done by rich young women. She had become an attorney. That Christmas she wanted something more. It wasn't money; he had always seen to it she had plenty of that. This time she wanted a real job with one of his companies: the chance to climb the ladder to the top.

Hunter Van Horn half smiled to himself at the memory. He wondered how he could have been so poor a judge; he usually had a knack for evaluating strengths and weaknesses. But not in his own daughter. What had begun as a discussion had turned into an argument and then a real fight. He had laughed at her ambitions, even mocking her law degree. He had advised her to marry well and get on with the business of raising a family. He had scoffed at her new desire for a real career in the family business and that had infuriated her. Her biting response had enraged him and their verbal battle turned vicious. That night she had stormed out of the apartment. He had never seen her in the flesh since, only her image in newspapers and magazines. She never asked him for another cent, and she had certainly proved him wrong.

He admired her, and he was surprised that he was affected so deeply by their separation. He considered trying to repair the breach, but he didn't quite know how to go about it. It was a matter of pride. He wondered if that might be the case with her too.

The jet touched down and roared along the runway. "You have a luncheon with Ambassador Lytle and his son."

Stewart Lytle was a member of the Vault. Van Horn knew Lytle wanted to promote his son into the Senate. Such a decision would take unanimous agreement of all the members of the Vault. The sole purpose of this lunch would be to sound Van Horn out, to see if he might be receptive to supporting such a move. Nothing more would be accomplished. Inasmuch as a particularly exotic and lush woman awaited him in her Sutton Place apartment, Van Horn was determined that the luncheon meeting would be very short.

His secretary interrupted his thoughts. "We have a few minutes.

Would you like a quick briefing on what can be expected at the Vault's next meeting?" She was the only nonmember he allowed to possess such information.

"No. Not now."

Only eight in number, the members of the Vault represented an enormous concentration of real wealth, what people called "old money." They husbanded and protected the vital interests of the city's ruling families, the rich and influential descendants of the original founders of New York and its commerce. Collectively, the members of the Vault had more power than any king. But most of the world never suspected the Vault even existed.

Hunter Van Horn had taken his father's seat on the Vault after his death. His father would have been proud that they had chosen him as their leader, although he found no pleasure in either the honor or the responsibility.

3

It had turned quite chilly, despite the optimistic weather predictions for a beginning of spring. Victoria Van Horn's apartment was warm and comfortable, but she felt a sudden need to venture out. She had spent all day with planners and architects. It had been busy, at times hectic, and she had longed for the quiet peace of her own place. But now that she had it, she instead felt penned up and restless.

Her maid had gone to bed. She had looked quickly through the newspapers, just glancing at the headlines. She seldom watched television, but she had the set on more for company than entertainment.

She walked to the windows and looked down on Gramercy Park. Despite the bleak weather, there were people about on the streets. She loved the park, available only by key to the people who lived in the posh buildings on its perimeter. A New York landmark, it formed a tranquil oasis set back from the rush and noise of Third Avenue, concealed like a jewel, hidden by bordering buildings.

She could see her own image in the glass of the windows, blending with the scene below, as if she were some disembodied spirit watching. She half studied her ghostly reflection; the features were hers, the now-famous Victoria Van Horn, but she wondered if she really knew the woman underneath.

Victoria made a face at her reflection. "You need a walk, ghost," she said aloud.

She took a warm jacket and slipped it on over her blouse and slacks. The coat had a high collar and she put that up against the expected cold.

No one was on the elevator. She smiled at Charley, the night door-man, who stood guard in the lobby.

"That's a good picture of you in that magazine," he said, smiling. "I showed it to my family. They were impressed I knew you."

"Thanks, Charley."

"Want me to get you a cab?"

She shook her head. "No, thanks. I'm just going for a walk."

Concern was reflected in his thick features. "I wouldn't go too far, Miss Van Horn. I think it's going to rain again. Maybe even snow if it doesn't warm up."

"I'm just going over to the park. I think I need a little air."

He smiled as if she had given just the right answer. "Good. I'll keep an eye on you from here."

"Stay inside the building. It's chilly."

He shrugged. "Hey, I like to get a little air too. I'll just stand under the canopy. It's no problem."

Victoria didn't protest. She appreciated his concern for her safety, but she wanted to be alone, outside, away from some of her problems. Still, it was late, not many people were venturing out in this depressingly damp weather. Even in the locked park it was best to play it safe.

"I won't be long," she said, pulling the collar tight against her face. She stepped out of the apartment door and felt the chill snap of the wind. Charley was right; it carried a real threat of cold rain.

Victoria thrust her hands in the coat's deep pockets and walked briskly, her head down against the chilly breeze. The park, fenced in high decorative iron, was kept in good repair. She unlocked the big gate, ice-cold against her ungloved hands, then closed it behind her.

The trees in the park had just the hint of buds adorning their otherwise stark branches. Despite the wintry weather, the signs of spring were beginning to show. Nature was a better predictor than any weather instruments yet devised. Spring in Gramercy Park was a rhapsody for the soul. She walked past the brooding statue of Edwin Booth. The park was well lit and she was quite alone.

She stopped and looked at the apartments. They all seemed so cheery, like giant Christmas trees, their lights a happy message proclaiming warm human life within.

But somehow the sight made her feel even more isolated and lonely. She sat down on a bench and bunched the coat up around her.

She was one of the most famous women in New York, and fast on her way to being one of the richest. She knew people considered her a true success, even envied her.

Victoria's eye was caught by a lighted window. A small child was being lifted by a bearded man, the child laughing in excited delight. Then they were gone; this unknown man and his laughing little boy.

She wondered if it would have made any difference to either the father or the son that a young, dark-haired woman had watched them. She wondered about the mother of the boy. Did she look at *People* magazine today and envy the woman she saw pictured there? Did she wish for the glamour, the wealth, the excitement?

Victoria squeezed down deeper into the coat. She looked again at the window, now vacant, and shivered.

She had no regrets, she told herself. She had chosen the path. It was what she wanted. And there was more to come, much more.

The feeling of loneliness seemed almost overwhelming.

The rain began, just a few drops at first, then it became a drizzle. She hurried to the gate, locked it and half ran back to her apartment house.

Charley was standing, still watching, under the canopy. She wondered what he thought he saw: did he see the hard-driving young woman who was the talk of New York, or did he see something else?

She thought about the unseen woman. Envy could be a two-way street sometimes.

Like his predecessor, Ed Koch, Mayor Al Felder was flamboyant, combining a finely honed sense of the public pulse with a shrewd understanding of media manipulation. Although new to the office, and to city politics, Felder exuded a confidence about running New York that was more in keeping with a well-seasoned city politician. He didn't look like a mayor, either. Felder was thickly built with a rough, street-smart face. Despite his Ivy League education, even his friends said he looked more like a cab driver than a Wall Street lawyer, which had been his profession for most of his life. He had come to politics late in his career. One term in the state assembly had led to the stunning upset of the veteran Koch. Felder had been in the right place at the right time. He had ridden into office on the crest of a citywide tax protest. He didn't like it when they called him a political accident.

"Send in Al Rossini," he commanded his secretary.

Rossini responded quickly. His formal title was special assistant to the mayor, but his real role was as the mayor's chief troubleshooter.

Rossini, like the mayor, was from Wall Street, on loan from the prestigious firm of Alesia and D'Amico. He, too, was a product of the Ivy League, but he looked the part, complete with carefully styled hair and tailored clothing. During the campaign, he had demonstrated a surprising grasp of the realities of politics and an ability to get things done. The mayor had "drafted" him. Although Rossini was concerned about his future with his law firm, he had nevertheless agreed to join forces with Gracie Mansion, fascinated with the chance to see government from the inside.

The mayor waved him into the office. "I have to make an appearance at some cocktail party they're throwing for the Italian ambassador tonight. He's in town for some United Nations thing. I want you to go with me."

Rossini grinned. "I'm Italian in name only. I can't speak the language and I've never been there. I won't be much help to you."

The mayor scowled. "I'm Jewish. You think that's going to help me with these people? I need to show off a prominent greaseball in my administration. You're it." Felder took a strange delight in using street language. "I need you to parade around there, that's all. Just let people see your name tag and your title. We'll only be there for a few minutes anyway. If someone tries to talk wop to you, just pretend you can't hear. Those goddamned parties are always noisy as hell. Between the usual music and the buzz of conversation, you won't have to pretend much."

"Do you want to present a proclamation, or anything like that?"

The mayor looked up. "For the ambassador? Hey, I only give proclamations to little guys, people the voter can identify with." He seemed to brighten. "Hey, I got an idea. How about the Italian ambassador giving you a commendation or a medal?"

"Me? For what?"

Felder used his hands a great deal when he talked. He now raised them heavenward as if in supplication. "You're a hopeless case, you know that? It's a natural for newspaper pictures. You know, 'Mayor Felder's Assistant Given Italian Honor.' If you get your picture in the paper, the Italians will see for themselves that I'm taking care of you people. It makes sense."

"Well, I . . ."

"Just line it up." There was a sudden coldness in the mayor's tone. "Debates I don't need."

Rossini nodded, then turned to go.

"Wait a minute," the mayor snapped. "How are the city planners coming along on that Van Horn broad's new proposal?"

"As far as I know, everything is in order. There's just a few procedural steps to complete, then they'll approve it."

The mayor leaned back in his large chair. He extended his right hand as if waving something away. "Pass the word, very quietly and very unofficially, that I want them to hold things up. I want them to check with me before they give final approval."

Rossini was startled. "It's a good concept. She did a fantastic job with her East Port project. She should be able to pull this off if she can raise the financing. It'll help revitalize that part of the city, and it would bring in added tax revenue. I thought you were all in favor of gentrification. Why do you want to hold this up?"

"Rossini, you're bright, but you have a lot to learn about practical politics."

"So?"

"Suppose everything goes through without a hitch, what happens? At best, that young lady might be grateful for an efficient city government. But more likely, she won't even notice and will just take it all for granted. But suppose things get sticky and she gets all wrapped up in bureaucratic red tape. Eventually, like it or not, she'll have to appeal to the mayor for help. She's a lawyer, she'll know enough to come and see me. And I predict that through my heroic efforts the little lady and her proposed project will be saved. I'll make damned sure she's grateful."

"Then what?"

Mayor Felder laughed. "I can read your mind. Are you thinking that I, a Princeton graduate, would sink to shaking down this beautiful young entrepreneur? Things haven't gotten that bad yet, Rossini. She goes on a special list of people ripe for campaign donations when the time comes. But mainly I'm going to try to use her to get a wire into her old man. And let me tell you, that could be really important."

"I doubt that will do you much good. I understand she and her father haven't spoken for years."

The mayor fluttered his hands as if waving away smoke. "Sometimes that kind of crap is put out just for publicity purposes. Maybe it's true, maybe not. You never know. Anyway, it's worth a shot."

"Why is Hunter Van Horn so important to you, besides the very obvious fact that he's enormously rich?"

"Well, it's always nice to have rich friends. And that conglomerate of his seems to own half the world. But that's not the main reason. He's head of the Vault, or so I'm told."

"The Vault?"

"Rossini, who do you think runs this city?"

The young lawyer looked puzzled. "You do."

Felder laughed. "It just looks that way. I take care of the nickel-and-dime shit, the daily diddly stuff. The really big decisions actually aren't made by me. The Vault runs the Big Apple."

"I've never even heard of this Vault."

Mayor Felder swung around in his chair and looked out the window at the magnificent East River. His brow was deeply furrowed in thought. "To say the least, they keep a low profile. But screw up something they're interested in, and out you go. They supply the juice that makes this city run. And you know what?"

"What?"

"If we handle the Van Horn girl just right, I might find a way to get in with her father. I might just find a way into the Vault. You know, Rossini, if I could find a way to get into bed with those guys, I just might end up running this city for real. And I think I'd like that a whole lot."

"Besides holding up her permits, what else do you want me to do?"

"Maybe give her a jump."

Rossini shook his head. "Hey, I'm a married man."

The mayor's rough face split into a toothy leer. "Ever see her picture?"

"Yes."

"Listen, with a good-looking bimbo like that, nobody's married. Not if they're in their right minds. And if you don't want to give her a jump, I will." The leer became even more pronounced. "God, why is it that I have to do everything myself?"

Chilton Vance watched his wife parade naked through their bedroom. A truly magnificent creature, she was tall, stately and full-breasted, with the ripe, lush look of an artist's model. She tossed her head, the movement causing her long, red hair to fan about like swirling ruby smoke. It was a habitual gesture, designed to call attention to her luxuriant hair. She stopped and looked down at him in bed, her green eyes challenging. He wondered again if the rumor that she had slept with Hunter Van Horn were true.

"We've been married almost a year now," she said, her voice deep and throaty, "surely you're used to seeing a red pussy by now."

He managed a weak smile. "I'm still an admirer."

She laughed and climbed into bed next to him. "I can see that."

He was fully erect.

"See what happens when you marry a younger woman?" she said. "You become young again yourself."

Her skin was silky to his touch. She had almost alabaster skin, not unlike the finest china. It was, she told him, a gift of her Anglo-Irish ancestors: vibrant red hair and milky skin.

His third wife, she had been born Roberta Fitzsimmons, the daughter of a prosperous Irish businessman in Dublin. The family had migrated to New York, and she had been schooled at the finest institutions, earning several degrees in economics. She now had her own successful business as a tax consultant.

Roberta fondled him gently. "When are you going to make your move?"

He laughed. "Against whom? You or Hunter Van Horn?"

She hurt him slightly as she jerked her hand away. "Van Horn, you asshole! Now is the right time. You'll never have such a chance again."

Whenever Van Horn's name was mentioned she became angry. And he was always surprised by the intensity of her reaction. Each time he became more convinced that she had once been Hunter's lover, despite all her denials.

Chilton Vance, the executive vice-president of Van Horn Enterprises, was second in command to Hunter Van Horn himself, but he had come to hate even the sight of the man.

There was no question that Roberta had had many lovers. She had a colorful reputation, even by New York standards. But he had married her anyway. Once again, looking at her, he felt the sick pain of jealousy. He loathed to think of anyone else possessing her, especially Hunter Van Horn.

Vance sat up and shook out a cigarette from the pack on his nightstand. He inhaled deeply before speaking. "We've been over this again and again. As I've told you, timing is everything in these matters. If I act too soon, I'll be the one destroyed."

She eyed his slender body as he sat naked on his side of the bed. "And if you wait too long, the opportunity will be gone. Life in a corporation is like a bouncing ball; you're either on your way up or on your way down. At the moment you're near the top of your rise, Chilton. But if you miss this chance, it'll be a long way down, and you know that."

He made no reply. She continued. "And Hunter Van Horn certainly is not the forgiving kind. If he finds out just how far you've progressed in trying to overthrow him, he'll come after you without mercy. There's no turning back, not now." She paused for effect. "And you can't afford the luxury of waiting anymore."

Chilton Vance stood up. Clothed, he was elegant, his tall, slender form a haberdasher's dream. His gray hair was carefully cut and combed; he was the picture of a leading corporate executive. But naked, he looked more like a scarecrow, with little rolls of wrinkled flesh around his middle, his body held up on spidery legs with knobby knees and oversized ankles. He had lost the erection.

He looked over at his wife. She lay on top of the sheets, her long legs akimbo. Although she was twenty-five years his junior and had the spectacular body of a call girl, he often thought she had the mind of a pirate.

"Roberta, you should have been born a man."

"I like the way I am. I have a man's interests and a woman's weapons. That, at least in my opinion, constitutes a most potent combination."

"I'll make my move when the Research Group makes its report."

"What difference will that make?" she asked. "They always lose money anyway. That won't mean anything to the board."

He took a drag on his cigarette. "This year it will."

Her fiery green eyes narrowed, reflecting her sharpened interest. "Why?"

"The company is about to be hit with a gigantic lawsuit. We have a small electrical research lab in Georgia. It employs only a few dozen people. Research technicians mostly."

"So?"

"They were working on a type of gas that would have been activated by a small electrical charge. If it had worked, it would have revolutionized the whole energy process from industrial plants to automobiles."

"And it didn't work, I take it?"

"Worse. The damn gas was poison, deadly but slow-working. At first there were no signs of what effect it was having. One of those kinds of things. But everyone who worked in the lab itself now has severe lung damage. Several have died. The rest of them will shortly."

"That's the price of progress. You can't make an omelette without breaking a few eggs, and so forth."

He stared at her, then laughed softly. "You're really heartless, aren't you?"

"No more so than any other practical business person. It's unfortunate, but these things do happen. There's no advance unless someone pays a price."

"The price is going to be extremely high this time. Those workers are all young, well educated and well paid. Courts award money on the basis of what the future could have held for people like that. Our lawyers tell me that when all the suits are filed, we could stand to lose well over a hundred million."

"That much?"

"Maybe more. Juries tend to be outraged in these circumstances."

"It's just a subsidiary company, isn't it? Declare it bankrupt and cut your losses."

He sighed. "When we opened up in Georgia, the locals were afraid we would be making atom bombs or some damn thing. They didn't want the research lab there in the first place, so we compromised."

"How?"

"We gave assurances that Van Horn Enterprises would stand good for any losses, and for whatever reason."

She rolled over on her stomach. The sight of the erotic curves of her well-formed hips always excited him. "So chalk it up as just one more political promise," she said. "It's certainly not binding."

He walked to the night table and crushed out his cigarette. "I'm afraid that it is. We entered into a binding contract to that effect with the state of Georgia."

"Who suggested that?"

"Guess."

"Hunter?"

He shook his head slowly. "Me."

She rolled to one side and propped herself up on one elbow. "Well, that tears it, doesn't it?"

This time his smile was genuine. "Not really. No one remembers that, except me. It's truly ironic. It was my mistake, but I'm the one who's going to profit from it."

"How so?"

He sat on the edge of the bed. His thin hand stroked the smooth skin of her long legs. "Van Horn Enterprises has five groups, right? Research Group will show the biggest projected loss in history. The Entertainment Group lost its shirt with a couple of bad movies. Our Manufacturing Group will post a small loss, mainly because of a new accounting system, but a loss nevertheless. The Transport Group will break even, although I expect there might even be a small loss there, too. Because we sold our French operation, the Foreign Group will post a gain, but it'll be the only one."

She took his hand and guided it between her legs. "Then this is exactly the time to move."

"Hunter has the full support of only a third of the members of our board of directors. The others either hate his guts or are terrified he may eventually ruin the company."

She was moving against his hand and her slow, erotic motion was arousing him again. Vance smiled down at her. "Of course all of them are afraid to move against him until they are reasonably sure of success. None of them wants him as an enemy, not if he still has power."

"How many times do I have to keep saying this? Now is the time."

"Not quite yet. As soon as the research people make their report, then the air will be ripe for a palace revolt. That's exactly what I'm waiting for."

She pulled him down next to her. She had a vitality and strength that he envied. And he knew it wasn't just a matter of age, it was something she appeared to have been born with.

"So you see, Roberta, I'm not afraid of Hunter. I'm just being prudent. When he goes down I'll make sure he will never get up again."

She began kissing his mouth, then his throat, moving slowly but steadily downward.

"God, Roberta, I love it when you do that," he whispered, catching his breath.

He was answered by a murmur of pleasure. He writhed as she expertly worked her tongue against his skin.

But the sound he heard was not entirely sexual, it was more a moan of exultation. Roberta Vance was contemplating her feeling of triumph when the great Hunter Van Horn would be brought down. Van Horn had thrown her out, the only man ever to do so. She wanted revenge, and now she was going to have it.

———

The big man signaled to the waiter for another drink. "I need someone who can talk to her. You can do it. Not just because you're a lawyer, but because you know her. I mean, you're in a position to really talk turkey to her, understand?"

"I haven't seen her for years."

"Craig, don't bullshit me. You used to live with her."

Craig Hopkins simply nodded. It was none of the man's business, but he was a client, a good one who brought a lot of work into the firm. Hopkins forced himself to put his resentment aside. He managed a smile. "We were, ah, roommates for a while."

"Look, that little Van Horn bitch has got me right by the short hair. I got an option on a building she wants, but my damn option is running out. She's just sitting there waiting for it to expire, then she'll buy it. I won't get a thing."

"Have you talked to her?"

"Sure. What kind of a businessman do you think I am? You think I'm scared of some little schoolgirl who got lucky? Hey, if I was dealing with her old man that might be a different matter, but I'm not. I even offered the bitch a partnership in the building, but she refused."

"Why don't you exercise the option?"

His client scowled. "I can't raise the money, if you want to know. The fucking bankers want my left ball, but I gave that away years ago. If I could bring Victoria Van Horn in as my partner I could raise all the dough I needed, just on her reputation, such as it is."

"Right now, it's pretty good," Hopkins said, taking his drink from the waiter.

The man eyed him warily. "Are you and she still a thing? I heard that was all over."

Hopkins looked at him. "That's getting a little personal, isn't it?"

"Who gives a shit? I'm talking real money here. I need to know. If that bitch hates your guts or something, I don't want you talking to her. It would do more harm than good. What happened between you two? Catch her screwing someone else?"

Hopkins felt himself color. "No."

"Don't get sore. You still carrying the torch?"

Hopkins studied his glass for a moment. He had often asked himself the same question. He wasn't entirely sure of the answer, but a man like his client would never understand that. "No," he said.

"That's smart. Women are like subway trains, if you miss one, another will be along in a few minutes. Come on, what really happened? She's a great-looking broad, and that's something a man doesn't walk away from, at least not without good cause."

Hopkins felt it demeaning that he should even have to answer such a question. Yet the man's legal business was important to the firm, and himself. "We had some differences. Nothing major."

"Differences? That little broad is worth millions, you know that?"

"I know."

"And that's just counting her money. Christ, when her old man croaks she'll probably end up a billionaire. If it was me, I'd get my ass over there and kiss and make up, quick. Money is hard to come by, pal. She's your gravy train. You don't get too many chances like that in life."

The man's eyes narrowed. "Do you have any contact with her?"

Hopkins shook his head. "We talk on the phone occasionally. We're both very busy. But we have mutual friends, so there are marriages, deaths, that sort of thing, to be discussed."

"Just like divorced people."

"In a way."

"Then give her a call for me, eh? Look, I'll be fair. I won't rob her. But she's got to give me a break here or my ass is grass. Hey, I'll even sell her the fucking option, anything. I'm desperate."

"I'll call her as your attorney. She might listen, but I can't guarantee anything."

The man lit a thick, long black cigar. His intense little eyes seemed to penetrate right through the dense smoke. "Listen, Craig, in this life nobody can guarantee anything."

"I suppose not."

His client again signaled the waiter. He slipped the man a large bill as a tip, but in such a way as to ensure that everyone saw his display of generosity. Given his client's dire financial circumstances, Hopkins considered the gesture both foolish and theatrical. The man shook hands with Hopkins, then strode through the rows of tables as though he owned the restaurant. In another age he would have been a gambler, betting all he had on the turn of a card. But he was a man of his time, a sportsman in a different game, a game where cards had been replaced by stocks, bond issues and development schemes.

Hopkins regretted his promise to contact Victoria. They were worlds apart now. It hadn't been like that in the beginning. They had become lovers in law school, and after admission to the bar they had lived together, a temporary arrangement until they could afford marriage. He had joined several other young lawyers in opening an office, a struggle that still continued. She had gone to work for a large law firm, assigned to real estate law. They shared their adventures without any sense of competition. They didn't have much money, but it hadn't mattered, not then. Their love had seemed eternal.

Memories assaulted him suddenly like an unbidden flood. He recalled vividly the details of their small apartment, the fun they found in life. It was almost painful to remember. He had watched her change. When they met she was a vivacious girl, rich but without pretension. Her deep beauty, her surprising sensuousness, was matched by a razor-sharp intelligence often concealed beneath a quick wit.

Their marriage plans had been put aside after the fight with her father.

Victoria had come to their apartment that night shaking, her eyes filled with tears of rage. An irrevocable rift had taken place between father and daughter. But he didn't realize the enormous effect it would ultimately have on Victoria.

At first, she had been merely moody. Then a lucky break at her law office—she had taken over a floundering real estate development and saved it—seemed to galvanize her into frantic action. She abandoned the practice of law as such and threw herself into large-scale development, the hurt of her father's reaction translated into a maniacal drive to prove herself in business. Craig was busy with his law practice and thought it would be just a passing phase. But it didn't turn out that way.

She opened a small office in the Village on borrowed money. They were both so busy that they seldom had a chance to talk. The apartment became merely a place to sleep in and occasionally make love in.

Then the quarrels began. At first it was over small things, such as who should do the grocery shopping. But the small things became symbolic to both of them, and the quarrels escalated to battles. But even that wouldn't have ended things between them, he realized.

It was her success that did it.

The love they had began to erode. He knew at the time he was jealous and was ashamed of it, but that didn't help.

It didn't end with an explosion, not even a whimper. One day they found time to talk and quietly agreed that what they had known was over. More than anything else, he recalled feeling sad.

She had moved out. The apartment held too many memories so he had moved too.

There had been other women in his life since. But no one was like Victoria. He wondered if she ever thought about him.

Craig Hopkins finished his drink. The firm really needed this man's business. He had promised to call her, and he would. But he regretted making that promise.

4

Bernard Thatcher physically resembled Margaret Thatcher, but they were not related. Both had been born in England and they were roughly the same age, but outside of sharing almost identical features, all other similarities ended there. As a youth, Bernard Thatcher had entered the British army, thereafter serving a succession of colonels as a batman, a military form of butler. He discovered he had a gift for the work and sometimes a perverse enjoyment in it. After his military service he managed to work his way up to butler in the household of a British merchant. Then he had been enticed away to serve a rich American woman who was enthralled by both his icy reserve and his implacable dignity.

Thatcher's career as a butler had been quite successful. He had been in America ever since, and had become a citizen. Moving from one rich employer to another, never once had he been out of work.

"How do I look, Thatcher?" his present employer inquired.

Thatcher coolly appraised the blond man. Eric Vogeldorf could have easily been a model adorning the pages of the slick women's magazines. Tall, broad-shouldered but slim-hipped, with blond hair cut and styled to perfection, he had the kind of good looks that seemed plastic. And although he was approaching his mid-forties, Eric Vogeldorf looked much younger.

"You look quite nice, sir," Thatcher said evenly. "My only reservation is your tie. Perhaps something somewhat more muted?"

"Do you think so?"

Thatcher quickly selected a maroon Italian silk tie and smoothly replaced the offender.

"That's a bit better, sir."

His employer's smooth face broke into a smile of dental perfection. "You really have an eye for clothes. Have you ever considered opening a shop? I'm sure you'd do quite well."

"I was born to be a butler," Thatcher replied, with a reserve that bordered on cool hostility. "It's what I do best." He picked an imaginary piece of lint from Vogeldorf's lapel. The other tie was just as good, perhaps even better, but Thatcher knew that being a butler required showmanship. It worked. Some of his "gentlemen" wouldn't have dreamed of even venturing outside unless they had first received his personal appraisal and approval.

"I may be bringing Miss Van Horn back here tonight."

Thatcher nodded. "Do you wish me to prepare something? It's cook's night off."

"No. We're going out to dinner. Maybe you could serve brandy and champagne when we get in." Vogeldorf grinned conspiratorially. "Then you can take the rest of the evening off."

"As you wish, sir." Thatcher helped Vogeldorf into his topcoat and then escorted him to the door and out of the apartment.

Thatcher always wore a black, conservatively cut suit. He unbuttoned the coat and let his waist expand. He was getting older, and looking trim and military was becoming more of a chore. He walked into the kitchen of the large penthouse apartment.

The cook, a stout British woman, was preparing to leave. She was dressed to go out. "Has Mr. Vogeldorf gone?" she asked.

Thatcher nodded. "Off in pursuit of his fortune, as they say. If he's lucky, he may talk his fortune into coming back here tonight."

"Has he gone to bed with her yet?"

"Not as far as I know."

The cook's chins shook as she laughed. "That's unusual for him."

She was relatively new to the household, but she had already been regaled with Thatcher's stories about the sexual prowess of their employer.

"This time the game is different. The Nazi is after much more than mere pleasures of the flesh, at least with this one."

"I don't think it's right that you always call him 'the Nazi.' He was a baby during the war."

Thatcher took out a cigarette and lit it. He never smoked except backstairs. "He was born in 1943, one of twin boys. His father was General Vogeldorf of the German General Staff . . ."

"That doesn't make him a Nazi, just because of his father!"

The butler pulled out a kitchen chair and sat down. "I suppose his father wasn't a Nazi either, at least not in the true political sense. He was a Prussian, a nobleman of sorts. He was accused of being in on the plot to kill Hitler. The Führer had him hanged."

"There, you see. He's from good stock, and his father was a general."

The butler allowed himself a wry smile. "His father had married a wealthy German heiress. That's how he secured his promotions in the army."

"What difference does that make?"

"All the difference in the world. It's a family tradition, don't you see? Our beloved employer has been bred to be a stallion, a blue-blooded stud. The idea is to find a very wealthy woman and, in exchange for impregnating her with nearly royal German stock, to enjoy all the wonderful benefits provided by her riches."

"Mr. Vogeldorf is a rich man himself," the cook protested.

Thatcher, who kept the household accounts, inhaled deeply on his cigarette before replying. "It would seem that way."

"A woman would be right lucky to have a husband like him," the cook protested loyally.

"Perhaps."

"There's no perhaps about it." She departed, in an apparent huff, her features set in a mask of self-righteousness.

When he was sure she was gone, Thatcher poured himself a stiff scotch. Although Eric Vogeldorf lived in a penthouse in the Murray Hill section of Manhattan and kept servants, he was far from rich. He was well educated—Harvard and Oxford—and enjoyed the best of everything, everything that is except a fat bank account. His money was running out.

His twin brother, Emil, who had married a California computer heiress, had made Eric a substantial loan, but now even that money was almost gone.

Thatcher could well appreciate his employer's predicament. Vogeldorf needed a strike soon, or he would be forced to settle for a life far different from that in which he had been raised—a completely new life, without servants, in which he would have to work for a living.

The Van Horn girl was beautiful, extremely so, but she was also smart. Thatcher had met her only twice, but he had been impressed by her quick ability to make shrewd appraisals. Eric Vogeldorf might fool a great many women, but not that one. But if she was in the market for a blue-blooded stud, he would succeed. If not, there wouldn't be a thing the strikingly handsome blond man could do about it.

Thatcher took the liberty of pouring himself another scotch. In a way it was his worry, too. Openings for the position of butler were not plentiful. He had a few more years to go before he could apply for Social Security retirement. Although he could have had a fortune from what he had stolen over the years, he had put very little money away, certainly not nearly enough to retire on. He liked very young Hispanic girls, and he liked good whiskey. Both had proven to be expensive habits. His plan upon retirement was to take a small apartment in the Miami area where he could quietly and frequently indulge both his interests. But that would take another year or two at least.

He hoped Victoria Van Horn would be ready to become a brood mare, to lie on her back and produce a lovely line of little blond, blue-eyed Aryans. She qualified. She was certainly rich enough on her own. And, if one counted in the possible slice of her father's estate in the future, she would be a worthy score for the dashing Prussian who had been born and bred to serve just such a purpose.

Bernard Thatcher swallowed the scotch. He knew he had to be completely sober when his employer returned, so it had to be his last drink of the day.

He had to stop drinking, but he wouldn't stop hoping.

———————

Congressman Barry Lytle came away from the lunch feeling like a small, rather incompetent boy. His father and Hunter Van Horn had talked about him as though he weren't there. And when they did pay any attention to him, it was patronizing, mere solicitude, as if he were some kind of retarded child.

He was furious. In Washington he was important, the chairman of a key subcommittee. There, people admired and respected him, and he was openly courted by lobbyists and other politicians.

But in New York he was simply Stewart Lytle's son, a somewhat graying child-man who had been given a public office to play with as though it were a toy, like a tricycle or a kiddie car.

The shaking had worsened at lunch. He felt reasonably secure that they hadn't noticed. At least their failure to pay any attention to him while they discussed his chances for the Senate had that benefit. As he listened to them, he wondered if his father would treat him any differently if the master plan actually worked and he did end up in the White House. He very much doubted it.

He desperately needed relief from the clawing and unremitting agony of his own emotions.

It had been almost two years since he'd felt the urge so strongly. That time had been in New York, too. He avoided Manhattan whenever he could, not only because being close to his father was demeaning, but also to avoid temptation. He never seemed to feel the cravings in Washington or the absolute need for release.

As he continued walking, he wondered if any of the other pedestrians could see, or perhaps even sense, his shaking. It was increasing. He stopped at a sidewalk pay telephone and dialed the remembered number despite a trembling hand.

"This is Barry," he said, cupping his hand around the mouthpiece. "I'm in town and I'd like to do some business."

He experienced immense relief as he was given instructions. Soon the torment would ease and the shaking would stop.

Harry Daniels expertly maneuvered the small Cadillac through the weaving lanes of late-night cabs and cars. He turned into a shabby street, driving past dreary piles of garbage and litter.

Like the street, the Beechwood Hotel was ancient and dingy. Two women standing just outside the entrance eyed them as they slowly drove past.

"Hookers," Daniels said. "They must have a stupid pimp. They won't do much business hanging around a junkie dump like this. Sex is the last thing an addict has on his mind." He parked in an open space in front of a fire hydrant.

A tall, heavyset man stepped out of a dark blue car and walked stiffly toward them. "This is my man," Daniels said.

Harry Daniels was head of security for the New York banking firm of Perry Stanley, and his contacts as an ex-police captain had come in handy more than once.

The man leaned over and looked into the car window. "Hi."

"This is DiVito, Sam DiVito," Daniels said. "He's one of the dicks in the Thirteenth Precinct."

The big man stuck out his hand.

"This is Ambassador Lytle." Daniels used his employer's title, as did everyone else, despite the fact that Lytle hadn't been in government since the days of Nixon.

The policeman's grip was strong, but his hand was slippery from perspiration.

"Pleased to know you." DiVito's voice was distinctively raspy. His breath carried the pungent echo of a recent garlic meal. "The kid's upstairs," he said simply.

"You got extra people here?" Daniels asked. "We don't want any trouble."

DiVito's heavy face creased into a smile. "Hey, Harry, you're the one who taught me the business. I have two men in the lobby and two more on the floor. All good men. And there's a scout car just around the corner in case we need uniforms."

"It's best we don't," Daniels said, climbing out of the car. "We don't want to attract attention."

DiVito opened the passenger door for Stewart Lytle. The small man stepped out into the street. His legs felt tired, cramped. He was glad to have the opportunity to stand up.

"Ambassador, you don't have to come with us." Daniels towered over his employer. "Sam can have one of the officers stay with you while we go up."

"No."

"This might not be pretty," Daniels said softly as they walked toward the hotel entrance.

"It never is," Lytle replied, snapping out the words irritably.

The two women moved quickly away from the hotel's entrance, aware something was happening and not wanting to risk becoming part of whatever it was. The lobby was small, musty and decrepit, with paint peeling from the walls and no carpet on the floor. A swarthy man in a flowered shirt eyed them as they passed. His dark eyes were like little black stones, giving no hint of his thoughts.

"That's the night clerk," DiVito said, nodding toward the man in the garish shirt. "He's cooperating."

The young men standing in the lobby looked expectantly at DiVito. Both were dressed in jeans and denim jackets.

"Stay down here, unless we need help," DiVito said to them.

The choking stench of urine seemed to grow more intense as the old elevator carried them up.

DiVito grinned. "Not exactly your fancy uptown place," he said. "But among junkies, this joint is their Ritz."

They stepped out into a dimly lit hallway. Two men waited in the shadows outside an open door.

DiVito nodded to them, then walked into the small hotel room. The single window in the room was open, but even that didn't help dissipate the odor. A single light bulb in the ceiling illuminated the scene.

A black woman lay face up on the bed, naked and unconscious. Her skin glistened with sweat, reflecting the overhead light. She was tall, and extremely thin. Her long limbs trembled involuntarily, and her breathing was labored.

A white man, clad only in his shorts, lay on the floor. DiVito squatted down and placed a practiced hand alongside the white man's throat. He looked up at the others. "He's out, but he's still okay. The pulse is a little thready, but he'll make it." He looked at Daniels. "Do you want me to call an ambulance now, Harry?"

Daniels's solemn face remained expressionless. "That won't be necessary. We'll get him medical attention. Help us get him dressed."

The white man had vomited. DiVito pulled off a graying pillow case and began to clean up the man as best he could.

The shabby room was littered with empty cellophane packets. Several syringes lay scattered on the floor. A scorched teaspoon and cotton balls lay on the top of the worn dresser. Daniels looked at several of the packets. "They were speedballing," he said. "Looks like China white to me."

The two plainsclothesmen came in from the hall to assist DiVito. Although it was an awkward task, they managed to dress the unconscious white man. He breathed noisily and snorted several times but gave no other sign of regaining consciousness.

Daniels looked over at the black woman on the bed. The shaking had subsided and her black skin seemed to be taking on an unhealthy, ashen color. "Wait until we get clear, Sam, then you better get the uniforms up here. This gal's going to need some help. They must have scored some really good stuff. Too potent for them, I suppose. This spade looks like she might just buy the farm."

The two big plainclothesmen hoisted the white man up and carried him between them like a drunk who had passed out.

The unconscious white man was practically a carbon copy of Ambassador Lytle, only younger. They were both gray-haired, both had identical jutting jaws.

Daniels scribbled an address on a scrap of paper and handed it to DiVito. "Have your men take him to this place. It's a private clinic. They'll be waiting for him."

"No problem."

Daniels slipped DiVito a roll of bills. "Make sure your people forget about this whole business."

DiVito looked hurt. "Hey, Harry, you didn't even have to say that."

The officers carried their burden to the elevator and they all squeezed in. When they reached the lobby, the policemen, like magicians, quickly spirited the unconscious man outside and into an unmarked car, whisking him away as though he had never existed.

Ambassador Lytle stepped out into the deserted street and breathed deeply, trying to clear his senses of the dreadful odors. "Let's get out of here," he said to Daniels.

They drove in silence for a while. "It's been a long time," Daniels said. "Almost two years."

"Do you think they'll be able to whip him back into shape?"

Lytle stared out at the shabby street. "It shouldn't be a problem. It shouldn't have happened in the first place. It's my fault, I became too trusting. I should have had his administrative assistant come along with him. That would have prevented all . . . this."

Daniels shrugged. "There's only so much you can do. After all, he's an adult in his forties, and he's an elected member of Congress."

Lytle's stern face didn't soften. "Yes, he's all of that, but he's also a junkie. That's what really matters in the final analysis. That's what has to be controlled." He paused for a moment. "They'll detox him again. He'll be fine physically. And I'll have to listen once more to his endless, bleating assurances that it will never happen again. But he's a drug addict. I'll just have to be more careful and hire a new keeper for him."

"What if this makes the newspapers?"

"It won't," Lytle said through clenched teeth. "Because it never happened, just like the other times."

Lytle stared out at the night in silence for a few moments. When he spoke, his voice was lower, more intense. "Understand this, Daniels, it is imperative that not a word about tonight leaks out. I don't want any member of the Vault getting wind of this. I don't want even a whisper of gossip. You can buy silence. You take care of it. I don't care what it costs."

"As far as the cops are concerned, everything's already taken care of," Daniels replied. He glanced over at his employer. Obviously the opinion of the members of the Vault meant more to Lytle than did his own son. Daniels wondered what kind of power an organization like that could have that would make it so important. He decided that he never wanted to find out.

They delivered the unconscious congressman to the small private clinic. Sam DiVito gave the two detectives part of the money he had received from Harry Daniels. He planned to take care of the others later. The two plainclothesmen offered him a ride back to the station, but he told them he had other business.

DiVito felt good. Being a policeman was interesting work, and if a man knew his way around there was always an extra dollar or two to be made. He approached the outside telephone booth. Even in school he had a trick memory for numbers.

He dialed and waited. The telephone was finally answered by a man who sounded extremely bored.

"This is Sam DiVito. I'm a detective assigned to the Thirteenth Precinct. I need to talk to the man."

"A lot of people need to talk to the man," the voice replied gruffly. DiVito recognized it instantly, even though he hadn't worked for the mayor's squad in years. Not since the trouble.

"Scarpini, you know me. I wouldn't be calling unless I had something really good."

"You can tell me, DiVito."

"Fuck you, Scarpini." DiVito laughed. "You'd use it yourself and forget I even existed. Don't screw around, this is hot. I tell the man or I don't talk."

There was a pause. "If this isn't good, DiVito, I hope you realize you'll be shoveling shit out of the police stable for the rest of your career."

"Don't fuck with me, Scarpini, it's good."

"Where are you?"

"A pay booth on Madison."

"Give me your number."

"Are you kidding? The fucking thing's been vandalized, just like everything else in this city. There is no number."

"Oh shit. Hold on a minute."

As he waited, DiVito became aware of just how chilly the wind had become. Long minutes passed, and he wondered if Scarpini had forgotten him. Then a new voice came on the phone.

"I understand you want to talk to me. Sergeant Scarpini tells me you have some information."

Suddenly DiVito found himself flustered when he recognized the voice. He knew he would have to be quick, his opportunity would be short.

"I'm Detective Sam DiVito," he said distinctly as if testifying in court. "I'm a detective assigned to . . ."

"I know all that. Go on."

"A couple of narcs stumbled upon Congressman Barry Lytle in the Beechwood Hotel. He was unconscious from an overdose of drugs. Looked accidental. He was in a room with a black woman. They apparently got into some good"—he was going to say shit, but changed his mind—"stuff. The congressman will make it. I'm not too sure about the black woman."

"Was the congressman taken into custody?"

"No. A few telephone calls were made and his father showed up with a former police official. Myself and two other detectives took the congressman to a hospital here, a private place. He was just admitted. There's no official record of the incident. Except for the black woman, of course. But the report will say she was alone. She's been taken to an emergency room."

"And you say Ambassador Lytle showed up at the scene himself?"

"Yes, sir."

The tone of voice on the other end of the telephone had changed from wary to friendly. "I understand, according to Scarpini, you were once a member of the mayor's special squad."

"Yes, sir."

"Don't say anything about this to anyone else, DiVito. Perhaps, if everything works out, you might be invited back to work at City Hall."

"Thank you, sir."

DiVito was about to say how much he admired the man when he heard the click as the telephone at the other end was hung up.

Sam DiVito had seen much of life. He knew real opportunities were rare, and when they did come they were usually sudden and unexpected.

He smiled to himself. It wasn't every day that a mere detective got to talk to the mayor of New York, and to do him a favor at that.

5

Victoria Van Horn liked Eric Vogeldorf. Always gallant and charming, he served as an occasional diversion from her busy business life. And he was amusing, often without realizing it. She needed a night out, so she had accepted his invitation to dinner.

The headwaiter at the Café des Artistes recognized Vogeldorf as a good tipper, so he made a theatrical production of escorting the blond man and his young lady to a good table. The woman was not only beautiful, she was famous. He had read a recent interview and profile about Victoria Van Horn in *New York* magazine. Mr. Vogeldorf usually escorted stunning women, but this one was different—she was rich and powerful in her own right. He placed them at a center table where the other diners could see them and be suitably impressed.

"This is one of my favorite places," Eric said, after giving the waiter their drink order. "I'm in love with the Howard Chandler Christy murals." The restaurant's walls were adorned with erotic paintings of supple nudes.

"My father brought me here several times when I was in college." Victoria looked around at the restaurant. "They've changed it since then, but I'm glad they had the good sense to leave the murals. They're a little campy, but I like them too."

Vogeldorf was full of curiosity about Victoria's father. She was always so guarded about discussing him. He decided to approach the potentially treacherous ground from a different angle.

"How's your new development coming along?" That seemed a safe question.

Victoria raised a quizzical eyebrow. "Why do you ask?"

He smiled and shrugged. "I'm interested."

"Well, so far so good. I believe I've finally lined up the necessary financing. I'm taking considerable risk, but I'm used to that."

"Risk?"

She was amused. He was sometimes so transparent. "Eric, I have put up every penny I have to get the Hudson River project off the ground. I am betting everything on its success."

His eyes widened, his expression a cross between shock and dismay. "Everything?"

She laughed. "The works."

"But what if it doesn't succeed?"

She shrugged. "Then I'm broke and back to square one. I've been there before. But I'm not worried. It will work."

His abject distress was reflected in his expression. "Vicky, that seems, well, so irresponsible. No one bets everything." Then he paused, an answer suddenly occurring to him. "Of course! You have no worries. Your father can bail you out."

Her eyes flashed with sudden anger, but only briefly. He couldn't be expected to understand the depth of her feelings. "You've forgotten, Eric, that my father and I don't even speak."

"But I'm sure he'd help if you were . . . well, broke."

"You just don't understand, do you?" she snapped. "I wouldn't take a dime from my father. What I have I've gotten all on my own. I plan to keep it that way."

He shook his head. "You're right, I don't understand. I've read about your problems with your father. You haven't seen fit to confide in me, but I read what's in the press. Vicky, I think you're just being stubborn. Whatever happened between you two can be patched up, especially if it looks like you might end up without a dime."

She laughed. "That prospect frightens you, doesn't it, Eric."

"My only concern is for you, of course. What did happen between you and your father to make you so determined? It must have been very traumatic."

Vicky smiled. "Well, not really. I suppose you might say it was no more than a family quarrel."

"That's easily patched up."

She shook her head. "No. He obviously considered me worthless, just another rich young woman with no purpose or ambition. He said some things that I considered unforgivable." She thought of her father. Despite everything, she missed him, very much. She often wondered what he really thought of her accomplishments, and whether they had changed his opinion of her. But there was no practical way to find out. She still couldn't bring herself to contact him, because of either pride or fear of rejection, she wasn't completely sure. She wanted to, but so far she hadn't been able to do so. And there were no family members who might act as informal ambassadors. She had only the most minimal contact with her brother, and if they ever discussed her it was never mentioned.

"What's wrong with being rich and idle?"

Her thoughts interrupted, she studied him for a moment to make sure he wasn't teasing her. His concerned look showed that he was expressing his true opinion. "Eric, I'm a human being with brains, perhaps even a little talent. I know how to work hard. I wanted the chance to prove myself."

"That seems odd, really. Why work if you don't have to?"

She shook her head in frustration. "You sound like him. *He* has the money. *He* has the power. *He's* the head of the Vault. Well, I wanted to show *him* that I was someone, too. I think I succeeded."

Vogeldorf knew it was risky to continue, but his curiosity overcame him.

"Well, if that's what you wanted, you got it, didn't you? Except now you may lose everything. By the way, what's this Vault business? I seem to have heard of it before. But I thought it was a Boston organization."

Victoria felt a slow anger, partly because of the remembered words of her father and partly because of the similar attitude echoed by the man seated across from her.

"The Vault consists of a few men who really run New York. The

Boston people, I believe, took their name from the Manhattan group, which my father happens to head, but theirs is much different, quite open and public. The Boston people operate like an elite chamber of commerce."

"You're joking, of course. I mean about the Vault running this city."

She really didn't want to discuss it with him, but his obvious disbelief goaded her on. "There's nothing really secret about it; the Vault just isn't public, that's all. The eight men who comprise it have the responsibility of protecting the business and cultural interests of the 'old money' families of New York."

Eric cocked a quizzical eyebrow. "How so?"

She wondered why she felt so defensive. "They function not unlike guardians. They protect tradition, and more important, finance and commerce."

"The whole thing sounds rather formidable."

She nodded. "Individually the members represent all aspects of commerce, even government. They are powerful men. In combination, they are what is commonly referred to as unstoppable."

"That sounds alarming, Vicky."

"Not really. They seldom interfere unless the issue is truly major."

"And your father heads this clandestine group?"

"He was elected head about ten years ago."

"Is that how one gets in, by election?"

He was trying to appear but mildly interested. But she knew he was posing. Money always interested him. It was more than annoying.

"No, there's no election. Usually the eldest son of a deceased member takes his father's seat. It's a tradition. Of course, if there's no son, or any reason why he can't serve, they select someone else, generally a nephew or some other qualified blood relation."

He smiled easily. "Strictly limited to family, then?"

His continued questioning was getting to be tiresome, irritating. "Everyone who serves as a member of the Vault is a descendant of one of New York's founding families."

"Then I would never be eligible, even if I married into one of those families?"

"That's absolutely right."

"A pity," he said. That answer had obviously ended any further interest for him. He patted her hand. "Allow me to order. The food here is superb, but they truly excel at a few specialties."

As he promised, the restaurant's chef performed a kind of magic with thin slices of veal and a simple, elegant lemon sauce.

After dinner Eric invited Victoria to his apartment for a nightcap.

In the taxi Vogeldorf suddenly drew her to him and kissed her. His movements were fluid, his mouth insistent. For a moment she felt herself responding, but then his ease and sureness became offensive.

Victoria Van Horn was a normal woman with normal desires, and it had been a long time since she had made love. But Vogeldorf's arrogant self-assurance annoyed her. She pushed him away.

He gently patted her leg. "Come now, Vicky. We're not a pair of teenagers out on a first date. We're adults."

She had made love casually at times in the past. And while she hadn't found it particularly fulfilling, it hadn't been awful. She wondered at the intensity of her own reaction.

She had been out with Eric Vogeldorf before, and not once had he made an advance. He was handsome, almost beautiful. In the past it had occurred to her that perhaps he was a homosexual. He seemed especially heterosexual now.

Vogeldorf's hand lingered, just grazing the top of her thigh. "I'm sure you realize I'm interested in you," he said easily. "We have the potential to form a great team, you and I. After all, I have been trained in finance."

"And I have the money, is that it?"

"Come now, Vicky," he said soothingly, his hand fluttering along her leg. "I'm hardly a pauper. We're both young, we're both attractive. In combination we could virtually stand this city on its ear. Let me . . ."

She started to laugh, then pushed his hand away. "Eric, don't be such a damned fool. I know more about you than you do yourself. You're down to your last dime. You have a superior education, that's true, but you've certainly shown no great enthusiasm for hard work. I know exactly the kind of partnership you want, and I have other things to do with my money than lavish it on you."

She was surprised when he, too, began to laugh. "You're a quite amazing woman. Am I as transparent as all that?"

"Somewhat."

This time he patted only her hand. "Vicky, I like you." He smiled. "Can we still be friends even if you insist on holding on to your fortune?"

She found his openness amusing and attractive. He might be a fortune hunter, but he was a charming one.

"Sure." She laughed. "I like you, Eric, but not as a potential husband."

He sat back and flashed his boyish grin at her. "Can you suggest someone else?"

"I beg your pardon?"

"Can you suggest some rich young lady who might be interested in making a good catch? As you say, I am down to my last dime." He laughed at her reaction. "Don't be shocked, my dear. I'm simply being brutally honest. This sort of thing goes on all over the world. Rich women need presentable showpiece husbands. I do consider myself rather prime breeding stock." He sighed. "I've found, at least among the very wealthy, it's a rather unromantic world, especially when it comes to fortunes and family. It's more of a business, actually."

Victoria gave the cab driver her address, then turned to Vogeldorf. "Eric, what you propose sounds quite unwholesome. I suppose you'd even consider giving me a commission?"

He wasn't offended and merely grinned. "You are different, Victoria. Even exceptional, I'd say—at least for a woman of your class. You're a lawyer. You work very hard at truly significant things, and you accomplish a great deal. That sort of pattern is more suited to a middle-class woman, someone on her way up."

"You make it sound completely demeaning. I don't think of it in the same light."

He laughed and shook his head. "Thank God, not all rich women think like you! My dear, you're a normal woman with normal sexual and emotional needs. Money doesn't change that. Women like you can't hope to find lasting happiness with an ordinary clerk who doesn't understand your world. So you see, I offer a very valuable commodity. I am an acceptable, eligible mate. I am an expensive item, to be sure, but I think well worth it."

Her laugh as she looked at him was robust and genuine. "Eric, you know something? Whoever gets you, deserves you. Your attitude stinks."

He grinned, apparently not offended. "Perhaps. But of the very best cologne, surely?"

When she returned to her apartment, Victoria couldn't sleep. Although she had been amused by Eric Vogeldorf and his philosophy, it disturbed her, too. She wondered if she were so very different, after all. Maybe he was right: women like her didn't throw themselves into all-consuming careers. Was it so important to be the total professional woman? She was driven, she knew that, and now, late at night, she wondered what her real motivations were.

For the first time in years she thought of her mother, a woman Eric would have thought quite typical. Her mother had never worked a day in her life, nor had she ever wanted to. Like herself, her mother had gone to the best schools, although she hadn't graduated from college. She had done all the expected things, both social and charitable, at the right places, at the right times, with the right people.

Victoria sat up and looked out the bedroom window. The barren treetops of Gramercy Park danced in the wind.

Victoria had read the faded and yellowed clippings of her mother's marriage to her father many times. It had been the society event of that year. Her mother's family hadn't had the great wealth of the Van Horns, but they were every bit as equal in social status.

The marriage lasted ten years, during which time she and her brother were born, or produced. Even the divorce was newsworthy, getting just about as much public attention as the wedding itself.

Victoria and her brother had been sent, like their parents, to the best schools. In her memory, her childhood hadn't been happy or unhappy. It just seemed like a procession of occurrences. She made friends easily, but never special friends. She had the usual schoolgirl crushes—first on movie stars, then on young men. Her life had been quite typical, she thought. But Vogeldorf was right, she was different.

She even liked her mother's second husband, although he was nothing like her father. While she was growing up, she had seldom seen either parent or their new spouses, but had felt no sense of loss because of it.

With a sigh Victoria got out of bed and walked to the window. Near the park she saw a young couple strolling arm in arm.

Even her love life had paralleled other women she knew in similar circumstances. She'd remained a virgin longer than the others, at least if the others had told the truth. She half smiled at the memory of her near-comic loss of maidenhood in the awkward arms of Allen Canaby.

She chuckled out loud. Her burning eternal love for Allen ended when she found out she was sharing him with Buffie Wheeler. It had all seemed so important at the time.

Except for the death of her mother, her life had been untouched by anything remarkable. Even the car accident that had killed her mother and stepfather hadn't seemed real. The only reality seemed to be accepting the difficult fact that she wouldn't be spending the holidays with them at their Florida estate. Later, perhaps in reaction to the death, she became much closer to her father. Her mother had been emotional, high-strung and unpredictable. Her father was just the opposite. He was in control of himself at all times. She had always felt more comfortable around her father. And she admired him.

The lovers on the street had walked out of view. A lone man walking a small dog was the only person in sight.

She wondered why the separation from her father seemed so much more agonizing than even her sense of loss after her mother's death.

Victoria was acutely aware, except for her work and business ventures, that indeed there was nothing and no one in her life. But she didn't feel deprived, at least not too often. Life is long, she kept telling herself. Eventually, there would be time for other things.

The man and the dog were gone, and now the streets were deserted. She thought once more about her father. It was foolish to keep on with this separation.

Victoria climbed back into bed, suddenly determined to find a way to renew contact with him. She experienced unexpected pleasure in the thought of that reconciliation, and sleep came easily.

———

The Habermann was hardly a household word in New York; there were so many larger and better-known museums. But within the elite international art community, no museum could match its reputation for quality. Its collection was housed in a building specially constructed for the sole purpose of exhibiting the most exquisite, and valuable, artworks in the world. Comparatively small, the museum was an almost perfect copy of a Greek temple. It had been built at the end of the century by the Habermann family—as a monument to themselves.

Other museums, even the largest, had financial woes, but not so the Habermann. It was financed almost exclusively by New York's "old money" families, some of whom could easily and readily trace their line back to the original Dutch settlers. Because some public money was accepted, for political and tax purposes, it was a public museum, but the Habermann never sank to such carnival displays as special exhibits or shows. It was a quiet place, known only to a discerning few.

The families not only donated rare and magnificent works of art, they used the museum as a hub for social contact. It formed the center of their confined and altogether elite world.

The Habermann, like most other museums, had below-street-level areas for such mundane uses as storage, repair and reconstruction. It was blessed with the best of everything, including a sophisticated computer that ensured that every inch of space was regulated at the perfect temperature to protect the aging oils.

Also concealed within the inner bowels of the museum—the nonpublic area—was a splendid conference room. The paneling had been brought over from a fifteenth-century English monastery. The room's centerpiece, a long polished refectory table, had served as the groaning board for a Florentine prince. The chairs, also Italian, would have been displayed anywhere else as rare artworks. The room was a quiet symbol of understated opulence.

Cecil Driker, the museum's new director, was busy fussing over a rather inappropriately dressed workman. Although his leather case contained tools and electrical devices, the man wore a conservatively cut three-piece suit.

"You must position those things so I can hear every word, even a whisper," Driker insisted.

"It would help a lot if you'd let me cut a small square on the underside of this table. It wouldn't be much larger than a dime. Then I could install a listening device directly in the center of the room."

Driker's small face reflected horror. "This table—as you so casually term it—is more than five hundred years old. It would be sacrilege to even scratch it, let alone," he paused, as if dreading even verbalizing the thought, "cut it."

The man in the business suit was sweating. He was obese and the suit was a heavy wool. "Okay, don't worry, I won't do anything to your precious table. I can set up a couple of these devices," he flipped a tiny metallic object in his hand, "on opposite sides of this room. These little babies may not look like much, but they're sensitive as hell. You should be able to pick up everything."

Cecil Driker, slight of stature but always dapper, was dressed in an elegant Italian silk shirt and tight designer jeans. Vain by nature, Driker was fifty, but looked younger. He had shaved several years off his official age. He frowned. "It won't be picked up outside, will it? That's all I need, to have a scout car crew come blundering in here to find out what they've been listening to on their police radio."

"No chance of that. These stone walls are too thick. Besides, I can adjust these things so the only one who can hear through them is you. It's the newest thing. State of the art, as they say. Of course, as I told you, all this requires very expensive equipment."

"Don't worry about the cost," Driker said loftily. "The museum is anxious to curb art thefts. It's all a justifiable expense." Driker planned to bury the charges among other bills for electrical work being done in another part of the building. No one would ever know.

The stout man worked quickly and expertly, installing the bugs in picture frames, then completely concealing them with putty that matched the wood of the frames. He was an expert, a former federal technician who specialized in planting and detecting listening devices. He assured Driker that not even the cleaning crew would know they were there.

"I can't understand why you people want this conference room bugged," he said while he was cleaning up the remnants of the putty. "It's been my experience that most thieves don't hold meetings, at least not in fancy digs like this." He ran his finger over a frame to make sure everything was smooth.

"The art world is different," Driker said haughtily. But he was thinking of the enormous advantage of being able to obtain secret information, the kind that could lead to insider trading. "These devices of yours will serve a very effective purpose, I can assure you."

The man wiped the sweat from his forehead. "Well, it's none of my business anyway. I'll go up to your office now and double-check the receiving equipment and the tape recorder. Wait a few minutes until I get up there, then talk or sing so I can check the sound."

Driker scowled. "All by myself?"

"You could always ask an employee to come in. Perhaps actual conversation would be a better test."

Driker quickly shook his head. "No, that won't be necessary. I'll do it alone. You just go on up to my office."

The man simply nodded, giving no hint of what he might be thinking. He picked up his leather case, wiped his face one more time, then left the room, quietly closing the door behind him.

The equipment did indeed cost a small fortune, but Driker considered it worth every penny. He wanted to hear every word spoken. The museum's board of trustees used the conference room, but he didn't care about them. Nothing they ever said or did was terribly interesting.

He had learned about the other group almost by accident. As director, he always had the schedule and he knew they met monthly. But he paid no particular attention, except to note the importance of the individual members of the group. Cecil Driker had attained his meteorlike rise in the world of art by carefully fawning over anyone who looked as if he had the least bit of influence. So out of habit he had made it a point to greet each of these men individually each month. That was even before he knew their collective importance. Now he fairly danced attendance upon their every wish and whim.

One of his assistant curators, a daughter of a prominent New York family, had told him about them. They were called the Vault and represented the families whose power and fortunes actually ran the city. They were the real owners of the Habermann, and they used the museum's conference room for their very private monthly meetings.

Cecil Driker began to sing self-consciously in his reedy tenor voice. He chose a Noel Coward song. He kept his voice purposely low as he moved around the room. It was of vital importance to ensure there were no dead areas. Even a whisper had to be audible.

If the electrical devices functioned properly, the Vault would have a silent and secret member who would be privy to everything that went on. The possibilities were limitless. To know exactly what the powers who ruled the city planned could be the magical formula to enormous riches. He would be able to obtain insider information without detection. He would be able to buy and sell stock without risk. If necessary, he could even bring in partners to finance schemes—schemes that couldn't fail. He had stumbled upon a golden opportunity and he planned to take full advantage. It was like owning Aladdin's lamp.

Cecil Driker began to do a slow fox-trot around the table of the Tuscan prince.

"I'll see you again, . . ."

Men were such fools—so easily captured, so easily dominated. She occasionally wondered if her low opinion of men might be some indication or expression of latent homosexuality. Cecelia had read of such things.

He lay there, his eyes closed, his facial muscles loose and relaxed after the recent explosion of pleasure. She looked up at his young face. He was handsome in a wispy way.

"You liked that?" she whispered as she moved up, running her hands beneath his shirt, the only article of clothing he still wore.

"Fantastic," he murmured. It was a word he used to describe almost everything, and she found it annoying, especially when he applied it to her lovemaking.

She sat up in bed and reached for a cigarette from the pack on the bedstand. "Only fantastic?"

"You know what I mean. It always seems to get better somehow."

She inhaled deeply, then turned to look at him. He was her husband's administrative assistant, a boy just out of college who had landed a job with a fancy title but who was really only a male secretary. But he had ambition.

Cecelia Van Horn recognized that she was just using him. But it was a fair exchange. This particular young man was looking for a promotion. Discreet sexual encounters with the boss's wife entailed the risk of discovery and discharge. On the plus side, of course, was that if this kind of indiscretion remained undiscovered, it was historically a sure avenue to rapid promotion.

She wondered if he were gay. He almost verged on being pretty. He seemed to prefer oral sex, but only if she was the one doing it. The reverse was always skillfully avoided.

She also vaguely wondered if she might be sharing him with her husband. Hunter Van Horn, Jr., had never shown any propensities that way, but something had arrested his natural sexual desire, at least where she was concerned. And he didn't seem to respond to other women. If he did, he kept that response artfully concealed from her. Human sexuality, she knew, was a puzzle, always. She studied the young man's smooth face. If Junior had turned gay, her new young lover might be enjoying an enormous joke. What a droll story to be told in certain circles—being blown by the boss and his wife, each not knowing about the other.

"Doesn't my husband ever wonder where you are and what you're doing during these long afternoons?"

The boy's eyes opened. "Oh, I always get my work done. I suppose he thinks I'm seeing someone." He ran a delicate hand through his hair. "But as long as I'm efficient, he doesn't seem to care."

Languidly resting on one elbow, she stretched out next to him. "Tell me, has my husband a little thing going on? He seems unusually understanding about your taking time off. Perhaps he has something going himself?"

The boy laughed. "You always ask the same thing. Your Junior has no girlfriend. I'm sure I'd know if he did."

She smiled, her eyes only inches away from his. "And how about boyfriends?"

For a moment there was fear in his eyes, but that moment passed almost instantly. "He's about as sexual as a piece of furniture." He was choosing his words carefully. "I think I'd probably know if he was, well, that way."

She patted his face with her free hand. "I'll bet you would," she said, letting him know by her inflection what she suspected.

"What do you mean by that?" He seemed to react just a little defensively.

Cecelia lay on her back and took another puff on the cigarette. "As his administrative assistant, you know everything he does and everyone he sees. If he were homosexual, I imagine you'd be the first one to know."

The boy sat up. "He's as straight as an arrow, at least as far as I'm concerned. I mean, as far as I know."

She reached out and stroked his cheek. She didn't want to upset him. He'd gotten his end of their little exchange, now it was time for her part of the bargain. There was information to be had, accurate information.

"Has Junior talked to my beloved father-in-law lately?" She made the question sound casual.

He nodded. "Yesterday. For a few minutes on the telephone."

"What did they talk about?" She continued the stroking.

He turned and looked down at her. She noticed that her nakedness had no visible effect on him. "Doesn't your husband tell you everything?" he asked.

She smiled. "Not quite everything."

"Well, it's just as I told you. Mr. Van Horn calls your husband about once or twice a month. Usually they just make small talk about the company, you know, business things."

"Do they seem to get along well?"

The young man climbed out of bed and stood up. As he retrieved his shorts from the floor, he turned to face her. He slid them up over his smooth legs. "It's strange. They seem sort of formal with each other. Your husband calls him Dad, and Mr. Van Horn calls him Junior."

"How do you know that? He certainly doesn't ask for 'Junior' when he calls, does he?"

"His secretary places his call," he replied.

"You could only know that he calls him Junior if you listened in." She giggled. "How naughty!"

The young man blushed. "It was accidental. I was on the extension when your husband picked up his phone. I heard the exchange before I could hang up. Then I was afraid to hang up in case they thought I was listening. I just had to sit there, and hold my breath. They didn't say anything important. Just the usual conversation about the company."

He pulled on his trousers. Expertly tailored, they were cut to fit very snugly around the crotch.

"How many times have you listened in?"

"Just that once."

She laughed. "I'll bet."

"Honest." He slipped on his highly polished shoes. "Listen, I've got to get back to the office."

Cecelia continued to drag on her cigarette, exhaling and watching the smoke spiral toward the ceiling. "It might be wise if you made it a point to always listen in when they talk."

"Why?"

"It certainly can't hurt, not if you're careful. And I'd like to know a little more about my husband's relationship with his father."

"Why don't you just ask him?" He adjusted his tie in the mirror, then quickly but carefully combed his hair.

Sometimes, she thought, he moved very much like a woman. "Because I suspect he sometimes withholds the truth from me. So from now on, I'll ask you. You'll always tell me the truth, won't you?"

He studied himself in the mirror. "Naturally."

"Good. Then use those gorgeous little ears of yours." She smiled. "I particularly want to know if they ever discuss my wonderful sister-in-law, Victoria."

"Why?"

"Just curiosity." It was an out-and-out lie. Cecelia Van Horn was terrified that her father-in-law might reconcile with his daughter. At whatever cost, it was the single thing she had to stop. "Just let me know," she said. "You won't regret it." Her voice was heavy with promise.

He sighed. "I'll do what I can." He looked at his watch. "Honestly, I have to run."

"Call me tomorrow. I'll be home in the afternoon."

"Will you be leaving soon?" He seemed worried. They couldn't risk being discovered by her servants, so they always met at his apartment.

"In a few minutes. What's the rush? Is there someone else coming in?"

His laughter was forced. "No, of course not." He touched his lips to her forehead, then left. Once he closed the front door, she listened to the silence.

Like a cat in the sun, she stretched her body. She was still unfulfilled; that was annoying. Despite this minor irritation, she considered these trysts well worth the effort. Two things counted: she not only had a direct line into her husband's business life, she—more importantly—was able to know and assess his relationship with his famous father.

She wondered if Junior was really doing his part. They were a mere heartbeat away from having immense wealth and prestige. Hunter Van Horn was the father of only two children, and he was estranged from his daughter, Victoria. They should be intent upon courting the old man, making damn sure they were the only ones in his will. They should be making it a mission to permanently cement Junior in as his heir-apparent.

If anything happened to Hunter Van Horn the elder, she could well become the most important woman in New York. Maybe even the most important woman in the country. Her father-in-law wasn't that old, and it was conceivable that he might remarry, or worse, effect a reconciliation with his bitch-goddess daughter. Either course had to be blocked. Cecelia would have gone to bed with the father if she thought it would have helped. But he was moral about some things, and probably fucking his son's wife was one of them. Cecelia considered that a pity. Certainly that path would have been the easiest. Now she would have to work hard to accomplish the same ends in other ways.

She sat up and crushed out the cigarette. If this young man was in fact gay, she thought almost nonchalantly, there could be the possibility of AIDS. Quickly casting aside that horrifying thought, she began to get dressed. There were more practical things to think about. She wondered if Junior honestly appreciated her efforts to safeguard his interests. To be married to a man with such unbelievable prospects and so little ambition was more than galling.

6

Franklin Trager took orders from no one except his secretary. Even though Janice McDaniel was extremely efficient and maddeningly capable, he strongly disliked the woman. She possessed a domineering quality that made his stomach churn. If it weren't for the fact that he had come to depend upon her for almost everything, he would have delighted in firing her.

Trager was a battle-tested executive who commanded not only a fast-growing network of retail stores, but also dozens of manufacturing plants. He had built it all, beginning with the original Trager's of New York—a Fifth Avenue shop that sold only the finest collections from Europe's exclusive designers. That store had served its purpose and was now closed. Then he'd gone to the other end of the economic scale. With outlets in every state, including Alaska and Hawaii, Trager's dealt in quick-turnover, discounted merchandise. The profits were immense. And he had branched out into manufacturing and producing low-priced electronic goods, also sold by his famous chain. Unrefutedly, Franklin Trager had become one of the richest men in America.

In his mid-sixties, Trager was broad but muscular, his perfectly tanned skin still without wrinkles. His excellent physical condition reflected an energy that had become legendary in the business world. When Franklin was still a young man, his father had died. Since that time, he had worked night and day to build the Trager stores into a potent retail force. In the process he had summarily crushed a number of rival retail networks whose names were now mere memories.

His manufacturing plants, both in America's South and in the Orient, used cheap labor to churn out a river of good-quality products. *Forbes* listed him near the top of its list of rich Americans. He pretended to be disdainful, but he was secretly delighted to be included in that exclusive company. He felt it proved to his fellow members of the Vault that Franklin Trager was no mere shopkeeper, but a man bursting with successful new ideas and innovative concepts.

He kept his headquarters in midtown Manhattan's Drysdale Tower. But there the rents continued to skyrocket, and his lease was due for renewal in a few months. He considered staying on as nothing more than a foolish waste of good money.

Trager's office, although enormous, was anything but pretentious. The vast space contained only a small desk, his chair and two straight-backed chairs for visitors. The only other piece of furniture was a padded table at the far end of the office, next to his small and modest bathroom.

"It's almost ten o'clock, Mr. Trager," his secretary reminded him.

Pushing himself out of his chair he walked over to the padded table and began to remove his clothes, systematically hanging them at the end of the table. His behavior was nearly automatic, his mind preoccupied with other things.

He stood completely nude as he looked down from his large office window at the city below. Anyone who might have been in a neighboring building, if he cared to look, could have seen the squat man standing in the buff, surveying Fifth Avenue below as though he owned it. The possibility that anyone might look at him never even entered Trager's mind.

His office door opened and Ernie hurried in. Graying but moving with an athlete's grace and wearing a white medical tunic, he looked like a doctor on his way to the hospital. He wore a brown topcoat slung casually over his shoulders and carried a large leather bag.

"How you doin', Mr. Trager?" He flashed a wide smile, exhibiting several shining gold teeth.

"Not bad, Ernie. You?"

Ernie slipped off the topcoat, tossing it carelessly on the thick carpet. He removed a collection of bottles and tubes from his bag, then began to rub his hands vigorously. "Jesus, it may be springtime somewhere, but it sure hasn't gotten to Manhattan yet. I'll just warm up these old mitts of mine so that you don't go screamin' out of the window."

Trager effortlessly climbed up on the table and lay on his stomach.

Once a professional boxer, Ernie had since become the masseur to the men of power in Manhattan. He was good, fast and stoutly masculine. Everyone felt relaxed with Ernie.

"Man, this freakin' city is getting worse all the time, you know that, Mr. Trager?"

Trager was paying little attention. Ernie's trained hands began to expertly knead Trager's flesh just above the shoulders. It was almost painful.

"I got held up last night," Ernie continued, making conversation that required no response. "I went over to Brooklyn to see my sister, the one who used to be a nun, you know. Anyway, I get off the subway and two punks pull knives on me." He snorted. "Just little punks, you know, but their knives were big enough. They grabbed my wallet and then took off like striped-ass apes. They didn't get much. Just a couple of bucks. But that's the third time I've been robbed."

"What did the police do?"

Ernie laughed. "What cops? Hey, they don't do nothin' anymore except give out parking tickets. I didn't even bother makin' a report. They'd just file it away. It's stupid unless you got insurance and want to prove somethin' happened. What a city, huh?"

Ernie sighed. "Of course, if you defend yourself, then you got plenty of trouble. Like the guy who shot those hoods on the subway. If you're a citizen, and not a robber, you got your choice of ways to lose. You can let them mug you, maybe even kill you—they'll probably get away with it— and if you defend yourself, you get arrested, hit the front pages, and everybody condemns you as a vigilante. You can't win, you just pick the way you want to lose. New York's no place to live for sane people."

Trager merely grunted. Ernie's words reflected certain plans that Trager had been preparing for quite some time. As far as Franklin Trager was concerned, New York was dying, and, in his far-from-humble opinion, sinking very fast. If people like Ernie got robbed, or even murdered, it was of no great consequence to him. Crime statistics merely added more ammunition to arguments he was eagerly polishing.

"Everybody who lives here just takes it for granted that they'll get mugged someday, or burgled." Ernie's fingers threatened to pull Trager's flesh away from the bone. It was as though Trager were being brought to the edge of pain but never quite over. Ernie was a genius at what he did.

"I read the stories in the papers," Ernie continued. "It seems that every couple months some politician starts yelling about street crime like he just discovered it was there. They get headlines but they never do any-thing. Hell, nothin' is safe in this city anymore. You park a car here, it's stolen before the motor gets cold. It's that bad, it really is."

Trager again grunted. Crime was one thing, a minor consideration. From his viewpoint, it was the taxes, expenses and inconvenience that were making New York untenable. It cost a king's ransom to do business in the city.

"And it's not as if living in New York was such a great thing anymore," Ernie went on. "The rents are out of sight. It costs a mint just to exist here. And the corner deli charges an arm and a leg for a lousy orange. And if you go into a bar, like I used to do, one drink can cost you almost as much as a bottle of hootch. That's a lot to pay, just to be sociable."

Trager merely nodded as Ernie's fingers dug into the back of his thighs. The masseur was right: a terrible imbalance was taking place. Only the rich had enough money to live in New York with any degree of comfort. And Trager thought the poor seemed to enjoy being jammed into their miserable squalor, living in places not unlike Dante's Hell, scrimping by on welfare and whatever else they could find. The middle class was being squeezed out.

"I got no choice. I got to stay on here," Ernie continued. "This is where I get my business. There's no place else where there are so many important executives like yourself. But believe me, if I thought I could make a decent living almost anywhere else, I'd go in a minute. I got another sister who lives in Cleveland. Now that ain't exactly paradise, either, but it's a hell of a lot cheaper. And a person can live in a suburb there and at least feel secure. Yes, sir, if it wasn't for my line of work, I'd pick up in a minute."

Trager evinced a half-smile. For different reasons, he had arrived at the same conclusions as had his masseur, but he intended to do something about it. New York no longer had any attraction for him. Manhattan was his place of origin, but he had houses in Palm Springs and the Bahamas. He still owned a number of commercial buildings in Manhattan, and they were at the peak of their value. Now was the time to sell.

Only his corporate headquarters remained in Manhattan. And he had made up his mind to relocate even that small part of his business. But he felt a duty to his fellow members of the Vault. They had always acted together, protecting their mutual interests. He felt at least he had to try to persuade the others to the same course. The city was becoming ungovernable, and the expense of doing business in it grotesque. Now was the ideal time for all of them to sell quietly and move away. He had even worked out a viable plan to accomplish it. They could all make a handsome profit by discreetly selling off their properties—there were plenty of rich Arabs and European buyers—then they could quietly slip away. It might take two years to carry it off completely, but it could be done.

"You know, Mr. Trager, New York's turned into a city of sleazeballs." Ernie worked his strong fingers deeply into Trager's calves. "Hookers, transvestites, bag ladies, bums—the whole place is just one big loony bin. God, I often wonder what the tourists must think when they come here. Everywhere you look there's strange-lookin' people talking to themselves. I'll bet none of those tourists would want to come and live here on a permanent basis."

Trager was deep in thought. He would find a way to put forth his idea to the other members of the Vault. But he knew realistically that as long as Hunter Van Horn was head of the group, his concept would have no chance. Van Horn's love of New York was well known. Despite that, Trager was determined to try. Perhaps Van Horn might change his mind. Then they could all leave.

"Did you ever think about leaving, Mr. Trager?" Ernie asked. "You know, just moving out, lock, stock and barrel?"

Trager slowly shook his head. He certainly owed nothing to Ernie. "New York is my hometown, Ernie. My family has been here since before the Revolutionary War. I could never leave."

Ernie chuckled. "That's what I figured. All true New Yorkers manage to stick it out somehow, no matter what."

Trager grunted. The city would be doomed if they all left, but it was doomed anyway. He would have to figure some way around Van Horn.

———————————

On the other side of the world another wealthy businessman stared out at the blue waters of the South China Sea as he weighed the relative merits of a number of hard choices. He had similar thoughts to Franklin Trager's.

Should they leave?

Like Trager, he too had to contend with a deep-rooted tradition. His decision would not only affect his family's fortune but many others' also. A wrong choice could spell disaster, and the end of a proud dynasty.

The sea was like a mother; he would not wish to be separated from such a parent who had always provided so much. If they did decide to move, it would have to be to someplace near the sea.

A white gull glided high upon the wind, its wings spread fully to catch the uplifting thrust of the shore breeze.

He watched it. The decision would have to be made soon. The Chinese would take over Hong Kong in a few short years. If they were to move, they would have to begin soon.

Jon Krugar wished he could be at peace like the solitary gull and float free from care, but he could not.

The decision had to be made, and only he could make it.

Ambassador Stewart Lytle sat across from his son in a small room designed to look and feel like a comfortable living room. Intended to be snug and inviting, it somehow retained its institutional air despite the hospital staff's best efforts.

"I'm sorry, father. It won't happen again. I can assure you of that."

Congressman Barry Lytle was dressed in casual trousers and a green polo shirt, his feet in leather slippers. He looked wan and tired.

The ambassador frowned at his son. "You always say you're sorry, Barry. You managed to survive this incident. I was able to keep all this out of the newspapers. People are more open-minded nowadays, but I doubt that even in these permissive times they would want a drug addict to be their next United States senator. Even New Yorkers. I think it's time you grew up, don't you?"

Congressman Lytle merely nodded.

"The Vault will meet tomorrow. Most of the members are aware that you may become a candidate for the Senate. I've not approached anyone directly, except Van Horn, but I'll start tomorrow."

"Perhaps you should wait."

The old man's steely eyes stared unblinkingly at his son. "Wait? For what? We have to lay the foundation now. It will take money, and, more important, the right kind of support. If the members of the Vault decide to back you, they can elect you. It's as simple as that. We don't have any more time to waste."

"And suppose they don't back me?"

His father sneered. "Even as a child there was always an air of defeat about you, did you know that? The only reason you've gotten anywhere is because of me. You'd better straighten out. I'm not going to live forever."

The congressman looked out the window and said nothing. If his father died he would welcome the freedom from his parent's domination. Yet that prospect also produced real fear in him. He was afraid of his father, but he also desperately needed him.

"The key will be Hunter Van Horn," his father continued. "If we can persuade him to back you, the others will follow. Hunter will be pivotal."

"Does he know about my . . . problems?"

His father's face was otherwise expressionless, but his eyes narrowed to slits. "That you're a drunk and a dope addict? I imagine he's heard rumors. God knows I've spent a fortune keeping all this out of the public eye, but people will always whisper. We'll just have to wait and see just how much he may have heard."

"I like the House of Representatives," Barry whined.

The ambassador's cold eyes filled with disdain. "You always like what's comfortable, what's easy. You're afraid of change, afraid of challenge. But this will be just like all the other changes in your life; you'll like the Senate as soon as you're settled in there."

"And then the White House, I suppose?"

Ambassador Lytle's mouth became a thin, grim line. "If you can ever control yourself, it's a very definite possibility," he snapped.

"So my future depends on what the Vault may do?"

His father stood up and glared down at him. "I'll have your administrative assistant fly in from Washington on Friday. The doctors tell me you can be checked out then. But I do not want you to leave his side, do you understand me?"

"I'm under house arrest then?"

His father's glare turned even more malevolent. "If you can't control yourself, you'll eventually be under a much different kind of arrest. And believe me, that will make this seem like living in a palace." He tapped the door. The attendant opened it and he was escorted out.

Congressman Lytle was returned to the main room, where, like himself, many of the patients were celebrities. He had come to like most of them, except for the television anchorman who was a true psychotic and needlessly cruel.

Lytle needed something—a drink or a hit—but both were out of the question.

One of the doctors, who, like the rest of the staff, was dressed informally with no badge of his calling, walked over to him.

"Everything all right, Barry?" he asked.

Barry Lytle's practiced smile answered him. "Just fine."

"Good visit with your father?"

"Sure."

The doctor chuckled as he patted Lytle's shoulder. "You're a fucking liar, Barry. Come on, I'll get you something to calm you down. I know you're trying to conceal it, but your insides are boiling."

"Is it that obvious?"

The doctor shrugged. "No. Only to someone like me who has read your file. Come on."

———

Victoria Van Horn was conscious of admiring glances as she strode along Lexington Avenue, moving with the noontime crush of hurrying humanity.

Craig Hopkins's telephone call had taken her by surprise. She had agreed to meet with him before she had time to really think about it. It had been almost three years since they had seen each other. After the call, memories came flowing back like a flood. Some of the remembrances were pleasant, some not. She regretted her impulsive action. But she always kept her promises, so she now battled her way through the lunch-hour crowds on Lexington.

Kenneth's was a small restaurant known to working city people, a place where only beer was served. The food was fast and good, if sometimes somewhat greasy, and inexpensive by Manhattan standards. The place was jammed as she pushed her way in.

At first she thought Craig had failed to show up, then she saw him wave to her from one of the back booths. Her first reaction was a rush of pleasure, and that surprised her.

She wiggled through the line of customers waiting for take-out orders, then slid into the narrow space of the booth.

He sat across from her. "It's been a long time, Vicky." His smile was tentative, as if he was unsure of how she might react.

"You've changed." It was an honest statement. He was thinner and looked older. The sure cockiness of youth seemed to have flown forever from his long, slender face.

"You're the same." He smiled affectionately. "Better looking, perhaps, but the same. How have you been? I've been reading about you."

"That publicity is all part of promoting my business activities." She studied him more closely. He was still handsome. "And how about you, Craig? How's the practice of law?"

"It has its ups and downs. That's why I wanted to talk to you, Vicky. It's on behalf of one of my clients."

"You said it was business," she replied evenly. "Go on."

His smile faded. "I feel like an idiot. Frankly, the only reason this client came to me is because he heard of our earlier relationship. At the time, it didn't seem improper to approach you. But as with so many things in life, now that you're here, I feel I've made one hell of a mistake."

Victoria twisted the napkin in her lap and tried not to show any emotion. "Business is business. It's been all over between us for quite some time, Craig. So you're really not trading on much, are you? Don't feel guilty. If it makes you feel any better, I talk to friends of my father for the sole purpose of advancing myself. Everyone does it. Now, who is this client of yours?"

Craig's manner became more relaxed. "You do business with your father's friends? I thought . . ."

She shrugged. "Nothing's changed. Dad and I haven't talked to each other in years, as you know. But that doesn't stop me from invoking his name, at least with those people who don't know any better."

"That sounds, well, rather exploitative, Vicky."

"It is," she replied coolly. "But no more than this little luncheon is exploitative. As I said, it's done every day. Now, what's on your mind?"

He reddened. "Forget it."

She had always found his clear blue eyes immensely attractive, and she didn't wish to hurt him. She smiled to lessen the impact of her words. "I see you're still the hopeless romantic. When you and I were living together I often found that the most charming thing about you, or the most irritating, depending on the circumstances. Look, this is strictly a business lunch. It's as simple as that. So go ahead." She kept her words purposely expressionless. She was a romantic too, and unexpectedly shaken by her feelings at seeing him again. It was very important to her not to appear weak in his eyes.

He slowly shook his head. "Okay, I'll get right to the point. My client is Martin Moran. Do you know him?"

She raised an eyebrow in mock surprise. "Who hasn't heard of the famous Bronx slumlord? And I know what he wants from me. He has an option to buy a building I need for my new development. He thinks I'm waiting until his option runs out and then I'll step in and buy the building."

"That's what he told me."

She smiled. "And he's perfectly right. If he could raise the money he'd exercise that option and buy the place himself. But he can't, and now he's trying to trick me into financing his adventure. I'm sorry, Craig, I'd like to help you out, but it's not possible."

Craig nodded. "Moran will be upset. But I'll pass along the message." He sighed. "Well, now that's over, let's have some lunch."

They gave their orders to the waiter, a young Greek having obvious difficulty with the language. They had to repeat everything slowly before he managed to understand. He hurried off toward the kitchen.

"You know, you really remind me of your father," Craig said.

Her eyes met his. "Oh, is that so? In what way?"

He smiled slowly, almost shyly. "That's not meant as a knock, Vicky. I'm impressed. You're all business, just like him. Same attitude, same drive and obviously the same talent. I'll wager you'll end up a billionaire too."

"I'm getting there," she said easily. "I hope you're not mistaken about the talent, Craig, but you certainly are about the drive. As soon as I've established myself and accomplished what I have set out to do, I'm going to sit back and relax. My father never stops. But I'll know when it's time to quit." She spoke the words confidently but she wondered if she would ever know when it was time to stop, or even what it was she really wanted. "It may look that way, but I'm not like my father at all."

He looked at her without replying and smiled, but there was a touch of sadness in his expression. "You really can't see it, can you, Vicky? You're cut from the same cloth. I'm sure you must realize that in your own way you're competing with him. I think you're out to show him, to prove to him that you have real worth."

"Calling Dr. Freud," she said lightly, but his words were disturbing. "I suppose there may be some validity in what you say, at least to a degree. But I'm in this for myself, primarily. It would be a nice side benefit, of course, to show my father that I'm every bit as good as he is. Proving yourself to your parents isn't exactly a new concept, you know."

"It is if you're trying to take over the world."

She wondered why she felt so defensive. "That's always been a problem with you, Craig. You never truly commit yourself. You want to play at life. And it's not a game, it really isn't. Either you devour it or it devours you."

"That's a rather pessimistic attitude, isn't it?"

The bustling waiter brought their food, setting down the cups of coffee awkwardly, spilling the hot liquid. He cursed in Greek, then quickly wiped up the mess with a greasy gray towel.

Victoria waited until the waiter left before continuing. "There's nothing pessimistic about recognizing reality. Life is competition, and I come from a long line of competitors."

Craig's blue eyes fixed on hers for what seemed like a long time before he replied. "You'd feel a lot better if you made it up with your father."

Her eyes became steely. "That's up to him."

He laughed. "Well, some things, it seems, never change."

Her stubbornness had caused arguments when they had lived together. She smiled at the memory. "My father's stubborn too. Perhaps one day he'll see the light and call me. But I'll be damned if I will."

"That's probably his exact attitude too."

"Maybe. Anyway, it's foolish to discuss it. Nothing's changed between my father and me. And I doubt if it ever will."

He took a bite of his dry sandwich, then a sip of coffee. His eyes were still on her. "So I take it, then, there's no chance you might change your mind about my client?"

"None whatsoever. That subject is closed."

Craig was suddenly tempted to ask her out. He felt an almost urgent longing, a return of feelings he thought long dead. He said nothing.

"How are your parents?" she asked, changing the subject.

"They're both fine."

"Say hello for me, will you?"

He smiled. "They really like you. I caught hell when we split up."

She took a hurried forkful of her salad. "I like them too."

They looked at each other, then both of them quickly looked away.

"Ah, Vicky," Craig said, breaking the awkward silence. "The Boston Symphony is in town tonight. I have tickets. Ozawa is conducting. Would you like to go with me?"

She was about to say she was too busy, which would have been an honest answer, but something stirred within her, awakening pleasant memories of other times. "Can you pick me up at my office?"

His shy smile spread into an enthusiastic grin. "I think I can manage that."

———

Hunter Van Horn, burdened with a heavy briefcase loaded with voluminous reports and projections relating to the Entertainment Group, climbed aboard his private jet. He was in the middle of a major corporate crisis, but it all had to be put aside to attend the monthly meeting of the Vault. He planned to use the flying time from Los Angeles to New York to study and prepare a course of action. The aircraft was a six-passenger

McCormick, reliable but aging. As soon as the company's fortunes improved, he planned to buy a new, larger one.

"What's the weather look like, Charlie?" he asked the pilot as he settled into a deep leather chair and fastened the shoulder harness.

"Not bad, Mr. Van Horn. It's clear all the way to the Rockies. They're having a snowstorm up there, but we should be able to climb over it. After that, clear skies almost all the rest of the way. It's drizzling in New York, but it should clear up by the time we get there."

"Okay, Charlie. I'm ready to go whenever you are."

"No staff coming?"

"No. This is just a quick trip to New York and back." Van Horn had assigned his various secretaries and assistants to more pressing company business.

"Then I'll crank this baby up. We'll be ready to request takeoff clearance shortly."

"Fine." Van Horn sat down and opened his briefcase on the convenient fold-down mahogany table. Things were in major turmoil. His company would need not only a steady hand just to survive, but also a very generous slice of luck. He knew he could provide the steady hand; it was the luck that bothered him.

They had crossed over the vast desert regions and were now high above the mountains and the storm below. The flight had been smooth and uneventful.

Hunter Van Horn found it difficult to concentrate on the reports. They merely outlined problems. It was up to him to provide solutions. He would have to fire a number of senior executives, many of whom had friends on the board of directors. That was certain to cause an uproar. It would be a risk. Lately he hadn't been very popular with the majority of the board. Such drastic action could inspire a move to unseat him. But it was a battle that had to be fought. Things were bad, and if the giant company wasn't dramatically turned around, eventually he would be tossed out anyway.

He glanced at the darkness below as they sped high above the Rockies. The storm had turned into a bona fide blizzard and was depositing record amounts of spring snow on the slopes of Colorado. The airplane seemed to be streaking just above the churning gray clouds.

Suddenly the jet rocked, then vibrated with a peculiar wiggling motion. Hunter would have chalked it up to air turbulence except for the change in motor noise; the engines became louder, their whine reaching a higher pitch.

Van Horn got up, using the seats as handholds as he made his way up to the front of the aircraft. His pilot was hurriedly adjusting the instruments, his hands fairly flying along the multilighted instrument panel. "What's wrong?" Van Horn asked.

"I'm not sure. The motors seem to be overheating. We'll have to put down at Denver."

"Is that absolutely necessary? I have important business in New York."

"Something's wrong, Mr. Van Horn." The pilot tried to keep a professional calm in his voice, but the trace of fear couldn't be disguised. "We may have a sick airplane here."

Van Horn slipped into the vacant copilot's seat. "Can I help?"

"I don't think so." The pilot radioed their position and requested permission for an emergency landing. The plane rapidly started to descend toward the dark clouds below.

Warning lights began to blink all over the instrument panel. Hunter Van Horn had been in danger several times in his life, and he had found he wasn't the kind of man to panic. He carefully assessed the possibilities.

They were close to Denver. In a matter of minutes they could begin their approach for an emergency landing at Stapleton, that city's huge international airport. But first they would have to get over the enormous jagged peaks of the Rocky Mountains, some reaching up thousands of feet into the sky.

Hunter Van Horn had never wasted time dwelling on dying. But suddenly he was seized with an overwhelming sense of sorrow that he hadn't reconciled with his daughter. The possibility of dying without coming to terms with Victoria seemed nightmarish, worse than death itself. It was something that just couldn't be allowed to happen.

Suddenly they were bouncing through snow. The storm's winds grabbed the jet and shook it like a toy.

"Jesus," the pilot whispered as he fought to keep control of the aircraft, "this is getting rough."

Van Horn could see nothing. The snow eliminated all visibility, rendering the windows useless. There was no feeling of movement. Without the help of the instruments they could be flying upside down or sideways and never know it.

He wished he could call Victoria. He couldn't put her out of his mind. It was like an obsession. There were so many things he wanted to say to her.

His death, if it happened, would embolden his enemies, both inside and out of the corporation. They would come on very hard and without mercy. He knew he had taken all the precautions. But the future was always a gamble.

The pilot swore softly as the jet continued to bounce in the turbulence.

Van Horn squinted and tried to peer through the snow. If they didn't make it, the Vault would certainly be thrown into turmoil. His sealed instructions to them weren't binding, but if the other members were smart, they would carry them out despite tradition.

He thought about his son. Junior had been such a disappointment. They had never been truly close. He wondered if his son would mourn for him if it happened.

His daughter, he thought sadly, would not. She would never know how much she meant to him or how proud he was of her. He was such a damned fool. He should have done something, said something to let her know how proud he was of her, and how much he loved her. It was a terrible price to pay for pride. The sorrow was almost crushing. In amazement he felt tears spill upon his cheeks.

Suddenly he felt the airplane shudder and heard the dying scream of its engines. Hunter Van Horn's last thought before the jet smashed into the side of a mountain was that it was so unfair; death was something that should happen to people who had nothing left to do.

The crash sent up a huge fireball that lit up the snow like a rising sun. But because of the storm, no human saw or heard anything.

The pilot had radioed his position and his desperate situation. When nothing more was heard, it was assumed that Van Horn's jet had crashed. The wreckage was covered by the falling snow. Despite an intensive search, the twisted metal and what was left of the two bodies weren't discovered for several days.

They had stopped for drinks, then Craig had brought her to her apartment. Victoria felt almost giddy with pleasure. The music had been majestic. It seemed as if she had stepped back in time, capturing again the spirit of the love she had known, all the conflicts, all the fights forgotten. She hadn't felt so good or so free from care in years.

"How about a nightcap?" she asked Craig.

He too was caught up in the mood. He grinned. "You've got a deal."

In the elevator he reminded her of an adventure they had shared when they had both been law students. She was still laughing when she unlocked the door to her apartment. But she was startled to see that her maid was still up, and that several lights were on.

"Miss Van Horn . . ."

Victoria wondered if the woman might have been drinking, for there was a red puffiness about her eyes.

"I thought you'd have been in bed long ago," Victoria said.

Her maid's face seemed to be twisting with emotion. "I was. The Colorado state police called. They woke me up."

Victoria was puzzled, but a vague foreboding tugged at her. "I don't understand. I don't know a soul in Colorado."

The woman looked at Craig as if imploring him for help. She opened her mouth several times before she could find her voice. "Your father . . ."

"What about my father?" Victoria's pulse was racing.

"It's been on the television already." Tears began to spill from the maid's eyes, trickling slowly down her wide cheeks.

"What? For God's sake, what are you trying to tell me?"

The woman swallowed. "The police, they say your father's airplane went down near Denver. They think. They think . . ." Her voice became a raspy whisper. "They think he's probably dead, Miss Van Horn."

It was as if the earth had suddenly stopped. Victoria seemed incapable of thought.

From a seemingly great distance she heard Craig say he would call the police and try to get details, but his words were far away, unreal.

Somehow it seemed to Victoria that she was the one who had died.

7

Enos Peacock had resigned the federal bench in 1958 to serve as a main partner in New York's prestigious law firm of McManus and Tate. However, everyone still referred to him by his former title. With his craggy face, brooding eyes hooded by bushy eyebrows, and a perpetually stern expression he looked like a judge.

"As you both know, I was your father's personal attorney, and for more years than I care to think about. I thought it best that I advise both of you privately as to the major provisions of your father's will."

"I presume this little meeting is only that, merely informational," Hunter Van Horn, Jr., said. "I have my own attorney. I would have brought him along except that you said you wanted this private."

"This is the purpose: information." Judge Peacock looked over at Victoria. "I trust you also have a lawyer? You know the old adage that attorneys who act for themselves have fools for clients."

She had known him since she was a small child. He had always come to family parties and seemed to be an important part of her father's world. He was more like an uncle to her than the family lawyer. Her mind continued to reject the reality of her father's death. She felt crushed under an unbearable burden of guilt. The estrangement between them, now never to be repaired, seemed like a sentence of doom. She could never tell her father now just how much she had loved him. Despite the pain that thought provoked, she could think of little else.

"You've always been the family attorney, Judge. I don't need anyone else." Craig had volunteered to come with her, but she felt it was something that she had to face by herself. She had clerked at McManus and Tate one summer between law school terms and she had expected to feel comfortable in the well-remembered offices, but she did not.

The judge nodded, his solemn face giving no hint of what he might be thinking.

Victoria presumed she would receive nothing: that her presence was only a courtesy. She didn't care. Money meant nothing. She felt sudden fear: her father might have used his will to release some of his anger against her. Her guilt was unbearable enough without recriminations from beyond the grave.

Victoria glanced over at her brother. If he shared her sorrow it wasn't apparent. He seemed changed, more confident, almost arrogant. Junior had taken over all the final arrangements, including the garishly elaborate and well-publicized memorial service held at Wall Street's Trinity Church. He handled every small detail of the funeral and burial, and he seemed to have relished it. He hadn't even consulted her about any of the arrangements.

Enos Peacock cleared his throat. "As you both know, your father was an extremely wealthy man. His holdings, chiefly in his own company, varied from time to time, depending on the market and other externals. At the moment, my best estimate is that his estate will be valued at about a half-billion dollars." His voice was as solemn as his expression. He paused, as if watching for a reaction. "That's a rough estimate, of course. It includes a number of trusts and other devices to keep taxes down, but I think that figure is reasonably accurate."

"I thought it would be more," Junior said, his tone surly, almost hostile.

Victoria was preoccupied with the possibility that some angry message might have been left behind for her. She didn't care about the amount.

The elderly lawyer peered over his half-glasses at Junior for a moment. Then he continued. "Your father left a number of specific bequests. He was, I think, rather generous toward his former wives. Of course, by doing so he has prevented them from fouling the estate with harebrained lawsuits. Each of them will receive several million dollars. If they contest the will in any way, they will lose all that. It's a provision often used in wills to prevent lawsuits. It works quite effectively.

"He also left a handsome amount to Yale to endow a chair for the study of business administration. Several other universities will receive similar bequests."

Junior shifted in his chair. "Get to the bottom line, Judge."

A frown played briefly upon the lawyer's craggy face. "In a minute," he said firmly. "Your father left additional liberal sums to various organizations, charities, museums, and so forth. And his servants were all well remembered."

Junior's laugh was harsh. "Lord of the manor, right to the very end. Well, I suppose it was to be expected. He always had an open hand for the people who worked for him," he said disdainfully.

The lawyer stared at him as though seeing him for the first time. "The rest and residue of the estate is left in trust."

Junior stiffened at the word. "Trust?" he rasped.

Enos Peacock nodded almost imperceptibly. "Yes. It is a trust created to save paying estate taxes, or at least part of them. Most of his fortune was already in that trust, including all of his stock holdings." The lawyer paused, looking briefly at each of Hunter Van Horn's children. "He has named me as trustee, with alternate trustees named in the event of my demise or inability to serve."

"Jesus, what the hell does that mean?" Junior snarled. "Does that make you the boss?"

"No. I merely carry out the provisions of the trust, to safeguard it, chiefly." The judge's tone was level.

Junior sneered. "Well, we'll see about that. Go on."

Victoria looked at him again. She saw nothing of her father in him, he was so different, and not just physically. His attitude seemed so reminiscent of their demanding and often emotionally juvenile mother.

Judge Peacock paused. Victoria wondered if he was dreading what he had to do, whether he was trying to shield her from what was to come, at least for a while. She searched his face for a clue but found none. She wished it was over.

"Let's get this done, shall we?" Junior's statement was more a command than a question.

The old judge nodded. "As you wish." He looked for a moment at Victoria, then his eyes rested on her brother. "The income from the trust, in other words, your father's fortune, goes to both of you equally."

"What!" Junior hissed the word.

Judge Peacock looked directly at him. "I said, it goes to you both, share and share alike." His face showed no emotion. "However, there are some differences."

Her brother's pallor suddenly became ashen.

Judge Peacock continued in the same even tone of voice. "Your father was quite explicit about this, both in the will and to me personally." He looked at Victoria. "Although the stock itself remains in trust, he has given full control of that stock, including the voting rights, to you, Victoria."

She wondered if those were actually his words or whether they were merely part of a self-serving daydream. Under stress the mind could often construct an unreal world as an escape from harsh reality. It was what she desperately wanted; some sign that in the end her father had loved her. It seemed so unreal, very much like a dream.

Victoria felt the sudden rush of tears. She buried her face in her handkerchief until she could control herself. "I'm all right," she managed to say to Enos Peacock, who watched her with genuine concern.

Her brother ignored her reaction. His words snapped out at Peacock like an angry whip. "When was that will made?" Junior snarled.

"Last November, five months ago."

"Something's goddamned fishy here! Really fishy!" Junior's voice was becoming shrill with emotion. "The old man had nothing to do with her." He glared at his sister. "She crapped all over him. They didn't even speak to each other. Why would he even give her a penny, let alone controlling interest in his company!" His voice had risen to a shriek.

Judge Peacock sat back, bringing his fingertips together as if in prayer. "Don't let this embitter you, Junior. After all, you do share equally."

"In the goddamned money, not the power!" He was trembling. "I had to run his errands and do the damned groveling, not her. I had to take his crap all these years. It isn't fair!"

Her brother's growing rage seemed distant, as if it were still part of a dream sequence. The unexpected expression of confidence by her father was to her nearly as shocking as his sudden death. Victoria realized she should be elated, but somehow it seemed to deepen the guilt and the sorrow she felt. He had expressed his love, but she had never done so. He had died not knowing. She bitterly remembered the fight that had started it all, and she wished more than anything in life that she could somehow undo it. But she could never do it now. That finality caused a depth of sorrow that was almost physical.

"I'm not going to stand for this!" Junior was red-faced and shouting. "I'll get this so-called will tossed out in court!"

"There are two very good reasons why that's not advisable," Enos Peacock replied evenly. "First, the provisions in the previous will were essentially the same. Your father just changed the amount of some of the educational bequests. The paragraphs regarding you and your sister remain the same."

"Then I'll get that one thrown out, too. I'll sue! I'll tie this up in court forever if I have to." Junior's face was trembling with exploding emotion.

Peacock's stony expression remained unchanged. "That's the other reason such a course of conduct would be ill-advised. Your father made a provision that if either of you was to contest the will, or any part of it, that person would lose everything. It's the same provision that applies to his former wives," he added wryly.

"What?"

Peacock looked over his glasses. "Junior, if you should bring any legal action contesting the will in any way, your father provided that you won't receive a cent. I suppose he anticipated that you wouldn't be pleased. Of course, the same provision applies to your sister."

"But suppose I am successful, and I do get the wills thrown out, then what happens?"

A hint of a smile ghosted upon the lawyer's thin lips. "You'll merely deprive some excellent universities of rather hefty endowments. Under law, you would still be entitled to only half, even if there were no will." The old man leaned forward, his eyes suddenly hard and piercing. "Even if you did win, which would be extremely unlikely, you'd still come up with the same amount. And if you lost, Victoria would get everything. Your share is roughly a quarter of a billion dollars. I hope you fully realize that. I doubt that anyone in their right mind would take such a risk."

Junior clenched his fists in rage. "That rotten old bastard! That miserable son of a bitch!"

Peacock's disdain was clearly visible. "Your father left you half his fortune. I'd be inclined to be a bit more grateful, if I were you."

Junior's face was a mask of hate. "Grateful? He left me the money all right, but he cut off my balls doing it! Now I'll never be anything, can you possibly understand that? I'll be able to buy anything I want, except respect. He's robbed me of that." He turned and glowered at his sister. "And it's all because of you, you bitch!"

"I'd advise you to restrain yourself, Junior." The judge's voice was stern.

Victoria felt numb. It was as if she were watching a play, not part of it, just a member of the audience. She made no response to her brother. She felt only pity for him.

"Something's wrong here, really wrong," Junior continued. "You'll be goddamned sorry before all this is over. You won't get away with this, Victoria, you can count on that. I don't care what that old cocksucker left in his goddamned will."

Victoria's guilt was suddenly converted into a seething rage. She stood up. "I'd be careful to be more respectful of our dead father, if I were you," she said quietly, carefully enunciating every word. "And don't even think about fighting me. It would be a very uneven contest."

"You may get the company, you bitch," Junior spat the words at her, "but I'll take his place on the Vault." He tried to smile but it ended as a snarling grimace. "And I'll use that position to destroy you. I'll get you back for this, both you and that old bastard!"

Peacock cleared his throat. "I'm afraid this just isn't your day, Junior."

Junior looked at him, his eyes widening. "What do you mean?"

Peacock's reply was almost kindly in tone, as if he felt sorry for the son. "Your father didn't think you'd bring much to that organization. He cautioned them to vote against your selection. They aren't bound by his wishes, but I'm sure they'll follow them in this case."

"Oh yeah? I'm his only son, his natural successor. They always go according to family lines. They'll have to select me. There's no other person eligible."

Peacock shook his head. "Your father did nominate someone to take his place. Who they eventually choose is up to them, of course. However, I understand they do give great weight to persons nominated under these conditions."

Despite herself, Victoria was curious. She could think only of her cousin in California, but he was a commercial artist living a laid-back West Coast life-style and therefore not a very likely candidate.

Junior sneered. "I don't care what my father told them, they have to pick me. Those old bastards guard their traditions like Fort Knox."

"Perhaps not this time," Peacock replied, with a hint of a smile.

Junior snorted. "Family is the name of their game. You'll see."

Peacock's eyes seemed suddenly cold. "You may be right, but they don't have to choose you."

Junior rose half out of his chair, his face fixed and angry. "Old man, there isn't anyone else. I'm it!"

"That's not entirely accurate," Peacock said sternly. "Sit down." He spoke politely but it was a clear command.

Junior resumed his seat, his cheeks flush with color. "I suppose there's some goddamned obscure relative that I haven't heard of. That would be just like him. All right," he snapped, "let's hear the fellow's name. Who is it?"

The sudden silence in the office seemed strangely eerie, as if they had been sealed in a soundless vacuum.

Peacock's stern expression never changed as his eyes remained fixed upon Junior. His deep voice seemed to echo as he spoke. "It isn't a fellow. It's your sister."

It didn't seem possible. Victoria was as shocked as her brother. She stared at Judge Peacock in disbelief.

Junior's face drained of color. A pulse throbbed visibly in his forehead. "Now I know you're lying," he snarled. "There's never been a woman member of the Vault. They won't buy that, even if it were true."

"What they do is up to them," Judge Peacock said. "But it's quite true."

Junior leaped from his chair. He looked about wildly. "I don't believe a word of this shit! I want a copy of that so-called will. I want my own lawyers to see it."

Enos Peacock reached into his desk and extracted a thick envelope. "I anticipated that you would. This is a photocopy. I have filed the original with the court."

Junior started to speak, then stopped. He stared at both of them, then snatched the envelope from the lawyer's hand and bolted out of the office, slamming the heavy oak door behind him.

"Judge, I must apologize for my brother . . ." Victoria began.

The lawyer shook his head. "I can't really blame him. It all came as a surprise, actually quite a shock. He'll be all right in time. Your brother doesn't possess the wisdom or ability to serve on the Vault, and he could probably never run anything as large as Van Horn Enterprises. I think, deep down, he knows that. Perhaps that's the real reason he became so angry. He knows when the chips are down he just can't measure up."

"And you think I do?"

The old man allowed himself the luxury of a small smile. "Oh yes, my dear. You've more than proved that. And, as you can see, your father thought so, too. I know you and he weren't talking for the past several years. He told me all about the quarrel." He chuckled softly. "But he was enormously proud of you. He was forever bragging to me about your accomplishments."

"I regret that I . . ." The tears she had been fighting came in a flood. "I wanted to see him but . . ." She found she couldn't speak without crying.

He handed her a tissue, then waited until she had regained control of herself. Peacock was obviously uncomfortable in the presence of emotional displays. He cleared his throat. "I think I know what you want to say. You loved your father. He knew that. In time you two would have made it up. He was stubborn, and being his true daughter, you are stubborn too. Death always brings such terrible feelings to the survivors. But I'm afraid you'll have to put those feelings aside. They are a luxury you can't afford at the moment."

She looked at the lawyer. Everything still seemed so unreal. "Why?"

His face took on its accustomed solemn dignity. "Victoria, your father has charged you with great responsibility. He wanted you to safeguard the company he built. You must take over for him."

"I can't." She began to cry again. "I have my own business, my own problems. I don't think . . ."

He shook his head. "You really have no choice, my dear. If Van Horn Enterprises is compromised, you stand to lose much of the fortune I spoke about. And not only your holdings but those of the other stockholders. I'm afraid there is no alternative. Your duty is clear. You'll have to take charge of your father's affairs."

"But . . ."

"And you may indeed find yourself a member of the Vault. That too is a weighty responsibility."

"My brother was right about that. They'd never accept a woman."

Judge Peacock half smiled. "It's a powerful tradition, I grant you. But we'll see; today women serve on the largest corporate boards, the Supreme Court, are even nominated to run for vice-president of the country."

"Perhaps if they did choose Junior, it would make him feel better."

Peacock's eyes were almost sad. "I'm afraid it's one of those things you can't walk away from, Victoria. They won't accept Junior. Your father expected you to take his place. A Van Horn has always served. It goes with the territory."

She took a gold compact from her slim lizard handbag and deftly powdered her face to cover the evidence of the tears. "If what you say about father's company is true, I won't have time for the Vault, even if they did offer membership."

"You have a great responsibility now, my dear. You must do what is best for a great number of people, not just Junior, or even yourself. All this is a great burden for one so young, but I know you'll carry it off. So did your father."

He gave her a copy of the will. It seemed as if suddenly she were quite incapable of independent thought, as if she existed in a vacuum.

Judge Peacock escorted her through the firm's offices to the elevators.

"Your father was very proud of you," the judge said as she stepped into the empty elevator. His smile was quickly gone, and again his eyes looked sad. "But I'm afraid from now on, Victoria, your life is entirely changed."

As the elevator doors closed, it seemed to Victoria as if the doors of her past life were closing too. Forever.

PART TWO

PART
TWO

8

The circus that her husband had produced and passed off as a funeral was finally over and Cecelia Van Horn was celebrating. Hunter Van Horn was absolutely dead and gone. Now Junior wasn't a junior anymore. He was the main man. But she continued to wear black for appearance's sake. Besides, she considered black to be flattering, accentuating her figure. But she let her sexy outfits hang in the closet, wearing only the most modest, though chic, designer clothes.

Junior was at the family lawyer's office. Just a formality, he had said. The king was dead, long live the king. And his queen. Cecelia had quickly noticed a significant change. At the funeral the photographers had taken a great many pictures of her. Victoria still got the lion's share of media attention, but that was to be expected. But this time the cameras had pointed at Cecelia too. And Junior. It was a welcome difference.

Cecelia had even been named in the long piece in the *Wall Street Journal*. The article, an overview of the Van Horn companies, featured both Junior and Victoria, but she had been prominently mentioned not only as Junior's wife, but also as his advisor. She knew her time had finally come. And she planned to savor every moment of it.

The company limousine was waiting for her as she stepped out of Tiffany's. She had always enjoyed special service at the famous Fifth Avenue store, but this time she could sense a subtle difference in the treatment afforded her. Just a shade more deference was paid, reflecting her new standing.

The chauffeur hurried around the long limousine and deftly helped her into its luxurious interior. Opulently equipped, it had been her father-in-law's car. She may have disliked Hunter Van Horn, but she admired his taste in cars. The chauffeur pretended not to see the long expanse of leg she flashed.

"Take me home." Cecelia spoke crisply to the driver. Their wildly expensive apartment, located in the choice Fifth Avenue area of the Seventies, was now not quite up to the standard of living expected of the man who would run the Van Horn empire. People expected queens to live in palaces. They would have to find something even more elegant, some place markedly more extravagant. The apartment wouldn't be home much longer.

Cecelia felt she had been specially groomed for just this particular destiny. Her family wasn't truly wealthy, but her mother had nevertheless given her an appreciation of the finest things money could buy. Her taste, although considered by many superficial, would become the measuring stick for the really important New Yorkers.

The doorman scurried to help Mrs. Van Horn from the limo and carried her packages up to the penthouse. Of Puerto Rican descent, he had the look of a man experienced with women. He never went beyond frank admiration; he knew his place.

But his swarthy, animal sexuality pleased her, and in a moment of delicious speculation, she considered asking him in. But that would have shocked her servants, so she quickly discarded the notion, instead merely thanking him by pressing a folded bill into his hand as her maid answered the door and took the packages.

"Any calls, Marie?"

"That lady columnist from the New York *Daily News* called again."

"She's a nuisance." Cecelia Van Horn would never lower herself to allow *that* woman to quote her in the *News*. She was above gossip columns now.

"And your husband's office called several times. That young assistant of his."

Cecelia wondered if Marie might possibly suspect their relationship. But it was unlikely. They'd been discreet. Still, it was odd that he had called from the office. She presumed Junior would have returned there after the meeting with the lawyer.

"Has Mr. Van Horn called?" she asked the maid.

"No ma'am."

Cecelia walked into her bedroom and sat on the edge of the bed. She lit a cigarette. Calling the office was risky. People could listen in. But perhaps he was only delivering a message from her husband.

She dialed the number and was put through.

"It's me," she said. "What's up?"

"I don't know," he answered in a near whisper. "I can't talk much now. Have you heard from, er, my employer?"

"I just got home."

"He was due here for a meeting, but he didn't show up. That's very unlike him, as you know."

"And he hasn't called?"

"No."

"He's seeing a lawyer today. He probably got hung up."

"Can I see you?" His words were an urgent hiss.

She smiled. She'd wondered if he was going to ask. They had no contact since the death. The little bastard sounded nervous, no doubt afraid of what the future might hold for him.

She crushed out the cigarette. He had served his purpose. "This isn't the time," she said coolly. "We'll work something out later."

"Please," he said, nearly begging.

Cecelia hung up without bothering to reply. He was old news. Besides, he hadn't been much of a lover. She had the whole world to pick from now.

She felt good as she got up and walked out of the bedroom. She felt like having a drink.

She heard him before she saw him. His voice was quarrelsome as he snapped something unintelligible at the maid.

Since the news of his father's death, he had grown more aggressive daily. It was as though he had been given an enormous dose of confidence. His new power might make it even more difficult to live with him.

Junior stalked into the dining room, then glared at her as if seeing her for the first time.

"How did it go?" She walked past him and went to the sideboard. She poured some brandy into a snifter, then turned and smiled widely at him. "Well?"

He roughly pushed her aside as he grabbed the brandy and filled a snifter almost to the brim, spilling some of the expensive liquor. He was shaking.

She was startled. He seldom had anything stronger than an occasional glass of wine. He disapproved of liquor and had often told her so, too often.

"I thought you didn't drink."

Junior gulped down a healthy portion of the brandy. Some of it dribbled down the corners of his mouth. He blinked at her, his eyes wide and watery. She quickly realized he was already drunk.

She had never seen him that way before, and she was suddenly frightened. "What's wrong?" Her question came out as a whisper.

He took another huge gulp, then flung his body into a chair. He leered up at her. "There's nothing wrong," he said, much too loudly. "Why should anything be wrong?"

"You don't usually drink. What happened?"

His chuckle was mirthless. "If you're worrying about the money, don't. We get half, exactly half." He stared at his glass.

"You can't mean he left the other half to that bitch of a sister of yours?"

"You mean Victoria?"

"Do you have some other idiot sister hidden away somewhere?" she asked sarcastically.

Junior drained the glass, then looked up at her. "You'd better learn to be a little more respectful, my dear. Victoria owns you now, too." His giggle sounded more like a sob.

"What the hell do you mean?" she snapped.

He lazily tossed his glass across the room, arcing it gracefully. The Baccarat crystal exploded into a glittering cloud as it hit the wall. "Bingo!" He laughed bitterly.

She felt the anger rising in her. "Don't be such a goddamn fool. *What happened?*"

"My father, my own dear father, whose ass I have dutifully kissed all these wonderful years, left full control of his company and everything else to my darling little sister. That's what the fuck happened."

Cecelia felt dizzy, as if suddenly there were no air to breathe. "Junior, you're drunk. You don't know what you're saying!"

He looked at her, grinned, then hiccupped. "Yes, Cecelia, I'm drunk, but I'm also very, *very* serious."

She finished her own brandy, shocked in the sudden knowledge that he was telling the truth. "Was that in the will?"

He nodded.

"Well, we'll sue the damn lace panties off your darling sister. We'll put that bitch up against the wall!"

He breathed in, then sighed, shaking his head. "My crafty old man anticipated just that. If we sue, we'll lose every goddamned cent." He bit his lip, his eyes brimming with tears. "This is the fucking pits."

"Is that all you're going to do? Just sit there and feel sorry for yourself? Jesus, even a rat will fight when it's cornered. You're absolutely spineless!"

"Oh I can fight, if you want. I can go to court, lose, and you'll have to suck off sailors for a living. But then, I suppose you'd like that."

She stepped across the room and slapped him smartly across the face.

He grinned as he wobbled to his feet. "Ah, my lovely Cecelia. You always know exactly the right thing to do."

She didn't expect it. He didn't look as though he had the balance to do it. His fist caught her solidly on the jaw. She reeled backward, then slammed down hard on the carpeting. She tried to get up, but his hard kick caught her thigh just below the buttock. He was laughing, as she tried to roll away from him.

He fell on top of her, tearing at the top of her expensive dress.

"I'll show you what I can do!" He was pawing madly at her as she attempted to push him away. The numbness in her jaw was giving way to throbbing pain. She wondered if it might be broken. He was snorting now, gasping for breath, bumping frantically against her. She realized he couldn't get an erection.

The servants who heard the commotion rushed in. They quickly pulled him off and helped her up. Junior sat on the floor, drunkenly mumbling to himself, his trousers bunched around his knees.

"Take him to his bed," she said through clenched teeth. Pain exploded with each spoken word. "Then bring me some ice, and call Dr. Daniels."

The maid brought her a towel filled with ice. She sat in a chair, wondering what she must look like. Her hands were trembling. Oddly, she felt no anger toward him. He was a mere object to her, occasionally useful, like a piece of furniture.

Her husband might be beaten, but Cecelia wasn't. There was always a way. It took a woman to fight a woman. And she was equal to it. She was so furious she hardly noticed the throbbing pain intensified.

Cecelia determined to destroy Victoria Van Horn, by any and all available means.

———————

Chilton Vance, sitting in Hunter Van Horn's chair, spoke quietly into the telephone. "Of course I'll pass along your condolences to the family. It's been a great shock to us all. I certainly appreciate your call, Harry. As soon as the dust settles we'll get rolling again. And we'll take another look at that idea of yours." Vance smiled to himself. The idea was as useless and empty as the caller. But there was no point in making unnecessary enemies. "I'll have one of my people give you a call when we're ready. Thanks again for the kind thought." He hung up.

He had moved into Van Horn's office the afternoon following the funeral. Nothing had yet been changed; there hadn't been time. However, he did replace Hunter Van Horn's girl with his own secretary. That move had caused some ripples in the executive suite. Joyce Spitz was classified as a senior secretary but she was paid the salary of a major corporate officer and was treated like a vice-president. There had been speculation that she might have bestowed sexual favors upon Van Horn, but Vance discounted such gossip. Van Horn, who preferred exotic women, could have had any woman he wanted and plain Spitz hardly filled that bill.

Vance had wondered if the Spitz woman might possess information embarrassing to Van Horn, but that also seemed unlikely. Whatever the reason, she was identified with Van Horn and had to go. But she was well liked and Vance didn't want to risk firing her outright, so he had assigned Joyce Spitz to the typing pool. It was such an insulting fall from privilege and income, he anticipated she would resign. He was informed the women in the typing pool were riding her pretty hard. But she surprised him. She had quietly cleaned out her desk and meekly reported to her new supervisor. But Joyce Spitz who had tasted life in the executive suite would eventually quit. And she was only the beginning. Vance wanted every one of Van Horn's key people out of the company. He planned to run the corporation his way.

His own secretary appeared at the office door. "There's an Enos Peacock on the telephone. He says he's the Van Horn family lawyer. Do you want to talk to him?"

She spoke as if she were part of a conspiracy. She obviously liked being executive secretary to the head man, and she was smart enough to realize that his future was her future too.

"Yeah, I know him," Vance replied. "Put him through."

"Mr. Vance?" The lawyer's voice was deep and vibrant.

"How are you, Judge?" Vance's tone was silky.

"I'm fine, Mr. Vance. I saw you at the funeral, but I didn't find an opportunity to say hello."

"I saw you, too. A sad occasion indeed."

"Very sad." But Enos Peacock didn't sound sad, merely businesslike. "These things happen. I thought I had better call and tell you what Hunter provided in his will. I have been authorized to do so."

Vance experienced a chill of foreboding, a chill that was fast turning into real apprehension. "Please go on."

"Hunter was quite generous to a number of educational and charitable institutions. There were other provisions, but the rest of the estate, the bulk of it, he left to his two children, equally."

"That surprises me, Judge. Hunter seemed proud of his daughter, but they were estranged, at least as far as I knew."

There was a pause. "That's correct."

Vance idly played with Van Horn's garish desk set. Gold and ivory, it was a gaudy item that would soon be replaced. "It's always nice if there are no bad feelings after a death."

"Hunter left his estate, everything, equally, but not the power."

"I'm not sure I understand you, Judge." Vance put the letter opener down and gripped the edge of the desk.

Again there was an infuriating pause. "The two children share the income from the estate, but not the voting power of his stock."

Chilton Vance smiled. Junior would be no problem. "I presume he left it to his son?"

The lawyer's tone was cool, almost distant. "I'm afraid your presumption is a bit faulty."

"Pardon me?"

"You flipped the coin the wrong way. Victoria Van Horn has been given all the powers possessed by her late father."

Vance felt the receiver tremble in his hand. Suddenly he felt like a trespasser in Van Horn's private office. He fought to keep emotion out of his voice. "That's quite interesting. I've never met her. I—er—came to the company after the trouble between Victoria and her father. Of course, like everyone else, I've read a great deal about her."

"She's an experienced businesswoman as well as an attorney," the judge continued smoothly.

"Since she now controls the largest single-owned block of voting stock, I have no doubt that she will want a hand in how the company is run."

"That's natural," Vance managed to reply calmly.

"I think it might be quite appropriate to give some thought to how her rather unique talents might be utilized."

"As a consultant?" Vance's voice sounded almost squeaky even to his own ears.

"The board of directors might consider electing her successor to her father. At least as an interim measure."

Vance sat forward and tried to concentrate. "Was that provided in the will?"

He was answered by a deep throaty chuckle. "No. It wouldn't have been binding if it were. I'm familiar enough with your corporate charter and rules. I helped draft them. The board elects the officers. Selecting her now as chairman and president would be a nice gesture." He paused again. "Also, she would bring great energy to the company, and new ideas. It's only a suggestion, of course."

Vance felt his head pounding. Somehow Hunter Van Horn continued to frighten him, even from beyond the grave. But he couldn't allow fear to rule him, not now. He had to be clever. Extremely clever. "I agree," he purred smoothly. "That would be a fitting gesture. If the young lady would be interested, of course."

"I think she might be persuaded."

Enos Peacock sounded very sure.

"Perhaps we can work something out. Let me sound out the board. Of course, I'll have to talk to Miss Van Horn first."

"That sounds like the thing to do. If I can be of assistance, Mr. Vance, please let me know."

Vance replaced the telephone receiver as gently as if it were a live time bomb. For a moment he sat perfectly still, not even thinking, just letting his pulse slow from its trip-hammer rate.

There was no legal obligation to name Van Horn's daughter to anything. If they refused and if she was angry, she'd have to wait until the annual stockholders' meeting to protest effectively. She could muster the support of only a third of the board; they were Van Horn's people. That would be all. She could easily be denied the presidency, and there wasn't a thing she could do about it, legally or otherwise.

It was damned bad luck that Van Horn had died. Chilton had set it up so perfectly; all cleverly planned and orchestrated. The report of the Research Group would have been the lever to unseat Van Horn. It would have worked. Vance would have been raised up as a savior. Now, if he took command, he would appear to be just another member of the Van Horn administration, not its opposition. Some hard-eyed and ambitious young man might knock him off just the way he had planned to do it to Van Horn. Being a savior was far better than being a successor, at least this time.

He began to relax. Victoria Van Horn knew something about developing, but she had been a lucky young woman, nothing more. She was really inexperienced in a rounded sense. Estranged from her father, she would know nothing of the inside workings of the company, nothing at all. He smiled. Perhaps, if she were named as interim president, he could still become the messiah.

But that could be dangerous too. What if the board began to like her, what then? Vance thought about how bitter Junior must feel. It was too bad that Van Horn hadn't picked his son for control. He was so different from his father. No one would have wanted to appoint him. Junior would have been such an easy target.

A plan began to form in his mind. Suddenly Vance laughed aloud. He had to admire his own inventiveness. It would work perfectly.

He stood up and walked to his office door. His secretary looked up.

He smiled at her. "There's been a change of plans," he said quietly. "I will be moving back into my old office." He walked past her, then turned. "Oh, please get Victoria Van Horn on the phone for me."

The secretary's eyes widened.

"She has an office," he snapped. "It's in the book."

There was no point in waiting. He would put the plan into operation immediately. His wife had seemed strangely depressed since Hunter Van Horn's death, as if his demise had cheated her out of some kind of revenge. Well, she would perk up now. She'd get her revenge.

And so would he. In fact, the prospect made him feel quite Machiavellian.

Cecil Driker was beside himself with excitement. The Vault had called a special meeting. He presumed Hunter Van Horn's death was the reason, but he wasn't sure. Driker had double-checked his concealed electronic equipment. Everything was functioning; he would be able to hear every word. He had discovered he experienced a surprising titillation when eavesdropping. He was even beginning to get erections.

As usual, Driker stationed himself at the museum's main entrance to greet each Vault member as he arrived. They all seemed so serious and preoccupied, a condition, he thought, that gave promise of a really stimulating session. He could hardly wait until he could race to his office, lock the door and turn on the receiver.

With Van Horn's death there were only seven of them now. John Robertson, the head of the famous brokerage firm, was the last to arrive. He walked up the museum's steps with difficulty, his enormous weight fast becoming more than his legs could handle. Puffing from the exertion, Driker escorted him to the conference room. As soon as Robertson stepped inside, Driker closed the big double doors and hurried to his office, trying to keep from breaking into a run.

Trembling with excitement, he locked his office door. He then fumbled with the small key to the wooden cabinet, finally managing to open the hinged doors. The installer had fixed it so none of the equipment had to be removed. He flicked on the switch and welcomed the familiar hum. He clamped on the earphones, then tuned in the disembodied voices in the conference room.

The clarity was superb.

"I thought it advisable that we get together as soon as possible." Driker recognized the voice of Sander Blake. The publishing magnate's voice had a distinctive nasal quality, with a hint of an Oxford accent. "We have two items of pressing business. We have to select one of us to be chairman of the Vault. And we have to choose someone to become a member of the Vault as Hunter's successor."

Driker heard grunts of agreement.

"As you know, I took it upon myself to call this meeting. By the way, the fact that I instigated this gathering doesn't mean that I'm running for chairman. Please understand that."

Driker heard some chuckles.

"We're all old friends here," Blake went on. "Unless there are any objections, I'll continue to conduct the meeting until we select a permanent chairman."

Driker leaned back in his high-backed leather chair and closed his eyes. He could conjure up their faces in the conference room. He felt as though he were in the room, but invisible to the others.

"I think we should first consider who's going to take Hunter's seat on the Vault. We can pick a chairman after that." Driker recognized the deep, aggressive voice; it belonged to Franklin Trager.

"There's no point to that." The high, reedy tone of Elias McKensie, the former secretary of state, crackled through the earphones. "First things first. We should pick a permanent chairman."

"I agree. We should first select a permanent chairman." Ambassador Lytle's tone was flat and forceful. "Anybody want the job?"

The silence seemed embarrassingly long.

"We're all busy men." Trager spoke again. "Chairing the Vault takes a lot of time and effort. It's a responsibility none of us really wants."

"Are you running for office, or what?" Elias McKensie's words ended in an asthmatic chuckle.

"No, I'm not. I say let's select one of us, if that's what you want, and get it over with."

"Anyone opposed to that?" Blake asked.

Again there was silence.

"All right. How shall we do this? The last time, as I recall, someone nominated Hunter, and he was selected unanimously."

"But he accepted reluctantly." Clifford Colburn, the head of one of the world's largest oil companies, spoke. His words provoked laughter.

"That's true," Blake said. "All right, I suppose we may as well begin. Who would like to make a nomination?"

"Gentlemen, I rise to that purpose." The wheezy voice of Elias

McKensie again filled Driker's earphones. "We all agree that none of us wants the job, and for good reason. However, it is a most important position. Not only does it require that rare quality, leadership, but above all, the man who assumes the mantle must be a diplomat."

"You were secretary of state, Elias, why don't you take it?" The voice belonged to Franklin Trager.

"I would, Franklin, but the man selected shouldn't be suffering from the slowing effects of advanced age. I plan to live at least another quarter century, but old age tends to leave one rather fatigued, I find. I have all the necessary qualifications and qualities except energy. We need a younger man. The man I propose has that."

"Elias, all due respect, but can we keep the nomination speeches to a half hour or less? I have things to do." The words were full of good humor. Driker could visualize the round, smiling face of John Robertson.

There was a pause and some laughter. Driker guessed that old McKensie was hamming it up, pretending to be affronted.

"I'll not be that long, John. At my age, a half hour is something to be treasured. I'll be brief, despite a lifetime of training to the contrary. I nominate a man who has the background, the energy, the interest, and the tact to do the job. I nominate and move the election of Sander Blake as permanent chairman."

"I second that," Robertson said loudly.

"Gentlemen, I appreciate the honor," Blake protested, "but as you know, I own and operate a number of newspapers throughout this country, in addition to my magazines. I'm gone from New York much of the time. I really think I'd be a poor choice."

"Do you decline?" Trager asked roughly.

"No, I don't decline, Franklin. I would ask, however, that you consider someone else."

"You're the man, Sander." Robertson laughed. "We realize no one wants the job. Unless you decline, it's yours."

There was a long silence, and Driker wondered if his equipment had malfunctioned. He was about to reach for the dials when Sander Blake spoke again.

"As we all know, it's a long-standing tradition that none of us will shrink from an assignment, at least not without very good cause. No one in this room has time for the job. I suppose one of us has to bite the bullet. I'll serve at your pleasure."

There was a polite smattering of quiet applause.

"No acceptance speech," Trager growled. "Let's get on to the next piece of business. I have a meeting to go to."

Again there was an uneasy silence.

"Before I came over here," Blake continued, "a messenger from Judge Peacock's office delivered a sealed envelope to me. As I'm sure everyone here knows, the judge was Hunter's personal attorney."

Blake paused, then continued. "The judge called and informed me that this envelope contains Hunter's personal wishes concerning his vacancy."

"How did Peacock know we were going to choose you?" Trager demanded.

"The judge knew I am a member of the Vault. That's all. Believe me, Franklin, I'm only the messenger boy. I haven't even opened the envelope. Peacock was acting on Hunter's instructions. As we all know, it's customary for deceased members to leave written suggestions concerning their possible successor."

Driker felt his heart thumping wildly as he listened. It was like one of those award shows when everybody waits for the secret winner's name to be plucked from the sealed envelope. He could hear the envelope being torn open.

"It's addressed to the Vault," Blake said. "It's obviously not very long, so I'll read it aloud."

He cleared his throat. "I have to admit this may seem a bit melodramatic, but here goes.

"'Gentlemen, when you read this, unfortunately, I will have died. I have asked my attorney, Enos Peacock, to draft my will and all other necessary documents in case of my demise. This short letter is such a document. The choice of the person who succeeds me and takes my membership is, of course, exclusively yours. Our tradition provides that it go to a family member, when suitable, usually a surviving son. However, that same tradition provides that the main qualification will be merit.'"

"Amen." Driker recognized the reedy voice of Elias McKensie.

Blake continued reading the letter. "'I leave behind two children. Ordinarily, my son would be the natural candidate.'"

Driker could hear the rising concern in Blake's voice as he continued. "'A member of the Vault should not only have good bloodlines but also a proven record of achievement. We represent much more than merely ourselves and our own interests. I have been proud to serve with all of you. None of you has been content to sit back and merely husband your family fortunes. Each of you, myself included, has made his own way in the world. We have proven ourselves. The hallmark of Vault membership has always been proven achievement.

"'Unfortunately, my son hasn't demonstrated any of these qualities. He is head of one of my subsidiary companies, but he performs as a simple caretaker. I am afraid, with my death, that he will abandon active business and be content to simply sit back and enjoy the fruits not only of my labor, but of those who went before me. I know some of you find yourself in similar situations. Children sometimes can be such a disappointment.'"

Driker found himself sitting forward, as if by so doing, he might speed things along.

Blake continued reading. "'I, therefore, strongly urge that my son, Hunter Van Horn, Jr., not be considered to fill my place on the Vault.'"

"I can agree to that," Franklin Trager cut in. "Junior always seemed such a pale washout, nothing at all like his old man."

"Franklin," Clifford Colburn muttered, "let Sander finish the letter."

"I thought he had."

"There is more," Blake said quietly. There was a different tone in his voice, one that carried a note of apprehension.

Driker found the suspense almost unbearable. He irritably turned up the volume.

"This is the rest of it," Blake said as he again began to read from the letter. "'I hope you will appreciate that I have given this matter great thought. Based on the criteria we seek in our Vault members, I nominate for my vacancy my daughter, Victoria Van Horn.'"

"What?" Franklin Trager's shout blasted Driker's ears. He quickly twisted the volume down.

"Sander, are you joking?" Colburn demanded.

Driker could hear the mutterings of several voices as Blake went on with the letter. "'I realize this could cause problems for some of you. It would set a new course. But these are new times. On that basis I most strongly recommend it.'"

There was a pause. "Hunter signed it," Blake said.

"I think this is some kind of a joke," Franklin Trager snapped. "The Vault has always been all male, and Hunter damn well knew that. I think he was having a bit of a leg-pull at our expense."

"We are based on tradition. I'm not a male chauvinist, but I think we should keep things as they are. The Vault should remain male." Driker identified the voice as belonging to Lucas Shaw, the newest member. Driker nodded in enthusiastic agreement.

He heard a long wheeze and knew that Elias McKensie was about to speak. The old man's voice was surprisingly firm. "As Hunter said, times have changed, gentlemen. Women serve as heads of corporations and as leaders of governments. This is not some male social club, some refuge for the consumption of cigars and brandy. The Vault is much more than that. We provide leadership for the city of New York. And as far as I know, gender doesn't count in that quality. I rather admire the young lady. And, after all, it is Hunter's last wish. I believe we should honor it."

"I call for a vote." It was Clifford Colburn. "I'm against it. Luke here is against it, and obviously Franklin is. That's three. Who else?"

Driker was outraged they would even consider putting a woman on the Vault. He knew how he would cast his vote if he had one.

Sander Blake's voice was emotionless. "It would take only one more negative vote to bar her. There's only seven of us."

"I'm for her," McKensie said.

Blake spoke again. "I realize that chairmen should only vote last, as tiebreakers, but I too am for her. I had great respect for Hunter's judgment, and that respect didn't die with him." His words were spoken with quiet dignity. "I will honor his wishes."

The sudden silence again caused Driker to wonder if his expensive equipment had failed him at a crucial moment.

"This is all quite unexpected," John Robertson said. "I've never even thought about such a thing, to tell you the truth. I'd like some time to think it over. I'm not prepared to vote."

Ambassador Lytle spoke. "I agree with John. None of us expected this. I too would like some time to consider it before making a decision."

"Suppose we meet here in a week?" Blake asked. "Will that be sufficient time?"

Driker heard a rustling of papers as the members consulted their personal calendars. "That's fine with me," Trager said, his words clipped and belligerent.

The silence indicated to Driker that the others had no objection to the adjournment.

"All right. We'll meet here at this time next week. Please be prepared to decide the question then."

Driker was furious that they should keep him dangling a whole week.

"No goddamned woman will ever sit on the Vault!" Franklin Trager's voice boomed into the headset like a crack of thunder. Trager apparently was standing near one of the concealed microphones. Driker's ears rang painfully.

"Absolutely!" Clifford Colburn echoed Trager's outrage.

"Be careful," Blake said icily. "Don't let this issue divide us."

"Divide us?" Trager replied, still angry. "We're already divided. This whole issue could destroy us."

"You can't really mean that, Franklin," McKensie said.

"Oh no? Well, when you people think about it, think on this." Trager's voice was almost a snarl. "The selection of Victoria Van Horn could mean the end of the Vault. Are you really ready to take that risk, just for her?"

"We'll vote on it next week." Sander Blake's words sounded like a declaration of war.

Driker tore off the headset, trembling with rage. "Damn that Victoria Van Horn," he said aloud. "She'll ruin everything."

9

It seemed strange to Victoria to be ascending in the executive elevator, whisked up toward the once so familiar executive offices. It had been more than four years since she had been in the building. She felt on the verge of tears as memories enveloped her, somehow underlining her sense of loss of her father, making the loss even more painful.

Childhood trips to his office had always been so exciting. In the halcyon days of her youth, she had proudly brought her school friends around, showing off, kind of strutting. She loved her father, who always took time to provide a tour for her wide-eyed pals, giving them a brief but exciting glimpse into the pulsating heart of one of America's largest corporations. And he always ended each tour with treats: ice cream when she was a schoolgirl, and as she grew older, though perhaps not wiser, cocktails for her college friends.

The elevator operator was new. Old Herb Jarvis was gone. His replacement was equally ancient, but very nervous. He stared at the instrument panel as though it had a life of its own.

The elevator slowed, then as the doors opened, stopped. It was immediately clear that the executive reception area had been redecorated. The walnut paneling that had suggested a private club was gone. Everything was now chrome and glass, glittering with reflected light from concealed fixtures. The changes enhanced Victoria's feeling of strangeness, making her feel as though she had never before been there.

Chilton Vance was waiting in the reception area. She extended her hand, and was startled when he gently embraced her instead. She had just met him for the first time at her father's funeral. Such liberties, on such short acquaintance, were distasteful to her, but somehow Chilton Vance's gesture was more comforting than cloying.

"Welcome, Victoria." He smiled. "I imagine things have changed since you were last here."

She swallowed before speaking. "A bit."

He laughed. "Your father developed a passion for redecorating. Every year we'd all be surprised to see new decor and furnishings. I think some of the executives resented it, but I personally found it adventuresome."

He opened the glass door to the executive suites and escorted her down the long hallway to what used to be her father's office. It was still located in the same place, but just like the reception area, everything had been completely changed.

She looked around. She had forgotten just how immense the office was.

"Everything is just as he left it." Vance's voice penetrated her thoughts.

Her eyes went to the desk. It was there—very much out of place among the modern furnishings, but it was there. She had given the desk set to him as a birthday present. At the time she had been fourteen, but even now she could remember the store where she had bought it. It was such an outlandish gift: two bone elephants guarding ivory pens, set in ebony marble, clashing with everything else in the room. So she had meant something to him after all. Otherwise, why would he have kept such a monstrous thing that clashed so with the modern decor? Tears welled and she quickly walked to the magnificent enormous windows and looked down at Manhattan. She managed to compose herself.

"Well, whatever else one might say about our executive offices," Vance said, laughing, "we do have the best view of the city, except, of course, for the Trade Towers."

She nodded, not yet trusting herself to talk.

"At times I find the view almost hypnotic," he continued, "especially at night. It's quite like a fairyland then."

She merely nodded her agreement.

"Victoria, may I offer you a drink?"

"Brandy," she said, surprised that her voice sounded normal. She turned and watched him as he touched a panel. It slid open, revealing a small but complete bar. He smiled at her.

"You remember, of course, how your father always loved gadgets."

"Of course."

He quickly splashed brandy into two Waterford goblets. The portions were more than just healthy. She wondered if that was part of some scheme or whether he had merely miscalculated in pouring.

Victoria accepted the offered drink, taking only a tentative sip.

"I'm so glad you could come," Vance said. "We have much to discuss." He led her to two forbidding-looking modern chairs, not in the best of taste. She found her chair, a combination of chrome and canvas, to be surprisingly comfortable.

Vance raised his glass. "Long life."

Victoria matched his gesture, then took another sip.

"Victoria, I asked to meet with you for a very important reason."

"And that is?"

"I've been contacted by some of the directors. They want me to sound you out on the possibility of becoming president of this company."

"Van Horn Enterprises?"

He nodded. "And chairman of the board."

She heard his words as if in a dream, a confusing dream. All she had ever wished was a chance to prove herself within the company, not head it. That dream had been the cause of the fight between her father and herself. Now other commitments would prevent her involvement. Once again, she would be denied. She felt shocked; her old dream now had nightmare qualities.

Vance smiled. "Well, Victoria, what about it?"

This time no one but herself would prevent her from the goal that she had once desired so desperately. It seemed so unreal. But there was no other course open to her. "Heading up my father's company would be completely ridiculous." She was surprised at the tone of conviction in her own words. "I know nothing about this business. My field is development. I have no background in any of the services or products offered by Van Horn."

He shook his head gently. "I beg to disagree. You've more than made your mark as a successful business executive. Whether it's development or anything else, it all boils down to a common denominator. Business principles are the same, no matter what the field. Executive ability doesn't change with the challenge, and you have demonstrated in full measure that you certainly possess that quality in abundance. The board of directors would like to employ your ability here."

"And what about you? Surely, you must have ambitions."

He laughed. "Of course, I do. I admit it. But at the moment, I tend to agree with the directors. I think you would be the very best possible choice for a number of reasons."

"And what are they?"

"Well, for one, your ability is a given, isn't it? However, there is something even more persuasive." He took a small sip of his drink. "Your father put this conglomerate together. He built it and it bears your family name. Given the size and complexity of this organization, any transition at the top can have enormous consequences all the way down. Bankers who did business with your father, businessmen who trusted him, and stockholders all over the world would be reassured if a Van Horn took over as chief executive officer; it provides a certain continuity. That way, you see, no one would be concerned that the company would be radically changed, or even broken up."

"I can't imagine anyone being quite that concerned. The company is healthy, isn't it?"

"Absolutely. Still, a banker in Europe who may have made loans to us will feel quite reassured if he sees a Van Horn continuing to run the corporation. Everyone understands family, Victoria. It's more important than you might think."

"What about my brother?"

Vance slowly shook his head. "Out of the question. Junior is a nice chap, but he has never commanded much respect within the company. Your father, I understand, felt the same way. You are the only one who can do it."

She looked around the office. Her father's presence was almost palpable, though she distrusted that feeling. She spoke slowly. "I'm undertaking a very large venture of my own, something similar to my East Port project, but even bigger. I couldn't possibly find time to serve as chief executive officer here."

His expression grew solemn. "Suppose I proposed a kind of partnership?"

"In what way?"

"If you'll serve as president and chairman, I'll run this company for you. You'll have only nominal duties. No one will ever know, except you and me."

"That seems unusually magnanimous."

"Oh, it's not entirely out of the goodness of my heart. There is, as with everything, a price tag."

"And that is?"

"Victoria, the company rather desperately needs the use of your name right now to show continuity. A year from now I think you could step aside, if you wanted to. By then, I would suppose that the loss of your father wouldn't mean so much."

"And then you'd take over?"

"Precisely. It's a logical step for me. It's a transition that I believe your father had in mind, eventually."

"And what if I decide then to continue as head of the company?"

He shrugged. "Where's the benefit in that? You wouldn't know any more about the internal workings of the business than you do now. You would have had the title, so you'd really have nothing to gain. It's not much of a gamble on my part. I think I'd be safe enough."

"Do you honestly think all this is necessary?"

His expression again grew serious. "I'm afraid I do. The unexpected death of the man who founded this company and ran it can only cause panic for stockholders, creditors and anyone else who looks to Van Horn Enterprises for their income, or a large part of it. It's happened before, as you know. Large companies, particularly ones where it has been something of a one-man show, have come apart when death has taken off the founder. I suggest that a peaceful, painless transition would be much superior to running that risk."

"Just how healthy is the company?"

He smiled easily. "Victoria, you understand the ups and downs of business as well as I do. Nothing ever runs entirely smoothly. Van Horn Enterprises has problems, but none are insurmountable. This is a rock-solid organization. Your father, as you know, was an extraordinary businessman. His company is sound in every way. I honestly don't anticipate any real problems, and I'll handle any that do come up."

"In other words, I'd be simply a figurehead president?"

Vance began to protest, but she held up a hand to restrain him. "Actually, Mr. Vance, that's about all I could be, a figurehead. The development I'm about to embark on here in Manhattan dwarfs my East Port. There's no way I could do both. If you feel it's to the company's benefit to continue to have the Van Horn name on the stationery for a while, I can agree to that. But you must run the business. I just want to be assured that you're fully prepared to do that. It's asking quite a lot."

Chilton Vance's slight smile masked his elation. "I shall have the board announce you as your father's successor. I will actually serve as the chief executive officer—in fact, if not legally. After a year, though, I will expect your support to legalize my position as head man."

She extended her hand. "Then it's a deal."

"Indeed it is."

His hand was unexpectedly moist, as though despite his cool exterior he had been exceedingly nervous.

"As soon as the announcement is made, I'll move into my father's office. I think it would look better. I can run most of my own operation from here."

"I presume you'll wish to bring over your own secretary?"

"She'll be more help back at my headquarters. She knows the business and I trust her judgment. Perhaps I can use my father's old secretary. I've forgotten her name."

"He had several secretaries lately." Joyce Spitz knew far too much about company operations, and he didn't want her anywhere near Victoria Van Horn. "Your father's last secretary left the company, I believe," he lied smoothly. "Marriage, or something like that. As I recall, Hunter wasn't enormously pleased with her work. Don't worry, we'll find someone tops for you."

"When will all this be made official?" Victoria asked.

Vance thought for a moment. "In order to maintain continuity it should be done as quickly as possible. I can contact the board by telephone and have an official meeting this Friday. Does that meet with your approval?"

"You're absolutely sure this won't interfere with my own business? I'm planning to enter into extensive mortgage agreements by Friday. I'll be putting up everything I own, so I'm in no position to gamble."

Vance put his arm around her in a paternal fashion and seemed to leave it there for an overlong fraction. Then he quickly changed the subject. "May I invite you out for a drink? We should mark this occasion with some sort of celebration."

She wondered if this were a feeble attempt at a pass, then dismissed the thought. He was probably just delighted with the agreement. "I'm afraid I can't, Chilton." She used his given name for the first time. "There's a meeting I just cannot afford to miss. Some other time?"

"Of course." He smiled. "My office is just down the hall. We'll have many opportunities."

He walked her to the elevator and waited until the doors closed after her. She seemed like a lovely young woman, and so pretty. He wondered if he should feel shame for what he had done, and what he knew he would be doing. But that was the nature of any competition: someone had to lose.

Victoria and her idiot brother were doomed. It wouldn't be quite the same as ruining Hunter Van Horn himself, but it would do.

He whistled softly. It was done. The plan was set in motion now and there was no going back.

———

Barry Lytle's gym clothes were becoming soggy with sweat. He was breathing hard, but he felt good. He made preparations to work out on the heavy punching bag.

Hiram Snow, the rotund Alabama congressman, grinned as he slowly trotted by. "What'cha all training for, Barry? The Olympics?"

"Just staying in shape, Hiram."

Snow laughed. "That looks too much like work for me. Good luck." He picked up his pace, awkwardly lumbering off for another lap around the congressional gym.

Keeping trim and fit had always been important to Barry Lytle, despite his appetites. The delights of the flesh constituted one of his main recreational outlets. The best bait always attracted the best fish. Women had always been attracted to him. And he wanted to keep it that way. Being slender and athletic helped.

Lytle pulled on the leather gloves over his wrapped hands. The big leather bag hung from its chain, its middle worn and beaten. He wasn't the only congressman who regularly vented his frustrations against the heavy bag.

He began slowly, moving around the bag, popping light jabs into the soft leather. Then, warming to the task, he began to hit harder, bringing his right fist across, feeling the jolt all the way up to his shoulder. He could almost imagine his father's face outlined in the cracked leather, and this image produced a flurry of blows, his fists smashing furiously against the swinging bag.

Gulping for breath, he danced away, enjoying a sense of exultation. If he could never do that to his father, as so it seemed, the bag was an acceptable surrogate.

He was his father's prisoner, and he knew it. Selected staff members were instructed to never let him out of their sight. His father, an absentee warden, was managing his son's life from New York. Now Ambassador Lytle wanted his son to meet Van Horn's goddamned daughter. There was nothing particularly subtle about this. Barry Lytle could sense a match being made. The rich Victoria Van Horn would be an asset to anyone on the road to the White House. His father had selected his first wife, for much the same reasons. He had been bound in a loveless marriage, set free only after his father had decided his wife might prove detrimental to the future of his son the congressman.

Lytle stopped the swinging bag with his left, then brought a smashing right hand into the middle of the leather. He grunted from the force, then followed with a fury of explosive blows.

Exhaustion finally made him stop. He stepped back from the swinging bag.

"Anyone I know?" Hiram Snow had made a slow circle of the gym.

Lytle smiled and pulled off the gloves. Despite the protective wrappings, both hands ached. "No one in particular, Hiram," he said. "Sort of a collection. You know how it is."

"Next time include my doctor on your list. He's the bastard who's making me do this."

"It's a deal."

The man from Alabama laughed and trotted off.

Lytle unwrapped his hands. He tried to shake out the throbbing, but he wasn't concerned. He knew that whatever pain and fatigue remained would be washed away in a nice steaming shower. Although he felt tired, there was a sense of fulfillment.

Lytle performed a few stretch exercises to cool down, then walked into the locker room.

The moist, steamy aroma of soap and sweat always seemed so masculine and comforting. His administrative assistant, dressed in street clothes, was seated on a bench near his locker, reading a report. He looked up.

"How did it go?"

"Good," Lytle replied, as he began peeling off the sweaty cottons. "If I get defeated, I may just open a health spa."

The man was always so serious. "You won't be defeated."

Congressman Lytle heard the words, but to him the words sounded more like a judge's dreaded sentence than an encouragement.

He grabbed a towel and headed for the showers.

———————

Cecil Driker stepped out of the cab in front of the San Carlos Hotel. His arrival attracted some curious glances. He wore no coat, but was dressed in a perfect cream suit, combined with a pale, robin's-egg-blue shirt, finished off with an exquisite red Italian silk cravat. From the top of his carefully groomed head of hair to the bottom of his Gucci shoes, everything about him seemed flamboyantly expensive. He haughtily walked past the doorman and made his way into the hotel. He was careful to conceal his excitement.

He took the elevator up, then briskly strode down the hallway toward his destination.

Enrico Pelegrine threw open the door. His fleshy but still handsome face split into a wide and toothy grin. "You look wonderful, Cecil. You seem to get younger every time I see you. How in the world do you manage that? And thin! God, how I wish I had your metabolism."

"Enrico, you know how I always look forward to seeing you. Do you have the painting?"

"Always so anxious, Cecil! Have patience. First, we take a little wine, then business. Ah, you still have much to learn about the fine art of being civilized. Only peasants and farmers hurry. Come."

He led the way to a table draped with expensive linen. Paper-thin wineglasses of the finest crystal and a deeply and luxuriously dark bottle of imported wine had been set out. "I took the liberty of tasting this before you arrived. It's quite nice. A trifle expensive, I suppose, but then, what is money for, eh?"

Driker accepted the offering and sniffed. The wine was more than merely expensive, it was rare. The first sip confirmed his initial appraisal.

"Did you unload the Titian?" Driker asked.

Pelegrine laughed. "Ah, the Titian. The one you thought stolen."

"I still think so. I'm surprised you were able to avoid the Italian authorities."

This time Pelegrine did not laugh. "As I have repeatedly assured you, it wasn't stolen. I sold it to a Texas gentleman, a rare man who is an expert in both cattle and art."

"Will he display it?"

Pelegrine's dark eyes gave the impression of being hooded, hawklike. "Ah, probably not. He delights in the privacy of his collection."

"So he doesn't care if it was stolen or not. No one but he will ever see it."

Pelegrine looked hurt as he sipped his wine. "You wrong me, Cecil. My clients trust me. My business depends upon my reputation."

"Your business, my dear Enrico, depends on the quality of the artworks you seem magically able to produce. Enough, Enrico, enough. May I please see the picture?"

Pelegrine heaved his large girth from the low-slung couch. "Come with me, Cecil." He led the way into a large bedroom, and pointed to a slender fiberglass cylinder on the bed.

Driker carefully extracted the oil painting from its container. He slowly and delicately unrolled the ancient canvas. There was sufficient light streaming in from the bedroom windows. He thoughtfully examined it.

"You like it?" Pelegrine asked, almost coyly.

"It's quite beautiful."

"It's a Montogna, one of his best."

Driker turned and looked hard at Pelegrine. "Don't insult me, Enrico. It is very good, but it's not a Montogna. It's by his pupil, Russo. I personally think Russo surpassed his master. But, of course, that doesn't affect the price. People pay for the master, not the pupil."

"If it were a Montogna, it would be worth close to a million," Pelegrine said grudgingly.

"But it isn't."

"No. More's the pity. I would need a hundred thousand."

Driker laughed. "Your needs are hardly relevant, are they? Give me a hard price on this, Enrico."

He was answered by a grunt of annoyance. "Cecil, you take the fun out of this. The price is fifty thousand. That's fair, I think you'll agree."

Driker studied the painting again. "Yes," he said at last, "that's fair. We can add this to the Habermann collection. I'm sure the board will agree. Of course, we will need to make the usual arrangement."

Pelegrine drained the last of his wine. "How much?"

"I'll tell the board that I agreed on a price of sixty-five thousand. You will provide a receipt for that amount."

"And pay fifteen thousand in cash to you?"

Driker nodded.

"Cecil, you make more profit from these transactions than I do. Suppose your board ever finds out."

"They won't," Driker said. "The price isn't that overinflated. This painting might well be appraised by experts for that amount. Besides, the museum has a great deal of money, and I don't."

"More wine?"

"I have to go." Driker carefully rolled up the picture and inserted it back into its container. "Ah, Enrico, you deal with many wealthy people, such as that Texan you mentioned?"

"I deal with other dealers, museums and private collectors. The collectors are very rich, of course. But you know all that."

"Suppose I came into possession of information that could prove extremely valuable. Insider information, as I believe the stock exchange people term it. Do you think any of your rich customers might be interested?"

Pelegrine escorted him back into the sitting room of the suite. The Italian poured himself some more wine. "What kind of information do you mean?"

Driker knew he had to be careful. He dared not divulge too much. "Let's suppose that I might from time to time come up with information, absolutely reliable, concerning financial events about to happen—inside information of the kind that would allow a large investor to profit enormously given that prior knowledge."

"If you have that kind of information, why not invest yourself?"

"To make real profits, it would take millions, Enrico. Unfortunately, I'm not in that league, at least not yet."

"And you would wish to sell this information?"

"'Sell' is a harsh word. I would pass along what I know for a piece of the action."

"And you wish to use my contacts?"

"Yes."

"What would I get out of this, beyond your undying gratitude?"

"A percentage of whatever I make."

"Such as?"

"Ten percent."

Pelegrine laughed. "It seems to me that if you are using my contacts I should share more equitably than that. I should get at least half."

Driker glared at him. "Don't you actually mean twenty-five percent?"

Pelegrine smiled. "At the very minimum, a full third."

Driker shook his head. "That's robbery, Enrico."

"I'm quite essential to your scheme. You can't do without me. That is my final offer, Cecil, a full third."

Driker sighed. "Oh, all right. I consider that outrageously unfair but I agree."

"Very good. When can we expect these miracles?"

"Soon, I think. It might be well to alert a few of your more wealthy clients that you may have something of value for them."

Driker paused. "But make sure that none of them are New Yorkers."

"Why?"

"I have my reasons." Driker worried that a member of the Vault might suspect where the tip was coming from. Eventually, it would all lead to him.

"My dear Cecil. I can't possibly approach my clients unless I can indicate more specifically the source of these wonders."

"Really?"

Pelegrine flashed his Cheshire smile. "Would you make a large financial commitment under such circumstances? I think not. Cecil, if we are to do business together, there must be some degree of mutual trust."

Driker was troubled. He hesitated to continue further, but Pelegrine did have a point. Well, he reasoned, all life carried some risk. "I have access to the Vault."

Pelegrine looked genuinely impressed. "I have heard of this Vault. How do you come by this access?"

"That's my business. Your clients will know about the Vault. That's all you have to tell them. But, for God's sake, be prudent."

Pelegrine savored his wine. "I am discreet in all things. And I will make some contacts. Cecil, I shall eagerly await your call. As you know, I do love adventure. Particularly if it pays."

"Oh, this will pay," Driker said. "We may both emerge from this inordinately rich."

Pelegrine beamed. "What a delightful thought!"

10

Victoria knew men considered her stunning. She had been told often enough and she did enjoy the attention, but she had quickly learned that beauty was often equated with being brainless. It was a handicap she frequently had to overcome by forcefully demonstrating her competence.

The meeting had taken up most of the day. The bankers and lawyers had all agreed on the contracts, but small points that required extensive redrafting kept being raised.

Victoria had to approve every word, every comma. Her legal abilities impressed her own lawyers. She made skillful and innovative changes in many of the provisions. The staggering amounts involved awed even the investment bankers, who were accustomed to juggling fortunes. At first, they tended to be patronizing, treating her as just another rich customer.

But soon they too began to rely on her judgment and expertise. Money generated one kind of power, knowledge another, and Victoria effectively exercised both. She enjoyed earning their respect. Since many millions were involved, the drafters treated the documents as though they contained the secret of life. The meeting turned into a mind-boggling, mind-numbing endurance contest. When it finally ended, Victoria Van Horn felt like a prisoner who had just escaped.

She quickly returned to her office.

"No calls for a while, Annie," she said to her secretary.

"You look bushed."

Victoria nodded. "I am. I think I may lie down for a while. Give me an hour, okay?"

"You push yourself too hard."

"Maybe." Victoria closed the door but didn't head for the couch. Instead, she walked to the window and gazed out at the gleaming buildings of her East Port project. She was proud of what she had accomplished. Fashionable shops, offices and restaurants stood where once there were only old and rotting warehouses. It seemed like an important part of herself. Now it was all pledged as security for her new venture. She was gambling everything she owned that another miracle could be pulled off, this one even bigger and better. This time it would be easier, she kept telling herself. She had an established track record; she had proven herself. But now, as she looked out at her glittering prize, she felt the terrifying clutch of doubt. She hoped she had done the right thing.

The telephone buzzed. Victoria walked to her desk and picked it up.

"I know you said no calls, but Chilton Vance is on the line and he's quite insistent on speaking with you."

"Put him through."

She waited for the call to be transferred. "Yes, Chilton, what is it?"

"Victoria, it's all legal. You are now the officially elected president and board chairman of Van Horn Enterprises. The board voted you in this afternoon. A few questions were raised, but generally it all went very smoothly."

Victoria felt her heart pounding. Fear, like a passing shadow, seemed to fall over her. "I thought it would take longer. I . . . I don't know what to say. I just signed the mortgages for my new construction."

He chuckled. "All you'll have to do is preside over a few board meetings, sign reports and authorizations, and look important. I promised you this wouldn't interfere with anything else you have planned, and as I assured you, I'll run the company. You haven't a thing to worry about."

"Thanks, Chilton. You've read my mind."

"Perhaps we could have dinner tonight?"

She paused without replying.

"That is, my wife and I and you, all three of us, of course," he added smoothly.

She wondered if Vance would have included his wife if she had responded more quickly. "I'll take a rain check, if you don't mind. It's been a long day and I'm exhausted. I'm going home and climb into bed."

"Oh, one more thing, Victoria. We should schedule a press conference. This will make quite an item for the *New York Times* and the *Wall Street Journal*. If ten o'clock tomorrow morning is convenient for you, I'll set it up."

She had scheduled a meeting with the architects, but she could be late for that. "Ten will be fine."

"Good. I'll have our PR people whip up something pertinent for you to say. They'll prepare a press kit. As I've said, Victoria, this job will be a breeze. Everything will be done for you."

"I appreciate that, Chilton."

"No need to. Well, get some rest. And congratulations again, Victoria. The Van Horn name will continue to make news." With that, he hung up.

She frowned as she sat down at her desk. He seemed genuine enough, and apparently her father had trusted him. Yet she wondered why she felt so uncomfortable talking to him. Wariness once again returned.

Because if Chilton Vance weren't trustworthy, she would be most certainly ruined.

Chilton Vance was pleased at the reflection that smiled back at him as he completed his inspection. The mirror in his office bathroom was large and well lighted. He brushed an errant strand of gray hair away from his forehead. Everything else was in good order. The tuxedo fit rather elegantly on his thin form. He winked at his reflection.

As he passed by, his secretary looked up admiringly. She remained at her desk, even though the work day was done. He had few set rules, but one of them was insistence that she stay until he left or gave her permission to go. "You can go home now, Jeanne. I'm off to that charity thing."

"Do you have your ticket?"

He nodded. The invitation in his pocket wasn't a ticket, but it did represent a pass into the opulent world of the select few who were always glad to exchange money for confirmation of their status as social and civic leaders.

The limousine picked him up at the curb. Traffic was snarled and slow-moving, giving him the opportunity to review the tactics he had so carefully planned. He felt ecstatic. Everything seemed to be falling so nicely into place.

The limo finally made its way to the front of the Metropolitan Museum of Art. The party was already well under way in the main hall, with almost everyone in black-tie.

It was what was known as a five-thousand-dollar crowd. Chilton Vance knew most of them. Lesser mortals could frequent inexpensive events, but the donation of five thousand dollars ensured that only New York's monied elite could afford to attend. For most, whether they were simply individuals or representatives of their companies, it was a tax writeoff and therefore reasonably painless. Others were so wealthy that the amount never really mattered. The usual buzz of polite conversation filled the air, becoming a hum of quiet elegance, broken only intermittently by short bursts of decorous and vacuous laughter.

Vance nodded to several acquaintances from the world of finance. He accepted a glass of champagne from the uniformed waiter, then surveyed the crowd.

But he didn't see the face he sought. The dining room was decked with large prints of photographs of sad, depressing children. Chilton Vance vaguely understood that the party was for a cause, in this case, Indian relief, so he had expected the usual pictures of emaciated figures cluttering the streets of Calcutta. It wasn't until he looked closely at the photos that he realized that it was American Indians who were being rescued by this particular gathering.

Vance moved from group to group, exchanging greetings but still intent upon his search.

He finally discovered him, nearly concealed in a far corner, standing quite apart, looking uncomfortable while awkwardly holding a glass in front of him, as though it wasn't altogether clear what he should do with it.

Vance slowly worked his way toward the corner. Rushing over would be too obvious. He practiced all the patience he could muster during his slow and deliberate trip. He hoped he would be found and greeted by the other man. It would be so much better that way. He carefully avoided any chance of eye contact.

"Ah, Chilton?"

It was like having a giant marlin strike a line. The fish was on the hook.

"Hello, Junior," Vance said, turning toward the voice. "I didn't know you'd be here."

Junior Van Horn shrugged. "I only stopped by for a few minutes. I really don't like these things."

"And where's the lovely Cecelia?"

Junior looked even more uncomfortable. "Cecelia took a bad fall and she's recuperating at a spa in California. A typical home injury, she slipped in the tub."

"Nothing serious, I hope?"

"Bad bruises," Junior said curtly.

"Lucky." Vance took a small sip of wine. "I haven't seen you since your father's funeral. I was quite surprised when you resigned from Demas Industries."

"Were you? It seemed the only logical thing to do, given the circumstances. Demas is one of father's companies. I'm sure she'd fire me."

"You mean your sister, I presume?"

Junior glared at him. "Of course. I understand she's going to be elected to succeed my father as chief executive officer."

Chilton Vance nodded imperceptibly, very slowly. "The board took that vote today, as a matter of fact. News certainly travels fast."

"I keep informed," Junior snapped.

"Of course." Vance took Junior's arm and guided him to an even more remote part of the room. "I confess I had some ambitions myself," Vance said, his voice just above a whisper. "Ah well, you never know how the ball is going to bounce, do you?"

Junior's face was beginning to color with emotion. "My sister doesn't know a damn thing about the company. She will screw everything up. Mind you, that's not jealousy. It's my honest opinion."

Vance pretended to look unsure, almost afraid. "Others have expressed the same opinion," he whispered.

Junior's eyes narrowed. "Who?"

Vance appeared to hesitate. "I'd rather not say."

"Come on, Chilton. You know you can trust me."

Vance sipped his champagne. "The choice was far from unanimous. Many of the board members expressed feelings not too dissimilar from yours."

"Still, they did elect her."

"It was—perhaps I'm talking too much—more of a symbolic thing. More of an honor to your late father, and his wishes, than anything else."

"She'll screw up the company, believe me. Someone should do something."

Vance played the part of a man troubled and concerned, seemingly caught in painful indecision. "They wanted a Van Horn to head the company. Victoria, of course, controls the voting rights to the stock left by your father. I think the directors thought they'd avoid a war if they picked her." Vance looked about with the air of a conspirator, then continued in a barely audible voice. "Some of the board, I happen to know, favored you for president."

"They did?"

Junior Van Horn's delight was just as intense as Vance had expected. It was almost too easy.

"Yes." Vance paused, as if suddenly fearful. "You must realize, Junior, that I'm in a very delicate position here. After all, I now work for your sister."

"But you're not happy with that, are you?"

Vance looked away. "Perhaps not."

Junior brought his face close to Vance. He was shaking with excitement. "Look, she'll fuck things up. I know she will. Someone has to protect the company. If they really want a Van Horn at the helm, I'm available."

"It could develop into a nasty fight. I'm sure you don't want that."

"I don't care. If they want my sister out of there, I'm their man. Chilton, let me be frank. If I should oust Victoria, I wouldn't want to be president forever. You could have the job after a while. I'd stay on as chairman of the board, but you could be the chief executive officer. You deserve it."

Vance pretended to show wary interest. "It could be dangerous for all of us."

It was as if Junior had become a new man. His eyes glittered with enthusiasm. "There's no danger, not if everything is kept under wraps until the right time. We could sweep my sister the hell out of the company before she even knew what hit her. It would work."

"I don't know." Vance purposely sounded hesitant.

"It would be easy. The first time she makes a mistake, all the people who were opposed to my father will fall on her like a pack of wolves. Then, if they really need a Van Horn, they'll have to turn to me. I've worked in this company all my life. I know every aspect of it. Of course, I'd still need your help running it."

Vance pursed his lips, as if in worry. "I can't really commit myself now, Junior. I'm sure you realize that. But I promise to think it over. As you say, it just might work. And, I confess, even on short acquaintance, I'm not particularly fond of your sister. She seems too arrogant, too irresponsible. I really don't think she intends to work at the job."

"Exactly! She'll end up ruining the company. You think it over,

Chilton. You have the contacts. If you decide to throw in with me, we can't miss."

Vance pretended to avoid his gaze. "I'll stay in touch," he said as he quickly walked away. He didn't have to look back to know the effect he had just made. Junior was transformed, completely intoxicated by the prospect of humiliating his sister.

But before he was through, Chilton Vance would get rid of both the Van Horn heirs. And Junior, all wrapped up and consumed by his chance for revenge, would never even see it coming.

Vance couldn't help smiling. It was actually going to be so damned easy.

Luke Shaw's office was a mass of clutter. Blueprints, tacked to the walls haphazardly, bore a multitude of notes and markings. Somewhere under a huge pile of rolled prints, maps and papers there was a desk, but it couldn't be seen.

"Allow me." Shaw picked up a pile of books and graphs, clearing a chair for her.

He watched her as she looked around his office. He laughed. "Benjamin Franklin said a disorderly desk was the sign of an orderly mind. That may not be true, but I've used it as an excuse for years. Few of my clients ever see this. We have conference rooms to impress customers. This is a typical working space for an engineer. It's messy, but everything pertains to a job, and believe it or not, I know where everything is."

Victoria Van Horn sat down. "Tell me, Mr. Shaw, are you usually so defensive?"

He shrugged. "No. But I know why you're here, and I need some of this clutter to explain our position."

"I need engineering studies done on my Hudson River development. It's essential to our timetable that they be done as quickly as possible."

He smiled. "Like immediately?"

She nodded. "Exactly."

"I told your architects that we have a dozen jobs, all equally pressing, scheduled before yours. It's first come, first served with us. We try to be fair."

"I wonder if my architects fully explained my problems."

"They talked to me." He wondered if she would try to use her feminine guile to her advantage. She was astonishingly beautiful, he had to admit that, and he knew that he was strongly attracted, as any normal man would be.

"You know my East Port project?"

"Of course. You did a beautiful job over there." It was sincere. He had been impressed with the ingenuity of some of the concepts.

"Are you a gambler, Mr. Shaw?"

He smiled. "No. Engineers are trained not to allow any margin for chance. Gambling sort of goes against the grain. By the way, unless it makes you uncomfortable, please call me Luke."

She nodded. "All right. My friends call me Victoria."

"Okay, tell me your problems, Victoria." He thought he saw a flash of annoyance briefly in her eyes. He hadn't intended the words to be condescending, but they did sound that way, even to him.

"My problems, as you put it, are extremely serious. In order to raise the money for the Hudson River development I had to put up every cent I had, plus I was forced to pledge everything I own, including East Port."

"I can see what you mean about gambling," he said.

She found his attitude irritating. He was a rugged man, quite handsome in a way, and his easy manner ordinarily would have been quite attractive. But she needed help and she wondered if he really took her seriously. "I'm not an engineer," she said. "But I think I've proved that I know what I'm doing in my field. Development, the kind I do, requires taking a risk. It would never be done otherwise."

"I suppose you're right. Now what is your problem?"

"My 'problem' isn't insignificant. I must meet a construction schedule in order to conform to the lending agreements. I have to meet obligations, payrolls, supplies, everything on a set schedule. Everything depends on your engineering studies, according to the architects. If you don't begin at once, I can't meet my schedule."

Luke Shaw wondered if she were telling the truth, or if it was just part of a manipulation. Perhaps she had used these tactics often. He was trying to be fair. Soon he would have to pass judgment on her admission to membership on the Vault. In a way he was trying to make that decision now.

He leaned back in his chair. "Our other clients have pressing needs too. However, I'm sure none is nearly as beautiful."

"Damn you," she snapped, her eyes angry. "Do you think I'm asking for consideration because I'm a woman?"

"Well, maybe not." He was surprised at her reaction. "But I'm sure it hasn't been detrimental in the past."

"In other words, I don't know my proper place?"

"You think I'm being sexist?" He was trying to remain even-tempered. She frowned. "Don't you?"

"I have some women engineers working for me. They've proven themselves capable. We even have women working on a number of our construction crews. Maybe I'm not as sexist as you might think."

"I'll bet those women had to overcome a lot before they were accepted. If they were."

He laughed, although he was irritated. "If you're implying that they are just 'tokens', they aren't. They earn everything they are paid."

"Do you work with any of them?"

He sat forward and looked at her. "You mean directly?"

"Yes."

"Well, it's none of your business, really, but most of them work in the field. I have some contact, although I'll admit it's minimal. I don't think that's relevant in any event."

Victoria knew her future depended on her persuading this man to do her a favor. But she couldn't bring herself to cajole him or even flatter him. He seemed to challenge her. In her mind she found an echo of her father's attitude.

"Perhaps you're right," she said. "Your attitude toward women has no part in this. This is strictly business, and all I ask is that you treat it that way. I don't want any special consideration because I'm a woman. But I don't want to be penalized either."

He was about to make an angry retort but checked himself. "That's the way it will be, I assure you."

"If what I request involves extra cost, I'll be happy to pay it. You can see what it means to me."

She really bothered him. Whether it was because he was so attracted to her and didn't wish to be or whether he resented her because she didn't conform to what he thought women should do mattered little. She was making him angry. "It sounds like you're offering a bribe."

"It's not a bribe at all, and you know it. If your people have to work extra hours, or additional costs are involved, I'll pay them. That's merely good business, Mr. Shaw. I am in a desperate situation."

He calmed himself before speaking. "All right, Miss Van Horn. I'll change our work schedule. If there are additional charges, I'll get the approval of your architects before incurring them. I trust that's satisfactory?"

She nodded. "I appreciate the consideration."

"Anything else?" he snapped.

She shook her head as she stood up. "We seem to have gotten off on the wrong foot, Mr. Shaw. I'm sorry."

"If you're worrying about the Vault, that's entirely separate from this."

Her cheeks colored and there seemed to be sudden fire in her eyes. "I know you're a member. I didn't ask to join, Mr. Shaw. I was nominated by my father. If I'm selected I will be pleased to serve. I also realize that no woman has ever been a member. It's always been a male bastion, and I suppose people who think like you will keep it that way."

He stood up and glared at her. "If you get in," he said, "it will depend entirely on your qualifications, not your sex."

"I'll bet."

He checked himself again. "You're the gambler," he said quietly. "Not me."

Victoria walked to the office door. She wondered why she was reacting so strongly to this man who was doing her a significant favor. She looked at him. He was so strongly handsome. Perhaps it was his obvious masculinity that brought out her competitiveness. "Thank you, Mr. Shaw."

"You're more than welcome, Miss Van Horn."

He wondered if Sander Blake had contacted her as he sat down at his desk again after she left. The meeting was set. She certainly hadn't tried to win his vote. He reluctantly had to admit he liked her for that. She was a strong-willed woman, but she seemed to possess integrity. He wondered how she would do with Trager and the others.

Luke Shaw tried to put her out of his mind, but he found that difficult. He had work to do. He had no time to think about some woman, no matter how beautiful or intriguing she might be.

He tried to concentrate on a blueprint that had to be checked, but somehow he couldn't focus on the specifications.

From the moment Hunter Van Horn's letter was read, Luke Shaw had planned to vote against Victoria as a member of the Vault. Now he suddenly wasn't quite so sure.

———————

It had turned pleasant, so Chilton Vance decided to walk. It was after six o'clock and blaring traffic choked the New York streets. He was excited as he headed across town toward Park Avenue. His wife was his only confidante and he had much to tell her.

He entered the Hyatt and looked around as the escalator took him up past the lobby's waterfall to the terraced lounge. The enormous glass panels of the walls and ceilings combined with the multitude of plants set among the tables gave the impression of a huge greenhouse.

He had no trouble spotting her. Roberta Vance's red hair was like a beacon. She sat next to a young man who had the look of an athlete. He was coatless and his tie and collar loosened. She was laughing at something her young companion had said.

The stab of jealousy Vance felt was almost physical. Although intellectually he had accepted that because of the differences in their ages, and her basic sensual nature, it was improbable that she would always remain faithful, the concept was emotionally unbearable.

They didn't see him until he reached their table.

"Well, here he is at last." His wife leaned over, offering her cheek for a kiss.

He merely brushed her cheek with his lips. The young man made no move to rise.

"This is my husband." She slid over, making room for Vance. "And this, darling, is Michael Jenning. Michael is a fast rising star at the Princeton Bank. He's vice-president in charge of their trust department."

The young man's grip was strong. He had a lopsided grin, and Chilton Vance wondered if he only imagined the sneer he saw in Michael Jenning's eyes.

"Michael's been helping me put together a portfolio for one of my clients." She reached over and patted Jenning's hand. "He's been a gem."

"Well, this gem has to leave," Jenning said, still looking directly at Vance. "I was only staying around to keep Roberta company until you arrived." He got up and slipped into his suit coat. He was quite tall.

"Can't you stay for just one more drink?" Her request sounded insincere as if merely for her husband's benefit.

"Sorry. I have an appointment." Jenning nodded to Chilton Vance. "Nice to meet you. I hope to see you again." He turned and was quickly gone.

"A very bright young man," she said, smiling at her husband.

"Have you been fucking him?" Even to his own ears the question sounded more like a desperate croak.

Roberta merely laughed. "I haven't, Chilton. And even if I had, do you suppose I'd tell you? But putting your jealousy aside, how was your day, my love?"

He felt anger but feared showing it. His greater fear was that he might lose her. He agonized that some of the young men she introduced him to might also be her lovers, a kind of sadistic joke on her part. But she was the most important thing in his life and he could not bring himself to any kind of confrontation with her.

Her expensive burgundy silk blouse was cut so that her magnificent cleavage was liberally displayed without being too obvious. She patted his hand. "I'm dying to hear the news, Chilton. Did you talk to any board members?"

He ordered a drink, then sat back, rubbing his throbbing temples. "I spoke with some of them, the ones who were originally opposed to Hunter Van Horn."

"And?"

"I planted the seed. They are as terrified about the prospect of Junior taking over as they were about his sister. Both Van Horns are unacceptable to them."

"That's a good start."

"It was to be expected." His emotions were returning to normal as he began to feel in command of himself once more. "They may not realize it, but they are tucked quite safely away in my pocket."

"And did you talk to Junior?"

He took the martini from the waiter. "You bet I did. He's really excited now. He can't wait to humiliate his sister. He would kill her if he could. I may have a problem controlling him."

"So your little plan is working?"

He grinned at her. "I know exactly what I'm doing. And I'm being as careful as if I were on a greased tightrope. I'm much too old a cat to make any wrong moves now."

"I'm glad to hear that."

He looked out the glass enclosure at the people on Forty-second Street. "You know, after a while—perhaps a year or two—I think I may be able to change even the company's title. The name Van Horn will disappear like smoke in a windstorm."

He could see she approved of that. Perhaps, if he could pull it off, he wouldn't have to put up with any more sneering young men. He sipped his drink. He was more relaxed, even expansive. "I feel a little like God. It's going that well."

"You'd make a great divinity," she half whispered as her hand caressed his thigh.

———————

Craig Hopkins toyed with his food. Pearl's was one of the most famous Chinese restaurants in the world, and the food justified that reputation. But Hopkins was too preoccupied to eat.

Although they had once been lovers, he and Victoria were both uncomfortable, as if they were strangers. Victoria had agreed to dinner but not the theater. She didn't have the time.

Craig spoke, breaking another awkward silence. "Well, how's the international world of corporate finance?"

She dabbed at her lips with a napkin. "I'm too new at it to make a judgment. Anyway, as I told you, I'm not running things. I'm just around for show. My development takes all my time. God, between bankers, architects and construction people, I sometimes think I'll go mad."

He put down his fork and took a sip from his small teacup. "You'll do fine, Vicky."

This was their second date since he had approached her about helping his client. In a way it was like being back in high school. She felt graceless and clumsy. "And how was your day, Craig?"

"Not bad," he said quietly. "Just the normal day of a practicing lawyer struggling to get by."

She smiled. "You make it sound so boring. I'm sure it's much more exciting." She found him as handsome as before, perhaps even more so. There was a quiet maturity about him now.

"You didn't stay with a practice very long, Vicky, so it couldn't have been so exciting for you."

She found his attitude puzzling. "You, of all people, know what happened. We were living together when it did. I had a lucky break."

He nodded. "To say the very least."

She was annoyed by his cool response. At the time it had been so unexpected and thrilling. She had been a low-ranked associate with a large law firm, assigned to their real estate division. Victoria had surprised everyone, including herself, with her flair for handling the deals in the complicated world of commercial development. Then one of the clients assigned to her had backed out of an enormous land development at the very last moment. Everything was in place: the documents, the financing, the plans. She had asked if she could take over, become the developer, and much to her amazement everyone had agreed. From that day on she had never looked back.

"I always found law fascinating, that's why I became a lawyer," she said. "I loved practicing law, but what I do now seems even more challenging. There's no basic difference."

He raised an eyebrow. "What kind of money did you handle today, Vicky?"

"What do you mean?"

"Did you sign any agreements, any big deals?"

She half smiled. "As a matter of fact, I did. I worked out an arrangement deal with a plumbing firm for my new development. They'll handle everything when the inside work is ready to be done."

"What kind of money?" he asked.

She shrugged. "Several million, why?"

He toyed with his teacup. "Today, I settled a negligence case. My client lost a few toes. There was a question of who was at fault. We settled for five thousand dollars."

"So?"

"I also picked up a divorce. It should be worth a couple hundred. Today was a good day for me."

"I don't understand."

He smiled wryly. "It hardly makes for scintillating conversation, does it? We're two lawyers, but we really have nothing in common."

"All this sounds very familiar," she replied quietly.

He reached across the table and took her hand. "Yes, it does. Just like the old days. I like you, Vicky. I may even love you. But there is such an enormous gulf between us we can never hope to come together. If we think otherwise, we'll just be kidding ourselves."

She nodded. She vividly recalled the fights they had had. But it had been so lovely in the beginning. Then life got in the way. "You're saying that things haven't really changed, I take it?"

He nodded. "Basically. We might as well be realistic." He released her hand.

"So you'll just drop out of my life?"

He smiled slowly, then laughed. "I think we've reversed roles. Isn't the girl the one who says 'We can always be friends?'—"

Victoria chuckled. "Times change, Craig. Even people."

He sighed. "Some things don't. Well, how about it, can we still be friends?"

This time she took his hand. The awkwardness was gone. "I can't promise I can control myself, Craig. But if that's the only way." She laughed. "Isn't that the way it's supposed to go?"

"Sounds good to me, Vicky."

She continued to hold his hand, both of them suddenly comfortable and relaxed with each other for the first time.

12

She had achieved celebrity status, the product of specialists she had hired to form and project just such a public image. Victoria Van Horn was accustomed to being stared at, but this time it was different.

From the moment she stepped from the taxi and walked into the Van Horn Building she was conscious of the people who followed her with their eyes. She was their new boss. They had watched her father walk through that door for years, and if they were making comparisons, she wondered how she might measure up to the business legend that had been her father.

She was whisked up to the executive level. A young blonde girl, very slender and all smiles, was seated at a desk in front of the office that had been occupied by Victoria's father. The girl didn't get up but seemed to become brighter, like a schoolgirl trying to please a difficult teacher. "Good morning, Mrs. Van Horn," she said.

Victoria stopped and looked down at her. "I'm not married. What is your name?"

"Linda."

Victoria checked her rising irritation. "And do you have a last name, Linda?"

"Oh yes, ma'am. I'm Linda Salem. I'm not married either." Then her eyes seemed to fill with a simple kind of joy. "But I do have a boyfriend."

"How nice for you," Victoria said. "Did you work for my father?"

"No, ma'am. I never met him. I'm new to this floor. I've been with the company for almost three months, but as a typist in the administration division."

"Are you a good typist?"

The girl seemed to possess only one expression, a sort of vacant-eyed smile. "Well, I'm learning. I have had courses in school."

"Do you know who was my father's secretary?"

"Isn't that the funniest thing, I do."

"Why is that funny?"

The girl made a fluttering gesture with her hands. "It's like a coincidence. She sat next to me in the administration typing pool. In fact, she's been helping me with my typing. It came as a surprise to all of us when Miss Spitz was demoted to being a mere typist. You know, after being head secretary to the main boss and all. Anyway, she's been a great help to me."

"What's her full name?"

The girl frowned, an expression that had the effect of a light being turned off from within, then she brightened again. "Joyce, I think. You see, everyone in the pool just called her Spitz. Some of them even made a sort of joke of it."

"Thank you, Linda. Now get me the head of personnel on the phone." The girl's smile remained fixed. "I don't know who that is."

"Make it a point to find out." Victoria's voice was clipped.

Victoria walked into her father's office and sat behind the desk, although she felt like a trespasser. She wondered if memories, which plagued her like ghosts, would continue to haunt her mind, causing recurring spasms of guilt. She wished her pride hadn't prevented her bridging the gap that had existed between her father and herself. It all seemed so foolish now. She idly glanced through a stack of reports neatly laid out for her signature. They seemed routine. Chilton Vance, as good as his word, apparently was handling the main problems of the business.

The telephone buzzed. She picked it up. "Yes?"

"Miss Van Horn, this is Harry Anderson. I'm director of personnel. I understand you wish to speak to me?" There was just a hint of fear in the otherwise confident voice.

"Where is my father's secretary?" She snapped the words. "Joyce Spitz."

"Ah, well, I'd have to, er, check that out, Miss . . ."

"Get her up here now." His stalling was obvious, and Victoria resented it.

There was a pause. "I think she may still be with the company. I'll have to check around and . . ."

"She's assigned to the administrative division typing pool." Victoria was annoyed. He was being deliberately evasive.

"Say, now that you mention it, perhaps that is where . . ."

"How long did she serve as my father's secretary?"

"A little over three years." There was no hesitation in giving that answer and she found that to be quite revealing.

"Mr. Anderson, I want Joyce Spitz in my office in five minutes." She was about to add that she wanted a report on how her father's secretary got assigned to a typing pool, but she thought better of that. She could get the details later, and if they warranted, take action then. She hung up the telephone.

She quickly glanced through the reports to ensure there were no hidden nuances in them, then she signed them. Her titles as president and chairman of the board had been typed under each signature line.

Finished, she swiveled in the leather chair and looked out on the view of New York. She wondered how many times her father had done the same thing. She could recall her visits as a young girl and being enthralled by the scene.

The city had its shortcomings, but she still loved New York. It was jammed, noisy and dirty, but it pulsated with a life all its own. The city had an almost hypnotic hold on her despite all the changes.

As she enjoyed the view she wondered if Hong Kong too had changed, and if those changes might have robbed that city of its magical charm. She would soon find out. She hadn't been in the Orient for years, but now she had to go. A Hong Kong businessman owned New York docks that were a crucial key to her Hudson River development. He refused to deal with anyone but her and he also refused to come to New York, pleading a fear of flying. She felt she could persuade him to sell. He was an old man, she had been told, quite independent, but he would have a price. And she would find out what it was. She was scheduled to leave on the evening flight.

The buzz of the intercom pulled her away from the view and her thoughts. "Yes?"

"Spitz is here." The young blonde's happy tone never seemed to vary.

"Please send Miss Spitz in."

A heavy-boned woman, not unattractive but dressed to emphasize her plainness, Joyce Spitz was about her own age. Victoria was surprised that she remembered her from the funeral. In a sea of people this woman's face had caught her attention. She had seen true grief in those broad features.

"You wished to see me, Miss Van Horn?" The woman was taller than average and wore low-heeled shoes to compensate. Her hair was neatly pulled back behind her head.

"Please sit down, Miss Spitz."

The woman sat primly on the edge of the chair. She seemed otherwise quite composed.

"You were my father's secretary, I'm told."

Joyce Spitz nodded slowly. "He had a number of secretaries. I was the main one, his private secretary. I served in that capacity for almost three years. Before that, I served in various company jobs."

"Were you assigned to the typing pool before or after my father's death?"

Joyce Spitz would have made an excellent poker player; she gave no hint of what she might be thinking. "After the funeral."

Victoria nodded. "That seems quite unusual. Did you complain?"

"Miss Van Horn, your father was a wonderful man and a wonderful person to work for. He was more than generous. I was given a great deal of responsibility and I was paid very well. I think that may have caused some resentment and jealousy, particularly among some people who now run the company. Complaining would have done no good, believe me."

"Why didn't you just quit? The demotion must have been a bitter humiliation."

A small smile played on Joyce Spitz's thin lips. "As I said, your father was generous. Despite my transfer, under company rules my salary can't be cut for one year. I have a number of pension benefits built up and about to vest. Another year would make them quite valuable. For financial reasons alone, it wouldn't have been wise for me to quit, Miss Van Horn. Besides . . ." She hesitated.

"Go on."

"I just didn't want to give certain people the satisfaction of driving me out."

Victoria sat back and silently studied the woman; she possessed an obvious intelligence. "You liked my father?"

"Very much."

"You knew, I presume, of the, well, differences between us?"

The woman's eyes seemed suddenly quite sympathetic and her tone was gentle. "Miss Van Horn, there never were any real differences between you, at least as far as your father was concerned. He followed your every move. He was very proud of you." She allowed that small smile to flicker briefly again. "Your father, however, was something of a stubborn man."

Victoria felt the threat of impending tears but managed to check herself. "Stubbornness is a family trait, it seems. Would you have any objections to working for me? To perform the same job for me that you did for my father?"

Joyce Spitz slowly shook her head. "I think I may represent memories of your father to some of the people in the company who were opposed to him. I doubt if that would be a wise move on your part."

"I didn't ask whether you thought it wise," Victoria said, instantly regretting the sound of her words. "I'm sorry, I don't mean to be testy. I'll worry about the possible consequences. Will you work for me?"

The woman nodded with a sudden smile. "I'd be delighted, of course."

"Good. You can start by getting rid of that brainless bimbo they installed out there as my secretary."

"Ah, Miss Van Horn, may I make a suggestion?"

Victoria wondered if she had made a mistake. Joyce Spitz might prove difficult to handle. "That depends."

"Well, Linda won't win any scholarships to Radcliffe, but she is a nice young girl, and eager to work. She befriended me when, well, some didn't. I wonder if I could have her assigned as my assistant." The smile flickered again. "I think I have her to the point where she may become a respectable typist. She could be a great help."

Victoria nodded. "Of course. Will you make the necessary arrangements?"

"Certainly, Miss Van Horn." Joyce Spitz stood up. "I imagine you may have some reservations about me; that I might not know my place. Please don't worry about that. I know which one of us is boss. I worked very well with your father, and you seem very much like him." The small smile was back. "And if you are like him, you may be wondering if I have the guts to crack the whip over the men who sent me to the typing pool."

Victoria laughed. "Well, something like that."

"When you give the orders, Miss Van Horn, I can not only crack that whip, I will take some small delight in applying it."

"When can you start?"

"Right now, if that's agreeable?"

"More than agreeable. I have to fly to Hong Kong tonight, but I'll be back in a few days. Meanwhile, you can set things up here as you wish."

Victoria stood up and extended her hand. Joyce Spitz's grasp was firm.

"I have one quality that may come in handy, Miss Van Horn. Your father appreciated it."

"And that is?"

"Loyalty," she said simply.

Cecelia Van Horn, her jaw wired shut, found it difficult to talk. She discovered, however, that if she kept her voice low and spoke very distinctly she could be heard quite clearly. It was one of the few times in her life when she had had to moderate any aspect of her behavior. It was necessary, but she resented it.

The maid showed Enrico Pelegrine into the living room. His dark olive eyes traveled over her in bold appraisal. Pelegrine was a tall, fleshy man, dark and swarthy. His round face glistened with perspiration. Although Cecelia enjoyed his obvious interest, she preferred her men lean, and dry, when possible. If he lost fifty pounds he might be handsome. She dismissed Pelegrine as a possible lover. She was bored, but not that bored yet.

"My dear Mrs. Van Horn." He grasped her fingertips. His lips were surprisingly dry against the skin of her hand. "They told me you were in an accident, but you still look absolutely lovely."

He received only a hint of a smile. She could manage no more than that without revealing the ghastly-looking wires. "Thank you, Mr. Pelegrine," she said tightly through clenched teeth. "I'm recovering nicely. Please sit down."

Pelegrine carried a large leather portfolio under one arm. He selected a straight-back chair near her, nervously placing the leather carrying case over his knees.

"Is that it?" She was glad he was close. She could speak only above a whisper.

"As I told you on the telephone, it is exquisite. As you know, I usually don't deal in the modern masters, but this came my way and I couldn't resist."

She had purchased the Matisse from him. Although at the time she realized it was probably stolen, it wasn't on anyone's missing list, and it had been authenticated by experts she trusted. It was very much like his famous *The Purple Robe*, full of rhythmic color, picturing a blonde woman with an explosion of flowers painted in the foreground. The Matisse served as the focal point in their large dining room. Pelegrine's reputation was somewhat odious in the art world, but he seemed able to deliver, and that was what really counted, odious or not.

"This was done rather late in Allen Brown's career. Brown, as you know, had problems with your income tax people, and a drinking problem. At the end of his life he did a number of paintings and hid them away from the tax people. This one has just surfaced."

"May I see it?"

He stood up and with a theatrical flourish opened the carryall. The painting was unframed but mounted. She recognized the distinctive splash of colors that had given Brown his reputation.

"It is breathtaking, no?" Pelegrine held it so that it caught the light. "At twenty thousand dollars it's a steal." He seemed to instantly regret the choice of the last word. "A bargain," he added quickly. "Bargains are very rare these days, dear lady."

Cecelia Van Horn, over the years, had developed a very astute eye for art. The painting was undoubtedly a Brown, but like many of his paintings from his IRS period, it was more an agony of alcoholism than artistry. He had turned them out like a factory, a bottle in one hand and a brush in the other. At the most the painting was worth a few thousand. It was unlikely to appreciate in value since Brown had done so many that he had saturated the market.

"He had a genius with color," she said, "but I think he wasted it on this canvas. If I can have it authenticated, I might go three thousand dollars."

Pelegrine slapped his forehead with exaggerated annoyance. "My dear lady, that would be out of the question."

"I do thank you for bringing it by, Mr. Pelegrine. I couldn't think of paying more. Besides, we already have a Brown, one of his earlier works."

He sighed, knowing she had correctly determined the true market value. There was no use in bargaining. He began to put the painting back in the carryall. He would find another prospect, less knowledgeable, whom he could persuade to pay much more.

"Perhaps soon I'll come across something that will tempt you." He wished to keep her as a potential customer. "One never knows in this business. A Titian may be right around the corner."

"Unlikely, but possible," she replied.

He looked down at her. "Oh, by the way, I met with a very interesting man the other day. He is a man connected with the art world, very reliable, very respectable." Pelegrine dismissed Driker's instructions to avoid New Yorkers. That was foolish. They were the obvious market, if a market really did exist.

Cecelia wished he would leave. She was tired and it sounded as if he was about to launch into promoting the sale of another painting.

"Your husband's father was a member of the Vault here in New York, I understand." Pelegrine finished tying the carryall. "Is your husband also a member?"

Cecelia was suddenly wary. "No. He is much too busy for social clubs."

Pelegrine beamed. "Ah! So that is what it is. I wondered. Perhaps my friend is getting a bit foolish. No one would be interested in any information about the Vault."

"What do you mean?"

"My friend says he has some kind of inside track to that group. Insider information, he called it. But who would be interested in some sort of club? It would be nothing, I suppose, but cigars, drinks and bragging."

Cecelia purposely shifted her position. She was aware that the silk dressing gown clung suggestively to her as she leaned forward and patted the couch. "Please sit down, Mr. Pelegrine. I was so interested in your painting I forgot my manners. Can I offer you a drink?"

He sat down, pulling a large handkerchief from his pocket to wipe his gleaming face. "Perhaps a little white wine?"

Cecelia rang the small silver bell to summon the maid. "Tell me a bit more about this information your friend has. It might prove to be quite droll."

"Gossip probably," he replied, his eyes glued to her waist where the sash was loosening. "But he claims to know exactly what goes on in this Vault."

"Did he give you any specifics?"

"No. He just mentioned he had access."

"Who is this friend of yours?"

"I'm not at liberty to say," Pelegrine dodged. "He prefers it that way."

She stretched, noting the effect it had on him. "Well, you can tell your friend that I might be interested."

The maid came in and Cecelia ordered a bottle of their best wine.

"You're a fascinating man, Mr. Pelegrine," she said. "We should get to know each other better."

Hong Kong hadn't really changed, at least not in its true essence. New tall buildings had sprouted, crowding each other like trees thrusting thirstily toward the sun. But the never-ending mass of humanity hadn't changed, nor had the noise, nor the almost gagging aroma of the Far East.

Victoria had completely forgotten the devastating odors, but she knew that she would quickly adjust, like everyone else, and not even notice the pungent air. A limousine took her to the hotel and she went directly up to her luxury suite. She had managed some sleep during the long Pacific flight but jet lag took its toll. She felt worn, disoriented and slightly irritable.

The Peninsula Hotel was just as she remembered it, regal and enduring. The pageboys were still dressed in immaculate white. And the gilded lobby with its ornate columns still seemed to be the center for the truly elegant members of Hong Kong society.

She had a magnificent view from her high-ceilinged room. Boats scuttled across the famous bay, the sails of the junks gliding like ghosts past the towering metal hulls of huge oceangoing ships. She watched for a moment, then lay down on the bed and closed her eyes.

The last time she had come to Hong Kong it had been a vacation, a graduation gift from her father. Other girls from school had gone to Europe, but she had often before toured the Continent. Hong Kong was new to her, and then there had been the promise of adventure with the young soldier she had arranged to meet there. At the time she remembered she was convinced she had found true love. Now everything was so different. She was no longer a carefree schoolgirl, her father was dead, and she couldn't even remember the soldier's name.

She had six hours to sleep until the meeting. She wanted to be sharp. It was an absolute necessity that she succeed. She took the flask of brandy from her flight bag and poured a healthy tot into the top that also served as a small silver cup. The liquor burned, but she felt more relaxed.

Victoria closed her eyes again and tried to force herself to review her approach to the Hong Kong businessman who controlled the waterfront property she needed. But her mind refused to function. Instead she seemed to drift off into a reverie, thinking of her long-forgotten soldier, of Hong Kong in that other time, and lastly of her father.

This time, the memories of her father did not seem to plague her with painful guilt. Now they were almost consoling. She could imagine him laughing, she could almost hear his voice.

It seemed like only minutes had elapsed when the telephone awakened her.

At first she couldn't get her bearings, then she remembered where she was. She picked up the offending receiver.

"Miss Van Horn, there's a Mr. Yee here." The singsong voice sounded indecently cheerful. "He says he is to take you to meet with Mr. Krugar."

She looked at her watch and sat bolt upright. She had slept the entire six hours. "I have to dress. Tell him I'll be down in about twenty minutes."

She hung up and headed for the shower. A residual memory of her father seemed to linger in her mind. And to her surprise it was not unpleasant.

Mr. Yee, a very small Chinese, was no longer young. His age could have been fifty or ninety, he had that kind of a face. He spoke perfect English, with just the faintest hint of a British accent.

"Miss Van Horn, if it's agreeable with you, Mr. Krugar would like to meet with you at his place of business in Aberdeen. I am instructed to drive you there, if you like."

Victoria nodded, as she glanced up at the hotel clock.

As if reading her thoughts, Yee spoke. "It is just a few minutes past noon, Hong Kong time. It's always difficult to adjust to a new time after a long flight, is it not?"

Victoria nodded.

"Lunch will be served when we arrive," Yee said. "Shall we go?"

Victoria wished she could return to bed. But this was no pleasure trip. Her time was not her own. "I'm ready," she said.

Yee led the way out of the hotel to a highly polished burgundy Rolls-Royce parked at the entrance. He assisted Victoria into the rear of the car.

Yee proved to be a competent driver, but the trip still seemed almost surrealistic to Victoria. They sped through narrow streets, parting battalions of pedestrians who seemed to barely step out of their way, as if their movements had all been carefully choreographed, rehearsed and timed. They passed through prosperous shopping areas, then drove into other sections teeming with ragged people who paid no attention to the luxury car as it went by them.

During the journey Victoria asked many questions about the surroundings and landscape. Yee answered them all. He was an affable little man, but she could get no information when she asked him anything specific about his employer.

She already knew a great deal. According to the information given her, Jon Krugar was nearing eighty, the multimillionaire head of a family that had begun as pirates raiding shipping along the coastal waters of China but had soon become a sea-based dynasty. Krugar was the product of various races, part Chinese, but mostly Dutch. He had commanded what had been the largest fleet of ocean luxury liners in the world. Now his income came chiefly from ownership of enormous oil carriers.

Krugar's liners had once been moored at docks, now abandoned and rotting, along the Hudson River. But he still had long-term leases on them. Victoria needed that water frontage. It was the key to her new development. It was crucial that she persuade him to sell his interest in those docks to her.

After about forty-five minutes, Yee slowed the Rolls and turned into a rough gateway cut through an ancient wooden fence. The big car rolled into a huge boatyard. Acres of land were covered with boats in every stage of construction. Armies of workers swarmed about each hull like ants attacking honey. Everything seemed to be noise and movement.

"This is Mr. Krugar's place of business?" she asked incredulously.

Yee chuckled softly. "This is a most famous shipyard. Years ago we made huge seagoing ships here. Now the market is for small luxury yachts for the world's elite. Mr Krugar believes in staying in tune with the times."

"Then this is his main business?"

Yee shook his head. "Oh, no. Shipping is still the primary business of the Krugar company. This is merely a very profitable sideline. Mr. Krugar lives in a small house at dockside here at the yard. His office adjoins it."

Yee carefully wheeled around a gang of workmen carrying a huge wooden beam. He chuckled again. "You see, Mr. Krugar is so rich he doesn't need to impress anyone. And, like his ancestors, he is more comfortable close to the sea."

Yee pulled up to a rambling wooden structure. It looked as if each part of it had been added as an afterthought, as an excuse to use up surplus wood. Old paint peeled from its rough boards.

"Here we are." Yee stopped the car and agilely skipped around the Rolls, arriving at Victoria's side of the car just in time to help her out.

Victoria's legs felt wobbly as she followed Yee to the front of the ramshackle building. A glass-enclosed porch looked out over the bay. Beyond, on the water, junks and motorboats moved crazily about with what seemed almost suicidal abandon.

Yee followed her gaze. "It's always busy. We are in the center of the water people. They live aboard thousands of boats, mostly junks. Like their ancestors, they make their living from the sea. It is quite beautiful, is it not?"

The sails were many and multicolored. Viewed together, they reminded her of an expressionist painting.

Yee led the way up a worn step to the porch and through a screen door.

A very old and exceedingly fat man looked up form his seat at an ancient rolltop desk. He struggled up, using the desk for support.

"Victoria Van Horn, I presume." His voice was surprisingly deep. He was stooped with age but was still well over six feet tall, and obviously weighed over three hundred pounds. A wispy gray beard protruded from the very tip of his fleshy face. His slate-blue eyes seemed astonishingly young. What little hair he had was white and plastered straight back on his round skull. His white suit was worn and wrinkled. He extended a puffy, veined hand.

"I knew your father quite well." He smiled. Most of his teeth were gold-capped. His breathing seemed labored. "Please sit down." He indicated a large bamboo chair. Easing himself back into his wooden swivel chair, he turned to face Victoria.

"I took the liberty of ordering lunch. I employ one of the world's best chefs, a Frenchman. He's a genius. May I offer you some wine? I favor a vintage Châteauneuf-du-Pape."

Mr. Yee had gone, replaced by a young and beautiful Chinese woman.

"My granddaughter," he said, nodding toward the girl. "Bring the wine, my dear."

Victoria smiled at the girl.

"She takes care of me. She has become my good right hand. My oldest son married a Chinese woman. They have eight children. She's the youngest."

"She's lovely," Victoria said softly.

He smiled with pleasure. "Isn't she? Now, Victoria Van Horn, what can I do for you?"

Victoria's tone became businesslike. "You know why I'm here, Mr. Krugar. I want to purchase your interest in your New York docks."

He nodded. "Yes."

"My agents here tell me you will deal only with me."

"There is a good reason for that. May I call you Victoria?"

"Of course."

"I own land all over the world, Victoria, as you have probably made it a point to find out."

"I have."

"The Krugar family made its fortune based upon shipping. My ancestors controlled vast fleets of commercial and passenger ships. The Krugars determined that they never wanted to be hostage to the whims of the shore people in any of the countries in which we did business. So, to avoid such problems, they set about buying up dock space. In those days it was a form of insurance."

"But your ships no longer put in at New York."

He chuckled. "Of course not. The nearest we come to Manhattan are the oil facilities in New Jersey. In which, by the way, we own a significant interest. Old habits die hard."

"Then you don't need the New York docks."

He sipped at the wine brought by his granddaughter, smacking his lips afterward. "I suppose I could tell you that we wished to hold on to the docks as a hedge against the future, but that's not true. Krugar is getting out of the shipping business, slowly to be sure, but it is inevitable. So you're quite right, we don't need those docks."

"Then why not sell your interest to me? You know of my East Port project. My plan for the Hudson River development is similar, only much larger. I can put that frontage to good use."

Krugar nodded, his face solemn. "I haven't been to New York in many years, but my people have told me of your success." He sighed. "I presume you plan to keep a nautical theme as you did with your East Port property?"

"Yes. That's proved quite successful, a blend of the past and the present."

"That's good. The sea is our mother. None of us should forget the past. Frankly, I like your idea."

"Then why are you resisting? Or are you simply trying to drive up the price?"

He laughed heartily, then wheezed from the exertion. "When I was younger, such things often interested me. But I have made enough money to last my family a hundred years. Profit, oddly enough, is not the prime consideration."

"I don't understand."

Krugar's granddaughter returned and placed a small portable table between them. She covered it with an immaculate white linen cloth, then set out dishes of the finest bone China, decorated with a delicate filigree pattern.

"Let's have our lunch. After that we can continue our little talk."

"I don't think I could eat if you insist on keeping me in suspense."

He chuckled. "I wouldn't want this food to go unappreciated. We'll continue as we eat. The money you offer is reasonable. As dockage, that property is almost worthless. As office space, shops, and especially housing, given the New York market, it could be turned into a rich vein of gold."

"Why then . . ."

"As I say, the sum you offer is acceptable. The problem is that you don't wish to pay cash."

"I try to keep cash liquid, Mr. Krugar. I have offered to buy you out over an extended period. I would think the interest I propose would make that offer quite attractive."

He waved his hand as if somehow that gesture would help to explain. "The amounts aren't the problem. It's the method that troubles me. You see, Victoria, I didn't wish to explain my reasons for refusing to anyone but you. Out of respect for your late father I thought this should be private."

"Why?"

He frowned for a moment. "I understand you've taken over as president of your father's company. Is that not so?"

"Well, yes. As you know, it's a huge company. It practically runs itself."

His granddaughter brought in a tray of steaming dishes. He smiled his approval. "Broiled duck breast," he said, as his granddaughter served generous portions. "A rare treat. Please eat."

"Mr. Krugar, what has my father's company to do with my development? They are entirely separate."

He chewed for a moment, his eyes raised heavenward as if in ecstasy. "As I grow older my taste buds become more blunted, but even so, this is quite remarkable." He took another forkful, eating with almost holy respect. He washed it down with wine. "If you offered to pay cash, I wouldn't hesitate to sell."

"Why cash? You'll be completely secured."

"Ah, but if your project fails halfway through, the other creditors and their lawyers will come flocking in. That dock property will be tied up for years in the courtroom wrangling that seems so popular in your country. It would be of no use to anyone. Now if I didn't own it, I wouldn't care. But since you propose buying it on time, as it were, I would eventually be drawn into the mess. And I have no time or inclination for that."

Victoria felt a vague shiver of fear pass through her. "You seem to believe my project is doomed. Why?"

He took another bite before replying, again chewing with relish. Then he spoke. "When Van Horn Enterprises collapses, you will go down with it. You are the president, after all. I'm afraid your wonderful project will also collapse. You see, you will lose all your credibility with the business world. Your money sources will withdraw." He took another sip of his wine. "I was most fond of your father. He might have been able to save his company, had he lived. He had the experience and the contacts. But even so, it still would have been touch and go."

"I don't know where you're getting your information. Van Horn Enterprises is absolutely sound." She was annoyed at his attitude, but he seemed so sure.

He chuckled. "Come now, Victoria. Surely you knew all this?"

"The company is sound," she snapped, but something in his tone frightened her.

His fleshy face reflected his concern. He put down his fork and pushed away his plate. "Is it possible?" He stared past her at the fleet of boats in the bay. He slowly shook his head. "Of course, I had forgotten. You and your father were estranged. You would have no way of knowing what was going on." His gaze came back to her. His eyes seemed sad.

She felt uncomfortable under his solemn scrutiny. "Mr. Krugar, I don't know where you got all this so-called information, but I . . ."

"Your father," he said simply.

"Pardon me?"

He spoke in almost a gentle tone. "Before his death, your father visited me. I own a sizable amount of stock in Van Horn Enterprises. In fact, one of my people sits on your board of directors. Hunter came all the way out here to ask my help in his plan to bail out his company. That was only a few weeks before he died." Krugar drew a long thin cigar from the pocket of his wrinkled suit. "Do you mind?"

"No. Please, tell me what you know." She had come about the docks; now that seemed so insignificant. Victoria prayed he was wrong, but she was terrified that he might be right.

He lit the cigar, sending up small gray clouds as he puffed it into life. He brushed away the smoke with his hand. "Victoria, I'm afraid I've blundered. I thought you would know everything about the company."

"I've read all the financial statements." She sounded defensive.

He again slowly shook his head. "On paper, it looks good, at least it did on last year's reports, which are what you read. However, those reports, my dear, should really be on a fiction best-seller list—they are more accounting art, than hard fact."

He studied the cigar for a moment. "Your father and I went back a good many years. We shared a number of connections. Hunter was a member of New York's Vault. I serve on a similar organization here in Hong Kong, called the Council. We often found ourselves to be allies in business."

Krugar's expression changed. The gentleness was suddenly gone. "When he came to see me, and explained what was happening, I told him I would wait to see what he could do about repairing things. If it looked possible, I would help. If not, I would sell my stock before the collapse." His eyes seemed fixed on hers. "I am, after all, a businessman."

"I stand in my father's place. I can do what he would have done." Even to her own ear, her words sounded hollow.

Krugar shrugged. "To be frank, I don't think so. So you can see why I must insist upon cash for my New York docks."

"Why don't you think I can do it? I have proved myself as a developer."

He puffed on the cigar, then spoke. "That's part of the problem. If you had only Van Horn Enterprises to worry about, there's a possibility, even with your inexperience, you might be able to save the company. But, I'm informed, you have totally committed everything you own, together with every bit of credit you could muster, to this new development of yours. You have your feet in two different boats, my girl, and I'm afraid they are about to sail off in opposite directions."

"I can handle both." Her words were brave, but spoken without real conviction.

He stared at her, his chuckle without mirth. "I wish that were so. But no one could. It looks to me as if you have been set up, my dear." He gestured to his granddaughter, who began clearing away the dishes. "I can understand your loss of appetite. I am genuinely sorry to be the bearer of such disastrous news."

She looked around at the ramshackle porch and at the boats beyond. Nothing seemed quite real. She wished it were a dream, but she knew it was not.

"Mr. Krugar, you apparently know everything about Van Horn Enterprises. Please take the time to tell me whatever you know. You will be doing me a great favor."

He relit the cigar, as if that gave him time to reach a decision. "Make yourself comfortable, my dear," he said as he sat back in his squeaky chair and again fanned away the smoke. "This will take quite some time.

"It all started with the troubles in your Entertainment Group," he began.

13

Thousands of feet below, the mighty Pacific seemed to stretch on endlessly. Victoria watched the empty ocean as the plane flew toward the United States, but she could not relax, her mind occupied with Jon Krugar's terrible revelations.

Krugar possessed all the facts, all the devastating details. Whatever doubt she might have had had vanished in the avalanche of his obviously credible information.

Van Horn Enterprises was in danger of collapse, its main divisions all in dire financial trouble. Krugar said her father had discovered the true condition of his company just before his death.

Her father had been cleverly set up, and it had to have been carefully planned and executed. Whether out of maniacal ambition or hate, her father's business destruction had been deliberately plotted.

And now it would be her destruction. Her father knew the company's operations, and he had only one business to worry about; he might have survived.

Victoria looked down at the water far below. She didn't know the company, and she had signed her future away in her commitments for the Hudson River project. She could think of no way out, no escape. Realistically, there seemed no hope.

It was obvious that Chilton Vance was the one who had brought it all about. Victoria wondered what might have motivated Vance into his treacherous action. There seemed no reason, after her father's death, why he had trapped her into certain ruin. It didn't make any sense.

She felt helpless and alone. Victoria wished there was someone in her life, someone she could talk to, confide in, who would share her concerns, perhaps even suggest alternative plans. She had always prided herself on her independence. Now that seemed quite hollow.

The magic between herself and Craig Hopkins that she had hoped would be rekindled had resulted only in resurrecting the old resentments and conflicts that had originally driven them apart. She liked Craig, but she knew she didn't love him. There was no one else; she was quite alone.

Her life in some ways seemed as empty as the vast ocean far below.

Timothy Burroughs had two reputations in the world of public relations. He was regarded as enormously effective, having been a working newsman for major papers. He had connections, good ones, and he had used them to become the unofficial mouthpiece of New York's elite. His second fame, self-proclaimed, was as a man who would do anything for money. Ethics and morality to him were merely words. The combination of that attitude and his true ability was making him wealthy.

Burroughs had agreed to meet Hunter Van Horn, Jr., but not at the office. Burroughs had specified a small bar near Times Square. Junior didn't like the squalid locale but presumed a man like Burroughs would be more at home there. Junior expected a newsman like those portrayed in movies: a rough, foul-mouthed cynic dressed in baggy, unkempt clothing.

Burroughs introduced himself after Junior took a seat at the bar. He was a clean-cut man, about forty, muscular, and dressed in a Brooks Brothers three-piece gray suit.

The bartender took Junior's order for a martini, and without asking, set a soft drink in front of Burroughs. They were alone in the place except for a wheezy old man at the end of the bar who was in deep study of a racing form.

"The bartender seems to know you," Junior said.

"He should. He works for me. I own this hole. My accountants are coming in for an audit, that's why it was more convenient for me to meet you here." He looked at the martini. "I don't drink. Never have. You can kill yourself with that stuff." He sipped his soda. "Now, what would you like me to do? Arrange the publicity for a charity event, maybe a wedding, what?"

Junior was about to sip the martini, but thought better of it. "It's a bit more substantial than that, Mr. Burroughs. I trust that what I tell you will be kept confidential?"

Burroughs shrugged. "If you're up to something illegal, I can't promise that. There's no privilege. I'm not a doctor or a lawyer, just a flack. But barring court intervention, my lips are sealed."

Junior wished he hadn't come. It had all been Cecelia's idea in the first place. "I'm sure you've read about my father?"

"A household name," Burroughs replied. "Just like your sister. People like me would be out of business if the world at large could get free publicity the way your father did and your sister does. Takes real genius."

Junior felt a rising sense of irritation. "Well, I'm not a genius, and I will need some advice, and perhaps help, in dealing with newspapers and television."

"Why?"

It was the last time he would listen to Cecelia. "I'm planning, well, a business move. I am about to try to take control of my father's company."

"You mean Van Horn Enterprises, the conglomerate?"

"Yes." Junior cleared his throat, then proceeded in a voice just above a whisper. "I need a publicity expert to ensure that the media handle it, well, the way I want it handled."

"Hey, I read that your sister is the new boss over there. Are you going to toss her out?"

"Crudely put, but correct." Junior felt himself coloring.

Burroughs grinned. "You want to look like the good guy, and make her look like a first-class bitch, right?"

Junior bolted down the martini. "In order to dislodge her, Mr. Burroughs, she must be put into something less than a favorable light."

"And you want me to kick her ass in the press. I can do that. Would that bother you? I mean, she is your sister. If it's done, there's no calling it back."

"It's necessary," Junior snapped.

Burroughs laughed suddenly. "Damn, this could be fun. It will turn into a goddamned circus, you know that. You'll be famous."

Junior began to see the wisdom in Cecelia's idea. "Time is a consideration." He looked around. No one was in earshot. "Can you make my sister look bad quickly? It's important."

Burroughs patted him on the back. "No problem. If someone is highly visible, like your sister, they're highly vulnerable, too. She's an easy target."

Junior tried to hide his delight, but Burroughs noticed his reaction.

"Of course, all this will be quite expensive."

Junior shrugged. "It's all tax deductible."

Burroughs laughed. "I'll need a ten-thousand-dollar retainer. I'll bill you monthly."

Junior stood up. He handed Burroughs his card. "This is my home address. You can send your bill there."

They shook hands and Junior started for the door.

"Don't worry, Junior. When we're through, your sister will have to change her name and leave the country. We'll knock her pretty little ass right off!" Burroughs called out after him, not knowing how much Hunter Van Horn, Jr., despised being called Junior.

———

The main offices of Perry Stanley reflected its history and banking philosophy. The furniture, carpeting and accessories were of the finest materials. Nothing had changed for almost a century. Electricity had been installed, of course, but everything was exactly as it had been at the beginning of the century. If a carpet became worn, it was replaced. And the replacement was not just in kind, it was identical. If it couldn't be purchased, it was specially woven. Everything, even lampshades, was duplicated exactly.

Perry Stanley was symbolic to an entire class, a rock in a stormy financial sea. Fathers brought their sons with them, and those sons grew up and brought their sons. Customers loved the old offices, and felt not only comfortable, but reassured.

Perry Stanley was a real bank, a place where deferential clerks had serious regard for money and its power. To the founding families of New York it represented an institution that did not change with every social tide. It was strong, solid, reliable.

The private office of the bank's chairman also never changed. Ambassador Stewart Lytle sat behind the ancient desk that had served his father and his grandfather.

Lytle studied his appointment book, then checked the engraved invitation once again. The name was on the list of sponsors. Sponsors were always expected to attend. It was timed perfectly. He dialed the special long-distance number.

"Carson here," the familiar voice answered.

"This is the ambassador," Lytle said. "I want you to have my son at a cocktail party here tonight."

"In New York?" There was a hint of apprehension in the question.

"Yes, in New York. At the Carlyle. It's a charity thing. You come with him and stay close to him. At least until I give you other instructions. Is that clear?"

"Of course, Ambassador. We can take the shuttle up. What time do you want us at the hotel?"

Lytle looked at the invitation and made a quick calculation. "Have him there no later than nine o'clock. It's for South American Children's Relief, by the way."

"Important politically?"

Lytle wasn't about to confide in an employee. "Just have him there," he snapped. "And I want him looking good."

"He's been absolutely straight."

"He better be. I want him looking his very best. I may even want him to enjoy himself."

"Would you like to talk to him? He's here in his office."

"No, it's not necessary. If he gives you any trouble about this, call me. Otherwise, I'll see you at the Carlyle later this evening."

Stewart Lytle hung up. He idly tapped the invitation on the expensive wood of his ancient desk. It was a good plan. Given a little luck, it could all work out quite well.

———————

Victoria had taken an extra day in Hong Kong to get all the information she could from Jon Krugar, and that extra day in the Orient played havoc with her schedule, robbing her of the time she had set aside to rest and recover from jet lag. There would be no rest now.

She resented having been scheduled to appear before the Vault and prove herself as if on trial. If she had been a man, it would never have been required. It was degrading, but her anger had made her accept. If she had to fight to become the first woman on the Vault, so be it. Other women had had to wage similar battles to achieve basic rights. But her anger wasn't so sharp now after the long flight. Her mind was on Krugar's information. She was depressed and tired, and she didn't feel equal to such a contest.

Before the Hong Kong trip, she might have cancelled the Vault appearance, even if it had meant she wouldn't be selected. But after discovering the true state of her father's company, she knew she would need all the help she could get. The members of the Vault were powerful. If she became a member she might be able to enlist them in her fight to save the company and herself.

She realized it might be clutching at straws, but she had to go.

She didn't wish to make an appearance at Van Horn Enterprises, so she went directly from Kennedy Airport to her own offices. She spent hours calling sources to check Krugar's information. Chillingly, it was all confirmed. Despite her fatigue the day passed quickly.

Krugar had been right: the company's situation was desperate. If she failed as president of Van Horn Enterprises, her own project would collapse too. Chilton Vance had led her into the slaughtering pen. She wondered why. Worse, she could think of no way out.

It was nearly time for the Vault meeting. Afterward she was scheduled to make an appearance at a charity party. She decided to cancel that but didn't have time to make the call.

She took a cab to her apartment where she quickly showered and changed. She selected a Chanel red two-piece suit made of the finest wool with the trademark frogs. She combined that with a deep navy shantung shirt and red lizard pumps from Bergdorf's. She deliberately chose red; it showed bold self-assurance and that she did not feel she had to imitate men by wearing a dress-for-success suit in gray or navy. If she didn't feel completely confident, at least she would look it. As she dressed, she tried to think of questions she might be asked at the Vault, but her mind seemed numbed. She would just have to rely on instinct.

Crosstown traffic to the Habermann was so congested that she left the cab and walked the last few blocks. The day was nice, a hint of summer in the air, and the walk helped to freshen her spirit if not her body.

Victoria had known the Habermann since childhood. It was familiar territory, but she didn't feel at ease as she rushed up the museum's steps. The door was opened by a smiling uniformed guard. Inside, she was met by a dapper little man who identified himself as Cecil Driker, the head of the museum. He seemed strangely excited, and, although he tried to conceal it, she sensed a hint of hostility in his voice and manner. He escorted her down to the conference room, closing the doors behind her as she entered.

All seven members of the Vault were there; they stood alongside ornate chairs placed around a long polished table. Sander Blake introduced her. She knew some of them, the others she recognized from newspaper photographs. She nodded to Luke Shaw. They seemed so serious and solemn, like judges who had to pass a sentence of death, that she began to regret having come.

Blake escorted her to a chair at the end of the table. Then he took his place at the head and everyone sat down.

"Victoria, as you know, your father nominated you to take his place." Blake broke the uncomfortable silence. "Traditionally, this has always been an all-male group. We took a vote, but it didn't decide the issue. Several members abstained and have since requested that you be invited here to answer any questions the members might have." He smiled, as if trying to reassure her. "I trust that's agreeable with you?"

Victoria was suddenly gripped by panic. She wanted to run. "I understand," she heard herself replying, and was surprised at the calm sound of her own voice. "I agree."

"Good." Blake looked at the others. "There's no formal order here. Who would like to go first?"

Several hands were raised.

"Elias, you're senior member. Why don't you start?"

Victoria had first met Elias McKensie when she was a child. She remembered a tall man with steely eyes and ramrod posture. He hadn't aged well. The elderly man who stood up was thin and stooped, but his eyes seemed as commanding as ever.

"I have known Victoria since she was a little girl." He smiled. "A rather nasty little thing, quite loud, as I recall. However, much to my surprise, she has grown into a lovely young woman. A woman, I might add, who has scaled the heights of the business world and who has proven herself absolutely capable in every way."

"Is this a question or a nominating speech?" Franklin Trager's tone was quarrelsome.

McKensie glanced over the top of his half-glasses as if seeing Trager for the first time. "Patience, Franklin," he said evenly. "If I'm long-winded, chalk it up to advanced age." He looked over at Victoria. "Do you understand the primary purpose of this organization, my dear?"

She nodded. "I remember what my father told me. The Vault represents and protects the major business and cultural interests of New York. It was started by the founding families."

"Exactly," he interjected. "Now, knowing that, is there anything in your private life or your business interests that would conflict with those simple but important duties?"

"No," she responded crisply, with assurance. "As I'm sure you all know, I operate a New York development firm and I was recently named as head of my father's company; I see no conflict in either capacity."

"Nor do I." McKensie looked at the other members, then sat down.

"You seem anxious to speak, Franklin," Blake said. "Why don't you go next."

Trager did not get up. He glared at Victoria. "I understand you were estranged from your father for a number of years before his death, is that true?"

Victoria felt a surge of anger, but kept herself in control. "That's well known."

"Why the falling out?"

McKensie spoke quickly. "That's a bit personal, Franklin."

"The hell it is," Trager snapped. "We have a right to know about a candidate's background. I know all about the rift; everyone in New York knows about that. But no one knows why. And I want to."

"I agree with Elias," Blake said. "I don't think . . ."

"That's all right," Victoria said. "I don't mind answering the question. After I graduated from law school I began working as an associate in a law firm. I liked the law, but I found that I liked business even more. The firm assigned me to commercial and business cases. Frankly, I believed I had a flair for it. My father owned one of the largest companies in the world. I asked him for a job and he refused."

"You wanted to start at the top," Trager said, smirking.

She took a deep breath to control herself. "No, Mr. Trager. As a matter of fact, I would have taken any job at all, but I wanted it to be a real job, not make-work. I wanted the chance to show what I could do. My father said I had no need to work. And he said he didn't favor hiring relatives."

"Reasonable," Trager said.

"Oh? My brother was employed by father's company. I told him he was applying two standards." As she spoke she could vividly visualize the scene. "He became angry. He said he had never been in favor of my becoming a lawyer. He told me my only worth was to help out in charities and raise children."

Trager laughed. "Well, a father knows his daughter, doesn't he?"

The anger was rising now, just as it had with her father. "Does he? I walked out of there and never returned. I had exactly eleven dollars in my purse. I never asked for or received a penny from him again. Without any help from my father I was able to start my own company. I borrowed money and paid back every cent. I have built East Port, one of the main attractions of New York City. I've gone from eleven dollars to millions, and every bit of it on my own. I think I proved my father wrong."

Trager's grin became a leer. "Maybe he was also wrong about nominating you for the Vault. Ever think about that?"

She knew he was trying to bait her into a violent reaction. She was determined to deny him the satisfaction. "That's for you people to judge, isn't it?"

Trager was about to speak, but Blake interrupted him. "That's enough, Franklin. Let's give someone else a chance. How about you, John?" He chose the stockbroker because John Robertson had been neutral at the first vote.

Robertson struggled to lift his huge bulk from the chair, then abandoned the attempt. "Do you mind if I call you Victoria?"

"Please do."

His fleshy face creased into a pleasant smile. "Victoria, I'd like to hear your view of New York."

"I don't quite follow you."

He nodded. "That is a bit vague, I'll admit. There's a number of people who think this city has no future." He looked over at Trager. "Many people, good people, are appalled at the crime, the lack of housing, and all the other problems that seem to be on the front pages of the newspapers every day. How do you feel about that?"

It was a subject she could warm to. "I'm in love with New York. I always have been. Talk, as we all know, is cheap, but I think my actions show how I feel. This is a wonderful city. We have all the problems that you spoke of, every city does, but we'll lick them eventually. My future is tied up in New York. I built East Port, and now I'm putting together an even bigger development on the Hudson River. I'm totally committed to this city. It's part of my blood. I'm not sure that's what you want to hear, but that's my position."

Their faces remained solemn; only Elias McKensie seemed to approve. She looked at Luke Shaw but found no hint of what he was thinking. She wished she knew. She was conscious of his eyes upon her.

Robertson nodded thoughtfully. "Well, you certainly have strong opinions." His tone implied that she might be strong-minded on all issues.

"I feel deeply about New York, yes." She smiled. "But I'm open-minded on everything else."

"What about women's rights?" Clifford Colburn's words were more an accusation than a question.

"What about them?" she snapped back.

"You're not applying here as some kind of advance scout for women's liberation, are you?"

Colburn's words drew laughter from several of the men.

"I was nominated," she said evenly. "I didn't apply. Is that what you see me as, a kind of token?"

He colored slightly. "How I see you makes no difference, young lady. This isn't some damn social club. This is very serious business."

"I take it, from that, you don't consider women capable of handling important business matters?"

Colburn's cheeks were suddenly red. "I'd like an answer, not another question," he growled.

"Take it easy, Clifford," Blake said.

"I can handle myself," Victoria said, trying to control her anger. "My father nominated me, I didn't seek membership. I believe I have proved myself to be the equal of anyone in this room." She took the time to make eye contact with each of them before continuing. "I come from a wealthy family, as did each of you. I made it on my own, without any family help. I don't think many of you can make that statement."

Clifford Colburn exploded. "How would you like to put up with this every time we meet?" He scowled at the others. "If we let her in, we will be turned into a debating society!"

"Hold on, Clifford," Blake said quickly. "Victoria Van Horn is our guest. She was invited. She's entitled to every courtesy."

"Clifford is right," Trager said loudly. "I can't stand aggressive females. She's provoked this. It has nothing to do with courtesy."

She looked again at Luke Shaw. He was merely watching, a bemused expression on his face. It seemed to her he might even be amused.

"Mr. Trager," she said, speaking each word distinctly, "probably hates every woman he has ever known. I know his type. You can put any number of words to it, but it finally boils down to plain prejudice."

"Wait just a minute!" Trager roared. "You can't come in here and act like that, not if you expect we'd actually consider you for membership."

Blake started to intercede, but she cut him off. "How did you expect me to act? Like some poor scared young woman trying for a job in the typing pool? Did you honestly expect me to come in here, sit with my hands folded in my humble lap and beg for your condescending approval? If you did, you're in for one hell of a long wait!"

"Good for you." Elias McKensie laughed. "You sound just like your father."

Trager's voice cut above the others. "I know all I need to know and I've heard all I intend to hear. I call for a vote!"

Blake stood up and glared at Trager. "You're out of order," he snapped. "Now, does anyone else have any questions of Miss Van Horn?"

"Sander," Ambassador Lytle spoke, "perhaps if we asked Miss Van Horn to step out for a moment, we might discuss this freely without risking embarrassing her."

Blake slowly shook his head as he looked at Victoria. "I wish to apologize," he said. "This has all turned out rather unpleasantly. It wasn't planned that way, I assure you."

Victoria stood up and looked at each of them. She had hoped Luke Shaw might speak in her defense, but he hadn't. His face was quite expressionless.

She looked at Sander Blake. "I'm here because I was invited. My father nominated me, and I am just abiding by those wishes. If I'm selected I will do my best. If not, I bear no grudges." She spoke with a calmness she didn't feel. "Thank you for your courtesy, gentlemen."

Victoria turned and quickly walked from the conference room. She closed the doors behind her, feeling a surprising surge of elation. She would never be selected now, but at least she hadn't allowed them to bully her.

She moved briskly up the stairs and out of the museum. She was glad to be outside. She felt she needed a drink. And she needed to be with people; people who appreciated her for what she had done in life. She changed her mind about the charity cocktail party. She would go to the Carlyle. She would show them they couldn't upset her.

At that hour she really didn't expect to get a cab easily, but to her surprise the first one she signaled pulled over. She gave the cabby the destination. She felt her pulse throbbing like an angry drum. They went several blocks before the tears began.

*   *   *

Cecil Driker had listened, his attention completely riveted on the exchange between Victoria Van Horn and the members of the Vault. He felt a sense of relief when Victoria stormed out of the meeting. That was the end of her. They would never agree to seat the bitch now.

Driker relaxed, as pleased as if he personally had banished the woman. He sat back to enjoy what was to follow. He hoped they would continue to wrangle. It was exciting.

Sander Blake's disgusted voice crackled into Driker's earphones. "I consider this entire episode appalling," he said.

"Bull," Franklin Trager snapped. "You saw how she acted, Sander. She's typical: another pushy woman trying to take over the world. It's a damn good thing we found out what she was like before it was too late." He sounded triumphant.

"I call for a vote." Driker recognized the dry tones of Ambassador Lytle's voice. Driker liked Lytle, he seemed a serious man.

"Second the motion." Driker wasn't sure who had spoken. He wished he could have installed video cameras. It was a pity they couldn't be concealed as easily.

"All right, if that's what you wish." Blake now sounded angry. "I'll start off. I vote to seat Victoria Van Horn."

Franklin Trager spoke. "I'm sure it comes as no surprise that I'm opposed. I vote no."

"You're next, Clifford," Blake said.

"I'm with Franklin," he growled. "I vote no."

"You can guess my position." Driker recognized the reedy voice of Elias McKensie. "I believe she's a fine young woman. I feel we owe it to her father. I vote yes."

"And you, John?"

There was a long pause. Driker was annoyed at the delay. Then John Robertson answered. "Well, to be frank, I like her. But, given how strongly some of you feel, I think her presence might be divisive. On that basis only, I vote no."

"Good for you, John," Trager said.

"Your turn, Ambassador," Blake said. "How do you stand?"

Driker smiled. Lytle was a conservative man who spoke rarely, but when he did, things made sense. Driker felt Lytle would never allow a woman to sit on the Vault.

"I've given a great deal of thought to this matter," Lytle said quietly. "Times change. I vote to seat the young lady."

Driker was shocked. He was angry. He determined that he would never trust Lytle again.

"That makes it three to three," Blake said, surprise reflected in his voice. "I'm sure you didn't wish to be put in this position, Luke, but it looks as if it's all up to you."

Again, there was an annoying delay.

"I wish to be quite frank," Luke Shaw said. "My company is undertaking some engineering work for Miss Van Horn's new development. If anyone feels this might be a conflict of interest I'll refrain from voting."

"I'm sure no one would think . . ." Blake started to speak but was interrupted by Trager.

"No offense, Luke but is it a big contract? I mean is her work a large part of your business?"

"Franklin, you go too far!" Blake's voice was strident.

"No problem," Luke said. "I'll be happy to answer. Her work constitutes only a minuscule part of what we do."

"Would it be a factor in your decision?" Trager demanded.

Shaw laughed. "No, Franklin. I can honestly say it would not."

Trager grunted. "Then I have no problem either. Luke can cast his vote, as far as I'm concerned."

"Anyone else have a question or an objection?" Blake asked. He waited a moment. "All right, I presume your silence constitutes agreement. You can feel free to vote, Luke."

Driker felt his pulse race with the excitement. Shaw seemed levelheaded, but he was young. And the Van Horn woman was pretty. He was trembling with suspense.

"Since our last meeting, I, too, have given a lot of thought to this. I wish it wasn't my vote that would decide it." Shaw sounded sincerely uncomfortable. "We have two conflicting traditions here. We usually follow the wishes of a departed member, and we would, except he has proposed his daughter. Our traditional membership has always been male."

Driker wanted to scream. He didn't want speeches, he wanted to know what was going to happen.

"It's a matter of balancing one tradition against the other, I suppose," Shaw continued. "I'm not interested in change for change's sake. But I am interested in continuity. I deeply respected Hunter Van Horn. I'm not sure his daughter can fill his shoes, but he obviously was. I intend to honor his wishes. I vote for her."

"What!" Franklin Trager and Cecil Driker both shouted in unison. Driker was shaking with anger.

"Luke, have you gone nuts?!" Trager exploded. "This will ruin everything."

"Hold it," Blake commanded. "All of you!" His steely tone reduced the room to silence. "It was a fair vote. The question is decided."

"Maybe for you!" Trager snapped.

"Are you thinking of resigning, Franklin?" Elias McKensie's voice crackled unevenly, but his delight was nevertheless evident.

Suddenly everything was very quiet in the conference room. Driker could hear a chair shoved back, as if in anger.

"I'm not going to make any snap decisions now," Trager said, his voice a low growl. "But I'll let you know."

"Wait. I'll go with you, Franklin." Clifford Colburn's voice was also angry.

"Unless there's other business," Blake said, "we stand adjourned."

Driker tore off his headset and threw it at the radio cabinet. "Damn her," he said aloud. Boiling with rage, he considered her election an intrusion into his own personal world. He vowed that somehow the bitch would be made to pay.

14

The trip to the Carlyle seemed to take forever as the cab inched along with the heavy traffic. The cab driver, an older man, made no attempt at conversation, content to stare straight ahead as he almost continuously sounded his horn with impersonal detachment.

Victoria was exhausted from the long trip to Hong Kong and back. She was disheartened by the nightmare revelations of Jon Krugar. That, plus the unexpected hostility she had found at the Vault, left her numb, as if the combination had propelled her into a state of emotional suspension, without time and without thought.

She felt like a rudderless ship, completely at the mercy of an unpredictable wind with no control over her ultimate destiny. She had put everything at risk. Her father's faith in her seemed betrayed.

The ride to the Carlyle took over half an hour. Someone in the lobby waved. She smiled an acknowledgment. Many of the men and women waiting for elevators were in formal dress. She wished she had taken the time to change, even if she did only stay a few minutes.

She went to a pay phone and was put through to Joyce Spitz.

"Joyce, I'm back at last. I stayed an extra day. Could you meet me for breakfast tomorrow? I want to discuss some things with you. And I'd prefer somewhere other than the office."

"Of course, Miss Van Horn. When and where?"

"The Dorset has a nice restaurant. I've eaten breakfast there before." She waved at a bank president who shouted a greeting. "Is eight o'clock too early?"

"That would be fine."

"I'll see you there."

Victoria hung up. What she had to confide in Joyce Spitz couldn't be risked at the office. Perhaps it was paranoid to take such precautions, but it seemed a wise thing to do, justified or not.

The crowd swept Victoria along, and she was jammed in with other guests for the short elevator ride up to the ballroom and the cocktail party. She had become accustomed to being stared at; it was the price of celebrity status, but she didn't enjoy the attention.

The party was in full swing. She took a glass of champagne offered by a waiter. The wine was a bit flat, but she was glad for anything that might help raise her spirits.

She quickly finished it, then accepted another. It served as a quick pick-me-up, something that allowed her at least the illusion of energy. She made polite responses to people who talked to her.

The decision to come to the party had been intended as a brave demonstration, but she regretted it. She felt completely exhausted both mentally and physically. The prospect of her apartment and some sleep seemed to call to her like an impossible dream. She decided to pay her respects to the chairman of the event, then slip away.

A handsome man seemed to be making his way toward her. She recognized him as Ambassador Lytle's son, a congressman rumored ready to run for the Senate. He was a younger, dapper edition of his father. Just the memory of Ambassador Lytle and the others at the Vault produced renewed feelings of anger.

Despite her bitterness, she had to admit that the younger Lytle was attractive. He possessed an affable, easy manner as he moved casually through the crowd. Barry Lytle's hair was full and thick but graying at the temples. His features were almost classical. Thin and slightly less than average height, he had an athlete's grace. He was tan and fit, and his infectious smile seemed quite genuine.

He walked up to Victoria. "We've met several times," he said. "I'm Barry Lytle."

"I remember. How are you, Congressman?"

He took a glass from an offered tray. "I'm pretty good. Also, I am a messenger from the gods."

"Pardon me?"

He laughed. "I suppose that does sound as if I'm a candidate for the rubber-walled room. Poorly put, perhaps, but true nevertheless."

She wondered if he might be a little drunk, or if he had made a joke she didn't understand.

He was amused at her reaction. "Well, another voter confused. If I can manage to do that statewide, I should win." He gently patted her arm. "I understand you just came from a little session with my father and his playmates?"

She nodded. "The Vault. Yes."

"How could a lovely, intelligent young woman like you associate with those old dinosaurs? As far as I'm concerned, most of them are a full century behind the rest of us. They are, however, the gods I spoke of."

"And you are their messenger?"

He drank the last of his champagne, then grinned. "I have no winged feet, I'm afraid, only Gucci shoes. We messengers tend to change to suit the times."

She suddenly felt dizzy. She hadn't realized just how much importance she had attached to the Vault.

He took her arm gently. "Victoria, are you all right?"

"I'm fine. But I haven't had a bite to eat all day, and not much sleep. It appears I'm paying for it now."

"Come on." He quickly led her through the crowd to an elevator.

"Where are we going?"

He continued to keep a grip on her arm. "To get you something to eat."

"I'd rather just go home. I need sleep more than food."

He smiled but shook his head. "Humor me, okay? There's an excellent restaurant just down the street. Parioli Romanissimo—it's Italian, obviously. With the magic of pasta and some good red wine, you'll be a brand-new person. I guarantee it."

She usually resented shows of male dominance, but this time she was grateful for help. He seemed very kind.

She began to feel better by the time they reached the street. The dizziness had lessened.

The small Italian restaurant, although elegant, was uncrowded, and they had no problem getting a table. She admired the abundance of fresh flowers displayed. She wasn't offended when he ordered for her without asking. Having someone else take responsibility again seemed strangely comforting.

The wine was excellent and the spicy appetizers awakened her hunger. She ate ravenously.

He watched with amused satisfaction. "And they say we Republicans don't care about feeding the hungry."

She smiled at him. "This was a very good idea."

"You were so starved that you forgot about my message from the gods." This time, she noticed, his smiled didn't seem quite as broad.

"I rather think I know how the gods have decided."

"Are you a betting woman?" He was without expression.

She patted her lips with a red-checkered napkin. "Sometimes. Usually for high stakes."

He laughed quietly. "All developers are gamblers at heart. What are the stakes to be this time?"

"If I win?" she asked.

"Or if you lose."

She sipped more of the wine. "What did you have in mind?"

He smiled. "Nothing sinister. If you're wrong, you have to spend the evening with me." The smile became a grin as he saw her reaction. "No, that's not what I mean, Victoria. We'll just enjoy a night out on the town, that's all."

"And if I win?"

He shrugged. "As soon as you finish dinner, I'll take you home and disappear from your life, at least for the evening. Is that fair?"

She remembered the hostility shown her in the conference room at the Habermann. "Seems fair enough."

"So? What message am I instructed to deliver to you?"

"I am to be told—politely, mind you—that after careful considera-tion, the Vault has decided to disregard my father's wishes that I replace him. My proposed membership is being quietly declined."

"That's it?"

"Oh, your instructions may require a bit more tact, but I think that's the nub of it: rejection, no matter how nicely sliced."

His expression gave no hint of his reaction. He sipped his wine.

"Where would you like to go tonight? I'm told they have an excellent combo at the St. Regis: authentic Chicago-style jazz."

She blinked at him. "I don't understand."

He raised his glass. "Tonight, you have become a legend, a significant moment in history. My father says they have selected you for membership. You're a member of the Vault."

Her napkin slid out of her hands. "Please don't joke with me, Barry. I can't believe they'd accept me, especially after what they put me through tonight."

He put the glass down and took her hand. "My father tells me it was close." He grinned. "My old man told me to tell you that he cast the deciding vote. But all politicians are the same. I wouldn't believe him about that, if I were you. However, the outcome is correct. He knew you would be at the Carlyle, so he asked me to find you and deliver the message. Congratulations."

Hot tears spilled involuntarily. She quickly dabbed them away with the garish napkin. "I honestly didn't think I really gave a damn, but obviously I do."

He nodded. "Just becoming a member of the Vault is an enormous accomplishment," he said. "And to be the first woman probably equals any miracle in the Bible." He paused. "Look, if you're too tired, Vicky, I won't hold you to our bet. I'll take a rain check."

She laughed, then finished the last of her wine. Their waiter hurried forward and filled her glass again. "I agree, Barry, it is a miracle of sorts. And it certainly merits a celebration. Maybe this signals a change of luck in my favor."

They touched glasses.

Barry Lytle's eyes sparkled with pleasure. His delight was evident, but it was not because of her triumph. His father had allowed him to slip the leash. It would be his first night out without a guard. He was toasting his own luck, not hers. He smiled at her, thinking that she might just prove to be his permanent ticket to freedom.

"Here's to the future," he said, beaming.

The jazz at the St. Regis was like a trip to old Chicago. The musicians seemed inspired as they wove their melodious magic. Lytle kept the very best champagne flowing. She knew she was getting high, but she was truly enjoying herself for the first time in weeks. The threatened collapse of her father's company and the possible doom of her own beloved Hudson River project seemed almost remote. She softly sang along with the music as the band smoothly swung into "Dardanella." Victoria forgot her worry and fatigue and became lost in the pleasure of the music, the wine, and Barry Lytle's laughing eyes.

She came gradually back to consciousness, drifting in and out of sleep, called back reluctantly by the street noises far below: a blend of faraway auto horns broken only by an occasional siren's wail. Victoria shifted her position and her hand touched smooth flesh. She was jolted instantly awake. Barry Lytle, his naked back to her, lay quietly sleeping. His breathing was easy and even.

She looked about her. They were in a luxurious hotel room. Sunlight streamed in through the partially closed drapes. Their clothes lay scattered around the room. She tried to get up, but head pain and dizziness forced her to lay back for a moment. She closed her eyes and tried to remember what had happened.

After the St. Regis, she foggily recalled a number of places. Barry seemed to know just where to find the best music, usually in exotic and sometimes squalid surroundings. She seemed to recall telling him of her business problems, and his soothing reassurances. Everything after that was a jumble of fragments. They had been at a private party somewhere in the Village. She recalled the collection of very strange people. And there had been cocaine, she remembered that. She had a hazy image of being urged to participate. She had a fear of drugs, but she wondered if she had.

Surprisingly, she had complete recall of their lovemaking. Barry had become more attractive to her as the evening progressed. His eyes, his voice, his touch, everything seemed to call out to her. She had gone to him without hesitation. Everything he did caused exquisite pleasure. He was strong, yet gentle. He seemed almost like a mystical figure.

She felt she had at last found someone whom she could rely upon, a strong man who offered love and support. She moved closer to him, feeling the reassuring warmth of his body. She was about to drift back into sleep when she remembered her breakfast appointment with Joyce Spitz.

Joyce Spitz arrived at the hotel's restaurant a few minutes early. She looked for Victoria Van Horn but didn't see her. She requested a table in the back, then she ordered coffee.

The last few days had been both exciting and perplexing: she was restored to her old desk, as the secretary to the president of the company, but without any assignments or duties. And she was being closely watched. Company politics were boiling as never before. She was back at the old stand, but this time she was an outsider. Only Chilton Vance loyalists were welcome.

No one knew Van Horn Enterprises the way she did. She had joined the company after high school. Working days, she had put herself through long years of night courses until she got her degree in business administration. She had worked at every level, and at almost every job. Joyce Spitz had made the Van Horn company her life; a conscious decision that she had never regretted. The excitement and challenge of the company had given her more than any man could ever offer. Her friends were all Van Horn employees. The hypnotic allure of power had more pull upon her than any need for a family or children. The corporation was her family.

Since her rescue from the typing pool and her restoration to the front office, Joyce had busied herself sounding out her contacts at every level, finding out what was happening and, more important, what was likely to happen. To a casual observer she would have appeared to be merely curious, but her activities, seemingly relaxed and without purpose, were planned and effective.

Her worst suspicions were confirmed. In the short period since Hunter Van Horn's death, Chilton Vance had quickly moved his own people into key positions. It had been fast, but it had been done very smoothly. No one was actually displaced. His tactic was to create new positions, just a step above the existing officers. The new people reported directly to Vance. Victoria Van Horn might have the title of president, but Chilton Vance had control of the company.

Joyce Spitz had been taught by Hunter Van Horn, a true master of corporate intrigue. It was obvious that Vance could not have moved so quickly and smoothly without a long-standing plan. She had questioned Vance's loyalty when Van Horn had been alive. She had heard the whispers. Now it was all confirmed. Everything was clear except Vance's reasons for backing Victoria's appointment to her father's position. He had held all the cards, and her selection could not have taken place without his blessing. It was a mystery that Joyce Spitz meant to solve.

She glanced at her watch. Victoria was late. Hunter Van Horn had had an obsession about punctuality, something obviously not passed on to his daughter. Joyce ordered more coffee and asked the waitress to bring her a newspaper. She sipped from the fresh cup as she glanced through the pages of the morning tabloid. She never actually read gossip columns, but she did scan them to see if she recognized any of the names printed in the dark bold type.

The name Hunter Van Horn, Jr., seemed to jump off the page.

It was only a small item near the end, by a gossip columnist who ordinarily covered only theatrical people. She read it carefully: "War drums are thumping as one of America's largest companies is about to become a battlefield for the two surviving children of a legendary business mogul. The gorgeous and glamorous Victoria Van Horn, new head of daddy's Van Horn Enterprises—that giant which seems to own half the world, darlings—is about to be challenged by her brother, Hunter Van Horn, Jr. He wants to take it all away from her. Wall Street is girding for a major conflict. It should be *the* story of the summer. Ah, the toys of the very rich. And we all know how vicious children can be, don't we? More to come."

Joyce reread the item. It had been planted, of course. Hunter Van Horn himself had been a master at that. Joyce knew some powerful publicity man had fed the item to the columnist with a promise of more to come. That part was obvious. The puzzle was who did it, and why?

Joyce was so intent upon the mystery that she failed to notice the approach of Victoria Van Horn until she was almost to the table.

"I'm sorry I'm late. I think something happened to my alarm." Victoria slipped into a seat, her eyes averted. She felt ashamed that she had to lie. And she felt guilty about Barry Lytle, which surprised her, since she was free and Barry's divorce was almost final.

"No problem," Joyce said, fumbling as she put the paper down to mask her astonishment. Victoria looked terrible. Her hair was still wet from the shower. And makeup couldn't hide the pallor. Her eyes, ordinarily so beautiful, were puffy and red. She had all the telltale signs of a major hangover.

Victoria ordered juice and coffee, but declined any food. Just the mention of bacon and eggs seemed to make her even paler.

"Are you all right?" Joyce asked.

"I'm fine. It's just the effect of the trip," she said as she downed the juice, then gratefully sipped the coffee brought by the waitress.

"Have you seen the paper?" Joyce handed her the newspaper. "You're mentioned."

Victoria read the item, then looked up at Joyce. "I don't understand? I was just elected president. I haven't had a chance to do anything, right or wrong. There's no reason for a change." She frowned. "I think this is just some harebrained idea of my brother's. He's quite upset."

Joyce wondered if Victoria was well enough to think clearly. She was surprised. She had heard a great deal about Hunter's daughter, but never a word about having a problem with alcohol. "I think it may be more than that, frankly."

"Please be candid."

"Are you up to it?"

Victoria nodded. "I must look a mess. But go ahead."

"I think you're being set up. To be honest, your father was the target of a takeover move. Things were in a bad way when he died. They haven't improved."

"So I've found out."

"It's only a guess on my part, but I think that newspaper item is the opening gun in a drive to remove you."

Victoria tentatively sipped at the coffee. "It doesn't make sense. If they wanted my father out, they got that when he died. Why should they elect me in his place? Besides, who would profit from all this?"

"Chilton Vance."

A frown of confusion crossed Victoria's face. "He asked me to take the job. I don't understand his motives."

Joyce paused before replying. "Much of what I have to say is conjecture."

Victoria forced a smile. "Let's hear it anyway."

Joyce drew in a breath. "Okay, it's my opinion that Vance wants complete control of the company. He can only do that if he has the majority of the board of directors solidly behind him. I think he was setting your father up, so that the board would toss him out and turn to Vance as a savior."

"He could have had the job when my father died."

"He could have, that's true. But he would have merely been a caretaker. He'd have to answer for all the problems of the company. Problems, by the way, I think he helped cause. If he can discredit both you and your brother, it will look as if the company is doomed. Then the board will turn to him, just as he originally planned. None of the problems will attach to him."

Victoria recalled what Jon Krugar had told her. It all added up. "That seems quite bizarre, at least in this day and age."

Joyce shook her head. "Not really. It's just another form of politics, really. Believe me, it's done every day in large corporations. Some are worse than others. The stakes are very high. People will take great risks for power and prestige."

"Why would Vance want control if the company is in such bad shape?"

Joyce smiled. "Well, for one thing, anything he does will look good, won't it? For another, there's plenty of strength left in Van Horn Enterprises. Some careful surgery can save the patient. He knows that."

"For example?"

"To begin with, the film company has to be sold, and right away."

"Prometheus Pictures? I've read it's healthy. They're about to come out with a big hit."

Joyce shook her head. "That's what they hoped. *Soul of Fire* was supposed to be another *Jaws*, but it's bombing at the previews. It is, I'm told, a major disaster." She smiled. "As I told you, I'm part of an 'old girl' network in the company. I have a source."

"If it's that bad, Joyce, who would want to buy that studio now?"

"I know some people your father was talking to. They could use it as a tax shelter. Of course, there wouldn't be any profit in the sale, but a huge liability would be taken off the company books."

"But I couldn't sell without permission of the board, right?"

Joyce nodded. "That's true."

"Apparently Chilton Vance controls the majority of the board, so we'd just be back at square one, wouldn't we?"

"You'd have to be as clever as he. It's all politics, when you get right down to it. You'd have to win them over; gain their support."

"Given what you tell me, I don't think I'd have much of a chance."

Joyce's usual expressionless face suddenly became animated. "You really have no alternative. He's going to unseat you by using your brother. And your brother will be just a sacrificial lamb, but he doesn't know that. Victoria, he's out to ruin you."

"What can I do?"

"The key is in the control of the board of directors."

Victoria paused, then looked directly at Joyce. "What would my father have done?"

Joyce met her gaze. "I'm not sure specifically, but I know one thing: he would have put up one hell of a fight."

Some color had returned to Victoria's face. She took a quick sip of her coffee, then motioned for the check. "If it's a fight they're looking for, they may not know it yet but they're in for a fight to the death. And it might as well start right now. Will you help me?"

Joyce Spitz grinned. "Do you remember what I told you is my chief asset?"

Victoria laughed for the first time. "Come on, Joyce, let's get going."

<hr>

The plane to Houston was about to board. Luke Shaw had to fly to Texas to explain his company's bid on the proposed African construction. There were tribal customs that had to be figured in with other costs. In Texas the practice was called bribery; in the emerging African nation it was called tribute. It was not easily explained over the phone or by letter. The trip was inconvenient, but it would be only an overnight stay. Well worth it if he could get the business.

He tried to keep his mind on the documentation that filled his briefcase, but his thoughts kept returning to Victoria. He had admired the spirit she had showed at the Vault meeting. But he was annoyed with himself. He was taking too much pleasure in the knowledge he would now be seeing her on a regular basis.

When the flight was called, he took his place in line as it moved slowly toward the loading gate. He would be seeing her at every Vault meeting, and in connection with her new development.

He felt that he couldn't allow himself to entertain such thoughts. The Vault had its function, and she was just another member now. The Hudson River project was business and should be treated as nothing else.

Luke Shaw wanted no more serious relationships. They had proved too painful in the past. He was determined that nothing more would come of his connection with Victoria Van Horn. He didn't have the time or the inclination.

Still he found it irritating that his thoughts kept returning to her.

<hr>

The telephone hadn't stopped ringing since the morning newspaper containing the gossip item hit the stands. Junior's maid screened the calls. Junior didn't return any calls, even those from nationally known reporters. Tim Burroughs, his publicity man, insisted all media information be orchestrated through him. Recognizing that he was out of his depth, Junior had eagerly agreed to comply.

The only call he did return was from Chilton Vance. Cecelia had come into the living room just as he made the connection, and she immediately knew something was very wrong. Junior merely grunted replies. When Junior was angry he had a habit of biting his lower lip. He now looked as if he might chew right through it.

Junior hung up, slamming down the receiver.

"Who was that? What happened?" Cecelia asked.

Junior stood up and stalked to the sideboard. He poured himself a large brandy. Her jaw seemed to throb as she vividly recalled what had happened the last time he had become drunk.

"That stuff won't help," she snapped.

He gulped the brandy down, then faced her. "You're absolutely right. But it feels like it helps, and that's important."

"Are you going to tell me what's happened, or must I find out for myself?"

He scowled. "That was Chilton Vance. He's heard that my delightful sister was elected to the Vault last night."

"That's ridiculous."

Junior poured some more brandy, but didn't drink. "I'm afraid it isn't. Chilton's information comes from Franklin Trager. Franklin is a Vault member. He was violently opposed to Victoria, so Chilton says, but they elected her anyway. It was a close vote, as if that makes any difference." His tone was hushed and flat, as if reporting a death in the family.

"I still don't believe it," she shrieked. "You've got to check it out!"

He nodded. "I know Franklin well enough to call him. It's not public information, but I'm sure he'd tell me." Junior sipped his drink. "This could be a major blow to our plans."

"Why?"

He sat down opposite her, but didn't look at her. "The Vault is very powerful. If she can get them to support her, we wouldn't stand a chance."

Cecelia snorted. "From what you've told me, the Vault exists to protect the old families as a group. Why would they support her?"

He nodded. "You're right. But Victoria somehow always seems to be able to work miracles."

Cecelia hadn't shown him any tenderness, or touched him, since the beating. But she now got up and came to him. "Don't worry," she said, gently stroking his hair, "if you just keep following Chilton's advice, her time is over. Being a member of the Vault won't help her."

He irritably brushed her hand away. "I'm not so sure."

"Is Tim Burroughs coming over?"

He nodded, sipping at the brandy again. "Yes. He has to handle all the telephone calls."

"Don't panic. Do whatever Burroughs tells you to do. By the end of the week you'll be riding the crest of a publicity wave that will sweep Victoria out to sea. Don't lose heart, Junior. This is our time, I know it is."

He nodded, but he didn't seem to be paying attention. Cecelia went into her bedroom. Just the thought of Victoria Van Horn caused rage to well up within her. If he couldn't stop the bitch, she would.

She checked her personal notebook and looked up the number. Perhaps he did have a friend who had access to secret Vault information, or perhaps he didn't. She was determined to find out. It would take more than money, she knew that. He was fat, but he did have nice eyes. One cock, she reflected, was about the same as another. She just hoped he didn't reek of garlic.

She dialed. "May I speak to Mr. Pelegrine?" she said.

15

Upon returning from the breakfast meeting with Joyce, Victoria called the hotel. She had left a note, but that seemed so inadequate.

Her call awakened Barry. The sound of his voice helped soothe the terrible hangover feelings and she quickly explained her reasons for leaving. He sounded disappointed but not resentful. His easy assurance seemed to lessen all her troubles. She wondered if she really was falling in love. It had been such a long time that she had forgotten what that feeling was like.

"Why don't you come down to Washington with me this afternoon?" he asked. "I think you'd enjoy yourself. I rate myself a pretty fair host."

It sounded like a wonderful invitation but she couldn't accept. "To tell you the truth, Barry, I'd love to chuck it all and go with you. But I can't, at least not today. As I told you last night, my little world needs some rather intensive care at the moment."

"You're carrying much too heavy a load, Vicky." His voice had a quality like smooth velvet. "You should delegate. That's the answer. Find some good people and let them do the work. You need some time for yourself."

"I really wish I could get away, honestly."

"Well then, how about this weekend? You could fly down Friday night and go back on Sunday. I'm sure the world wouldn't come to an end. I can show you some places on the Chesapeake that are pure magic." He paused. "You need a break now and then, or you'll go stale. Chalk it up as part of doing business."

"Put it in the 'I'm doing it for my morale' column?"

He chuckled softly. "Something like that. Can you make it?"

She desperately wanted to say yes. But she couldn't just walk away. Not now. She had never ducked a challenge in her life. Still, something might be worked out. At least she could try. "I'll let you know in a couple of days," she demured.

"I really hope you'll come." He wasn't making a demand. It sounded like a gentle invitation. "Well," he laughed, "if the republic is to survive, I suppose I had better get back to the Capitol and save it."

"Important work?"

"Not really," he answered. "I have a subcommittee hearing later this afternoon. The whole thing is mostly for show, but I'm the chairman, and I'm expected to show up."

"I could have the company limousine take you to the airport."

"Thanks, Vicky, but that's too much bother. I'll just grab a cab. Want to come with me? At least as far as the airport?"

"Barry, you know I want to. But I can't."

He again chuckled. "Well, promise me you'll try for the weekend."

Before she could answer he had hung up. She replaced the receiver and sat quietly for a moment. Everything in her life was happening so fast. Nothing seemed real somehow.

Barry Lytle sat back in the taxi, feeling comfortable and relaxed. He watched the people on the streets of Manhattan as the cab driver fought to find a quick and easy way to La Guardia.

Victoria Van Horn had proved to be a delightful surprise. It had been his experience that truly beautiful women allowed love, rather than gave it. Restrained, even cold, they seemed to imply that beauty was enough in itself. But Vicky had been passionate, even wild at times. Lytle knew his limitations, but when it came to women, he considered himself an expert.

Victoria Van Horn was a rare find.

This time, for a change, his father's dominance over his life might prove beneficial. She would be an ideal combination: a wife who was both beautiful and rich. They would look good together in photographs, and voters loved good-looking people.

She had a career and would live in New York. He could commute from Washington on weekends. She wouldn't interfere with his life-style or his appetites.

If Victoria didn't come to Washington, he would content himself with his new secretary. She was equally passionate, although not nearly as attractive. But he hoped Victoria would show up for the weekend. He could weave a romantic fabric that no woman could resist.

The cab raced along the FDR Drive. He looked out at the East River and felt truly pleased with himself. It had been a wonderful time. His father had allowed him freedom; he had even snorted a little coke, but who didn't in these times. And he had made love to a gorgeous woman.

Things finally seemed to be turning his way. Thinking of Victoria, he started humming "You Are My Lucky Star."

Being mayor of New York suited Al Felder just fine. He loved the trappings of office: the speeches, the salutes, the parades, everything. To him it was like being king. He relished power, and although it happened infrequently, he hated the occasional episode when even he was obliged to bend a symbolic knee.

But most of all, he disliked Asa Myers.

Myers, the boss of Brooklyn, had welded together a machine not unlike the powerhouses of old; an organization built upon a foundation of honest graft plus promises of pieces of the political pie. Myers ruled over an army of neighborhood leaders, union presidents and other Brooklyn power brokers. He was the only man in the city who could actually deliver a vote; something Myers never let any other politician forget. The Brooklyn boss always operated legally, sometimes stepping very close to the line, but never quite crossing over. Asa Myers never had to leave home—everyone made the pilgrimage to Brooklyn, including the mayor.

Although titular head of a small legal firm, Asa Myers no longer practiced law. His firm was tucked away in a squat pre-Depression building that housed a variety of lawyers and accountants. Myers's name was on the door, but he used his office as a headquarters for generating Brooklyn political power.

Myers didn't even bother to get up as Felder was escorted into his office. The Brooklyn boss was a small pudgy man who peered at the world from old-fashioned metal-framed glasses. His eyes were narrow and hard, and his fat face seemed quite incapable of smiling.

Felder reached across the desk and shook Myers's offered hand, then took a seat opposite him. "You're looking great, Ace," Felder said, using Myers's nickname, which he knew Myers liked and encouraged.

"Don't smoke that damn thing in here," Myers growled as Felder took out one of his big cigars. "Jesus, I'd have to get this place fumigated."

It was well known that Myers didn't like Felder. The Brooklyn boss had supported his election because of political realities, not admiration.

"What's up, Ace? I always like coming to Brooklyn, but I assume you want something more than just one more look at my handsome face."

"I want to get rid of you as mayor," Myers replied.

Felder felt a flush of both anger and fear. If there was a smile hidden in Myers's fat features, he couldn't find it. "That might take a bit of doing," Felder replied, but without conviction.

Myers shrugged. "You're a pain in the ass, Al. I can work with you, but I really don't trust you. I want one of my own people downtown. The mayor's office is important to my operation here in Brooklyn."

Felder, shifting uncomfortably in his chair, mentally reviewed the recent past, wondering if the toadlike man might have stumbled upon some juicy scandal.

Myers seemed to enjoy Felder's discomfort. "I just got back from Albany," he continued. "We had a meeting of state Democratic leaders up there. We even managed to get down to some really important business."

"Oh? Like what?"

The little man leaned back in his large leather chair and put his hands behind his head. That was as relaxed as Asa Myers ever got. "Like who will succeed Senator Bannon."

Felder hid his surprise. "Well, I suppose the Republicans would really whip him if they came up with the right candidate. Bannon's been on the wrong side of some touchy issues."

"That was the consensus of opinion," Myers said. "Bannon's a liability to the party."

Felder laughed. "Maybe so, but you'll never get him to step aside."

Myers rocked back and forth a bit, then lowered his arms and sat forward. "Bannon isn't going to run again."

"What?" Felder's surprise was genuine.

"He's got cancer. Bad." Myers's tone implied that God was punishing Bannon for being a weak candidate. "He's in the hospital now. That's not public knowledge. They did a bilateral orchiectomy on him."

"What's that?"

"They cut off his balls," Myers replied.

"Oh God!" Felder experienced a squeamish sensation in the area of his own groin.

"They tell me they didn't get it all. He'll have to have chemotherapy.

He might beat it, but he'll be in no shape for a major campaign. He knows it. He's through."

"Jesus!" Felder, still shocked, hoped nothing like that would ever happen to him.

Myers tapped his stubby fingers on his desktop. "That changes everything. With Bannon we figured we'd probably lose the Senate seat in November. But now, if we pick the right candidate, we might not."

Felder's attention swung like a radar screen, going from the awful fate of Senator Bannon, and zeroing in on the words now being spoken by the fat man behind the desk. Suddenly he was glad he had come out to Brooklyn.

"Like I say, I want the mayor's office," Myers continued. "So I put your name up as a candidate to succeed Bannon. There's some opposition, but I think I can overcome that. First, I have to know if you'll run."

Felder began to relax. Horse-trading was one thing he understood and enjoyed. "I'm happy as mayor," he said. "I don't have any other ambitions."

"Don't give me that shit, Al," Myers growled. "You'd sell your mother to Arabs if it would help get you elected to the United States Senate. Right now, in your mind, you're trying on the title to see how it sounds."

"Koch ran for governor and got his ass knocked off statewide," Felder said. "New York mayors haven't done too well in state races."

Myers chuckled humorlessly. "That was Ed Koch. He made fun of the farmers and all the other people upstate, then he had the nerve to ask them to vote for him. Chutzpah will carry you only so far. Sure, Ed Koch lost, but other mayors have gone on to bigger and better things. And like Koch, even if you lost, you'd still be mayor. And you'd have had a hell of a lot more exposure."

Felder nodded. It was all quite true. "Who are the other candidates?"

Myers allowed himself the ghost of a smile. The fish was hooked. "Alice Kearney, the judge. Also Johnny Russo." Myers scowled. "It isn't Johnny's year. He's a comer, but we want him for the governor's chair. It's important that we hold on to that office. Russo will come to heel, don't worry about that." Myers's little eyes seemed to become even more malevolent. "And Alice has a drinking problem. She'd never make it."

Felder nodded. "Okay, let's talk a little business. You've never been my greatest supporter, Ace. What do you want?"

Myers's face gave no hint of his thoughts. "You're a lucky man, Al. You came along at just the right time, and in just the right election. Maybe some of us weren't wild about you, but you've shown you know how to go along when it counts, and that's important."

"So? What do you want?" Felder repeated.

Myers nodded slowly. "I told you. I want the mayor's office. If you win for Senate, I want you to support Sullivan, he's my man."

Felder made a mental note to perform a political orchiectomy on Danny Sullivan. He wanted no one around City Hall who might one day run against and beat him. "That's no problem," Felder said cheerfully. "I'd have no trouble with that."

"Then you'll run?"

Felder reached across the desk and extended his hand. "You've got a deal."

"It won't be easy." Myers shook his hand reluctantly. "We can easily take the primary, but the Republicans will smell blood. The general election will be the main battle."

"Who do you think they'll put up?"

Myers shrugged. "A couple of people, but my money's on Barry Lytle. He's got the name and the bucks. He'll probably wind up as your opponent. The other bums you can whip, but Lytle will be tough."

Felder could feel his heart racing with excitement, but he kept his face expressionless. "Well, you never know, Ace. Like they say, the bigger they are, the harder they fall."

Myers squinted at him. "That little prick Lytle is well connected. His old man is on the Vault. If he should get them to back his kid, then Lytle could beat anyone, including you."

Felder stood up. He took out a cigar but didn't light it. "Like you said, Ace, I'm a lucky man. And if you have to choose between brains and luck, go with luck every time."

Felder was grinning when he left Myers's office. He had a lot more than just luck where Barry Lytle was concerned, a hell of a lot more. When he reached the street he lit the cigar, then looked around. Brooklyn, he decided, wasn't so bad after all.

Since Junior had learned of his sister's elevation to the Vault, his moods seemed to swing violently from sorrow to rage. He spent much of his time brooding.

Cecelia Van Horn had better things to do.

"Going out?" he mumbled. If he noticed her clingingly provocative silk dress, he gave no sign.

"Shopping," she replied. "Then I'm having cocktails with Wilma Fischer."

She anticipated a stinging response. He hated Wilma Fischer. Wilma wasn't even in town, but he would never know that. Cecelia had no intention of wasting such a stunning dress on another woman.

"Say hello for me."

His depression had to be very deep if he had a good word for Wilma. "I will."

They had long abandoned any signs of affection except for the perfunctory kiss. But her jaw was still sore and she was damned if she'd ever get that close to him.

Cecelia took a cab instead of the chauffeured family limousine. She often took cabs so she could go to her little assignations without detection or backstairs gossip.

Pelegrine's hotel was in a fashionable area near Central Park. The doorman, a tall, gray-haired man with an expressionless face, helped her out. Her skirt rode up, but he showed no reaction.

Pelegrine's suite was like a small art museum, its walls tastefully decorated with expensive prints.

Pelegrine, dressed in tight stretch slacks and a knit shirt open at the collar, beamed a welcome. A collection of gold chains and charms rode atop his thick curly chest hair. His dark fleshy features were a combination of subservience and lust. His hand was warm and moist.

"An honor," he said, escorting her to a low-slung couch. "Please sit down. Perhaps a glass of wine?"

Enrico Pelegrine definitely was not gay. His reaction to her long legs was near adoration. He reluctantly tore his eyes away, hurried to his kitchen and returned with two large goblets of white wine.

Cecelia considered herself an expert on wine. She sniffed the bouquet and found it pleasing. A taste told her it was well aged and very expensive.

Pelegrine sat opposite her, his eyes riveted upon her display of thigh. He gulped half his drink. "I have some very good things here," he said. "A few might please you."

"I look forward to seeing them," she replied, amused at the direction of his gaze. "Who knows? I may become one of your best customers."

"You would be the loveliest, by far." His trembling baritone had dropped to a seductive whisper.

She almost laughed. "I anticipate enlarging our family art collection. Art can be a very sound investment. Of course, I would need expert advice." She paused. "And someone to serve, well, as my agent."

"In Europe such a thing is done all the time. Wealthy people employ experts to seek out the very best for them. They, how do you say it, root out treasures, real bargains."

She recrossed her legs as she sipped from her glass. Little beads of perspiration appeared on his cheeks. He had lovely eyes, dark and large, not unlike a deer's. "Of course, everyone loves bargains," she said. "But I'm more interested in quality. My husband and I never begrudge paying full price if something is truly worthwhile. We anticipate spending a great deal to expand our collection. As I say, it's a good investment."

He licked his lips, then quickly finished his wine. "You are wonderful, you and your husband. Real art, the best, is truly priceless. But you will need someone to make sure you pay no more than what is fair." He was already thinking of the potential for enormous commissions.

"More wine?" His trousers were cut so tight that little was left to the imagination when he stood up.

"Not yet." She smiled up at him.

He raced into his kitchen and returned with his goblet refilled almost to the brim. "I could be of great service to you." He forced his gaze from her legs to her face.

She smiled slowly. "I'm sure you could, Mr. Pelegrine." She took a sip from her glass. "I think we might work out very well together."

He grinned nervously, then downed half his wine.

"To be quite frank, Mr. Pelegrine, I'm here for more than just a discussion of art."

His eyes grew wide with curiosity.

She set the wineglass on the coffee table. "You mentioned a friend of yours who has access to the Vault. I might be interested in some inside information, in a manner of speaking."

Pelegrine was wary. "The Vault is just one aspect. He is very well connected. My friend can also be a very good source of finding good works of art."

"How nice. When can I meet him?"

Pelegrine's face clearly reflected his determination not to reveal his source.

"He has, well, a position of some trust. I don't think he would wish to deal with you directly. But I would, ah, be happy to serve as go-between."

"For a fee, of course."

He puffed up his large chest as if indignant. "Never, my dear lady! It would be a service, a favor."

She smiled. "How nice. But wouldn't that arrangement be a bit awkward?"

His quick breathing seemed caused by rising excitement. His face was now gleaming with perspiration. "Not at all. You merely tell me what you would like to know, and I can get it from him. It would all go quite smoothly, let me assure you."

Cecelia picked up the goblet again, knowing that her skirt had now crept almost up to her hips. She had no doubt she would obtain the informer's name before she left. "This suite is quite lovely. Two bedrooms?"

He smiled broadly, obviously relieved that the subject had been changed. "Yes. Although I use one as a storage place for some of my paintings. Allow me to show you."

She stood up. Even at two thousand dollars the dress was a good investment. His eyes seemed to consume her. "Actually," she said in a tone that was unmistakable, "I'd rather see *your* bedroom."

When they got into the bedroom they kissed. Pelegrine was so excited he had difficulty getting undressed. She wondered if he was really experienced at all.

But Cecelia was surprised and delighted. Although overweight, he had a pleasing body, heavily muscled and smooth. And nature had been generous to him, even by vaunted Italian standards.

His lovemaking had been passionate and strong. In her pleasure she had almost forgotten the reason for her visit, but not quite.

It was almost midnight when she left and took a cab home. Pleased and satisfied, she would see a lot more of Enrico Pelegrine; he was very good. But, like all men, he had been quite easy to manipulate. She had obtained the name of Cecil Driker and knew he was the director of the Habermann Museum.

The Vault met at the Habermann, and it didn't take a very keen mind to guess that Mr. Driker was bugging their meetings. She smiled. Driker's information might be the key, a tool they could put to very good use. Cecelia felt content; she had done Junior a very good turn.

Mortimer's on Lexington Avenue was packed with young men and women, upward-bound executives, meeting after hours over drinks to discuss the ebb and flow of office politics. Chilton Vance could remember when he was just like them: young, eager, believing the world was easy prey.

But he had quickly discovered that nothing came easy. Success in business, at least for him, had been like climbing a giant, sometimes dangerous, jagged mountain. The footing was loose, the handholds perilous and any fall fatal.

But he had managed to survive the climb, and now he was nearing the top. He could almost touch the success he longed for. He had reached the point where if he pulled the right strings people jumped. He found that enormously rewarding.

Bradford Lewis, located at a far table, signaled to him.

Vance admired the lush young women he passed as he made his way through the crowded bar.

Bradford Lewis, a brokerage firm president, also served as a member of the board of directors of Van Horn Enterprises. Tall and gangly, he was approaching middle age, but not gracefully. His hair was thinning. His gaunt face seemed to become more craggy almost daily. Lewis looked decidedly out of place in Mortimer's.

They shook hands and Vance signaled a waitress. "Gin martini. Straight up."

"Too noisy for you?" Lewis asked.

Vance shook his head. The loud talk and laughter, although distracting, also served as a protective screen for a private conversation. They could not be overheard, and Vance considered that important.

"I don't know why I continue to come here," Lewis said, gesturing awkwardly with his long arms. "I met my second wife here. Good-looking, but a first-class bitch."

Vance nodded. "Nice of you not to hold a grudge."

Lewis shrugged. "Hey, it's still a good place to find a little action, if you're in the mood. But now I'm older and wiser. No more wives. Too painful, and far too expensive."

Lewis waved to a stout young woman who waved back. "Well, what's up, Chilton? We usually only see each other at board meetings."

Vance accepted his drink from the waitress. She was a little heavy in the thigh, but not unattractive. "I need some advice, Brad."

"Investments?"

"No, this is Van Horn company business, I'm afraid." Vance sipped his martini. It contained a bit too much vermouth for his taste. "I think I made a mistake in urging the selection of Victoria Van Horn to succeed her father."

"Oh?"

Vance sat back, his attitude designed to show he was relaxed and casual. "Based on the girl's reputation, I thought she might take charge and bring the leadership we need to the company."

"And that hasn't happened, I take it?"

Vance sighed. "To be blunt, no. She's never at the office. I think she believes the job is honorary. I do the mechanical things that have to be done, but I can't get a policy decision out of her no matter how hard I try."

Bradford Lewis frowned. "Given the company's rather hazardous position, that could be serious."

Vance pretended to force a smile. "Or worse, fatal. You heard what happened at our movie studio, I presume?"

Lewis tried to conceal his embarrassment. "No. But then I've been so very busy at the firm."

Vance nodded, as if that was explanation enough. "They previewed *Soul of Fire* and it's a complete flop."

"*Soul of Fire?*"

"That's the new picture Prometheus has made. I thought everyone knew about it. The damn thing cost more than any other movie ever produced. It's terrible, and they say it can't be saved. Every cent we spent will be lost." Vance knew the broker didn't know or care about movies, but he was passionate about money. "When the smoke clears we could be out over a hundred million dollars."

"Jesus Christ!"

"Add that to the other losses at the studio and it puts a real drain on the rest of the company."

"Who approved such an outrageous expense?" Lewis demanded.

"You know how Hunter was, always extravagant." It wasn't true. Hunter hadn't even known the extent of the project. Vance's man at the studio had conceived the entire disaster. But no one would remember that. "And I'm afraid Hunter's daughter is cut from the same cloth." He sighed, sipping again at his drink.

"Then we'll have to get rid of her," Lewis exploded. "This just won't do! She could ruin the company."

Vance studied the olive in his martini. It was just the reaction he wanted. "Victoria controls her father's stock. The other members of the board will be sensitive to that interest."

"It's not a majority interest. We have a duty to the other stockholders. We'll just have to vote her out. My God, this could be one of the greatest corporate disasters in American business. We must take action."

Vance nodded slowly, as if reluctantly agreeing with Lewis's wisdom. "If we do it, we would have to be very careful. Whoever we select to replace her would have to have credibility. I even thought about offering myself, but that's out of the question. I'm well known to everyone on the board, but not to the public. We need a name the stockholders would recognize, and hopefully trust."

"What about Hunter's son? I know Junior. He seems level-headed. And he's a team player. He's worked within the company structure. I think the market would accept him as a replacement." Lewis paused. "Of course, if the board had its way, Chilton, you'd be the natural choice."

"Thank you, Bradford. But things are a bit too dicey for that at the moment. However, you've come up with an interesting idea. I have heard rumors that Junior would like to take over from his sister. I suppose, as in many families, there may be some friction between the siblings."

"So true." Bradford Lewis swung his long arms about. "I hate my sisters, always have." He calmed down a bit. "I think we must remove the lady and replace her with Junior. I just hope to God Hunter's lack of business sense doesn't run in the whole family."

"I don't know of any directors who would dare lead the charge against her. Harry Armstrong hates her, but even Harry wouldn't make that move."

"I will," Lewis said.

"Too risky," Vance said, smiling slightly. "She may be doing business with your firm."

"As a matter of fact, she isn't. She does a great deal of business with the Chase and some of our other competitors, but not us. So there's absolutely nothing to stop me. In fact, I'd like to do it."

Vance reached across the table and patted Lewis's hand. "Bradford, you are a very brave man."

"Nonsense. I'm only acting in the interest of the stockholders. As I say, we do have a duty."

Vance studied him for a moment. "I do know some of Junior's friends. May I contact them and let them know how you stand?"

"Of course."

Vance raised his glass in solemn salute. "Here's to the last of the real knights."

It was so damned easy. Being a puppet master was a wonderful thing. In a matter of weeks the Van Horns would be destroyed and he would have complete control of the company. Vance downed the rest of the martini.

Preston Shaw was engrossed, his complete attention riveted on the book he was reading. He was unaware even of the food he was eating. He was equally unaware of the approach of a man laboriously using an aluminum walker as he made his way across the dining room of the Oseola Club to Shaw's table.

"What the hell are you reading, Preston?" a creaky voice demanded.

Startled, Preston Shaw blinked, then looked up at the intruder.

"Have you gone dotty? It's me, Knowlton Nash."

Shaw managed a weak smile. "I know it's you, Knowlton. What is that you're leaning on?"

"It's a walker. You've seen them before. My damn knees won't support the weight of my body. It's the damned arthritis."

"So that's why I haven't seen you at the club lately, you've been ill."

"Not ill," Nash bristled. "My knees won't work, other than that I'm perfectly healthy. May I join you?"

"If I said no, would that stop you?"

Knowlton Nash groaned as he eased his body from the walker into a chair. "What's that book you find so interesting?"

Shaw sighed. He closed the book and lay it on the table.

"It's a rather fascinating history of the royal families of France."

"Before they lost their heads, I presume?"

"Of course." Shaw looked at his table companion. "And to what do I owe this honor? I'm sure you haven't hobbled all the way over here without some purpose."

"You're an old friend, and I wanted to talk to you."

"For old times' sake?" They had known each other since childhood, but a mutual dislike had always existed between them.

"What do you think about this ugly Van Horn business?" Knowlton Nash extracted a thin black cigar from inside his coat.

"You're not going to smoke that thing, are you?"

Nash chuckled. "Let's not be nasty, Preston."

Shaw hoped he would go away, but he knew he would not. "What about the Van Horns? You seem to be up to date."

"Bad business," Nash replied. "Our people, eh? Old family. Old money. But everything is certain to be ripped apart and paraded before an eager public. It could hurt us all in the long run. Shouldn't have the dirty laundry about, and all that, eh?"

Shaw leaned back in his chair. "What can we do about it? It's not like the old days, Knowlton. Everyone now is free to do their own thing, as the saying goes." Shaw signaled to the waiter. Knowlton Nash was an old bore, and he would need a drink to endure him.

Nash frowned. "Damn it, man, there's still the Vault, isn't there? The young Van Horn woman is a member, just elected."

"So?"

"Your son is a member too."

Shaw nodded. "That's true."

"Have him put a stop to this business before it begins."

Shaw chuckled. "Luke may be my son, but he's his own man. In any event, how could he possibly stop any of this?"

"He could harness the power of the Vault. They could step in and make sure things didn't get out of hand. That's part of their function, isn't it?"

Shaw nodded slowly. "Social arbitration? I suppose it used to be. I doubt they serve quite that way anymore."

"Something has to be done or one of our leading families will become the laughingstock of the great unwashed. It just won't do, Preston, it really won't." Nash reached across the table and tapped his fingers on the closed book. "Look what happened to those French aristocrats, eh? It starts with laughter but ends with anger, believe me."

"You want me to talk to my son?"

"Yes."

Shaw took a sip of his drink. "The public eye can be devastating."

Nash snorted. "Once the public gets a peek behind the velvet curtain, so to speak, things can go very sour quite quickly. Please talk to your son."

Shaw wondered just how he might approach Luke. He wondered if his son would understand. He questioned if anyone really realized the need for the old rules, or if anyone was even interested anymore. But Nash was right, much would depend on what the Vault might choose to do. "All right, Knowlton, I'll talk to Luke, although I don't know if it will do any good."

"Good." Nash struggled to his feet and used the walker to move awkwardly across the nearly empty dining room.

Preston Shaw sipped again at his drink. Social order depended on a stable class structure. Protection of privileged status, whether earned or inherited, depended upon the maintenance of that structure. And that required constant vigilance. He would talk to Luke, but he doubted that his words would have any influence.

16

Despite the family name, Victoria was apprehensive in the Van Horn Building, especially in the executive offices, which she knew were the heart of the enemy. She still felt like a trespasser in her father's office.

Joyce Spitz was elsewhere in the building, using her contacts to attempt to discover the direction of Chilton Vance's attack. Joyce's protégée from the typing pool poked her blonde head in the door. "There's a Craig Hopkins here to see you. He says he has an appointment." She winked, her voice dropping to a near whisper. "He's a real hunk. If you don't want him, I'll take him."

Victoria tried not to laugh but failed. The girl had a mindless impudence that was more amusing than offending. "Show him in. And find your own hunks." Victoria was surprised at her own pleased reaction that Craig had come.

Craig walked in, looked around at the large office and then at Victoria. "You could play basketball in here." His grin was boyishly attractive.

"The ceiling's too low. Please sit down, Craig." Now that they both knew they would never be lovers again there seemed to be an ease between them that had never existed before. She felt comfortable with him, and she sensed he felt the same way.

He took a chair. "What's up?"

"Craig, I'd like to hire you."

He grinned. "Retain is the word. Have you forgotten? You're still a dues-paying attorney. Lawyers are retained, not hired."

Victoria shook her head. "This is different, I'm afraid. Because of my father's business, I can't find time to run my new project. It has to be done. I need someone who I can trust. I want you to do it."

His surprise seemed genuine. "I'm flattered, Vicky, I really am. But I don't know the first thing about real estate development. You're right, you can certainly trust me. The only problem is that I'm not qualified."

"As I recall, Craig, you handled a development, back when you and I were together."

He laughed. "Small potatoes compared to what you do. It was just a small apartment on Seventy-sixth Street."

"One building or many, the means and methods are the same. You could handle it, if you wanted to."

He shook his head as he seemed to relax. "Vicky, I have a law practice. I just can't walk away from that. I have responsibilities to my partners. Besides, I've read about your Hudson River project. It's enormous. Millions are involved. You need someone with real experience. Yours is no game for amateurs."

"Suppose you took it on as legal business? Your partners could have no objection to that, could they? The fees would be substantial."

He studied her for a moment before speaking. "Why don't you tell me what's really going on? You never were very good at concealing things, Vicky, at least not from me."

She stood up, walked to the window and looked out. "In order to obtain financing for the new Hudson River project, I had to pledge my entire interest in East Port."

"So?"

She turned and looked at him. "That's everything I've earned, Craig. I've risked everything, every last cent." She returned to the desk and sat down. "When I did it, I believed I'd be able to devote all my time to the new project. And even then it still would have been risky." She laughed softly, but it was without humor. "I was assured that this job as president of my father's company would be only honorary; that I was just lending my name to reassure the stockholders. I was told the place would run itself."

"And it doesn't, I take it?"

She nodded. "Far from it. Van Horn Enterprises may collapse unless someone takes charge and turns it around. My father was in the process of doing just that when he died."

"It sounds like you were badly taken in by someone. However, the answer seems simple enough."

"And that is?"

He shrugged. "Quit. Especially if the company looks as if it's going down. Why risk your own business?"

She sighed. "I've thought about it. But if this company collapses many of the stockholders will be ruined, including me. And perhaps even more important, my father put his trust in me. I feel honor-bound to justify that."

Hopkins, more than anyone else, knew Victoria's relationship with her father had been complicated in life. Now that Hunter Van Horn was dead, everything had probably been accentuated by grief and guilt. Death had a way of bringing feelings and attitudes to a painful boil.

He chose his words carefully. "Vicky, I can understand, but self-preservation is still the first law of nature."

She shook her head. "Even if I quit here, Craig, I'd still be ruined. My development depends on my credibility. Quitting would cause my backers to lose confidence in me. I'm caught in a no-win situation; that's why I need your help."

"Vicky, I'm not qualified, so it wouldn't be fair to you. And it certainly wouldn't be fair to my partners. I'm sorry, but I can't."

Her expression became even more determined. "Look, Craig, I'm desperate. I'll retain your whole damn firm, if I have to."

"There's only five of us. I know the others wouldn't agree. This just isn't our field."

"Craig, I'll pay a million dollars to your firm as a retainer. I won't need the others, just you. They can run your law firm while you work for me. How many clients do you have who will pay a million dollars up front?"

"My God, is this all success has done for you: reduced everything to dollars? Don't you know that I can't be bought?"

She quickly swiveled her chair around, turning her back to him so that he couldn't see her desperately trying to fight back the tears. He had never seen her cry, not even when they had lived together.

"Victoria," he said softly. "You really are in a fix, aren't you?"

She remained facing away from him. "Yes, Craig, the worst mess I've ever faced."

Victoria quickly dabbed at her eyes, then turned to face him. "I'm sorry, Craig. I shouldn't have asked you. I shouldn't have presumed on . . ."

He held up both hands as if in mock surrender. "Whoa. You win. I may not be a Wall Street lawyer, but I don't come cheap either. I'll charge you by the hour, the same as any other client. You can keep your million dollars. Look, I'll do my damnedest for you, but I can't guarantee I won't screw things up. This is not my field, but I'll do what I can."

"All this because I cried?"

He shook his head. "Not really. I know you, perhaps better than you do yourself. You always try to do everything yourself. You don't ask for help easily, Victoria, you never have." He sighed. "And you're right, my partners can handle our regular work. I'll take over your project until you can free yourself from this business. After that, you're on your own. Agreed?"

She wanted to run around the desk and kiss him. As if reading her thoughts, he laughed. "This is a business deal, Vicky, that's all. I'll make money. Now, what do you want me to do?"

As if a great and troubling cloud had been lifted from her mind, her thoughts were suddenly clear and organized. Turning businesslike, she quickly outlined her plans and the steps that would have to be taken to carry them out.

The romantic love they had known was gone forever, they both knew that. They would go through life as good friends and that was all. Craig Hopkins would make someone an ideal husband, but it wouldn't be her. Still, it felt secure to know she had such a real and reliable friend.

As she watched him take notes as she talked, she realized she had almost forgotten what it was like to have just a little hope.

Franklin Trager walked through the sliding doors to the pool in his Palm Springs home. The palms stood out clearly against the clear blue sky, their fronds moving gently in a light breeze. Everything was so beautiful, so tranquil and, even more important, safe.

To Trager, the election of Victoria Van Horn to the Vault was just one more unsettling example of the changes taking place in society in general, and New York in particular. Only fools remained committed to staying in New York. It was as if everyone were blind. The need for the old central city no longer existed. Everything soon could be done by little electronic machines, and from anywhere in the world. Most of the founding families had little except tradition to tie them to the city.

And time was running out on all of them. Soon New York would be nothing but a dangerous cesspool of poverty and perversion, owned and run by devious foreign interests. He could see it happening; he wondered why the others could not.

Trager eased himself into a beach chair and sipped at the fruit drink prepared by his cook. He no longer drank alcohol. It caused him to gain weight, and health had become important to him. It was no good having money if one couldn't live a long time and enjoy it. The sun felt pleasantly warm on his already tanned skin.

The weather, the trees, the tranquility of the pool, all were so soothing. He was the only Vault member who didn't maintain a main residence in New York. But with the tide of social and technological change, those apartments, worth millions now, would soon be next to worthless. The city was doomed.

He reached for the poolside telephone. The others, like ostriches, hid their heads in the sand to blind themselves to the coming danger. He had to find a way to show them what was happening, to open their eyes. The Vault's ancient purpose was to preserve and protect. He had always taken that responsibility seriously.

It was people like Victoria Van Horn—people who went ahead and built in that dying city as if it had a future—who lulled the others into a false sense of confidence.

There had to be some way to awaken them.

What had the Van Horn girl called her new adventure? The Hudson River project? Trager scowled. Even if she succeeded, it would all be so foolish. And if she failed . . .

Trager smiled slowly. That just might be what he needed. Then the others might recognize the realities they faced. Even her membership in the Vault could turn out to be a good thing. It would make it more personal to all of them. Her foolish project might be just the thing he needed to persuade the others to leave New York. But only if she failed.

Trager quickly dialed his New York office. His secretary was as officious as ever, and he relished the prospect that one day he would be able to fire her.

"I'll be flying in tomorrow morning," he said. "Get me everything you can on the Van Horn girl's Hudson River project. You know the one?"

"It's been all over the newspapers," she snapped. "Do you think I'm stupid?"

She was still too valuable, so he controlled his anger. "Get what you can," he said between clenched teeth, "then set up a meeting with Harvey Sloan, the investment banker."

"What time?"

"Any time that's convenient to him. Tell him I'll need an hour." Harvey Sloan would know where Victoria Van Horn was vulnerable. He would know the places where the right kind of pressure could crush her.

"Are you thinking of investing in it?" she asked. "You haven't put a dime into this city in years."

He was furious. It was none of her business. "I'm just interested," he managed to reply evenly. "But I'll need some more information."

"Do you want me to arrange for a limousine to pick you up at the airport?"

Women, they could always find an easy way to waste good money. "You know I never use them," he snapped. "I'll take a taxi as usual."

He hung up. Even his secretary's attitude failed to dampen his enthusiasm. Victoria Van Horn might prove to be a gift from the gods, a kind of ritual sacrifice. Her ruin would cause the others to examine their own futures. But it would have to be a dramatic ruin.

He closed his eyes and let the sun and the sea breeze work their miracles.

On the other side of the world the breeze from the South China Sea carried the hint of an impending storm. Jon Krugar looked up at the fast-moving clouds and knew it would hit before he finished lunch.

He did not often leave his home, but when he did, he preferred familiar surroundings such as the quaintly traditional Luk Yu Tea House, where time seemed to have stood still and the old values and ways of Hong Kong were forever preserved.

Krugar lumbered to a table at the rear of the restaurant. The smoke from his cigar wafted up, stirred by the motion of the wooden blades of the slow-turning ceiling fans. Everyone paid deference as he passed.

Harold Moy, the banker, rose to greet him. Almost as old as Krugar, he was small and wispy thin. They shook hands and then Krugar eased himself into a chair.

"I appreciate your coming," he said to Moy. "I know how busy you are."

"Always a pleasure to see you, Jon," Moy replied, his ancient face expressionless. "And your mysterious invitation has whetted my curiosity."

Krugar accepted tea, then turned his attention once again to the banker. "Between the two of us, we control a very large share of Hong Kong's wealth. Is it not so?"

Moy nodded, his dark eyes intense with interest.

"And we are both ranking members of the Council, responsible for ensuring stability and protection for Hong Kong's commerce," Krugar said. "It is in that capacity that I wish to speak to you, Harold."

"I am a good listener, as you know."

Krugar sipped his tea, then spoke. "The Chinese will take over Hong Kong from the British in a matter of a few short years." He smiled, but without humor. "They may decide at that time to take us over too."

Moy shook his head. "Probably not. They could have seized this island any time they chose. They need us, Jon. We are a window on the world for them, at least commercially."

"And you're willing to bet everything on that? Your future, your family's future?"

Moy shrugged. "What else can we do?"

Krugar's eyes met his. "We can leave."

The ghost of a smile flickered across Moy's thin lips. "Where? This is our home, yours as much as mine. Here we have power, influence. We can protect ourselves. But only here. We cannot leave."

"I am going to urge the Council to consider leaving," Krugar said.

"That has been discussed, of course. They will not agree."

Krugar nodded. "I will ask, nevertheless. In any event, I have made up my mind to go."

Moy looked at him. "We are both old men, Jon. It isn't likely we'll even be alive when the Chinese take over. Why worry?"

Krugar sighed. "I am just one in a long line. I don't wish that line—my family—to stop with me. I must protect those who come after me."

Moy shook his head. "And where will you go? Here you are one of a few who control destiny. Anywhere else you will merely be another wealthy businessman. Without power, you or those who come after you will not be able to protect that wealth for very long."

Krugar looked up at the fans. "There may be opportunities elsewhere."

"You cannot duplicate your influence here, Jon."

"I will make my argument to the Council. If they do not agree, I shall move my own interests. But I feel that honor demands I inform them."

Moy shrugged. "A nice gesture, but they won't agree."

"Then the Krugar family will withdraw." He smiled at Moy. "My dear friend, it may be different with you. You are Chinese. I have some Chinese blood, but I'm afraid I would stick out if mixed with our friends from Peking."

"But where would you go, Jon? You could never hope to equal your power here."

Krugar frowned. "That is a problem I am working on. I admit it is difficult but not impossible."

Moy raised his teacup in salute. "I wish you luck, of course. But I'm afraid you are as much a prisoner of your past as we all are." He chuckled. "I can understand your concerns, we all share them. But there are problems to which there are no solutions, Jon. I'm afraid this is one. You will never leave Hong Kong."

Krugar smiled, an enigmatic Oriental smile. "We shall see, Harold. Fate, sometimes, is a very surprising lady."

Joyce Spitz buzzed Victoria. "Congressman Lytle's on the line. Do you want to talk to him?"

Victoria felt a rush of pleasure. "Put him through, Joyce."

She heard the click as the call was transferred. "Hello."

"Vicky, how are you?"

"I'm fine, Barry."

"I've been thinking about you," he said.

"Have you?"

He chuckled. "Can you make it down here this weekend?"

Suddenly her pleasure became anguish. "I can't, Barry. Oh, I'd really like to, but there's so much I have to do here, I can't possibly get away."

"If I came up there, could you sneak away for at least a quick dinner?"

She felt her pulse quicken. "I think that might be arranged. But that's asking an awful lot of you. I . . ."

"I know my priorities," he said softly. "I can fly up Thursday. Could you meet me?"

Thursday would be hectic. She was scheduled for a meeting with two friendly members of the board, plus a crucial confrontation with the head of the Research Group. "It would have to be on the late side."

"Just name the time."

She thought for a moment. If everything went as planned she could be through by eight o'clock. But she wanted time to go home and dress. She wanted to really impress him. "How about nine?"

"That sounds good. How about the Russian Tea Room? I'll use your name to get a good table."

She laughed. "I think you'd do quite nicely all on your own, Congressman. The Tea Room it is. I look forward to it."

"I'll see you then," he said, then paused. "Victoria, I think I'm in love with you."

Before she could reply he hung up.

She sat back, breathless, wishing that Thursday would come quickly.

Barry Lytle smiled as he patted the telephone. They were all so alike, so predictable. Of course, that's what made it so easy. His father would be pleased. That in itself usually would have annoyed him, but not this time. Victoria Van Horn was a good lay, even a great lay. For once, he didn't resent his father's interference.

Thursday looked promising, very promising indeed.

17

Sander Blake's communications empire was composed of many parts. He owned radio and television stations. And newspapers by the dozens. But the foundation of his holdings was his magazines.

Sander Blake was recognized as America's magazine king, with periodicals covering everything from stock market reports to cooking tips. He seemed to collect magazines as some men collect stamps. And he always made them profitable.

He had purchased *National Nova* for two reasons. It had an enormous circulation and a huge potential, not yet realized, to attract lucrative advertisers. The second purpose, which would help with the ads, was to reform the weekly magazine from a scandal sheet into a more respectable form of journalism.

When Sander Blake took over a magazine he sent in an expert team to cut away any dead wood and generally redesign operations to make it profitable. The team had fired most of the staff of *National Nova*. They brought in new editors and writers who would keep the weekly as entertaining but make it less lurid and more responsible.

But they didn't touch Pete Hooper, even though he was a nasty, mouthy drunk who viewed the world with the eyes of a venomous snake. He was an alcoholic but he never missed work. Loathed by his coworkers, Hooper was indeed mean, but it was that character trait that had brought him fame late in his checkered career.

Pete Hooper was the *Nova*'s number-one gossip columnist. His column, "Hooper's Alley," was the most-read item in the weekly. Millions delighted in his acid characterizations and malevolent humor. The team not only left him alone in the reorganization, but assigned him assistants to help check out tips and leads.

Hooper, the last of a vanishing breed, was an old-fashioned newspaperman. He was a master of the English language, although he had never been graduated from high school. He had been trained by men of his own kind who never forgave or forgot. Before he was sixteen he had learned from masters. No one could check a story better, or write one.

The trail of his long career looked like the line of an interstate highway imposed on a map of America. He never got along well with editors, so he never lasted long in any one place.

While his masters had taught him the art of communication, they had also shown him the underside of human nature, instilling in him a permanent cynicism. And they had taught him to drink.

Editors hated him, but he was beloved of bartenders, fellow boozers, prostitutes and other denizens of the night world that he had embraced as his natural environment.

The job at the *Nova* had seemed to be the very last rung on his way down the ladder: hacking out stories about two-headed children for a lying, sleazy rag pandering to the worst in man. He knew he had reached the gutter of journalism.

But then they had tried him out on the column. Graying, half sick all the time, with a liver like a boulder, he had at last found his niche.

All those saloons, all those bartenders, all the night people had become his own personal CIA, a network whispering of the steamy delights and disasters enjoyed or endured by people of prominence. New York was his headquarters. After dark he hunted like a voracious animal, moving from bar to bar, party to party, watching, listening. Hearing from his contacts all the wonderful whispers that would be translated into the hot little items of "Hooper's Alley."

But Pete Hooper also knew that his peculiar talents were unique to the *Nova*. No other publication would ever touch him. So, despite his popularity, for the first time in his life he made an effort to hold on to his job.

The Van Horn story was typical.

A drunken lawyer had entertained some ladies from his law firm. It was confidential, of course, but they had all found it amusing. It was interesting. The bartender, a friendly fellow who seldom talked but was a great listener, relayed it to a producer who was a regular customer. The producer, knowing Pete Hooper's power and wishing to curry favor, called the newspapermen and passed it along.

Hooper took nothing at face value. He went to work checking it out. Truth was a hell of a good defense to libel actions. It wasn't long before he had unearthed Junior's publicity man.

Pete Hooper knew he had struck gold. The publicity man was anxious that the story be kept under wraps until Junior's lawyers started the suit to unseat his sister. Timing was all. In exchange for Hooper's forbearance, he gave him all the details. The story had everything, money, power, sex, family, the works. Hooper got enough to keep his column boiling all summer. He was assured he would be the first to explode the story.

The war between the two Van Horns would be lively and juicy. But Hooper knew the girl had just been selected as a member of the Vault. That too was inside information. Of no use to him, since none of his readers knew about the Vault, or cared. But the big boss, Sander Blake, was also a member.

Pete Hooper meant to keep this job.

He called Sander Blake.

Blake had taken notes. He disliked Pete Hooper and was somewhat ashamed of being his employer, but he had to admit the man had gathered an impressive mass of information. Unfortunately, it all rang true.

Junior was planning a massive attack against his sister. His lawyers would bring actions in all levels of the courts, all of it orchestrated by a public relations man. Junior did not intend to win in court, only to discredit Victoria.

Given the extent of the attack as reported by Hooper, he would succeed.

Blake wondered if Junior realized fully what he was doing. Such a thing would drag him through the same mud. But more importantly, it could bring the Vault itself into the baleful public eye. And all the members. Even the system itself.

Somehow it had to be stopped.

Blake began calling the other members of the Vault. They would have to have a meeting, this time without their newest member. Perhaps they would have to reconsider their reaction in naming Victoria to her father's vacancy. It was regrettable, it wasn't her fault, but there was more at stake here than one person's reputation.

It could all end in disaster.

Eric Vogeldorf's situation was fast becoming desperate. Although his brother reluctantly had provided another small loan, Eric knew without asking that it was the last he could expect. The California heiress his brother had married was tiring of supporting two blond Germans, royal or not.

His efficient butler, Thatcher, was a good money manager, but even with adroit penny-pinching he had only a few months left to market himself as a husband to a rich woman. Beauty and age didn't matter to him anymore. If Vogeldorf failed he would no longer have a butler, or much of anything else. Worse, he would be forced to work. No male in his direct family line had ever labored for wages. It was more than economics; his family honor was at stake.

He began campaigning like a maddened ward heeler, frantically running from one society gathering to another, exhibiting his face, form and charm to any woman who might be a possible prospect.

His quest took him to attend a private exhibit at the Whitney. It was the type of event that attracted the rich and powerful, their daughters, discarded wives and about-to-be discarded wives. Vogeldorf had been schooled in the finer things, and he considered art one of his specialties. For him, it was a promising hunting ground.

A striking dark-haired woman was engaged in an earnest conversation with Cecil Driker. Vogeldorf knew Driker, having attended a number of functions at the Habermann Museum, where Driker was director. Driker, a pompous little man dressed in clothing more colorful than the paintings at the exhibition, was fawning over the tall brunette. Vogeldorf recognized that as a sure sign the woman had either money or position, or, more likely, both. She stood with one hand on her hip, a pose that showed off her good figure and excellent legs. Vogeldorf's practiced eye noted that she wore very expensive clothes with flair.

He worked his way toward them. "Cecil!" he said, as if just discovering the presence of the little man. "What a pleasure to see you here."

Driker was preoccupied, but he smiled automatically as he looked up. "Ah," he said, lingering long enough to finally recall Vogeldorf's name. "Eric. How nice."

Vogeldorf stepped closer to the handsome woman. He glanced down at Driker and waited.

Obviously annoyed at the interruption, Driker snapped out a curt introduction. "Mrs. Van Horn, may I present Mr. Eric Vogeldorf."

The woman's smile was perfunctory, but her eyes seemed to appreciate what she saw as she made a quick inventory of the tall blond man.

"Mr. Vogeldorf is a patron of the arts." Driker stammered slightly, as if nervous.

"The name Van Horn is quite illustrious," Eric said, allowing her the effect of his full smile. "Any relation to the famous family?"

"My husband is Hunter Van Horn, Jr." Her voice possessed a sultry, almost raspy, quality.

Vogeldorf was disappointed. He wasn't interested in rich wives, unless they were planning a divorce and had the prospects of a handsome settlement. However, in his desperate straits she certainly merited investigation.

"I was sorry to hear of your father-in-law's death," he said with just the proper solemnity. "A great loss to your family, of course, as well as the business community."

She nodded, but he sensed her hesitancy to agree. Perhaps there was more here than met the eye. He decided not to mention his acquaintance with Victoria until he knew more of the situation. Timing, he knew, could be everything.

"Mr. Driker and I were just discussing some business," she said. "I'm considering buying some foreign paintings and I want his expert opinion."

"Ah, business." Vogeldorf bowed slightly. "In that case, I'll leave you two alone."

She touched his sleeve. "Actually, we've completed our transaction. Haven't we, Cecil?"

Driker nodded without enthusiasm. He seemed increasingly anxious. "As soon as I have anything, Mrs. Van Horn, I'll be in touch." He made a nervous little smile, then strode off quickly, as if escaping something.

"Odd little man," she said. "Do you think he's gay?"

Vogeldorf wondered if her question might really be about him. Because he was blond, handsome and single, he knew some people wondered just that.

"I have no idea," Vogeldorf said evenly. "I only know Cecil from dealings with his museum."

She smiled. "So many men connected with the art world are that way, don't you think? It must have something to do with the creative process."

Vogeldorf laughed. She was curious about him and that was a good sign. Mrs. Junior Van Horn apparently had a roving eye. He decided to abandon his hunt for the evening and to concentrate on the provocative Cecelia.

"I have friends who are gay," he said. "Some are in the arts, but some are lawyers, some accountants. There are no more stereotypes. I'm happily heterosexual myself, but I consider the other an acceptable preference if one chooses, don't you?"

Her eyes reflected her growing interest. "Oh, of course. What do you do, Mr. Vogeldorf?"

He smiled. "I have been trained at Oxford and Harvard to be a businessman, but I suppose I'm what some might term a playboy. An archaic term, but I try to live up to it." He took her arm. "Let's sneak out of here, shall we? I'm dying for a real drink."

"You're a man after my own heart, Mr. Vogeldorf."

"Eric," he said easily. "Please call me Eric."

"And I'm Cecelia to my friends."

He guided her toward the marble staircase. "Cecelia, I hope you'll allow me to become your very good friend."

Married to Victoria's brother or not, she was a hot property and well worth his time. She possessed that essence of pleasurable evil he always found so attractive.

It promised to be a very interesting evening.

The first thing Sander Blake did after he flew into New York was to put a call through to Junior Van Horn. He had met Hunter's son several times and he hoped Junior would listen to reason.

"Sander Blake, Junior. How are you?"

There was a pause before he received an answer. "I'm just fine, Sander."

"I wonder if we might meet for a few minutes?"

"Why?"

"Oh, for a frank discussion of mutual interest."

The reply was a bitter chuckle. "And what mutual interests could we possibly have, Sander?"

"I'd prefer to talk in person, Junior."

"How's the newspaper business? Do you still have your fingers on the pulse of America?"

"I try."

"Look, Blake, I have no quarrel with you. I'm disappointed I wasn't selected as my father's replacement on the Vault. But I don't consider that decision personal."

"I appreciate that, Junior. Can we arrange to meet?"

"Why? So you can try to dissuade me from knocking my sister out of our family company?"

"There may be some repercussions you haven't considered, frankly. I think we should talk."

"There's nothing to discuss, unless you wish to have your newspapers support my position."

"I don't know what your position is," Blake replied.

"Well, you can read all about it soon in your own journals. Then, if you wish, we can talk. I won't be stopped, Blake. I'm determined on a course of action here. I mean to obtain justice."

"Junior, I . . ."

"Don't try to con me, Blake. I know you're speaking for the Vault. You are all scared shitless that a Van Horn fight might spread into areas that could threaten all of you." Anger crackled in Junior's voice. "Well, you just might have cause to worry. But don't come to me. My sister is now a member of your precious Vault. If you're so damned worried, talk to her. If she will resign from my father's company, I'd be satisfied with that."

"Is that what you want, control of Van Horn Enterprises?"

"Of course. If she resigns I can take over without any unnecessary bloodshed. If not, this could get very sticky before it's all through. I don't blame you people for being worried, but you're talking to the wrong Van Horn."

"Junior, I would like to . . ."

"I'll talk to you, Sander, when my lawyers advise me to, not before. Nothing personal, you understand," Junior said as he hung up.

Sander Blake shook his head. If a major war couldn't be averted, something else might have to be done, perhaps something unpleasant.

But first he would talk to Victoria.

Cecil Driker was excited. Something was in the wind. The Vault had scheduled a special meeting, something very rare. He trembled with anticipation. He would record the proceedings as usual, but this time he had a very special buyer for his tapes.

He dialed Cecelia Van Horn. The maid called her to the phone.

"Cecil Driker," he said softly.

"Oh yes." She sounded surprised. "How are you?"

"I'm fine. You asked me to call if those special art buyers ever got together." They had agreed to be guarded on the telephone in case anyone might be listening.

"Yes, I did." Her heart pounded in anticipation.

"They plan to meet Wednesday night. That in itself is unusual."

"Do you think anything of value may come of it?"

He nodded, as if she could see. "Quite probably. This just isn't their normal method of doing things. Something's up."

There was a pause. "You'll let me know what happens, as we discussed?" She was reminding him of her offer to buy the tapes.

"Of course."

They both hung up. He had worked out the details. There would be no direct payment to him. Everything would go through Pelegrine. In case of trouble, nothing could be traced to Driker. She would buy a painting at a grossly inflated price. Pelegrine would get his commission as a reward for his part in the transaction, but Driker would get the real profit. Of course, he realized the information had to be worth the money.

Cecil Driker never drank at the museum except on special occasions. He happily locked his office door, poured himself a healthy brandy, then double-checked his prized listening and recording equipment.

Wednesday seemed so far away. He felt like a child waiting for Christmas.

"Craig Hopkins is on the line," Joyce Spitz said. "He sounds excited."

Victoria picked up the telephone. "Yes, Craig?"

"I hate to bother you, Vicky, but I think we've run into major trouble."

"Go on," she said, drawing a deep breath.

Craig did sound agitated. "The engineering firm you hired to do the foundation work claims your architect's plans can't be carried out. They say it's impossible, something about the proposal of the successors to the Westway people and the condition of the footings. Frankly, I didn't understand what they were talking about."

Victoria's mind was full of facts and figures concerning Van Horn Enterprises; she found it difficult to shift gears and concentrate on something else.

"That's Lucas Shaw's company?"

"Yes."

"Just what are their specific objections?"

"Victoria, when I took this job you knew I was a lawyer, not a builder or an engineer. They told me over the telephone, but I couldn't understand a goddamned word. Maybe it would help if you talked to them? I hate to bother you with this, but apparently it's vital, and, as I said, I'm out of my element."

"I'll take care of it," she said. "Did you talk to Luke Shaw himself?"

"I started out at the bottom and worked myself finally to the top. That's a big company, as you know. Shaw was trying to be patient, but I think he became a bit disgusted when I couldn't comprehend what he was trying to tell me."

"Okay, I'll talk to him."

"Vicky, I know I was hired to take all this off your back, but in this case I honest-to-God don't know what to do."

"Relax, Craig. I'll get back to you."

Victoria mentally reviewed the project plans, then asked Joyce to get Luke Shaw on the telephone.

"Mr. Shaw, this is Victoria Van Horn." She decided to be formal despite their being fellow members of the Vault. "I understand you have some reservations concerning the foundations proposed for the buildings on my Hudson River project?"

He paused before answering. "'Reservations' isn't quite the right word. What your architects propose can't be done."

"You mean in light of the old proposals?"

"No. It's just the proposed supports for your river towers. Everything else seems okay, based upon our first investigations and tests. But the towers can't be built."

"And why not?"

Again there was a pause. "This is a bit difficult to explain over the phone. I have charts and graphs in my office, but I think it might help explain things quicker if you could meet me at the site."

"Mr. Shaw, will this take long?" She had so much to do. Some of it could be delegated to Joyce, but most could not. She resented having to spend the precious time. Still, the towers were the key to her project, so it boiled down to a matter of priorities.

"Can you meet me in an hour? It shouldn't take too long." He sounded annoyed. "I'll bring along some of your architect's drawings. They might help you understand."

"Where shall we meet?"

"Do you know the old Sperry warehouse? The abandoned one just south of Thirty-fourth Street?"

"I should. I bought it." She regretted the inflection of her answer; even to her own ears she sounded arrogant, even pompous.

"Then you won't have any problem, will you?" His tone was flat, almost angry. "Meet me on the Thirty-fourth Street side, near the pier."

"I'll be there. Please be prompt. I have a number of things to do today."

"It might surprise you to know you aren't the only busy person in New York. I'll see you in an hour."

She was about to apologize, but he hung up. She supposed Luke Shaw, although intelligent and attractive, was another one of those men who feared women. She had seen the type before, the rugged out-doorsman who really longed for another time. But if he thought he would be able to parade his supposed masculine superiority past her, he was in for a big surprise. She knew a great deal about building, and foundations, all of which he would soon find out.

Victoria calmed herself. Anger was only self-defeating. She considered calling the architects and asking for one of their experts to come along.

But her pride was involved, and she was determined to handle it alone. She had no doubts of her own competence.

She asked Joyce to come into her office. "I have to go to a meeting about problems with my Hudson River project. I'm expecting a call from Adam Robins, the head of Prometheus Pictures. I want a bottom-line figure on the losses we can expect from that new movie, *Soul of Fire.*"

Joyce nodded. "I hear they are staggering."

"Do you think I might be able to trust Robins?"

"Yes and no. Robins knows he will get axed, no matter what; it's expected when a studio produces a bomb of that magnitude. He can only hope for a favorable settlement of his contract. He isn't considered one of Vance's men, so that's in his favor. He'll be looking for support. You won't be able to trust him totally, but I think he'll want your goodwill."

Victoria nodded. "All right. Also ask him to get me an estimate of the studio's probable worth. Tell him it has to be absolutely confidential."

"Are you thinking of selling Prometheus?"

"It's a possibility. Some drastic surgery is going to be needed to save this company."

Joyce smiled, an expression rare for her. "You remind me more of your father all the time."

"Impress on Robins the need for privacy. If Chilton Vance gets wind of this, we can expect real trouble. Vance still believes that I have no interest in company affairs."

"You can trust me to handle it," Joyce said. "Anything else?"

"See if you can find out what's really happening with the Research Group. Use your company contacts. I can't seem to get any hard dollar figures from them. I suspect Vance is up to something. This company doesn't need another disaster."

"I'll see what I can do. I think it would be better if I made calls from outside the office."

Victoria looked at her. "Do you think we might be bugged?"

Joyce shrugged. "I don't know. It would be wiser to presume that we are. I know Chilton Vance hired a security firm just after your father's death. They are experts at finding bugs, but they also have quite a reputation for installing them."

"Joyce, you aren't becoming a bit paranoid, are you?"

"Your father used to say that industrial spying was far better organized and developed than international intelligence systems. He employed a firm that specialized in that sort of thing."

"Industrial spying?"

Joyce shook her head. "No. He used them to protect against it."

"Would Chilton Vance have known about them?"

"No. Your father always played that sort of thing very close to the vest. That expense was hidden away in other budget items. I saw to that."

Victoria nodded. "I want to make sure this office and our phone lines are clear. Could you get them to work for me?"

"Of course."

"And hide the cost the same way?"

"It's as good as done," Joyce said. "I'll see to it while you're away. Anything else?"

"No. I'll be back soon. I just have to settle a macho-man's hash, and that won't take too long."

Victoria got a taxi almost immediately. Even the traffic moved quickly, and she arrived at the Thirty-fourth Street area earlier than she had planned.

The Sperry warehouse was just one of many abandoned, decaying buildings that had once served the river commerce. No one had bought them for development because the anticipated Westway route might run through the property, and any money spent might be lost. The successors to the Westway plan made it just as chancey. As cargo ships moved to newer, more efficient docking areas, there were no other uses for the buildings and they were allowed to rot. Only a few blocks away, gentrification was being accomplished, old structures being remodeled and new ones being built. But, despite the renewal nearby, the old river area had a deserted, nightmarish quality to it.

When Victoria paid the taxi driver, his expression showed his opinion that any woman who would walk alone in such a lonely and dangerous area was taking a foolish, even fatal risk, but he said nothing. As the cab sped away, she regretted being early.

A wire fence enclosed the rear of the Sperry structure and yard. Useless, rusted padlocks held a sagging gate together. The fence had been ripped open in several places, making entry easy. She gingerly stepped through one of the gaps, being careful not to tear her clothes. Broken pieces of stone, glass and wood littered the ground. She picked her way through the rubble, moving along the side of the building, working her way onto the pier.

Sea gulls wheeled above her, their cries rising above the distant sounds of the city, adding to the illusion that she had stepped into another world. Everything else was eerily quiet. Suddenly she froze, too frightened to make another move. A huge gray rat, barring her way at the side of the building, stared at her.

The rat showed no sign of fear. This was its world, and it knew it. After a casual appraisal, the fat gray animal waddled a few feet along the side of the building, then disappeared through a hole in a rotten board.

Victoria tried to control her involuntary trembling, then forced herself to continue toward the pier, but this time farther away from the building. She moved slowly and cautiously.

She stepped out onto that part of the pier that extended beyond the building but went no farther. Some planks were missing and she could see the Hudson's dark murky water far below her. The ancient dock, long neglected, was tilted at an angle, as if it might collapse under the slightest strain.

Victoria looked out at the river. An enormous freighter was maneuvering toward the New Jersey side. The blood-red hand painted on its stack identified it as belonging to an Irish line. A sleek motor yacht passed it, its prow cutting through the water, leaving a bubbling white wake behind it. The pungent odor seemed a salty clash of the clean sea air with the corruption of the dark river, compelling yet slightly offending, a blend that seemed a symbolic reflection of the city itself. A sailboat bowed up and down as the slight wind took it across the wake of the yacht.

"Beautiful, isn't it?"

Startled, she spun around.

"Sorry," Luke Shaw said as he joined her. "I didn't mean to frighten you." He wore no hat or tie, just a rough jacket over a plaid shirt. He looked more like a workman than the head of one of the world's largest engineering firms. The light breeze ruffled his hair slightly. Reluctantly, she had to admit to herself that she found him good-looking. He carried a rolled-up blueprint in his hand.

"Now what's all this about the foundations?"

Without asking, he took her arm and led her out along the rotting pier extension. "It's safe enough if you know where to step," he said. They walked about halfway out. "According to your specifications, this is about where you propose to sink the foundations for your two towers, right?"

She looked at the dismal sagging buildings along the shoreline. It was so desolate, and so very different from the dreams she had for it. "I suppose so. I'd have to check the specifications to be absolutely sure."

He grinned. "Take my word for it. According to the plans sent to me, this is where they go."

"So?"

"You propose to build two fifty-story towers here. Judging from the renderings I've seen, they'll constitute the central feature in your development. On the architect's drawing, they look like two guardian angels."

She frowned. He seemed to take the whole thing too lightly. "The towers are important, but they are designed to blend in with everything else. It's the entire concept that matters."

He shrugged as if entirely indifferent to it. "Well, according to the tests and studies we made, everything but the towers can be done. But if you build those two babies they'll slide right into the river eventually."

She glared at him. "Manhattan Island is a rock. That was the original reason they could build huge skyscrapers here. You'll notice the Empire State Building is still standing."

He grinned. "It wouldn't be if they had built it here. And in case you haven't noticed, this is the Hudson River." He gestured toward the water below them.

"We made provision for landfill. It's all in the plans, if you had read them. Even the courts have approved the proposed landfill here. We won't be harming any fish or interfering with shipping. The Westway successors have approved our plan for landfill."

"That's not the problem. The concept is very nice. Hell, the drawings make it look like paradise. Landfill or not, you happened to select one of the few places on this little island that won't support buildings the size of your towers. The rock shelf below the water isn't thick enough to accept the weight. You could move the towers to the present shoreline, or you could make them much smaller. But you sure can't build them the way you have them now." He laughed.

It was his attitude that provoked her anger. "Is this some sort of boyish way of getting back at me because I cracked the gender barrier in your precious little men's club? Aren't you looking for ways to get even since they took me into the Vault?"

His eyes narrowed. "Look, toots, I don't care if they make you the pope. You hired my firm to make certain evaluations. Our findings have nothing to do with your being a woman, a member of the Vault, or the Queen of Sheeba. We deal only in scientific fact. If you build your delightful towers here, they will fall into the goddamned river. Is that clear enough for you?"

"This is some kind of personal vendetta on your part." She realized she was shouting. "I'll get another opinion!"

He started to unroll the blueprint as if intending to prove his point, then, disgusted, he changed his mind and tossed them into the river below. He glared down at her.

She hadn't realized he was so tall.

He spoke in flat angry tones. "I will submit our findings in writing, together with our bill for services rendered. I would not only suggest you get another opinion, you can get another engineering firm. We only deal with customers who have confidence in us."

Victoria knew she had foolishly overreacted and felt herself color with embarrassment. She realized that he was probably right about the foundations. Her anger had been provoked by his condescending manner. But his firm was the best, and she didn't want to lose their services. "If what you report is correct, I see no reason why you shouldn't stay on . . ."

"No way," he snapped.

Despite herself, anger flared again. "If that's the way you want it, that suits me."

"I'll escort you back," he said icily.

"No thanks," she snapped. "I'm quite capable of taking care of myself." She turned and stalked off. A board gave way and she lost her balance. Her foot crashed through a rotten plank, and she made an involuntary cry.

He grabbed her and effortlessly lifted her up. "Are you okay?"

She looked down. Her leg was scraped. Her stocking was torn but there was no blood. It stung like a burn. "I'm fine," she said haughtily. "Now, if you'll get your hands off me, I can find my way back myself."

"I'm sure you can," he said, his tone disgusted.

She knew he was watching so she tried to walk with dignity as she gingerly picked her way back to the shore. She walked very slowly past the place where she had seen the rat, and was relieved to finally reach the street.

She wondered what it was about him that made her react so violently. She didn't like his attitude, but he hadn't been unreasonable. And if he was right about the foundations, he had done her an enormous service, perhaps saving the project itself.

Her anger past, she considered turning back and apologizing, but she was too embarrassed to do it. She climbed through the fence, walked a block on her throbbing leg, and finally hailed a cruising cab.

Luke Shaw was disturbing. She was offended by his masculine self-assurance, but she knew she perversely found it attractive at the same time. She resolved not to think about him. After all, he was just another man. But, somehow, she still couldn't put him out of her mind.

18

Barry Lytle telephoned shortly after Victoria's return to the office, to remind her of their date. After the row with Luke Shaw, she craved some show of kindness. Barry's earlier invitation to dinner had been perfectly timed. She looked forward to an evening away from the feverish concerns of her world. There was so much work to do, but she knew she had to have some time for relaxation.

She had just finished dressing when her doorbell rang. Squinting through the peephole she saw he had an armful of roses. As they shared a quick drink she reflected that Barry, although compact, possessed the kind of build that would delight any tailor. In his case, the man made the clothes.

Victoria didn't object when Barry kissed her while they waited for the elevator. It was a romantic gesture; his touch not presumptuous but graceful and pleasant.

He had a limousine waiting. Barry held her hand as they drove through the Manhattan traffic, still heavy but moving well. Spring was finally arriving and the evening was warm. Victoria felt wonderful.

As their limo moved with traffic across Fifty-seventh Street, she noticed the cluster of people waiting on the wide sidewalk in front of the Russian Tea Room. It was one of her favorite restaurants.

"Looks like the press is out in force," he said.

"I wonder why."

He laughed. "Well, practically every Hollywood mogul uses the place as a headquarters when they're in town. We'll probably find the place crawling with celebrities."

The limo slowed and pulled to the curb. Victoria saw two television crews waiting by the door. The gathering of photographers and newsmen had attracted a small crowd of curious onlookers.

Their driver came around and opened the door.

The television lights went on and flash bulbs popped.

"They must be practicing up," Lytle laughed. He waved at the cameras. "Vicky, you go on in. I have a reservation in my name. I'll deal with these folks." He grinned at the assembled faces. "It's all in a day's work for a politician."

He deftly led her to the door, then closed it after she entered the restaurant. He turned and smiled as the cameras continued to click.

"Well, Congressman, how about it?"

He knew the reporter very well. Several microphones were thrust forward to catch his remarks. "How about what?"

"Is there a romance in the air?"

He managed a shy smile. "Miss Van Horn and I have known each other for a long time. We're friends."

"You two look like more than just friends," a woman commented. She wore a television button on her lapel.

He tried to look solemn. "Obviously, I'm not in a position to say what the future might hold. Victoria Van Horn is a lovely and famous woman. Any man would be honored to have her for a wife."

"Cm'on, Barry. Are you two going to get married?" As the question was asked, the microphones seemed to be thrust even closer to his face.

"All I can say is, anything's possible." He laughed conspiratorily. "Maybe I haven't even asked her yet. If she was to say no, then where would I be? Just quote me as saying it's a possibility."

"Will she help you in your campaign for the Senate?"

He bowed slightly, as if embarrassed by the question. "I haven't yet said that I might run, as you know. If I did, Vicky and I are old friends—I would hope she would support me." He posed for a few more pictures. "Now, if you'll excuse me, I'm starving."

He pushed past them and walked into the restaurant. He was surprised at the coverage. It had all been planned by his office. But none of them had expected this degree of success. It must have been a slow night. He had recognized many of the newsmen, including photographers from two national magazines. That, combined with the television crews and the photographers from the tabloids, made it quite a successful turnout. Lytle was pleased. It must have been the romance angle that brought them out. That always worked.

They had seated Victoria at one of the so-called power tables near the front of the restaurant. He joined her.

"What was that all about?" she asked.

He smiled and patted her hand. "They're out there to snap pictures of some bunch of UN diplomats who have been avoiding the press. They got a tip, or so they told me. Bad timing for us. You're always newsworthy. But I got rid of them so that we can dine in peace."

"How did you manage that?"

"A politician's secret, my dear, a trade secret of sorts." Lytle grinned at the waiter, who hovered near the table.

"Let's start off with champagne and caviar," he said.

The producer of the nightly television news watched the short video of Junior Van Horn's bitter attack upon his sister. The camera, set up in Foley Square, used the columned majesty of the federal courthouse as stage background while Junior explained why his attorneys had started a suit to unseat his sister from control of the family's international company.

"This looks like it might turn out to be just the thing for a long dull summer," he said to his assistant. "Ah, life among the rich and famous, eh? Everybody loves a family fight. This should be a pip."

Junior was denouncing his sister as incompetent and unfit to run Van Horn Enterprises, pompously explaining he was acting only out of unselfish concern for the stockholders. He was determined to protect them against the ruination sure to be caused by his wicked playgirl sister.

"Daddy always liked her best," the producer said, laughing. "I suppose we'd better give it some coverage. His lawyers or somebody wrote a good speech for him. We can use practically any part and still tell the story. Clever."

Their woman reporter took over, explaining that although the judge had refused to issue a temporary order removing Victoria Van Horn as president of the conglomerate, he had set up a future hearing on her brother's petition. Her face shining with sincerity, the reporter said the family fight promised to delve into the very heart of one of the nation's largest companies, and into the deep, perhaps dark, secrets of one of America's most visible families.

The producer liked the tag ending. It had potential. He had screwed the reporter when she had first hired on, but she was interested in marriage, so he had quickly dropped her. Despite that, he had to admit she did a good job on camera.

He turned to his assistant. She showed promise. Fresh from Columbia, she was intense, had good legs, and seemed receptive to his initial advances. The intense ones were usually the best fucks. "Didn't we have some footage from last night about the Van Horn girl? We didn't use it, but I recall something about her and a politician."

"I thought you might want to see it," the girl replied, delighted to show her ability to anticipate his wishes. She nodded to the technician. He hit a button and a new clip flickered on the monitor.

The camera zoomed in on a long gray limousine pulling up to the Russian Tea Room. The famous Victoria Van Horn showed a nice bit of leg as she climbed out. She was being helped by a very handsome, dapper man. The scene reminded the producer of fancy magazine ads for the good life. The Van Horn girl was pleasant to look at, the producer thought, although she stared at the camera as if surprised. The whole shot, only a few seconds, seemed to be just what her brother had just described. A rich, beautiful woman who lived for the delights of the flesh, without concern for anyone but herself.

"Shit, this is pretty good stuff," the producer said.

Congressman Lytle's comments on the romance were recorded just before the clip ended.

"Okay, this is how we handle it. First, we use about ten seconds of brother Junior in front of the courthouse. I want that part where he goes after her on a personal level. We'll have Harry do a little intro tonight about the coming family fight. After the brother, use the whole thing from the reporter, only make it voice-over for a few seconds to show sister showing her legs in the limo. Then close with the pompous little tag at the end. Have someone write something sort of funny for Harry to sum up. You know, something cute about families being the same whether rich or not. It might make a good lead into the sports."

"You want it as a lead item, or as a close?"

"Things are slow today. It would fit as a lead, but I sort of like playing it at the end. Make it sort of a joke. The fuckers have been kicking the shit out of us, saying our news team shows no humor. Yeah, have the writers use it as a tie into the sports." He paused. "Who was that guy with her?"

"Congressman Barry Lytle. He may be the Republican candidate for the Senate."

"Cut him. Who's interested in some moth-eaten politician? Everybody loves show biz. Go for the glitz."

Ambassador Stewart Lytle was a man of well-fixed habit. He worked late at the bank, as always. His supper, if he had no social obligations, was a sparse meal, designed more for health than enjoyment. A widower, he was alone except for servants who were always careful to stay out of his way.

It had been a busy day, although not productive. Lytle felt a lingering frustration. He opened a book on foreign finance he was reading, dull but informative, and read for an hour. He continued to follow his usual ritual: preparing himself for bed, taking up the snifter of brandy set out for him, and settling himself in his comfortable chair. He then used the remote control device to switch on the national news. He would make the brandy last as long as the news, then he would retire.

Sometimes it seemed to him he was watching reruns. The usual strife in the Middle East and Orient was reported, with pictures of the usual government troops moving through the usual devastation. A traffic problem had blocked many of Manhattan's streets for the early part of the day, and he listened to the accents of outraged commuters as they vented their anger into the camera.

He found it all quite boring until the anchorman began a snickering introduction to what he described as the Van Horn family fight. Stewart Lytle used the remote to turn up the volume.

Lytle was surprised at Junior Van Horn's sharp performance. Someone had polished him to a high gloss. His comments were terse, incisive and persuasive. Whoever Junior had hired as an image maker was very good. Lytle felt a sense of growing apprehension.

Then he saw his son, Barry, helping Victoria Van Horn out of a gray limousine. She was dressed like a movie star in a frock that showed too much leg. Stewart Lytle hardly paid any attention to the voice-over commentary by the television reporter. The picture itself was devastating enough. It was as if she were acting out the accusations her brother had made against her. She looked like a caricature of a spoiled society girl; no brains or talent, existing merely for the pleasure of the moment. He knew that wasn't true, but it made no difference. People tended to believe the worst, especially about the very rich.

Barry wasn't identified. Lytle considered that both a blessing and an omen. If his son stayed with Victoria Van Horn he would become a little, well-dressed moon circling about the society playgirl. People wouldn't vote for anyone who reminded them of the little man on top of a wedding cake.

The family fight between the Van Horns was certain to blow up into a media volcano. It held all the promise of a real-life soap opera, with wealth, power, greed and sex. Lytle knew from experience that it would be the summer's sensation; not only in New York but nationally.

The newspapers would cover the story in much the same way as the television stations. The tabloids would ballyhoo it all over page one with photographs of Victoria's long legs.

Stewart Lytle snapped off the set and finished the last of the brandy. He felt no particular emotion. He genuinely liked the Van Horn girl. She would have made Barry an excellent wife, providing a touch of glamour and glitter, just the right salt to help with the campaign.

But no more.

Now, quite suddenly, she was a liability to Barry. She would have to go.

It would have to be done immediately. He picked up the phone and dialed the special Washington number.

Usually Eric Vogeldorf took great pride in his sexual prowess, but Cecelia Van Horn seemed insatiable. At first it had been great fun, but then her strenuous sexual games became tiring, and their sweaty sessions became more like endurance contests. Cecelia knew every nuance of sex, and seemed to enjoy everything enthusiastically. Vogeldorf drew the line only at physical cruelty, which seemed to disappoint her. But he knew which one of them would end up shedding blood, and pain held no thrill for him.

They had been together almost every evening since they had first met. Cecelia expressed cold disdain for her wealthy husband, but never his money. Divorced, she would be a rich prize. He hoped she was considering ridding herself of her spouse.

Vogeldorf lay naked on the bed, exhausted and relieved that she had broken off the action to take a cigarette break. He was actually becoming sore, a condition he had doubted could ever occur.

"Hmmm," she purred. "That was very good. I enjoy the old-fashioned way every now and then." She extended her free hand and stroked his aching genitals. He resisted the impulse to cry out.

At least she had finally agreed to come to his apartment. His hotel bills were becoming monstrous, and Thatcher warned him American Express was threatening to cut off his card, despite its "fatherly" commercials. He had persuaded her they would be more comfortable at his place, assuring her that his servants were all quite discreet. Since he had been forced to let the cook go, Thatcher was his only servant, but she didn't know that. And Thatcher was as keen on Vogeldorf snagging a rich wife as he was himself. There was no worry about backstairs gossip.

Much to his relief, Cecelia released him and stood up. She walked across the bedroom to the table on which were two bottles: vodka for her and scotch for him. She poured a healthy splash of vodka into her glass and gulped it down like water. Vogeldorf was amazed that the liquor never seemed to have any noticeable effect on her. He needed his expensive scotch as a crutch to supply much-needed energy.

Cecelia flicked on his large color television set. The brilliant picture flowed into view. Naked, she stood with her back to him in an easy pose, one hip carrying most of her weight. She reminded him of an artist's model, her body supple and inviting. But he felt he could no longer respond.

"My husband may be on tonight's news." She flipped the dial just in time to catch the segment devoted to Junior's attack upon his sister. They watched the screen as the tape showed Victoria being assisted from the limousine.

Cecelia watched motionless until the broadcast switched to sports. She drained the vodka, then poured some more.

Turning to face him, her smile was more of a suggestion of evil than lust. "Well, for once Junior did himself proud. He looked good, didn't he?"

Vogeldorf lifted himself up on one elbow. "Was he really serious? From what I've heard, his sister is the one who has all the power. He seems to be making a dangerous move."

She padded back to bed, her eyes sparkling. "He can attack her as company president, lead a move to oust her. That way he can damn well ruin her without any danger."

Vogeldorf watched with unaccustomed apprehension as she climbed back into his bed, being careful not to spill her drink.

"I thought there was something in your father-in-law's will against that sort of thing?"

She laughed, a low, almost threatening sound. "We would lose everything if we even questioned the will. This way we don't have to. Junior can take control of the company away from her and we won't be risking a dime."

She cuddled close as she kissed him, her tongue hot and searching. He could taste the vodka.

"You seem to hate her," he said. "Why?"

She stopped, putting down the drink as she lit another cigarette. "Over the years she managed to make my husband look very bad. Junior was always like a puppy, doing everything he thought daddy wanted, always in the background and always dependent on darling old dad." Cecelia blew out some smoke. "His sister, on the other hand, turned herself into a national figure, a celebrated success. I think she probably fucked her way to the top; nevertheless, she made it. Junior never did."

"I can see why your husband might, ah, dislike her, but why should you?"

She scowled. "Society, at least the people who count, treat Junior like some kind of middle-aged wimp. As his wife, I get accorded the same treatment. It's galling, and all because of his damned sister." She stared off in space for a moment. "You can't possibly imagine what it was like. We were never invited by the right people, never asked to serve on important committees." She stopped, as if secretly recalling specific humiliations. "But that's all going to change. Junior will topple her. Then we'll be treated quite differently."

"If that should happen, what will become of us?" He tried to make it sound like a joke, although his concern was real. "Your husband will probably become irresistible to you again and you'll have no place in your life for me."

She seemed to relax. "Eric," she said, "I married Junior because it was the logical thing to do; a sort of merger. For a while—a very short while—we were passionate. But now he can't even get the damn thing up. He's tried. Gotten drunk you know, pitiful really. But he's impotent. Even if he brings Victoria crashing down, that thing of his just won't work anymore. And you know my needs. So don't worry; nothing will change between us."

"Have you ever thought seriously about leaving him?" Vogeldorf again tried to make his inquiry sound lighthearted.

She snorted. "Sometimes, in the past, it was like an obsession. But I stayed with him, thinking he'd take his father's place eventually. And, in those days, if I divorced him I wouldn't have gotten very much. Now, of course, I'd get millions, more than even I would ever need. But I still wouldn't get the kind of respect I want. I will when he takes over the company. I'll stay for that, if nothing else."

Vogeldorf felt his heart sink. Time was running out and the prospects were just too dim. He'd have to break off with her.

She laughed. "Don't look so worried, Eric. No matter what happens, I'll always be yours." She reached down and playfully grabbed him. "I couldn't get along without this," she said.

Suddenly she came at him like a wild animal. The news report seemed to have given her new vigor.

He tried to smile, despite the pain, but it occurred to him that if she pulled any harder they would both have to get along without it.

———————

"Have you seen the newspapers this morning?" Ben Tatem's voice had a funereal ring to it, as if announcing a death.

"I've read them." Chilton Vance smiled as he cradled the telephone against his ear and lit a cigarette. This would be the first of a fleet of calls he expected; an eventual roll call of most of the Van Horn directors. He knew they would all be horrified about the family fight and what it could do to the corporation.

"This could drive the stock down, maybe even ruin the company," Tatem continued. Ben Tatem was one of the directors whom Chilton Vance had classified as independent. His vote might be the one to turn the trick.

"The company's going through some rough weather," Vance replied evenly, his tone friendly, "but I think we can survive. You're right about the stock, of course. Publicity of this kind always tends to panic investors."

"Chilton, we must do something, and fast."

Vance inhaled as he looked out the office window at New York's skyline. It promised to be a beautiful clear day. "What do you suggest?"

"For a start, Victoria Van Horn has to go. It's unfortunate, of course, but even if she was the best businesswoman on earth, she can't bring this fight into the company. She may be entirely blameless, but we just can't afford to keep her on as president of this organization."

Vance kept his tone reserved to show he was neutral. "I've heard that some of the directors propose ousting Victoria and replacing her with her brother."

"Jesus," Tatem exploded, "that's going from the fry pan into the fire. He's determined to ruin his sister. She won't stand for what he's doing; she'll return the fire."

"Don't forget the Van Horn stock, Ben. It's a very large block and Victoria controls the voting rights. We would have to contend with her at the next annual stockholders' meeting."

"Who cares? By that time she'll be nothing but a national laughing-stock. Good heavens, Chilton, the public loves these open family wars. This thing will be on the front pages for months to come. We have to put some distance between the company and the warring Van Horn children. If we don't, I'm not so sure we're healthy enough to survive."

Vance crushed out his cigarette. The time had come. "Well, let's suppose Victoria was removed as president and that Junior couldn't muster enough votes to replace her, what then?"

"We need a calm and experienced hand, Chilton; someone who could restore public confidence, someone who we would all trust."

"So?"

"I think it's time you became president, Chilton. You deserve the job. We should have done it after Hunter was killed."

Vance knew he would have to word his reply very carefully. "I'm flattered, of course, Ben," he said smoothly. "But I'm not so sure the other directors would go along with it. And, to tell you the truth, I'm not so sure I'd want the job."

"Why?"

Vance smiled but kept his tone serious. "Even without this family fight, things have become quite messy in the company. Most of it, I think you know, was Hunter's doing. The man who takes over will have to take radical action, and that will call forth a storm of criticism. I'm not sure that I'd want to expose myself to all that."

"Chilton, I realize it's asking a lot, but I think you must do it, for the company's sake. Honestly, I can't think of anyone better suited to the task."

Vance leaned back and put his feet up on the desk. "I do feel a strong commitment to the company," he said slowly, "but I still don't think it would work out."

"Why not?"

Vance idly examined the fingernails of his free hand. They were in need of a trim. He would have it done after lunch. "In order to be effective as chief operating executive I'd need the support of the board, and not just a simple majority. Also, I'd need some assurance of job security. I'm sure any executive hired in, under these circumstances, would want as much. You can't do a really good job if someone is looking over your shoulder or you expect to get the sack at any minute."

"Suppose you had more than just a majority of the board, say two-thirds? Would that satisfy you?" Tatem didn't wait for an answer but continued. "Suppose you were given a five-year contract, with perks, stock options, including bonus escalators based upon production and performance?"

Vance grinned. It was all working out so well. "I really don't want to get mixed up in this, Ben. I like both Victoria and Junior. Of course, if the board were determined to get rid of both Junior and his sister, and I could be assured of more than just token support, I might be persuaded to consider it. But I would do so only under those conditions."

There was a pause. Vance wondered if he had misjudged, perhaps gone one step too far in his demands. He was about to modify his statement when Tatem spoke again.

"I'm not just a mere spectator here, Chilton. Some members of the board asked me to sound you out. I'll make some phone calls and get back to you. Just promise me that you'll keep an open mind until then, all right?"

"Okay, but there is one thing."

"What's that?"

"Please make sure that anyone you may talk to understands this isn't my idea. I'm opposed to ejecting the Van Horns. However, if that's what's going to happen anyway, then I'll have to consider what you've spoken about. I just want to ensure that my position is made clear to anyone you contact."

Tatem chuckled. "Of course, Chilton. That's what everyone likes about you: you're loyal, honest and up-front. You were always loyal to Hunter, and I can understand your feelings about his children. We need that kind of integrity at the helm of this company. I'll get back to you. If not today, by tomorrow at the latest."

Vance thanked Tatem, then hung up. It was working, it really was. He would not be just Hunter Van Horn's successor; he would be hailed as a new force in the company, a savior. Vance inhaled deeply, then casually began to blow small rings of smoke toward the ceiling, watching them with pleasure, as if somehow they were symbolic of his complete triumph, not only over Van Horn's children, but Hunter himself.

And for him, that would make victory even sweeter.

19

After receiving his father's telephone call Barry Lytle had made a tour of a number of Washington bars. He had only a dim memory of trying to rip a blouse from an overripe waitress. He had been taken home by the capital police. In Washington, congressmen were a protected species.

Awakened by an enormous headache, he had dressed and gone directly to the congressional gym, plunging into the pool, in the hope that the healing effect of the water and strenuous physical exercise would purge him of his monumental hangover. He forced himself to swim vigorous laps.

It helped, but only physically. He showered and dressed, and still felt the cold clutch of depression. The dread feeling had enveloped him after his father's call, and he couldn't shake it. His first analyst had easily discovered the reason; he hated his father. Despite that knowledge, he remained strangely dependent. His angry resentment conflicted with his acknowledgment that life without his father's direction and protection was too frightening to even contemplate. So he took what steps he could to make himself feel better, without ever really risking his father's ultimate wrath.

When he returned to his office he called Victoria. Get rid of her, his father had commanded, and fast. He would obey, as always, but first he wanted one more time with her. Making love once more was just a petty act of defiance, but it would help dispel some of his rage. And his father would never know.

He explained to Victoria that he would be coming up to New York for the evening, and invited her out for a late supper. She understood, as women do when they are in love or think they are, more than dinner was involved.

After the call, he stopped and chatted with his administrative assistant, his watchdog. He was no longer being closely monitored, presumably on his father's orders.

Lytle told his assistant he would be attending a cocktail party at the French embassy that night. There was such a party and he had indeed been invited. If anyone went to the trouble, it would all check out. Only he wouldn't be there.

For the other telephone call he chose a pay phone far away from prying eyes and ears. If he faced a future as a prisoner, of sorts, on Capitol Hill he felt entitled to at least one more night of freedom, just one. It would help chase away the anger and depression. But this time he would be careful and not overdo it.

It was easily arranged. He could pick it up after arriving at La Guardia. There would be no risk, and no sordid neighborhoods or hoodlums. It would be all very safe and very discreet.

Barry Lytle felt much better when he returned to the halls of Congress. He looked forward to a busy day, but it was the evening he anticipated with real pleasure.

He was determined to make it a night to remember.

———————

Sander Blake waited until Ambassador Lytle arrived, then he closed the doors to the conference room. Only two of the Vault members were missing. John Robertson was in Europe and couldn't attend. Victoria Van Horn wasn't there, but she hadn't been invited.

"I asked everyone to come," Blake said, "but informally. I suppose we can consider ourselves a committee. We aren't here to take formal action as the Vault, only to explore some problems." He looked at their serious faces. "This may be the first time the Vault has faced such a situation."

"Not altogether correct," Elias McKensie said in his high reedy voice. "Before my time, believe it or not, a Vault member was once involved in a major scandal at the turn of the century. A stock fraud matter. Angst Merriweather was accused of watering stock in his company."

"I presume he was chucked out," Franklin Trager said.

McKensie shook his head. "On the contrary. The Vault, I'm told, closed ranks and used its power to see no prosecution resulted. They even helped get his company back on a firm financial footing. After it all blew over, Merriweather quietly resigned as a Vault member. He sold his interest in his company and retired to Spain, where he later died."

"That's not of much help here," Blake said dryly. "We have a much different situation. Victoria has committed no crime. Her only offense, it seems, is being in the eye of a publicity hurricane."

"That's certainly putting it mildly," Clifford Colburn snapped. "Look, that brother of hers is going to use the front pages to charge her with everything from A to Z. People love that crap. He'll get a lot of ink. I don't care if she's a saint, she's going to be splashed with so much mud you won't be able to see her. And some of that could cause us embarrassment, even hurt our prestige. I, for one, don't want that."

"No one wants that, Clifford," Blake replied. "This meeting is to explore alternatives."

"Why don't we just ask her to resign?" Colburn continued. "She's a sensible person. She should be able to see where all this leads. She might even agree."

"I'm against that," McKensie protested. "I think we should throw our considerable weight behind her and go after that damned brother of hers. After all, he's the one who is causing all this fuss."

"This isn't going to blow over," Stewart Lytle said. "We stand in real danger if we are drawn into this sordid affair, no matter whose fault it might be. I think someone should approach Miss Van Horn and sound her out. She may prove quite reasonable."

"Just for the record," Luke Shaw said, "I'm against it. At least now. I agree that this whole thing could blow up into a nightmare, but it hasn't yet. The Van Horns may come to an agreement. You never know about families. I think we should wait and see what happens."

Blake sighed. "Well, for the record, I agree with Luke. I think the request would be inappropriate at this time."

Lytle held up his hand. "Sander, you're outvoted, I'm afraid. I'm not advocating anything except approaching her and discussing the problem. We don't have to take any action until we know where everyone stands. But I think you should talk to her."

Blake nodded slowly. "We depend on settling matters through mutual cooperation. We'll continue that way. Although I'm opposed, I will talk to Victoria. I'm not going to ask for her resignation, but I will discuss that possibility with her. Does that meet with everyone's approval?"

Franklin Trager stood up. He took a minute to look at each of them. "What I have to say ties in with what we were just discussing. Victoria Van Horn represents New York City to a lot of people. I think we should distance ourselves from her." He paused for effect. "And I think we should distance ourselves from this city too."

"I beg your pardon," Elias McKensie said.

"Look, I had planned to bring this up later when I thought the timing might be better. But this Van Horn thing's propelled the whole question into the forefront. This isn't just the Van Horns and their dirty laundry, it's more than that. As I say, they represent New York."

"We all do," Sander Blake said quietly.

"No. For instance, Sander, you don't. You own newspapers all over the country, and magazines, but none of them here, not in the city itself. Few of us have any real vested interest in this city anymore. Look, the old families who helped found this damn place have moved, and most of their businesses have moved too. I feel it's about time that we recognized reality."

"Are you advocating disbanding the Vault?" Elias McKensie's voice was surprisingly sharp.

"No, not at all. But this isn't our city anymore. Years ago we controlled New York because we wanted to protect our business interests, and the interests of people like us. But now everything's changed. Why control this place at all? It doesn't put a nickel into any of our pockets anymore. Most of us have national or international businesses. There's no point to staying here." Trager looked at their faces. They looked shocked. He found no sign of support. He continued with frantic vigor. "This place has become a cesspool of the very poor. They call it the underclass now. Foreign investors own half the place. It's dangerous here.

"Why stay? It's a terrible place to live. Most of us own property in the city. That can be sold now, quietly, and we can all get top dollar. If we're cautious we can quietly abandon this godforsaken place and make a nice profit at the same time."

No one, not even Clifford Colburn, looked at him. They were all opposed, he could see that. There was no use in trying to persuade them. At least he had tried.

"I say we move out of New York." Trager's words were almost a defiant shout. Then he quietly took his seat.

Sander Blake stood up. He looked at Trager, smiled and sadly shook his head. He sighed. "I'll talk to Victoria, and let you know what happens."

Upstairs, Cecil Driker had hung on every word. He had even taken notes. His heart was pounding with excitement. He heard them as they left, just snatches of neutral conversation, nothing more. It was over.

The echo of Franklin Trager's words seemed to ring in his mind. Driker, since he couldn't see the faces of the other members, assumed that Trager had stated their unspoken decision.

He was shaken.

Driker was purchasing his luxury apartment. And he had made other investments in Manhattan property. Now, if he didn't act quickly, it would all be worthless. He felt perspiration dampen his thin face.

And if the Vault left New York, they would leave the Habermann Museum too, probably relocating its priceless artworks to other cities. He would then be the director of a third-rate museum. He shuddered. They might even make it a public museum.

He began to calm down. He blessed the day he had installed the listening equipment. It had saved him. He would not be left holding the bag, not now.

But he would have to be quick. A smart man, one who moved fast, could turn this disaster into a golden opportunity. His mind raced with the possibilities.

He would need cash.

Driker put the wheels into motion.

First, he called Enrico Pelegrine.

Then he called Cecelia Van Horn.

The world was there for the taking if a man knew what to do and when to do it. He might even become rich.

His shock was turning into excitement.

No one was going to leave Cecil Driker behind.

———

Sam DiVito liked airports. The veteran detective enjoyed watching the passing dramas—joyous family reunions, tearful partings, clusters of hard-eyed businessmen on their way to battle—people flowed in and out like human tides. There was always something interesting. Bus stations were dismal but never airports. He particularly liked La Guardia.

DiVito glanced down the long concourse. Barney Harper was at his post, almost out of sight but not quite. Harper too was a member of the mayor's squad; a young cop, but one with well-developed street sense. DiVito's recent transfer to the mayor's special squad had come as a direct reward for his information about Congressman Barry Lytle. And it was because of that connection that he found himself waiting at the airport for the arriving flight from Washington.

DiVito knew Lytle on sight, but the congressman didn't know him; the only time the two had had contact, Lytle had been unconscious. DiVito often wondered at the random occurrences that seemed to have such impact on all lives, his own included. An unsanctioned telephone tap had tipped the narcotics people, who had the good sense to alert the mayor's squad. The narcs didn't want to bust a political friend of the mayor. That would be unwise, especially since everything would have to be checked out first. Anything else was a challenge, and an invitation to an unwanted transfer, or worse.

Sam DiVito had taken control of the case, dismissing the narcs from any further responsibility. They pretended annoyance, but they were really delighted. Politicians could be bad business. No one ever received a medal for arresting a popular public figure.

DiVito kept careful watch as the passengers from the Washington flight deplaned. He didn't see the congressman. They had checked at Washington's National Airport—all quite unofficially—and Lytle had been booked on the flight. DiVito wondered if the information might have been wrong. His anticipation turned to anxiety.

A stewardess helped an aged woman up the ramp from the airplane. There didn't seem to be anyone left aboard except the crew.

His apprehension vanished as Barry Lytle came striding up the ramp, unencumbered except for a thin briefcase. Lytle smiled and said something to the stewardess and the old lady as he passed them. The stewardess laughed, but the woman seemed only confused at the unexpected attention.

Lytle walked briskly along the long concourse. DiVito waited a moment, then began to follow. Barney Harper, dressed in jeans and blue shirt, like an airport maintenance man, took up a swift pace just in front of the congressman.

Short but athletic and dapper, Lytle was the picture of a fit, energetic man destined for success. DiVito vividly recalled the rag doll form he had seen lying in that cheap junkie hotel and reflected that clothes really did make the man.

Trailing the congressman's cab was easy. They used two cars, but they really didn't need them. Lytle's driver took him into Manhattan by way of the bridge and FDR Drive. Traffic, although heavy, was moving well.

Lytle got out at the Trump Tower on Fifth Avenue near Fifty-seventh Street but didn't go in. Instead he walked a few blocks, turned down Fifty-fourth Street, then hailed another cab. DiVito, who had been following on foot, got back in one of the unmarked cars. Again, following him was easy. The cab drove straight to the Village. Lytle got out on Sixth Avenue, walked another few blocks, turned into a small courtyard, then disappeared.

DiVito, again on foot, strolled into the courtyard, going through an open wrought-iron gate. It was a pleasant oasis, like a tiny park. Several buildings faced on the courtyard. Lytle could have gone into any one of them. DiVito swore softly to himself.

Barney Harper joined him. "Our boy likes cocaine," he said, almost languidly.

"This guy likes everything, including powdered cat shit. What makes cocaine stick out?"

"That end unit, the one with the red door, just past the iron bench, see it?" Harper asked.

"Yeah."

Harper smiled easily. "That's home for Averill Kittle. You know him?"

"This wasn't my territory," DiVito said defensively.

"Mr. Kittle is well connected in a number of ways. He deals cocaine to the very well-to-do. Strictly the carriage trade."

"How come nobody busts him?"

Harper grinned. "Sam, you sound like a virgin. Kittle's cash contributions are always gratefully received by a number of our brother officers. Besides, Kittle keeps his nose clean, and he has a cousin in high places. And, maybe most important, he's a nice little source of information for friendly policemen. Everybody likes Averill Kittle."

"How come you know so much about him, Barney? You never worked narcotics."

Harper shrugged. "I never even heard his name until I was assigned to the mayor's squad. Like I say, he's well connected. He does favors and he's discreet. The big boys like him."

"It's always nice to have friends," DiVito replied. "Lytle will be coming back this way. We better wait in the car."

They had just reached their unmarked car when Lytle reappeared on the street. He looked both ways, then moved off again at a vigorous clip.

"Shall we bust him?" Harper asked. "He's either got the stuff on him or in that briefcase."

"And what grounds do we use to justify the arrest, jaywalking?" DiVito laughed. "We have to wait until we can find an excuse that will look good in the newspapers."

"Is that what the mayor wants?"

DiVito looked at him sharply. "That's none of your business, Barney, and you know it. I had better hop out here and tag after him on foot."

Harper shook his head. "Why bother? He thinks he's being cute. He'll walk a couple of blocks and grab another cab. You'd just be wasting shoe leather."

DiVito hesitated, then nodded. "You may be right at that."

As Harper predicted, Lytle hailed a cab at Tenth and Greenwich. They followed him to the Sherry Netherland Hotel on Fifth Avenue at Fifty-ninth Street, where he got out. He didn't go in but walked up the street to the Desalle Hotel, older, smaller and even more expensive.

DiVito hopped out and made it into the small lobby just ahead of the congressman. The detective inquired about a nonexistent guest and waited while a clerk tried to locate the customer. Lytle checked in at the nearby reservation desk. DiVito noted both the room number and the name the congressman used. The clerk apologized to DiVito. He was unable to locate the phantom guest. DiVito thanked him for his trouble and left.

DiVito gave instructions to Harper to pass along to the rest of the crew, then followed Lytle again on foot when he came out of the hotel. He had apparently left the briefcase in the room. It was getting dark, but the streets were still busy, which made DiVito's task easier. Lytle went into a dark, nondescript restaurant. DiVito, dressed in a decent suit and tie, went in after him and took a seat at the bar.

He recognized her as soon as she came in. She was as beautiful as her photographs. DiVito had a good view of the dining room from his seat at the bar. He nursed his drink and watched as she joined Lytle.

Sam DiVito had seen much in his many years as a policeman and considered himself a shrewd judge of mankind, in all kinds of situations. Victoria Van Horn displayed real affection when she quietly greeted Lytle. But the congressman, despite a more expressive show, to DiVito's practiced eye, seemed more like a man on the make than one really in love.

DiVito wondered if the Van Horn girl was a heavy drug user too. They'd soon find out. DiVito slowly sipped several drinks as he waited for them to finish dinner. He was getting hungry, but he ignored it. He had a job to do.

The detective studied her in the mirror at the back of the bar. She was a beauty. Naked, he speculated, she'd really be something to see. He decided he would give them extra time if they went back to the hotel. Perhaps, that way, she'd be undressed when they went in.

Besides, DiVito reasoned, it would be a better story that way. And that's what the mayor wanted—a real front-page zinger.

From the first moment they entered the hotel room Barry Lytle seemed entirely different. Before, he had been a gentle lover, full of consideration and grace that had made love a joy. But this time he seized her roughly, kissing her with such force that it caused pain. She tried to break free, but he gripped her more roughly, then forced her down across the bed. His kisses were like assaults, hungry and demanding. Finally he stopped.

"Barry, what's the matter?"

He sat up, looked down at her, and then laughed. "I just got carried away, Vicky. Passion, lust, whatever the hell you want to call it. I'm told some women secretly love the rough stuff."

"I'm not one of them." She moved to the other side of the bed.

Lytle made no reply. He stood up and walked to the dresser. He put his briefcase on top and opened it. His back was to her and she couldn't see what he was doing, but he seemed to be working at something.

"What are you doing?" she asked.

"This is a party, Vicky. I'm whipping up something to put you in a better mood. I'm setting up a few lines. This stuff will make you feel great."

She climbed off the bed. He had poured out several thin lines of white powder on the glass top of the dresser.

"Cocaine?"

"It isn't talcum powder. This is the good stuff, the very best."

"I don't do drugs, Barry."

"It's time you started. You don't know what you've been missing." He rolled up a paper to form a thin straw. "Everybody uses this stuff, Vicky. It's the new martini. You've seen me do this before."

"I have, but that was at a party. I thought you were, well, just going along to be polite."

He snorted up one line, sneezing as he finished. He laughed. "Damn, this is really exceptional. Of course it should be, it cost enough." He inhaled through the straw to draw up another line of cocaine, then turned to her.

"Come on. This stuff makes you feel great. It's better for you than liquor and there are no hangovers."

Victoria shook her head. She had tried cocaine in college, but she hadn't liked the effect. Since no person could know what his or her tolerance might be, drugs were to be feared. Anyone could have the hidden potential for real addiction. She had long ago decided that nothing was worth that risk.

"We haven't needed drugs before, Barry. Why tonight?"

He stripped off his tie and loosened his collar. "I'll call room service and have them send something up. Vodka, whiskey?"

"I don't want anything." She suddenly felt cold, emotionless.

He nodded, then inhaled the last line. She could see he had much more in a small envelope on top of the dresser. He snorted noisily, his breathing fast. "Hey, loosen up." He turned and grabbed her roughly, his hands strong and insistent, his fingers inflicting the beginning of pain.

"Barry, you're hurting me." There was an edge of fear in her voice.

He had a half smile on his face as he pushed her across the room and onto the bed once more. He reached down and pulled up her skirt as she fell. Then he was on top of her, biting at her neck and face with force not hard enough to break the skin but sufficient to cause real pain.

"Barry, stop!" she screamed.

"Bullshit," he whispered in a low growl. "You love it." He tore her blouse, ripping it away from her shoulders. She tried to wrench free, but he was able to pin her with the strength of his legs.

"Please!" Panic was giving way to anger. His hand went to the top of her bra and he ripped it away, hurting her as he did so.

"Damn it, stop!"

"I'm going to fuck your ears right off," he giggled. He was breathing fast, excited by his efforts.

She brought her leg up hard, catching him not quite fully at the crotch but close enough to cause him to wince.

"Bitch!" He grabbed at her throat, jamming her even harder into the bed.

"Damn you!" she screamed.

Lytle was about to hit her with his free hand and didn't hear the door open, but she did.

A stout man, dressed in a rumpled suit, grabbed Lytle's hand before it descended.

"Let's think things over, shall we?" The man sounded amused. Lytle turned, his eyes wide with surprise. "What the hell is this?"

The man kept a firm grip on Lytle's arm as he exhibited a gold badge with the other hand. "We're police."

"You have no right here," Lytle snapped, his eyes on the other men coming into the room. "You have no search warrant."

"We heard someone screaming." The policeman was smiling. "And we apparently stumbled into a crime being committed. Looks like rape to me." His eyes wandered to Victoria. She quickly covered her bare breasts with the tattered remnants of her blouse. She struggled off the bed and tried to seek the safety of the bathroom but one of the other men, younger and dressed in workman's clothes, effortlessly stopped her, holding her almost gently as he casually examined the top of the dresser. "Looks like drugs are involved, Sam. There's some white powder here that looks awful familiar." He tentatively dipped a finger into the envelope on top of the dresser, then tasted it. "Cocaine. Hmmm, good stuff too." He grinned at Victoria.

The man held her firmly. She was shaking, her heart beating at a trip-hammer rate. She was a lawyer and she tried to remember what she should do, but her mind refused to function.

"You have no right here," Lytle persisted. "My identification is in my wallet in my coat over there. This is all some kind of a mistake."

Before he could continue a photographer stepped into the room and began taking pictures, his flash blinding as it went off repeatedly. The policemen did nothing as he took shot after shot.

"Hey," the policeman in the work clothes finally said, as if just discovering the cameraman, "this is a police matter. Get out of here."

The photographer smiled, but continued to take pictures.

"Get that camera out of here, or I'll jam it up your ass," the policeman holding Lytle said, but he didn't sound really angry.

The cameraman nodded, and this time respectfully retreated out the door.

"Funny how those guys seem to know when something's going on." Sam DiVito tried to sound upset but couldn't. He had set the whole thing up. Respectable newspapers wouldn't have touched it; besides they couldn't be trusted. But the tabloid he had selected specialized in sensation. A deal had been quietly arranged. By morning, the spicy pictures would be plastered over every newsstand in New York. And that was what counted.

"Well, who belongs to the dope, or vice versa?" the policeman in work clothes asked. He released Victoria, but she was still trapped between the wall and the rumpled bed.

"It's hers," Lytle said quickly. He kept his eyes averted from Victoria. "She brought that stuff up here. I told her I wouldn't use it, and I didn't. She uses it all the time."

Victoria thought herself incapable of additional shock, but she couldn't believe what she was hearing.

DiVito nodded solemnly as if Lytle was speaking an obvious truth. "How about that, Miss?" he asked. "Is that stuff yours?"

It all seemed like a dreadful nightmare, the kind that made you hope to wake up. But it was no dream. Her initial fear was fast being replaced by a growing sense of rage. Keeping her body primly covered, she glared at Lytle. "You lying bastard!"

"It's hers," Lytle repeated. "Oh, she won't admit it, but she brought it up here."

The policemen released Lytle's arm. "I recognize both of you now," he said. He looked at Lytle. "You're some kind of public official, as I recall."

"I'm Congressman Barry Lytle."

DiVito turned to Victoria. "And you I know from the papers and magazines. You never did answer my question, Miss Van Horn. Is that stuff yours?"

Victoria shook her head. "No!" she snapped. She could remember her father's lectures from years before, his advice to her when she was in college about what to do if she got in trouble. "And I want a lawyer," she said firmly.

DiVito shrugged. "That's your right. Speaking of rights, I had better give you both our standard patter. You have a right to remain silent, you have a right to counsel . . ." He continued his little litany, watching their faces, his own expression one of amusement.

When he finished he spoke directly to Victoria. "By the way, Miss Van Horn, you may want to charge him with assault. It sure looked like an attempted rape when we came through that door."

Lytle's eyes grew wide. "That's ridiculous!"

DiVito took off his suit coat and gently put it around Victoria. "If you charge him, Miss Van Horn, it might look better for you. You know, considering the dope and all." He sounded like a kindly uncle.

"I wish to have an attorney," she repeated. She was becoming more furious than frightened.

"I demand a lawyer, too," Lytle whined. "I'll sue all of you and the city before this is over."

DiVito shrugged. "That's your privilege, Congressman. Now, under the circumstances, I have no alternative but to arrest both of you for possession of cocaine. You'll have to come with us. You can call lawyers when we get to the station."

"You can't arrest me. I'm a congressman! I have immunity!" Lytle's voice was high but wavering. He sounded more scared than angry.

DiVito nodded. "I seem to remember something about that. But I think that's only if you're on your way to the Capitol to vote—something like that. We have attorneys, too. They'll tell me if I'm wrong."

Lytle was shaking visibly now. "You'll regret this, all of you, every day of your lives."

"Congressman, if you know something I don't, maybe this is the time to tell me," the stout policeman replied. "Now, as I said, you don't have to talk to me, and you are entitled to a lawyer, but if you have a reasonable explanation, I'll be glad to listen to it."

Lytle said nothing.

The policeman continued. "To tell you the truth, it sure looked to us like you were trying to strangle Miss Van Horn here. She's yelling, and she's got half her clothes torn off when we come in. That doesn't look too good, Congressman. But, like I said, there might be a plausible explanation."

Lytle's face had started to twitch. "I was invited here. She was like that when I got here. She was crazy, screaming and carrying on. I was just trying to calm her down when you came in. I suppose it was all those narcotics she was using. I'm entirely innocent."

DiVito again nodded as if listening to the true gospel. "Is that really true?"

Lytle seemed to be regaining some of his composure. "Absolutely! I was afraid she would hurt herself or something. I was trying to help."

"Or something?" DiVito asked. "Like what?"

"Suicide. Who knows? She was like an animal."

DiVito turned to Victoria. "Like I told you, Miss Van Horn, you don't have to say a word. But maybe now you might want to?"

She stared at Barry Lytle. He kept his eyes averted. His face was twitching again. Victoria felt sick and ashamed. He was pathetic and she wondered what she had ever seen in him. It was like finding something beautiful only to discover it was completely wormy and rotten inside. She felt as if she might vomit.

Despite her revulsion, anger and fright, she resisted the impulse to panic. She recalled her criminal law professor saying the human mouth was the most dangerous instrument in the world. "I wish to have an attorney. My lawyer will say anything that needs to be said."

DiVito grinned. "Class act," he said in admiration. "Okay, enough of this. Let's go downtown. You can get all the lawyers you want there. I'm just a working man, and my working day is almost over." He turned to the younger officer. "Bring the evidence, Barney."

"You had no right coming into this room," Lytle persisted as they prepared to leave. "You have no warrant."

A tall man dressed in a well-fitted suit waited in the hall. "Hotel security," DiVito said, nodding toward the man. "They asked us to assist in another matter. We were on our way to another room when we heard the screams. I'm a cop, mister, I can't walk away from anything like that." He turned to the hotel man. "Did you check out that other room?"

The tall man shrugged. "Empty. The tip must have been wrong."

DiVito grinned. "Isn't that always the way? Here we get a tip that a guy is dead, or maybe dying, and we're on our way to check that out when we hear the screams. Hell, if it wasn't for that tip, we'd never been in this hotel, or on this floor." He lit a cigarette. "Well, that's the breaks, eh? Maybe we stopped a rape, maybe we didn't. Anyway, we did stumble into a nice little felony bust."

"You'll regret this, I promise you," Lytle snapped.

DiVito shrugged. "Miss Van Horn, I'm afraid I'm going to have to put handcuffs on both of you. It's department rules. You have to do it when transporting prisoners. We'll take 'em right off as soon as we get to the station."

He gently cuffed Victoria's hands in front of her, sneaking a look at her breasts as he did so. The woman had a magnificent set of jugs, he thought to himself. "Just keep a good hold on my coat there and you'll be covered, Miss." Her face was crimson with humiliation and rage.

He was less gentle with Lytle, enjoying the man's grunt of pain.

"Let's go."

The same photographer was waiting in the lobby. The policemen told him to move away but did nothing to prevent him from taking pictures of their two handcuffed prisoners.

"Newspaper people," DiVito sighed. "They're all a real pain in the ass."

He led the way toward the street. The hotel security man, an old friend, had cost a great deal, but DiVito didn't think the mayor would mind. And they hadn't needed to use their invented story; the screams were justification enough. It had all worked out very neatly, all nice and almost legal.

He grinned at Lytle. "You know, this is like any other business, some days you just get lucky."

PART THREE

20

By the time Enos Peacock got her out on bail Victoria Van Horn had been subjected to all the bureaucratic indignities inflicted on anyone being processed as just one more item in the New York City criminal justice system. She had been searched, all pride stripped away by impersonal matrons as they made their inspection. She had been fingerprinted and photographed. She had suffered the vulgar jibes of other prisoners and jail employees as she made her journey through the penal maze; celebrity status enjoyed no privilege in the stone and steel of the cells.

Victoria had studied the justice system in law school. It seemed so logical, so ordered; at least that's how the law books made it sound. As a practicing lawyer, Victoria had never been involved in the criminal courts. Now that logical, ordered system she had studied seemed chaotic, frightening and designed to destroy.

The system, vast and computerized, had no machinery to distinguish between the class, color, economic circumstances or educational background of its customers. Prostitute or princess, it made no difference—the system ground along, processing a seemingly endless stream of humanity.

Enos Peacock had retained Albert Baron, the best criminal defense lawyer in New York, to defend her. But despite Peacock's impressive reputation and Baron's knowledge of the system, it still took over an hour before a judge set bail.

Victoria was dressed in clothes brought from her apartment by Enos Peacock. Her maid had selected an outfit suitable for a public execution. Somehow the woman had managed to choose the dreariest dark navy Bill Blass suit in her closet and mismatched it with a taupe Nipon shirt.

A clamoring army of newsmen and cameras crushed in upon them as they exited the criminal courtroom. Hands reached out to stop her, microphones were jabbed at her face as a jumble of voices shouted questions. Victoria thought she was beyond fright, but the pressing mass of frantic people terrorized her. She clung close behind Baron and Pea-

239

cock, who, together with some policemen, forced a path through the pushing, shoving tumult.

Her world seemed reduced to one continuing nightmare.

They finally reached the safety of Judge Peacock's limousine and sped away from the crowd that had followed them out to Centre Street.

For the first time since it all had begun, Victoria cried.

Judge Peacock put a comforting arm around her shaking shoulders. "I think it best, Victoria, if you stayed with my wife and me for a few days." His voice was gentle, but commanding.

It took her a few moments to compose herself. She looked out at the night scene as they passed through Little Italy. Everyone seemed so happy. She shook her head.

"Thanks, Judge, but I can't take any time off. I have a business to run, things that have to be done."

Peacock patted her shoulder, as one might that of a child. "At the moment, Victoria, your presence would only make things worse. As you can imagine, your arrest will be front-page news. It's the job of the media to get the story. If they know where you are, they will hound you." He paused. "Also, all this will give fuel to the people who were already calling for your ouster. Now they will come after you in full cry."

"But I'm innocent," she protested hotly. "Those drugs weren't mine."

"I have no doubt of that," Peacock said dryly, "but innocence or guilt makes little difference at the moment. Like it or not, this is one of the year's biggest news stories. At a time like this, the best tactic is to hide, at least for a while. It helps cool things down a bit."

Albert Baron sat next to Peacock. A middle-aged man with silver hair, he had remained quiet. Now he spoke, his voice deep and gravelly, a voice perfectly suited to addressing juries. "Miss Van Horn, the judge is quite right. Despite the law, people do tend to think anyone who is arrested is guilty of the charge. That's not true in a courtroom, as you know, but that's the public's general attitude. Our fight will be not only in the law courts, but also in the newspapers. We have to find a way to reverse this whole matter."

"How?" she asked in a voice filled with defeat.

Baron's expressive face looked especially solemn. "If those drugs weren't yours, then they had to belong to Congressman Lytle. It's as simple as that."

"They were his," she said firmly. "I saw him use the cocaine."

Baron nodded. "Unfortunately, at this point it's only your word against his. Obviously, whoever sold it to him isn't about to rush forward. Somehow we'll find a way to prove the truth." His tone reflected his lack of optimism. "These cases are always difficult."

"What can we do?"

Baron's eyes narrowed as he considered the possibilities. "First, talk to no one about the case unless you clear it with me. Don't think your legal training will protect you. You're human, the same as the rest of us, and words can be twisted. And I'll have my office start an in-depth check of Lytle. We may come up with something."

"If you don't, will I be convicted?" For the first time there was genuine fear in her voice.

Baron slowly shook his head. "I doubt it. They haven't much of a case. It's just Lytle's word against yours and your previous history is spotless. And there's something very odd about that search and arrest, too. It's not your acquittal in the courtroom that worries me."

"What do you mean?"

Enos Peacock spoke. "You're good copy, Victoria. The press will have a field day with this. It has all the elements: people in high places, a beautiful woman, drugs; it's the kind of thing some editors dream about. You see, my dear, Mr. Baron is quite right: just being acquitted isn't good enough. Somehow we have to demonstrate to the public, beyond any legalities, that you are completely innocent, one hundred percent."

"But that will take time. My business has to be . . ."

"Victoria," Peacock cut her off in midsentence, "I think you have to face up to some rather unpleasant realities."

"What do you mean?"

"The board of Van Horn Enterprises will have to demand your resignation. If you refuse, they must vote you out. No matter what the final result of this episode, at the moment you are notorious and a definite liability to the company. They have no other choice."

"That's not fair."

Peacock nodded. "Unfortunately, that's true of so much in life, my dear. I agree it's unfair, but they'll have to get rid of you, and quickly. I imagine Van Horn stock will dip seriously tomorrow on the basis of the newspaper reports. The market is a very delicate instrument, and it reacts to the slightest provocation. In order to restore confidence in management, the board has to act immediately. They have to protect the value of the stock. You're a businesswoman, I'm sure you can appreciate their position."

"I suppose Junior will take over. Well, at least he'll be happy."

Peacock shook his head. "Junior is a mere dupe. Someone else is using him, pulling his strings. Whoever it is won't need your brother any-more."

"I never wanted to head the company. Now, at least, I'll be free to run my own development." They were passing shoppers strolling past the international stores of midtown Manhattan. Victoria watched them with envy. They looked as if they didn't have a care in the world. "That's a plus, I suppose."

Peacock cleared his throat, as if dreading what he was about to say. "That's another area where you can expect trouble, I'm afraid."

"Why? I own my business. I'm my own board of directors."

Peacock's usual stern expression seemed to soften. "I understand you've pledged almost everything you own as security for your new pro-ject, is that right?"

"Yes. What difference does that make?"

He seemed to hold her just a bit tighter, as if guarding her against the effect of what he had to say. "Bankers are very conservative people, as you know. I rather think they'll try to foreclose on the mortgages, using today's incident as a reason."

"They can't! I haven't missed a payment. I'm not in default!" Victoria realized she was shouting.

Peacock sighed. "I haven't seen the documents, of course, but any good draftsman will usually insert a clause protecting the investment if good cause can be shown that it's threatened. That's rather standard procedure. Do you recall such a clause?"

"Yes. As you say, it's standard language. I never contemplated any-thing like this." She slowly shook her head. "Then I'll lose everything?" she asked quietly.

Again Peacock patted her shoulder awkwardly. He was obviously unac-customed to any display of emotional support. "As far as the security pledge, it's a distinct possibility. But not all is lost."

"It sure sounds that way to me."

"You're still a lawyer. They won't disbar you unless you're convicted. And you still have the stock your father left. Unless the Van Horn company collapses, you're still an enormously wealthy young woman. When all this blows over, you'll have a very solid base upon which to begin again."

"This will never blow over, never completely, Judge." They were passing the elegant apartment buildings bordering Central Park. It all looked so peaceful. "After this, do you honestly think anyone would ever again take me seriously? I worked very hard to earn my place, but that's gone now. Everything I've done won't matter. They'll only remember the headlines."

There was an uncomfortable silence in the car. What Victoria said was true, and both Peacock and Baron knew it.

Cecelia Van Horn agreed to pay an outrageous price for the small Monet watercolor, fifty thousand more than it was really worth. Despite the price, she considered it a bargain. The money really wasn't payment for the painting anyway, it was to purchase Driker's information. Cecelia would have paid directly, but the dapper little man insisted on doing it his way; getting his money from the exorbitant price paid to Pelegrine for second-rate artwork. Enrico Pelegrine, she knew, was getting only his normal commission, but she was introducing him to sexual adventures that even that worldly and robust Italian never suspected existed—she considered both men well rewarded for their services.

When she returned to the apartment she found Junior at his desk in his study intently writing, his pen flying along the lined paper. She knew he would resent her intrusion into his den; it was his exclusive place. They had no formal agreement, it was just something that was understood.

He looked up, surprised and annoyed as she entered.

"What is it?"

She smiled and sat on a chair near the desk. The dress fell open, as it was designed to do, but he failed to exhibit even a flicker of interest.

"I have a bit of news." She lit a cigarette, aware that smoking also annoyed him. But she felt playful. She enjoyed his expression of disapproval as she exhaled a long stream of smoke. "What are you writing, a letter?"

He scowled. "What is this news you claim to possess?"

"It's about Victoria. But then, perhaps you're not interested."

"Damn you, Cecelia. Please stop these silly games of yours and tell me what you know."

She laughed. "It seems the members of the Vault met but didn't invite your sister. A sort of executive session, they called it."

"How do you know this?"

"Never mind my source, it's valid enough," she said. "They want her out. And all this was even before her arrest. So I think you can forget worrying that the Vault might take her side. They're going to toss her out." She inhaled deeply and expelled another cloud of smoke. "She deserves it, the bitch."

He laid down his pen, then turned to face her. "That's very important news. More than you know."

"Oh?"

"You asked what I'm writing. I'm preparing my acceptance speech. The board of directors of Van Horn Enterprises is meeting tomorrow. Chilton Vance says they will oust Victoria and name me as president. And, by the way, all this also happened before she got herself arrested."

"Junior, that's wonderful!" Cecelia's enthusiasm was sincere. Now it would come flowing to her after all, everything she wanted, the prestige, the social leadership, it would all be hers. She felt exultant.

"Oh, there's one other thing. Do we own much property in New York City?"

"Some. Why?"

"The Vault members are planning to sell their New York holdings. They plan to leave the city."

"What?"

"They're convinced Manhattan is all through as a city, even as a center of commerce. They are moving their businesses too. I thought if we have any real estate here we should get rid of it fast. If they go, this place will sink, foreign money or not. Anyway, I prefer Palm Beach. There's so much more of interest happening there. And that's where everyone seems to be going, the people who count."

Junior frowned. "This business about moving out of New York sounds ridiculous. Are you sure you have it straight?"

She stood up and looked down at him. He was such a bore, everything about him seemed to be shaded gray. She preferred colorful men. "The information is accurate. You can do what you wish, but I thought you might be glad to hear how the Vault regards your sister."

He nodded. "I am." He made an attempt at a smile. "Thank you, Cecelia."

She shrugged. "I've been busy and I've worked up a tremendous thirst. You go ahead and finish your little speech. I need a drink."

She left him in the study. If things went well, even if they stayed married, they wouldn't have to see much of each other: just another convenient arrangement. She would prefer that. And she could continue as she always had, perhaps with just a bit more discretion—she wouldn't want to be disgraced, to be splashed across the nation's front pages like her sister-in-law. Cecelia would be quite content at being photographed exclusively for the society pages.

That was where she properly belonged, and where, from now on, she would stay.

First, Cecelia prepared a martini, then she called Eric Vogeldorf. She decided she merited a little reward herself.

———————

Cecil Driker knew exactly, to the penny, just how much of the museum's money he could lay his hands on. He even planned to dip into the Habermann's operating funds. That, combined with the several million available to him from the museum's trust for purchase and repair of artworks, came to a nice round sum: just a fraction under six million dollars. He wished it could have been more, but it would just have to do. Time was of the essence.

Enrico Pelegrine met him at Flood's. It was an airy, pleasant restaurant, and Driker asked for a table at the back. It was early, the dinner crowd had not begun to come in, so they had the place almost to themselves.

Driker ordered a good wine. Pelegrine seemed quiet. Although he had earned substantial commissions as part of Driker's scheme, the Italian seemed almost depressed.

"I wish to purchase some more of your paintings," Driker said, "for the museum."

Pelegrine's eyes narrowed suspiciously, although he managed a professional smile. "I'm delighted, of course. Which ones did you have in mind?"

Driker sipped the wine. It was excellent. He loved true luxury; it always made him feel so good, so confident and relaxed. "The Corot you showed me, for one."

"Ah, you always have the great eye," Pelegrine said. "It is one of his finest works."

Driker sneered. "It is one of his worst, and we both know it. He was in his teens when he painted it. It's no more than an exercise canvas."

Pelegrine's face took on a professional solemnity. "I would argue that, of course. But even if you were correct in your assessment, his name alone makes it worth a great deal."

"How much?" Driker asked.

Pelegrine hated setting a price without preliminary negotiation. It seemed shocking to set a price so early, like sex without foreplay. It was crude. "His use of light and shadow . . ."

"Enrico, I asked how much."

"I represent a client, who owns the painting, as you know. The owner is an Italian nobleman. He is . . ."

"How much?"

Pelegrine sighed. This way, it was like selling fish. He set a price in his head—one the owner would like—then doubled it. "Two hundred thousand," he said, his voice sounding quite insincere even to himself.

"I'll pay half a million."

"Oh, I can't possibly . . . what?"

Driker's small mouth curled into a wry smile. "A half million, my dear Enrico. Of course, your client will see only one hundred thousand of that. I'll pocket the difference. And I'm sure your client will be delighted to pay you your commission."

"One hundred thousand? And the rest is kicked back to you?"

"Of course. After you take your share, obviously."

Perspiration began to dampen Pelegrine's face. "Listen, I have a reputation. I can't . . ."

Driker's eyes were like slits, his words almost a hiss. "Your reputation is extremely fragrant, Enrico, as we both know. Despite that, I will pay you a third of what I get. You will come out a hundred thousand to the good. That should help soothe any abrasions to your delicate good name."

Pelegrine's dubious expression reflected his uneasiness. "Cecil, where are you getting all this money?"

Driker frowned. "That's my business, but it is, I assure you, quite legitimate."

"You realize, of course, that kickbacks can be considered a criminal offense?"

"A questionable practice perhaps, but not criminal. Other museum directors often overpay for art. It's subjective, a matter of judgment. If my appraisal of value is proven wrong someday, so what?"

"You'll be fired, for one thing."

Driker finished his wine, then signaled the waiter for more. "I'll be leaving the museum soon. Of my own free will, by the way."

"That could be a bad move. They always do an audit under those circumstances, as I'm sure you know."

Driker felt expansive. "The Habermann is controlled by a very exclusive group of wealthy men." He was about to add a woman, but soon that would be no longer true. "They are planning to disband the museum. Therefore, I doubt any serious audit will be done."

"Still, it is a risk."

"Perhaps. If it bothers you, I can always find someone else to handle sales to the museum. I shall be buying other artwork, by the way."

"More?"

"Yes."

"Under the same, er, circumstances?"

Driker smiled. "Exactly, my dear Enrico. I shall be spending almost six million dollars. If you cooperate, you could possibly earn nearly a million in commissions. However, if all this truly offends you . . ."

Pelegrine's sweaty face split into a grin for the first time. "Please! A risk implies something wagered, doesn't it? Well, when the stakes are that high, an intelligent man will take a greater risk than he might normally."

"Then you'll supply me as I wish?"

Pelegrine stood up and reached out for Driker, awkwardly embracing him despite Driker's efforts to wiggle free. "My dear Cecil, for that kind of money, I'd go over Niagara Falls in a barrel. You have, as they say in this country, a deal."

The Italian released Driker, then picked up his glass, almost shattering it as he toasted their agreement.

"Here is to a most delightful and profitable arrangement!"

Driker hated public shows. He scowled. "I'd appreciate it if you didn't advertise it all over town." He nodded toward the waiters. "What we do must be kept as secret as the . . ."

"The grave!" Pelegrine said loudly, raising his glass once more.

"A rather inappropriate comparison," Driker snapped. "But it must be secret. If not, the risk will become a certainty."

"I understand entirely. When do we begin these transactions?"

"Within the next few days. We must move quickly."

Pelegrine grinned. "For each transaction I shall need a check for the true owner, certified, of course."

"Of course."

"And as for my commission, I should like cash."

Driker frowned. "Cash might be awkward."

Pelegrine chuckled. "Not if one had to leave town suddenly. After all, we really shouldn't keep any record of these transactions between you and me. Canceled checks have an ugly way of turning up at the wrong time. Yes, I think it must be cash."

Driker's mouth became a thin angry line. "You don't trust me?"

"Do you trust me?" Pelegrine grinned.

Driker sighed. "All right. Cash it will be."

Pelegrine raised his glass once more, then drained it with lip-smacking pleasure. "Cecil, we shall make a great team. We will do all this in grand style."

Driker looked at the big grinning man. For the first time he began to question the ultimate wisdom of his plan.

All the newspapers had given the pictures front-page coverage. The *New York Times* carried the photograph of Lytle and the Van Horn girl as they were led to the waiting police car. She was covered in that shot.

Mayor Felder went from the diplomatic reception to an Irish wake, and then returned to Gracie Mansion. He was delighted with himself. It had all worked out, even beyond his wildest hopes.

The other papers, especially the tabloid with the exclusive, weren't as charitable as the *Times*. The tabloid's entire front page was the photograph of the congressman in bed with the girl. Her bare breasts had been blacked out with printed strips that only served to make the picture even more shocking and titillating.

If Barry Lytle had been the only obstacle barring his way to the Senate, Al Felder now had a nice clear road.

Felder called Ace Myers, the Brooklyn political boss. "I take it you saw the newspapers?"

"Telephones can be tapped," Myers replied coldly. "You had better be careful what you say. If what you are referring to turns out to be a frame, it will be hung around a certain party's neck. If that happens, that person should plan on spending the rest of his life in Thailand, or some other faraway place. Got it?"

"Hey, Ace, relax! I had nothing to do with any of that shit. That's why I can make this call. Lytle got caught snorting some coke and getting some ass. I can't take credit for that, can I?"

There was a pause. "And you had better not. If somehow the congressman should beat this and show it was something else, like a frame, the public is going to scream for scalps. This kind of shit, if that's what it was, is like pissing into the wind; it has a way of blowing back at you."

"You worry too much. God, what's happening out there in Brooklyn, is everyone becoming paranoid?"

Again there was a pause. "Lytle's old man is on the Vault." The words were spoken quickly, as if just to say them was painful. "If this turns out to be something other than a straight deal, forces like you can't even imagine will come down on you like an atomic bomb."

Felder laughed, but he no longer felt so triumphant. "Jesus! I thought you'd be overjoyed. He was the main Republican opponent, wasn't he?"

"Yeah. This will end that. But just remember, if you poke a bear with a stick, you may get more attention than you want."

"Ace, you worry too much."

"And maybe you don't worry enough."

Felder was about to reply when Myers hung up.

He replaced his own receiver, got up and walked to the window. But the beautiful view of the river failed to soothe him. He assured himself that nothing could go wrong. They had the goods on Lytle, even if he did claim the drugs belonged to the girl. If things started to look bad, they could always leak the information about his previous hospitalizations for drug abuse.

It was that damn Van Horn girl. If only she hadn't been involved. It made for better copy, but he was suddenly worried about the price to be paid.

Myers was getting to be an old lady. So the Vault was involved, so what? Al Felder was still the mayor. What could the Vault do anyway?

He knew it. Myers knew it. They could destroy him, that's what.

21

Luke Shaw joined his father in the main lounge of the Oseola Club. Meant for large gatherings, something that never happened at the club anymore, the room was usually deserted. Most members preferred the cozy smaller lounge. Although cavernous, the empty main lounge was the perfect place for a private conversation.

Preston Shaw started to struggle from the giant leather chair. Luke restrained him by shaking hands. He took a seat in a matching chair.

"Your message sounded urgent," Luke said.

"I hope I didn't take you away from anything important."

"Nothing that won't keep." He had been reviewing final specifications on a job beginning in the morning. It still would have to be done. He found the interruption annoying. "What's up?"

"I've been following the story about young Lytle and the Van Horn girl."

"You and the rest of the world. It's on the front page all over."

"That's why I called you here. I'm concerned about that girl."

"Are you serious?" Luke sat back. "It seems to me you were the one who warned me about Victoria Van Horn. Something, as I recall, about her being a Magnusson woman; hot-blooded and all that."

"Which could account for her being in that hotel room with young Lytle. Passionate: the whole bunch of them. However, that aside, she seems to be an outstanding young lady, too ambitious perhaps, but obviously talented."

"I was to do some work on her new river project," Luke said. "I have to admit she's knowledgeable, but a bit too forceful for my tastes. She's known for hard work, a real dynamo. Maybe she's been using drugs to keep herself going at that frantic pace."

"Then you think Lytle's right."

"What I think makes little difference, doesn't it? Besides, whether the cocaine belonged to her or not, she was probably snorting it anyway."

"What do you know about Barry Lytle?"

His son shrugged. "Not much. I'm acquainted with his father, the Ambassador. As I'm sure you know, he's a member of the Vault. Barry Lytle has the reputation of a middle-of-the-road Republican. I understand he planned to run for the Senate. This arrest will put an end to that ambition."

Preston Shaw nodded. "Don't you think that all this is just a trifle too convenient for anyone who might wish to contest that seat?"

"You aren't trying to say he was framed?"

Preston Shaw leaned back in the leather chair. He looked tired. "My friends—those few who are still alive—gossip. It's our only remaining vice. Like all gossips, we talk about people we know—the rich, the establishment families of New York City."

"So?"

His father pursed his lips, as if carefully planning the words he was about to speak. "Barry Lytle has been quite a trial to his father, from the time of childhood, I understand. His father has always guided his career. Stewart Lytle is an extremely competitive man, and he likes politics. He arranged his son's election to Congress, despite young Barry's problem."

"Problem?"

"Barry is a drug addict, and has been for years."

Luke laughed. "Come on. I certainly would have heard something, if that were true."

"No, really, Luke. Stewart Lytle knows how to keep things quiet. He's had a lot of practice, and he's become quite good at it. But up here at the club, we know. After his son's last escapade, Stewart arranged to have him detoxed at a very exclusive local establishment. Barry, it seems, is quite a lady's man; absolutely charming, irresistible, or so they say. Anyway, a niece of one of our members—the poor girl is an alcoholic—was in there at the same time. It seems quite a torrid love affair bloomed in that tony drunk tank. It ended when he was discharged. The girl thought marriage was just over the horizon, but it was obvious that young Lytle was only using her, just a convenience for him, I suppose. I suspect the Van Horn girl's situation might be quite similar."

"That she was being used? Victoria Van Horn is an adult, a sharp businesswoman. I doubt she would allow herself to be tricked like that."

His father half smiled. "Ah, Luke, you know so much about so many things, but you are something of a boob when it comes to women."

His son laughed. "I've never claimed to be an expert in that field, but I don't think I can be classified as a boob, as you put it."

His father seemed to pay no attention to his reply. "Stewart Lytle probably desired a match between Victoria Van Horn and his son. A rich, famous and good-looking wife would be an asset to any national candidate. He may have set them up originally."

Luke Shaw listened. His father always seemed to display a surprisingly shrewd eye, no matter what the subject.

"Until she got tangled up with young Lytle, the girl's reputation was spotless, and impressive." Preston Shaw smiled sadly. "It's quite ironic. Instead of her usual publicity about building things, she's pictured for the first time enjoying herself, making the café rounds with the dashing young congressman. Then her brother charges her with being frivolous and incompetent. His lawsuit plus the pictures were like exploding dynamite."

Luke nodded. "Very damaging. As a matter of fact, because of all that she was going to be asked to resign from the Vault. Now, with her arrest, it's a foregone conclusion."

"But suppose she's truly innocent, Luke? Shouldn't that affect the outcome?"

Luke shook his head. "I suppose it depends on your definition of innocent. After all, she was up in that hotel room with Lytle. They were in bed. Drugs were out in the open. Innocence can be quite subjective."

His father chuckled. "I do believe you're jealous, Luke."

He felt himself coloring. "Not at all. Even if you're right and Lytle is a snake, and an addicted one, she should have known that."

"So she will get just what she deserves, is that it?"

Luke shrugged. "Victoria isn't some high school kid. She shouldn't have allowed herself to be caught in a web of circumstances."

His father's face became solemn. "From all I know about her, gathered from our rather effective gossip network, she is quite a normal young woman. I suspect she was searching for the right man, someone who could match her drive and abilities. At first blush, Barry Lytle would appear to fill the bill."

"Well, it seems she certainly picked the wrong card."

His father's smile vanished. "I submit to you that the Van Horn girl is one of us, our class, and of our background; she is in very deep trouble. She may be forceful and independent, as you say, but she appears to be honest, hardworking, and at the moment, very much alone."

Luke chuckled. "With the money her father left her, I think she can probably buy whatever she needs, including friendship."

"But can she buy back her honor? I think not."

Luke studied his father for a moment. "Perhaps not, but while she may lose everything she's earned on her own, she'll still be a rich woman, thanks to her father."

Preston Shaw snorted. "And what good is that? Where can she go? She's known the world over. She's a rather remarkable woman, not some empty-headed society girl. She deserves better. Something should be done to help her."

"And you want me to be the one to do it?"

Preston Shaw's eyes seemed to burn with intensity. "I think you should try. She merits your efforts. You're a member of the Vault; you have power, Luke. For heaven's sake, use it now for a good cause."

Luke was about to refuse, but he thought again of Victoria Van Horn. He recalled their argument on the pier. His father was right, she was an unusual woman.

Luke stood up. "I have to go, father. I'll do what I can. I can promise effort, but no results. Even a Vault member can't work miracles."

His father smiled warmly. "I'm pleased, Luke." He reached across and patted his son's hand. "I sincerely wish to see Miss Van Horn helped, but perhaps more than that, I would like to see you explore your own horizons. You may find them surprising."

It was a nice day, cloudy but not chilly. As Luke Shaw left the Oseola Club he walked along Fifty-seventh Street thinking about what his father had said.

Preston Shaw had given voice to thoughts that had been haunting Luke. Like his father, Luke had been worried about Victoria. He didn't really wish to be concerned, but he had to admit that he was. He realized that jealousy might have been the root of his failure to do anything. For some reason, just thinking about Victoria seemed both upsetting and compelling at the same time.

His father said Barry Lytle had a drug problem. Preston Shaw might have fashioned a remote existence for himself but he always surprised his son with his remarkably accurate knowledge of events and people. If the drugs belonged to Lytle, then Victoria was suffering a horribly unfair fate.

Luke crossed Fifth Avenue with a horde of other coatless people enjoying the soft weather and its promise of summer. He knew he should get back to his office, there was always so much to do. But normal work now seemed out of the question.

He called from an outside telephone. Victoria Van Horn wasn't in. The woman he spoke to sounded competent and professional, but Luke thought he detected more than just a note of concern in her voice when she spoke of Victoria. Victoria hadn't come in and no one seemed to know where she was. Luke told the woman he would call again.

He continued to walk, this time in the direction of his office. Luke promised his father he would do something to help, but he wondered if he was acting merely because of duty or because of something else.

Luke thought of how lovely Victoria was, and how interesting he found her. He hadn't seemed to have thought of anything but Victoria since their first stormy meeting. He made a firm decision to put such feelings aside; they were dangerous.

He would help her, but he resolved that his sole motivation would be duty, nothing more.

———

Joyce Spitz spent most of the day trying to contact Victoria to tell her that a special meeting of the board of directors was being convened, but with no success. Victoria had declined Enos Peacock's offer to stay at his apartment. He hadn't seen her since and she hadn't returned to her own place. The nervous maid reported that newsmen were laying siege there. Craig Hopkins told Joyce that Victoria hadn't gone to her other office. No one knew where she was.

A small squad of media types was camped in the executive waiting room. Local and national news services kept calling, all hoping to interview Victoria. Lucas Shaw had telephoned. Joyce presumed it was a business matter, although he did seem personally concerned, and very insistent on locating Victoria. He had subjected Joyce to vigorous questioning on where Victoria might have gone.

Enos Peacock called regularly, as did Eric Vogeldorf. They shared Joyce's growing anxiety over Victoria's disappearance.

Joyce watched as Hunter Van Horn, Jr., was escorted to Chilton Vance's office. The special board meeting and the appearance of Junior Van Horn, in Joyce's estimation, added up to only one possible conclusion. This would be Victoria's last day as president and chairman of the board.

It would be Joyce's last day too. This time she wouldn't be allowed to remain, even in the typing pool. Not that she would want to stay on.

Chilton Vance came down the hall and stepped into her office. "Any word from Miss Van Horn?"

She shook her head. "No."

He shrugged, as if that was really unimportant anyway. "Miss Spitz, as I recall, you take excellent shorthand, correct?"

"I'm pretty good."

"Since Miss Van Horn won't be here I'd like you to sit in on the board meeting, and make a verbatim record of everything said. This won't be for company purposes. As you know, we have both a stenographer and a recording system. But, in case of any doubt, I think Miss Van Horn would like an unquestionable report by someone she obviously trusts." He smiled, but his eyes were icy.

"I'll be happy to do that. When is the meeting?"

"Right now," he said. "In the boardroom. Oh, by the way, I'd like a minute of your time when the meeting is over."

Joyce knew what that meeting was for. She had already cleaned out her desk and sent the contents to her apartment. "I'll be right there."

She waited until he was gone, then tried Victoria's apartment once more. The maid, now nearly hysterical, still hadn't heard from her employer.

Joyce gathered some sharpened pencils and a steno pad, then walked down the long hall past the row of executive offices. They were all there, every board member but Victoria, all seated around the oblong board table, their expressions uniformly grim. Junior was seated near the head of the table, next to Chilton Vance.

Vance stood up and opened the meeting, rapidly going through the usual formalities. The board quickly sanctioned the special meeting.

Joyce, seated at the foot of the table, took down every word as Vance had requested. But she knew Vance's action wasn't out of kindness or consideration for Victoria; he wanted to ensure that the insult was recorded, and that Victoria would read every word.

Her pencil flew as she took down the heated speeches concerning Victoria's conduct and troubles. She was heartened that some of the board members who had been loyal to Hunter Van Horn were also loyal to his daughter. But they were in the minority. Most of the board was openly hostile toward their absent president. Victoria was described by a few as a prostitute and a dope addict. Some long-repressed hatred for her father poured out in the form of vilification of the daughter.

Joyce glanced several times at Junior. He looked as if he enjoyed hearing his sister's name smeared in the vilest terms. Joyce wished she could slap his smug face.

Finally, Chilton Vance, acting as chairman, cut off further debate.

Bradford Lewis, who Joyce knew was one of the directors friendly to Vance, stood up. "I wish to make a motion that Victoria Van Horn be removed from all offices in Van Horn Enterprises, effective immediately. She is a disgrace to herself and to this company."

Vance's face was impassive, giving no hint of his thoughts. "Without any further comments, is there a second to that motion?"

It was immediately seconded by another director who was friendly with Vance.

They voted quickly. Only two directors were opposed to the motion. Joyce jotted down their names. Victoria would want to know.

"Well, that's it," Vance said. "We are without a president and chairman of the board. Are there any nominations?"

"I nominate Hunter Van Horn, Jr.," one of the directors said.

Bradford Lewis stood up. "May I say something before any other nominations are made?"

"Any objections?" Vance asked.

Silence was his only answer. "Go ahead, Bradford."

Joyce thought she detected a slight sinister quality in Vance's voice, as if something secretly planned was about to be carried out. It seemed almost rehearsed. She looked at Junior. His smug expression seemed to become even more exaggerated.

Bradford Lewis made eye contact with each director before speaking. "I think this company is at a most crucial and dangerous crossroads. Like some of you, I've had some advance word on what we may expect when our various groups report. I understand it will not be good news. Not only the value of our stock but even our basic ability to do business may be greatly threatened if what I've heard is true. Allow me to be quite frank. I didn't think Victoria Van Horn was a suitable candidate in the first place. She didn't know the company, and, as we have seen, her character obviously leaves much to be desired. I felt so strongly about it that I approached Junior here," he nodded toward Junior Van Horn, who smiled in return, "to consider a move to unseat his sister and become president himself."

Lewis paused for a moment before continuing. "This was, of course, before all this unfortunate publicity about his sister. I still consider Junior to be a fine gentleman, and a businessman. However, I now believe we must distance ourselves from the stigma of his father, who, before his death, managed to run this company almost into the ground. And we must distance ourselves from the immoral reputation and conduct of his sister. In other words, despite our company name, I don't think we can afford to have a Van Horn at the helm at this time."

He looked down at Junior, whose face was no longer smug. "Nothing personal, old boy. We must think of the company first."

Lewis again searched the faces of the other directors. "We desperately need someone who Wall Street will recognize as a mature leader. We need someone who has been tested, and who has the necessary experience to save this company. I nominate Chilton Vance to be president and chairman of the board."

"Second," one of the other directors quickly called, as if on cue.

"What?" Junior's startled expression reflected his sudden confusion. "What's going on?" he blustered.

"I'm afraid you're out of order, Junior." Chilton Vance's tone was suddenly quite different, commanding and cold. "You're not a member of the board, so you haven't any official voice in these proceedings."

"What the hell do you mean, no voice?" He stared at Vance, then turned to the others. "I was to be your new president. I was told this meeting was only a formality."

Bradford Lewis had remained on his feet. He looked at Junior. "As I said, there's nothing personal in this, Junior. But everything has changed, literally overnight. Right now, because of what's happened, we can't afford to have any of your family members running this company. I should think that would be obvious. Actually, you benefit from our decision since you own a large block of stock. I know you want us to protect that. But to use an old movie line, this just isn't your night, Junior."

Joyce Spitz knew she should enjoy watching Junior brought down, but she felt only pity. He seemed to be coming apart. His facial muscles were jerking, and it looked as if he might burst into tears.

"You can't do this to me," he said, his voice rising. "The media will make me look like an idiot. They were told I was going to be named president. Now my lawsuit against my sister will make me appear like some vindictive fool."

Bradford Lewis looked at him with unconcealed disgust. "That's really not our affair, is it? We're charged with protecting the future of this company, and we must do what we think best. I'm not saying it's true, but at the moment, I'm afraid the public perceives you and your sister as two rich and very spoiled offspring of an indulgent father. If we appointed you, the public and the investors would think we were merely taking sides in this sordid affair between you and your sister. We'd be the ones who would look foolish."

Junior's mouth moved but words didn't come. His eyes were wide and wet. He stumbled to his feet, looked around in apparent panic, then rushed from the room.

There was an awkward silence. One of the directors got up and closed the door Junior had left open in his flight.

"My motion to elect Chilton Vance president and chairman of the board has been seconded. I call for a vote," Bradford Lewis said.

Joyce recorded the votes. The two Van Horn loyalists were the only ones opposed.

Chilton Vance's acceptance speech was designed to serve as a nice handout to the press; obviously prewritten, edited, and meant to appear on the nation's business pages the following day.

Joyce sat quietly while most of the directors crowded around Vance. He accepted their congratulations with a polite coolness. He was in charge now, and he wanted to make sure everyone knew it.

Joyce waited. Finally they left, and only Chilton Vance remained.

He sat at the head of the table. "Did you get all of that?"

"Yes."

"Please transcribe it immediately. I'd like a copy when you're finished."

He smiled, but again there was no warmth in his expression. "By the way, Joyce, speaking of being finished, you must realize that you are, at least with Van Horn Enterprises. This is your last day. You'll receive the usual two weeks' severance pay."

"I have vested rights here. I will bring action to protect them. You have no reason to fire me, and you know it." There was plenty of spirit in her voice.

His chuckle was without humor. "You can bring all the lawsuits you want. You can't hope to match the legal firepower of this giant corporation. I think you're smarter than that. The official reason for your termination will be poor work performance. Of course, we both know the real reason: you hitched your wagon to the wrong star. Even if I sent you back to the typing pool, I'd always feel the Van Horns had a spy on the inside. I'm afraid you have no friends at court."

"Mr. Vance, do you honestly think you'll get away with this?"

"Don't you?" He laughed quietly.

Joyce Spitz stood up. She felt no anger, and that surprised her. "Junior has no control over the stock; that belongs to Victoria exclusively. That block, together with only a few others, will be sufficient to vote out most of the directors at the next annual meeting. In fact, with the help of a lawsuit, perhaps even before then. A new board's first act will be to get rid of you, surely you realize that?"

His widening grin became a chuckle. "Your Victoria may be in prison when the next annual meeting is called, did you think of that? And any lawsuit she might bring now, given all the publicity, would be laughed out of court. I just loved those photographs of Victoria in bed with the congressman, didn't you? I must admit there is a possibility, however slight, that I might have to look for other employment after the next annual meeting. Maybe."

"There's no 'maybe' about it."

He shrugged. "You never know. This company is teetering on the brink of financial disaster. If I manage to save it, the other stockholders would raise hell with anyone trying to throw me out. I doubt if Victoria could stand that kind of heat." He laughed. "But I don't want you to worry about me, Joyce. The annual meeting is almost a year away. By that time I will have built up such a reputation that even if I am tossed out, every major company in America will be clamoring for my services." He gestured as if bestowing a blessing. "It's regrettable that you picked the wrong horse, but these things happen. As soon as you've finished typing up your notes, pack up your things and get out."

She returned to her office. A security guard stood at Victoria's office door, his embarrassment evident. "I'm sorry, Miss Spitz, but Mr. Vance says I'm not to let you into Miss Van Horn's office. You can use the typewriter at your desk; but that's all."

"What about the telephone?" she asked.

"Nothing was said about that. Use it if you want."

Joyce Spitz made several calls, but no one had yet heard from Victoria. She glanced at her watch. It was getting late, very late. Soon it would be dark. It seemed childish, but somehow the approach of night seemed to increase Joyce's feeling of dread.

Jon Krugar sat on his porch and idly watched the colorful water traffic. His body was old, but he had always retained the resiliency of a young mind. He accepted the necessity of change. He would miss Hong Kong.

First, there were arrangements to make, people to see. He found himself relishing the challenge.

Mr. Yee sat quietly in a chair a few feet away. Krugar turned and looked at him. "I shall need to go to New York," he said.

Yee merely nodded. "When?"

"As soon as possible. Please make the arrangements. I shall take two of my granddaughters and yourself." Krugar watched a bird skim close over the water. "It's been years since I was in New York. You know the city, Yee. Does the Sherry Netherland still stand?"

"Much has changed, but that hotel remains."

"Still good?"

Yee smiled gently. "Very nice. Very old, but still elegant. Would you wish to stay there?"

Krugar nodded. "I have fond memories of the place. We shall need adjoining suites, perhaps a floor."

"And the method of travel?"

Krugar chuckled. "I'd prefer a boat, but there isn't time. We have much to do. We'll fly. Charter a private jet, one with suitable comfort."

"As you wish," Yee replied.

Krugar took out a cigar and sniffed it. "Does that distant New York relative of yours still live, the one-armed man with the fragrant reputation and the rather, ah, interesting connections?"

"No Wing Moy, my cousin," Yee said, "is in good health and prospers. I shall contact him and alert him to your arrival."

Krugar nodded. "Good."

Yee stood up. "How long shall we be staying?"

Krugar looked up at him; his eyes seemed to pierce the smoke. "That, my dear Yee, will depend on the outcome of a number of things. It may be a short stay, or something considerably longer. What is to happen is in the laps of the gods."

Yee smiled gently. "We seek our fate, then?"

Krugar's huge body shook as his rumbling chuckle echoed across the wide porch. "That, Yee, is what life is all about."

Cecelia had demanded that he come to her party to celebrate Junior's election as company president. Eric Vogeldorf usually enjoyed small cocktail parties, but there was an unpleasant flavor of danger connected with this one. The party was a surprise for her husband. Since Eric had been sleeping with Cecelia, he supposed his invitation was some womanly gesture of revenge upon her husband for neglect, real or imagined. He was one of seven who had been invited. Two women, lovely and well dressed, came to the party together. As promising targets in his quest for a rich wife, Eric attempted conversation, only to discover that while they were indeed well off, they were obviously interested only in each other. The others were two couples who were friends of the Van Horns. They seemed almost interchangeable, good tans, good tennis bodies, and a certain disdainful air that seemed to proclaim they had never had to sully their well-manicured hands with work, and never planned to. One of the women shamelessly flirted with Vogeldorf. Her husband noticed but seemed entirely indifferent.

The Van Horns' apartment was decked out in racing silks, complete with the traditional wreath of roses presented to a winner. A gaudy banner, suspended from the ceiling, proclaimed congratulations.

Vogeldorf know he was drinking the Dom Pérignon a bit too fast, but it helped curb his anxiety. This would be his first meeting with Junior Van Horn and he considered it embarrassing to meet the husband of a lover. It had happened before, usually by accident. On those occasions, if Vogeldorf discovered he liked the man, he found the encounter depressing and guilt-producing.

He slipped away to use the phone in Van Horn's study. He called once again to see if Victoria had been located. He knew how Cecelia felt about her sister-in-law, so he had to make the calls in secret. Joyce Spitz told him there still was no word.

Vogeldorf took an extra moment to look around at Van Horn's den. It had a spartan look, with just a few bookcases filled with fancy leather-covered books, more for show than use. A small desk contained a compact home computer and a telephone. A large seascape was the only wall decoration. He studied the painting; he had been trained to know good art. An original by a well-known American, it would be valued at more than a quarter million, he knew. Van Horn could well afford it, he thought. Vogeldorf, who had become an expert in evaluating other people's wealth, estimated Junior's fortune at close to a quarter billion. If

Cecelia did divorce her husband, the settlement would make her the perfect candidate to become Mrs. Eric Vogeldorf.

When he rejoined the party Cecelia was laughing a bit too loudly. The possibility that she might be becoming drunk, and possibly indiscreet, made him even more anxious.

Vogeldorf had just accepted another glass of champagne from the maid as Junior Van Horn entered. He recognized him from pictures. He had even made love to Cecelia in Junior's bed one night when Van Horn was out of town. That had been Cecelia's idea. Women, Vogeldorf thought, could sometimes be such nasty little savages.

Van Horn stood in the doorway, his eyes moving slowly over the banner and the other decorations. His guests began to applaud.

Cecelia threw her arms around him. "Congratulations, darling!" she said brightly, kissing him despite his obvious reluctance.

He tried to push her away, his cheeks suddenly flaming. "This, I take it, was your idea?"

She beamed. "Yes. How does it feel to be the head of Van Horn Enterprises?"

"I really don't know, Cecelia. You'll have to ask Chilton Vance." Although Junior's voice was steady, he seemed to be developing a twitch below one eye.

"What do you mean?"

He made an attempt to smile, but it flickered out. "Business, as the saying goes, can be a jungle. The board didn't want anyone from my family in control. They felt it might adversely affect stock prices. So they chose Vance."

"My God!" Cecelia shrieked. "What are you going to do about it?!"

He studied her with cool detachment, even though they were almost chin to chin. "There's not a great deal I can do about it, my dear."

"You asshole!" she screamed. "You flaming asshole! Be a man for once, smash your enemies!"

He half smiled, then sighed. "For once, Cecelia, you just may be right."

Vogeldorf sensed a peculiar note in Van Horn's voice, something like a warning signal. He put down his glass and tried to hurry forward.

"I agree I should do something," Junior went on, his smile becoming almost dreamy. "I think I'll start with you."

Vogeldorf was just a split second too late. Junior landed a quick left hook to his wife's jaw. She lurched back a step, then sat down hard on the thick carpeting.

Vogeldorf meant only to step between them, but in so doing he jostled Van Horn, who was already off balance. Junior stumbled, then he too fell to the carpeting.

"If you've broken my jaw again I'll kill you!" she screamed, holding her face with both hands.

Junior looked up at Vogeldorf. "You must be that German chap she's fucking," he said quietly, almost pleasantly. "You'd be doing me a great favor if you'd get her out of here."

Cecelia struggled to her feet, her eyes narrowed in hate. "You goddamned useless worm, I've had it with you! I'm going to divorce you. I'll take you for everything you own!"

Van Horn appeared almost comfortable sitting on the carpeting. He smiled up at her. "Whatever it costs, getting rid of you will be more than worth the price."

Vogeldorf didn't know what to do. Everyone else in the room stood as still as if they had been turned to stone.

"Perhaps it would be best if we left," he said to Cecelia.

"I'll get some things," she snapped, then stalked from the room.

Vogeldorf waited until she had disappeared, then he offered a hand to Junior, who seemed grateful to be helped up.

Eric Vogeldorf had been trained to remain calm no matter how embarrassing the social situation. "I'm sorry to meet you under these, er, circumstances," he said.

"Me too," Junior replied. He looked at the other guests. "I realize all this is quite shocking, but you're invited to stay, if you like."

Suddenly the remaining guests remembered other pressing engagements. Vogeldorf quickly escorted Cecelia from the apartment before anything else erupted.

He helped her into a cab, then gave the cabbie his address. "How's your jaw?"

She leaned against him and squeezed his arm. "It's sore, but not broken. I think you're wonderful, you know."

"Oh?"

"Knocking him down like that after he struck me. Not too many men would do something like that. You really are my shining knight."

He was about to explain he had merely touched Junior who was on his way down anyway, but thought better of it. Vogeldorf's mind worked like a computer.

He took her hands and gently kissed them. "Cecelia, you need someone to protect you. After your divorce, I would like you to become my wife."

Her eyes suddenly passionate, she drew him to her and kissed him, and, at the same time, reached down and began to gently massage his crotch. "Mrs. Eric Vogeldorf," she whispered. "That has a nice ring to it."

He knew what he was getting. She was beautiful, but she was promiscuous and a drunk. He would be sharing her with friends, servants and even strangers. But she would come away from the divorce with at least a third of Junior's fortune; something close to one hundred million. All in all, some allowances had to be made.

22

Victoria Van Horn kept walking. She had walked aimlessly since morning. She could think of nothing else to do. Incapable of any other thought or plan, she moved along, barely aware of other walkers in the continuing stream of sidewalk traffic. She found a sense of solace in the sounds of New York; the cacophony of horns, voices, construction machines; the rising throb of noise seemed endless. She realized she had walked all the way to Battery Park. She paused to watch the water traffic.

She tried to assess her situation. Her life had suddenly collapsed, and there seemed to be no future. She couldn't muster the will to even consider alternatives. Everything seemed too painful to confront.

She turned and began walking once more, headed back toward midtown Manhattan, but with no specific destination or purpose. Once again she concentrated on the physical act of putting one foot in front of the other, thinking of nothing else. She was only dimly aware of the areas she passed through. It was getting late, but time meant nothing. Walking was like dreaming, with no present or end.

She hadn't eaten and had no desire to do so. Darkness had come and the streetlights had been turned on. She kept walking, as if to stop might propel her back into her own personal nightmare.

At first, she had failed to recognize the area or even realize she was close to the Hudson River. Then she found herself moving toward the old waterfront buildings that were to have been the site of her proud new development.

She passed a seedy bar. A group of young men standing near the open door called lewdly to her. She didn't even notice them. Two of them began to follow but abandoned their pursuit as a police car came cruising lazily down the street.

As if drawn by a force she didn't understand, she turned down the narrow street and recognized the old Sperry warehouse. She was alone.

She returned to the hole in the fence. The streetlight enabled her to see well enough to climb through. She moved through the rubble like a sleepwalker.

The night seemed to accentuate the odor of the river. There was no light and she had to pick her way along the abandoned pier.

Like a graveyard, it was a place that belonged to the dead past, a place of memories, and perhaps sorrow for things lost. It could have been so different, so wonderful. But that dream was over.

She moved past the building out onto the part of the pier that extended into the river. A huge ship glided by, the reflection of its running lights shimmering on the surface of the dark water.

She dimly became aware of soft sounds behind her. She remembered the rat and quickly turned.

As her eyes adjusted to the gloom, she saw shapes, or thought she saw them, between herself and the abandoned warehouse building. They were large and moving at an odd shuffling gait, converging toward her.

"Who is it?" she called out guardedly.

Her only reply was a guttural obscenity. She took a step backward, almost falling as she caught her heel on a broken board.

They continued to move toward her. Victoria wondered if she might be hallucinating, perhaps losing her mind. The shapes were too large to be animals, yet they didn't look human. They advanced slowly and awkwardly.

Something came whistling through the air and she ducked instinctively. An angry grunt of disappointment came from the shapes.

"Get out of here," a voice rasped. "Go away!"

"Drown the cunt!" An angry growl came from one of the advancing shadows. "Throw her ass in the river."

Victoria turned and tried to run but fell, landing painfully on her hands and knees. Her heart was thudding as fear seized her.

"You scummy cunt." The raspy voice spoke again. "You got no business here."

She stumbled to her feet. A steel-like claw gripped her arm. A cloud of rotten breath choked her as a whisper sounded in her ear. "We're goin' to feed you to the fuckin' rats!"

She screamed.

Suddenly a flashlight beam played over the things that surrounded her. Illuminated, they seemed even more frightening. They were filthy, dressed in mounds of rags. She couldn't tell if they were men or women. Some had no teeth. They blinked as they tried to avoid the light.

"Let her go!" a strong male voice snapped. "Get back to your god-damned holes. Now!"

They scurried away, scrambling toward the darkness of the warehouse, their voices an angry muttering babble.

"You're rather difficult to find, Victoria," Luke Shaw's voice came out of the darkness. She felt faint as he grabbed her and pulled her to him. "Relax," he said gently, "they were just trying to scare you. Let's get out of here." He led the way back toward the street, holding her and using the flashlight to light their way.

"What were they?" she asked in a whisper, afraid they might reappear if she spoke too loudly.

"They're your tenants," he said.

"What do you mean?" she asked, trembling uncontrollably.

"Poor crazy people. Bag women, bums, psychopaths, they live here at night."

"But the rats . . ."

"It's a tough world, Victoria. The city has shelters, inadequate per-haps, but available. These people, most of them insane, prefer living here. At night, this is their home. You were trespassing."

He helped her through the fence. Three young boys, just entering their teens, lounged near his Mercedes. They looked at Shaw, then at the long-handled metal flashlight. As if having made a silent assessment of their chances, without a word spoken between them, they turned and walked away.

"It's as tough out here on the street as it is back there," he said, "and probably a hell of a lot more dangerous."

He helped her into the car. Every joint in her body now seemed an aching agony. Even her feet throbbed. Luke quickly got behind the wheel, locked the doors and started the car.

"You look like hell," he said, looking over at her. "Where have you been?"

She felt so tired, nothing seemed important, not even the pain. "I've been walking."

"All day?"

"Yes."

He guided the car through the dark streets, then turned on Forty-second Street, blending with the moving traffic, past the seedy glitter and the staring, suspicious faces.

"I'll take you to my place. With some food, a bath and some sleep, you'll be as good as new."

He turned to look at her when she made no response.

She was already asleep.

As usual, Sander Blake began his morning with coffee and the newspaper. For him, the major story of the day was on page one of the business section. He avidly read the article, an in-depth report of the purge of Victoria Van Horn from the management of Van Horn Enterprises.

Any experienced businessman like Blake would read between the lines of Vance's acceptance statement and know he was encouraging a bid for a takeover by another company. It was a clever move, Blake thought; a buyout would allow Vance to escape the revenge of the Van Horns and he could write his own ticket with the new owners.

The article was highlighted with a photograph of Victoria and young Lytle. The details of their arrest were repeated once again.

Blake felt sorry for Victoria. He wished he didn't have to deliver the Vault's request for her resignation. On top of everything else that was happening to her, this seemed particularly cruel.

Blake reread the story, thought for a moment, then dialed the editor in chief of his weekly news magazine.

To Harry Westlake, the editor, a call from Sander Blake was not unlike a direct call from God. Blake paid very well, but he expected a high standard of performance. Failure meant instant dismissal.

Westlake never felt entirely secure, despite the magazine's fast-growing circulation and its surging challenge to *Time* and *Newsweek*. He was on a first name basis with Blake, but his telephone calls still worried him.

"You're up early, Sander." Westlake hoped he sounded cheerful and confident. "What can I do for you?"

"What have we found out about Victoria Van Horn's arrest? I wonder if everything was really on the up and up."

Westlake was instantly relieved. Only ten minutes before he had talked to the investigative reporter assigned to the story. It was an ideal situation to score some points with the boss.

"You should go into the crystal ball business, Sander. You're right on the money. Something's very fishy. The New York narcotic cops didn't make that arrest. The policemen who did belong to a special squad assigned to the mayor. That's very peculiar for starters. Then there's Congressman Lytle; he looks good on paper, but there's a rumor in Washington that he's got a drug problem. We're checking, of course, but if it all turns out to be true, it certainly looks like the Van Horn girl may be taking a very bad rap."

"What's this mayor's squad?"

"It's a special outfit. Some mayors do away with it, some use it as a kind of personal guard service. Felder, we suspect, has the cops acting as a sort of local CIA, loyal only to him." Westlake chuckled. "Sander, you New Yorkers sure elect some very colorful people."

"It's a failing of long standing. Harry, I have something of a personal interest in what's going on. Could you keep me advised? I'm particularly interested in discovering who might be behind all this, if that turns out to be the case."

"Your wish, as you know, is my command. How much muscle do you want us to put into this?"

"Pull out all the stops. Make it a major effort, Harry. Also, have your business writers dig a little into this Van Horn purge. It may all be tied together."

"If we go all out, our esteemed rivals will be alerted. We'll lose any chance at an exclusive."

"Let me worry about that," Blake replied. "Harry, you're experienced in this sort of thing. Based on what you know so far, what's your opinion?"

"I can't say definitely yet, but something sure smells rotten. If something's wrong, Sander, we'll find it. I'll keep you advised as we go along."

Blake hung up. He was troubled. Even if Victoria was being unjustly harmed he wondered how much help, if any, the other members of the Vault might want to give her.

———

The morning sun streamed in through the windows of Luke Shaw's apartment, giving promise of a bright spring day.

"I'm sorry I'm a bit late," Joyce Spitz said. "I stopped by Victoria's apartment and picked up some clothes for her."

Luke Shaw nodded. "Good. She's still sleeping. Can you stay with her?"

"At the moment, I'm one of the unemployed, so that's no problem." She sensed the intensity of his concern. "Are you going to help her?"

"I plan to do what I can. I can't promise anything. But I'm on my way to see someone who might be of real assistance. I'll check back with you every so often."

"Don't worry, I'll take good care of her."

Shaw frowned. "Look, I don't wish to sound melodramatic, but don't let her out of your sight, okay?"

"She may have taken quite an emotional smashing around," Joyce replied, "but she's a pretty tough lady. I doubt she's the kind who might take the easy way out; she's too much like her father. As soon as she gets back on her pins, she'll be up and ready to go. She's a survivor."

"Survivor or not, let's not take any chances, okay?"

Joyce smiled warily. "It's none of my business, I admit, but what's your interest here? Romantic?"

Luke colored slightly. "She's a client. My company is to do some work on her new project. My interest is strictly business. That, plus she's a fellow member of the Vault."

Joyce Spitz remembered first hearing his name when Hunter Van Horn had mentioned that Luke Shaw had been nominated to take his deceased uncle's place on the Vault. But she didn't expect that he would be quite so young or so handsome. "And what do you members of the Vault have in mind for Vicky?"

"Some want her to resign," he replied.

"Are you one of them?"

He cocked an eyebrow. "You're certainly blunt enough. No, I'm not."

"So I presume then that you're in Vicky's corner?"

He didn't reply at once, as if reluctant to commit himself completely. "I have to go," he said. "Keep an eye on her, a close eye."

Joyce closed the apartment door after him. She looked around. The place was neat but completely without frills, a typical man's apartment, with no clues as to the character of its resident. But they would all soon find out what kind of a man Luke Shaw really was.

Al Rossini walked into the mayor's office. As he closed the door behind him Felder looked up from his desk.

"Did you forget to knock, or what? At least have the girl announce you. Christ, I could be scratching my balls or getting laid. Even a mayor is entitled to some privacy." For the first time he noticed the anxiety in Rossini's expression. "Oh, to hell with it. What's up?"

"They have people digging into the role of the mayor's squad in the arrest of Lytle and the Van Horn girl."

"Who the hell are 'they'? Anyway, so what?"

"Magazine writers are crawling all over the place. These are national guys; one of them is the reporter who broke that story on the Miami contractor kickbacks."

"So what? This isn't Miami."

"A lot of people went to jail. They will try the mayor next month. This is the guy who started that ball rolling. They have a lot of questions about the arrest, and they want to know more about DiVito."

Felder grinned. "Rossini, you're close enough to know that I'm not on the take, right? So what's to worry? Look, tell 'em DiVito is a precinct dick. He called in my squad, tell 'em." Felder thought for a moment. "Yeah, that would sound about right. A precinct detective stumbles on a narcotic case involving a congressman; he's scared and he doesn't want to step on the wrong toes. He calls the mayor's squad because he knows they are sharp and honest—use some bullshit like that. The squad comes out and makes the arrest. That way, DiVito looks good, the squad looks good, and what's more important, I look good. Go tell them that."

Rossini slowly shook his head. "I can't."

"Why the fuck not?" Felder demanded. "What's wrong with that?"

"They have copies of the paperwork transferring DiVito to your special squad."

Felder felt a rush of anger. "And just how the hell did they get that?"

"From police headquarters, I suppose."

Felder stood up, his voice rising with emotion. "Find out who the fuck let them have that stuff, Rossini. Then let me know. I don't give a shit if it's a captain or a commissioner, the son of a bitch will wish he had never been born."

"At the moment, I don't think that would be such a good idea."

Felder's eyes narrowed. "Are you telling me what is a good idea and what isn't? What happened here? I'm not the mayor anymore? Tell me, was there a special election and you got in, is that it?"

"No. But those media people are digging, and I mean, really digging. Someone in high places is interested in this, and in a big way. If we start shaking up the police, or anything like that, it will just fan the flames. I think we should come up with a real explanation why your squad made that arrest."

The anger left Felder as quickly as it had come. "They're cops. It's their goddamned job to make arrests when a crime is being committed. That's explanation enough."

Rossini frowned. "I don't think so. Look, even I don't know how all this happened, and I'm on your staff. That squad works exclusively for you. I understood its job was to check city departments, to keep everybody honest. That's what you told me."

"Have they talked to DiVito?"

Rossini nodded. "They've talked to just about everybody. The reporter who broke the Miami story says he's even talked to the guy who sold the drugs."

"Fuck, he's bluffing. What pusher in his right mind would talk to the press?"

"I don't know, but judging from their questions, the reporters believe you set Lytle up. The writers say you want to run for Senate and that Lytle was in your way."

Felder sat down. He turned and stared out at the river. "They're just baiting you," he said, but his words carried no real conviction. "Duck the fuckers. This kind of thing always blows over quickly if everybody keeps a low profile."

"That's what Nixon said about Watergate," Rossini replied quietly.

Felder turned and stared at him. "Okay, I don't have to take that kind of shit! I'll overlook it this time, Rossini, but don't try to pull that kind of crap again, get me?"

Rossini shrugged. "That brings up another point. I've been thinking it's about time that I returned to my law firm. This seems as good a time as any."

"You don't trust me?"

"It's time to leave, that's all."

Felder got up and walked around the desk. He put his arm around Rossini and hugged him. "Hey, who loves you, baby? Don't be pissed. I got a little testy, that's all. Hell, I've done that before. Let's not let ourselves get too touchy, Rossini." He laughed. "Besides, I still need the wop vote." He squeezed a bit tighter.

Rossini waited until Felder released him. "There's another thing."

"Oh Christ, you're just full of good news. What is it?"

"The guy from Miami says the cops themselves are looking into why your squad made that arrest."

Felder threw his hands in the air. "That's just talk, fuckin' talk. He's trying to get you to react. Get my man, that new deputy commissioner, on the phone. I'll get that shit killed quick, if it's true."

Rossini nodded. "I'll have your girl telephone him."

"Why not you?"

Rossini's usual placid expression reflected a shadow of disdain. "I have my own questions about all this. As I said, it's time for me to go back to the firm. You'll have my letter of resignation within the hour."

Felder sat down again behind the desk. "It's just as well you're quitting, Rossini. I don't want anyone around me who doesn't have any guts."

Rossini looked around at the large office. "I must admit, all this has been quite an experience." He walked to the door and carefully closed it behind him.

Felder again stared out at the river. Everything had gone so well in the beginning. He wished he hadn't decided to go after Lytle. He wished Ace Myers had never suggested the Senate race. Most of all, Al Felder wished he too could quit and go back to law practice.

But he couldn't, and there was no place to hide.

Al Baron took a booth in the back of the small restaurant. It was almost deserted. A lifetime of courthouse coffee had ruined his stomach so he ordered only milk while he waited.

Baron, Manhattan's most famous criminal lawyer, had developed a network of people who owed him favors. Some were criminals, others police officers. His network had become an important tool of his trade, and through it he knew everything that was happening in New York.

The man he was expecting came in. Tall, lean and black, he moved with an easy grace, his shoulders bobbing in time to a beat only he could hear. His long face was decorated with a gold stud in one nostril and a straggly goatee. He looked dangerous.

"What's happening, Al?" He slid into the booth and grinned at the attorney, displaying several sparkling gold inlays.

"Jimmy," Baron said, shaking his head, "you get more bizarre every time I see you. Maybe it's time to ask for a transfer. One of these days you may forget you're a cop and actually start dealing. You know, like an actor who can't stop playing the part."

The policeman signaled to the waiter for a cup of coffee. "The newspapers say you're the lawyer for Victoria Van Horn. You're really moving up in the world, Al."

"She's a nice young woman." Baron's reply was noncommittal. He waited to hear why the policeman had asked to meet him.

The cop's face was totally without expression. "The mayor's squad made that bust. Some of our narcotics people were standing by as backup. One of the young guys who works for me was in on that thing."

"Come on, Jimmy, don't fence with me. What do you know?"

"You realize that all this is strictly between you and me? These are my people. I can't end up testifying."

"This conversation never took place. Go on."

"Whatever their reason, the mayor's boys have been keeping a close eye on Congressman Lytle. The word has it that Lytle is a heavy user. My man tells me Lytle bought those drugs from a well-placed and discreet dude who supplies the uptown crowd. They didn't arrest Lytle when he made the buy because the dealer cooperates with us."

"Licensed?"

Jimmy grinned. "Sort of. He deals light stuff, weed, cocaine, but he lets us know what the heavies are doing. That way we keep a nice little history on how certain rich folks blow their dough. It's a convenient arrangement for both sides, dig?"

The policeman sipped his coffee. "An old detective named DiVito choreographed that arrest like he was a Broadway director. He even had a newspaper photographer there, as you probably already guessed."

"In other words, a frame?"

Jimmy shrugged. "No, at least not in the usual sense. Lytle is a real user and the buy he made was real, nothing was planted or set up. They didn't care about the drugs, they just wanted to ruin his ass. And they did. Of course, your client got ruined as well."

"From what you know, Jimmy, is Victoria Van Horn a user?"

"How did I know you were going to ask that?" The policeman grinned. "Hell, she's better known than the president. If she was buying, my boys would know." He chuckled. "Apparently her only vice is being a congressman fucker."

"It sure would help if I could prove Lytle bought the drugs," Baron said.

"It all comes down to a matter of ethics. I can't give up the dealer, Al. I'm sorry. He's an informer and a lot of people like him trust us with their lives."

"I understand." Baron nodded.

Jimmy finished the coffee, then stood up. "There *is* one thing I can do for you." He reached into the pocket of his tailored jeans and pulled out a folded paper. He handed it to Baron. "My boy made a copy of this when DiVito wasn't looking. I think you'll find it interesting reading. Just don't say where you got it."

As the narcotics officer left the restaurant Baron unfolded the paper and studied it for a few minutes. It was a photocopy of a typed list of hospitals and dates, much of it in abbreviations. He whistled suddenly as he discovered the key. It was a list of treatment centers where Barry Lytle had been admitted for detoxification and treatment for drug abuse.

The last entry, handwritten, identified a recent stay at a posh uptown clinic that catered to the very rich and specialized in treatment of substance abuse. A signature had been scrawled at the bottom to ensure the signer got proper credit for the information. It was Sam DiVito's signature.

The information would be the means to destroy Lytle's story, and thereby help prove Victoria Van Horn's innocence.

Baron slowly finished his milk, relishing the cooling smoothness. It *was* nice when things went well.

23

Joyce Spitz realized it was foolish to sit by the side of the bed as Victoria slept, but she found some comfort in it, although she was fighting off a tendency to close her own eyes.

Victoria stirred, then opened her eyes. She looked around at the unfamiliar surrounding.

"Good morning. You're in Lucas Shaw's apartment. He tells me you took a gold Olympic medal for wandering last night."

Victoria made an attempt to sit up, groaned, then lay back again.

"As I figure it," Joyce said, "you must have walked for over fifteen hours straight yesterday. If you're sore, that's the reason."

Victoria made another, much slower effort and managed to pull herself up and swing her legs over the side of the bed. "'Sore' is hardly the word. I feel like I've been run over by a truck."

"Why don't you go back to sleep? It would do you good. It'll take a couple of days, at least, to recover from your little jaunt."

Victoria shook her head. "I don't have the time."

Joyce watched as Victoria cautiously stood up. "What's so important that you must do it now?"

Victoria tried a few tentative steps. She was dressed only in her slip. "My feet feel numb."

"They don't do that much marching in the Foreign Legion."

Victoria walked stiffly around the bedroom. "Well, I certainly don't feel like going dancing, but I can get by." She steadied herself. "Joyce, I hate to ask, but could you run over to my apartment and get some clothes? As I remember, what I had on last night took quite a beating."

"I stopped by on my way over. Newsmen are as thick as flies over at your place, but I managed to sneak out a complete outfit."

"Good girl. I'll pull myself together and get going."

"What's the rush, Victoria? Luke Shaw asked that you stay, at least until he returns. That seems sensible to me. I'll get you some food and coffee. Just relax."

"Where did he go?"

"I don't know. But I think he sincerely wants to help. We should wait." She smiled conspiratorially. "I think he likes you."

Victoria sat on the bed and rubbed a foot. "I don't know if he likes me or not, Joyce, but if it wasn't for him last night things might have turned out very badly. He may have saved my life."

"Then you should do what he asks." Joyce paused. "Don't you like him? He's quite attractive."

"Every time we meet we seem to end up in an argument. I don't think that offers much hope for romance."

Joyce shrugged. "You're probably both of a type, strong-willed. He's unmarried. He was divorced a couple of years ago. Maybe if you gave it half a chance . . ."

"Joyce, there's no place in my life for marriage, not now. I'm fighting for my life. Even if Luke Shaw was the greatest catch in the world I just don't have the time. And, speaking of time, I have to get going."

"Take it easy, Victoria. You need a rest, and your attorney told you to stay out of sight for a while. Let Shaw carry the ball for a change."

"What did he do, appoint you as palace guard?" Victoria laughed. "Listen, I'm hitting on all cylinders again, Joyce, or at least most of them. You don't have to worry about me. I'm not suicidal. If anything, I'm homicidal. I want to see Chilton Vance's hide flying in tatters from the Van Horn flagpole, just above the flapping skin of the wonderful Barry Lytle. If you have to be concerned about anyone, worry about them."

Joyce Spitz found it eerie. Although young and female, Victoria was speaking just like her father had, using the same gestures and inflection, taking the same attitude. It was almost unnerving. "You need some time to think, Victoria. Shaw said . . ."

"Joyce," Victoria said, smiling, "one small question. Who do you work for, Luke Shaw or me?"

Joyce laughed. "Well, technically, no one. Chilton Vance fired me last night. As the actors say, I'm at liberty at the moment."

"Not anymore. I'm hiring you right now as my executive secretary. If you want some other title, make one up. Now, I have to get cleaned up."

"You know the board fired you too, don't you?"

"They didn't waste much time, but then, I didn't expect anything else. I presume they put my brother in my place?"

Joyce shook her head. "No. He was at the meeting but he got the surprise of his life. They double-crossed him at the last minute. He was so upset I thought he might break down and cry. They elected Chilton Vance as president and chairman. Your brother stormed out of the place."

"They made a fool of him, in front of everyone?"

"Yes."

Victoria was silent for a moment, lost in thought. Then she looked at Joyce. "I'll take you up on that coffee. In the meantime, I'll take a shower."

After Joyce left the bedroom, Victoria stood up and stretched. Every muscle in her body protested. She hoped a nice hot shower would help ease the pain. Then she looked at the telephone.

She hadn't called that number in years and was surprised that she still remembered it. She dialed and a maid answered.

"This is Victoria Van Horn," she said. "I would like to speak to my brother."

———————

Sander Blake sat quietly on the terrace of his large New York apartment, sipping his morning coffee. The visit from Luke Shaw troubled him. Luke's cup remained untouched. He wished he could have offered more assistance, but he felt he could not, at least not yet.

He wondered how involved Luke had become with Victoria Van Horn. She was staying at his apartment, and that led to some inferences, despite Shaw's denials.

Blake allowed his butler to refill his cup. Now that he knew where he could reach Victoria he had no excuse not to deliver the Vault's request for her resignation. It was a job he didn't want to do, but it would have to be done.

Perhaps Luke had been right, and a terrible injustice was being done to Victoria. Still, the Vault had the duty to protect itself. Blake had heard Luke Shaw's argument in favor of Victoria. He even agreed with much of what was said. Blake's people were busy proving the drugs that caused her arrest actually belonged to Barry Lytle. But even if they proved it, she was a detriment, and her continued membership, innocent or guilty, would be an embarrassment.

And that raised another problem. If young Lytle was shown to have a drug problem and that he had tried to put the blame on another, the Vault could be seriously compromised by his father's membership. Shaw had asked for the Vault's help for Victoria, but to do that could hurt Stewart Lytle. Ambassador Lytle had to be protected too. Blake would have to consult with some of the others. Things were fast getting out of hand.

Blake had gently suggested that Shaw had fallen in love with Victoria, but Luke had denied it. He wondered if Shaw was really denying it to himself. The situation was becoming dicey all the way around.

His butler announced his second visitor of the morning.

Blake stood up to greet Jon Krugar. He had never met Krugar before and tried to hide his startled reaction to the man's appearance. Krugar lumbered onto the terrace, his huge body encased in a wrinkled suit more suited for the tropics. He moved surprisingly well for a man his age, even with the enormous weight he carried.

Krugar was far too large for the narrow terrace chairs, and the butler hurried in with a flat stool. The old man sat down and mopped his perspiring face. His wispy gray beard shook slightly as he chuckled. "Good man, that," he said, referring to the butler. "He saved me from embarrassment with such easy grace. If you ever decide to fire him, let me know."

"There's not much chance of that," Blake replied. "I'm delighted to meet you after all these years. I've certainly heard a great deal about you."

The butler brought Krugar a cup of coffee. He smiled his gratitude. "I know you're busy, Mr. Blake. I've read a great deal about you too. So let me come quickly to the point of my visit."

"As you wish." Blake tried to hide his aroused curiosity.

Krugar nodded. "As you know, my family controls a healthy share of the world's commerce. It has taken several hundred years and a number of Krugars, but our success speaks for itself. I am the present patriarch of that line, and while my health lasts, I control our varied interests."

"So I've heard."

Krugar chuckled. "The Krugar family started as pirates. It's a well-known story. Perhaps because of those questionable beginnings we have always tried to protect our interests as much as possible. I suppose only a pirate can fully appreciate a good stout fortress, eh? We have always had our fortress in Hong Kong, as you know. No matter what flag flew there, the Krugars made sure they were members of whatever organization really ran the place." He paused to take a sip of coffee. His eyes peered at Blake over the rim of the cup. "Like your organization here in New York."

"The Vault?"

Krugar nodded. "Yes. I am a member of the Council, the actual ruling body in Hong Kong. As you know, our friends the British have seen fit to agree to give Hong Kong to China. We have only a few years until that becomes a fact."

"And you don't think you can make an arrangement with the Chinese government?" Blake asked.

"To be frank, I don't wish to take the risk. I propose to remove our headquarters from Hong Kong. This shift of one of the world's major commercial forces, as I'm sure you're aware, would have major impact on international commerce."

Blake nodded. Krugar was right. Such a move could affect history itself.

"I should like to relocate here in New York," Krugar said. "I find it comforting that it is a port city."

Blake tried to conceal his excitement. It would be a tremendous story. He wondered to whom he should assign it. "When will this take place?"

Krugar put down the cup. "It depends. Certain arrangements must be made. As I say, I have to ensure my family and our interests will be safe in the new location. I shall need a new fortress. That's why I've come to you."

"Oh?"

"There are many rich people here in Manhattan, some foreign, like myself. They have money, but not influence. I need something more than just a line of credit, Mr. Blake. I must seek to duplicate the power I enjoy in Hong Kong." Krugar looked out at the city, as if seeing it for the first time. "I wish to become a member of the Vault."

Blake was startled. He searched to find the right words. "Mr. Krugar, the Vault is a small group of men, and one woman—but that is a temporary thing—people who have come to membership by reason of family. It was founded well over a hundred years ago, and membership is passed down through families. There has never been an exception."

Krugar smiled. "I made inquiries, of course. And I know what you say is correct. But we exist in a constantly changing world, Mr. Blake. Perhaps the Vault might be induced to make one small change. I admit I am the descendant of pirates." He chuckled. "But some of your members are the descendants of some rather notorious smugglers."

Blake forced a smile. "That isn't the issue, Mr. Krugar. We have only eight members, it's traditional. Soon there will be a vacancy, but that's an unusual circumstance."

"Miss Van Horn, I presume?"

"Yes. Her replacement will come, most probably, from her family."

Krugar nodded. "Then she is still a member?"

"As of the moment."

Krugar held up his hand when the butler started to refill his cup. "I must be going, Mr. Blake. I understand your position, of course. Tradition governs us all, but it is not the final law. Would you do me the courtesy of sounding out the other members as to my proposal? Of course, they must realize all this is in confidence."

"I'll ask, and I can assure you your privacy will be honored. However, I have to be honest. I don't think you can expect a favorable answer."

Krugar awkwardly stood up. He again mopped his face. "All I can ask is due consideration." He extended his hand. "I'm staying at the Sherry Netherland, Mr. Blake. You can contact me there."

Sander Blake walked him to the apartment door. He was surprised to find two elderly Chinese waiting for Krugar in the hallway. One was dressed in a black silken blouse and had only one arm.

"I shall look forward to hearing from you," Krugar said as he and the two Chinese stepped into the elevator. "You might wish to start with Mr. Franklin Trager. He's a long-time business associate of mine." Jon Krugar smiled as the elevator doors closed.

Sander Blake stepped back into his apartment. The request was ridiculous. Still, Krugar was an important man. Blake decided he would go through the motions as a courtesy. But the matter of Victoria Van Horn would have to be settled first.

Her brother agreed to meet Victoria at a small restaurant near Seventy-ninth Street. It was a place their father had often taken them when they were young, and both had agreed they would feel comfortable there. More important to Victoria, there was little chance of being discovered by the press.

Junior was waiting when she arrived. She was surprised at his appearance. He wore an old sport jacket over an open-collared shirt. She couldn't remember when she had last seen him without a tie. He looked drawn; dark shadows seemed to encircle his tired eyes. He stood up awkwardly as she approached his table. It was too early for the luncheon crowd, so they had the place almost to themselves.

Junior looked at his sister, then quickly averted his eyes as she sat across the table from him.

He continued to look away from her as he spoke. "What can I say?" His voice was almost a whisper. "I'm sorry for what I did to you. I fucked up, and I've proved myself quite the fool doing it."

Even across the table she could detect the alcohol on his breath.

"If it's any consolation," he continued, "I called my lawyers this morning and told them to withdraw that lawsuit. I asked them to make a public apology to you."

"You really are feeling bad, aren't you?" Victoria said.

His chuckle sounded as if it were close to a sob. "Let's be frank. We're brother and sister, but we've never been friends. I suppose we've been competing against each other for years. That's not unheard of in families, but I think we—I—have overdone it. I've read about your other troubles," he said quietly. "I feel very badly."

"The fact that Chilton Vance made a fool of you last night didn't help either, I presume?"

Her brother shook his head very slowly. "Yeah, that was pretty bad. It turned out to be something between a humiliation and an execution." He met her eyes for the first time. "You've been the shining success, Vicky. I suppose I wanted a turn at the glory. I went into that meeting with the confident expectation that I would be kicking you out and taking over. That was a good feeling, to be candid." He paused; his eyes looked wet. "But, instead, I was exposed as a horse's ass."

She tried to interrupt her brother, but he half smiled and put up his hand, insisting that he wanted to go on.

"You can't imagine what it was like. Right from the start I was always in father's shadow. And, for the past few years, I have been in yours." He again shook his head. "That can be tough to take." He looked away. "Withdrawing that lawsuit may look like a weak gesture. I'm ashamed I got conned into bringing it. Anyway, for what it's worth, I'm sorry."

"What does Cecelia think about all this?"

He shrugged and made a gesture with his hand as if waving away something unpleasant. "As soon as she heard what happened, she left me. I anticipate being served with divorce papers, perhaps even today. I don't know what it will finally cost me, but whatever the price, getting rid of her will be worth it."

Victoria suddenly, for the first time, felt pity for her brother. She began to understand his bitterness toward her, an attitude probably fanned by his flagrantly unfaithful wife.

He signaled a waiter who quickly brought him a martini.

"Isn't it a bit early to start drinking?" she asked quietly.

He laughed. "Hell, I haven't stopped since last night." He took a healthy gulp. "And I don't plan on stopping, ever." He again looked directly at her. "The funny thing is that it doesn't seem to help. I'm not drunk, although I'd welcome the oblivion. It just doesn't come."

"What are your plans?" she asked.

He shrugged. "I don't know, really. I'll probably get out of the country for a while, go somewhere the name Van Horn isn't known, someplace where the company doesn't have any interests."

"That might be hard to find."

He snorted. "Yes. Peculiar, isn't it? The Van Horn name is known everywhere. Once I was so damned proud of that, now it's turned into a curse."

Victoria watched as he downed the martini. "Did you wonder why I asked to meet with you?"

He pushed the glass away. "I thought you might want to call me a few choice names. I would, if our positions were reversed. I'm a schmuck. The worse thing is, I just found that out."

"You're wallowing in self-pity."

"Wouldn't you?"

She laughed. "Well, brother of mine, perhaps you've forgotten, but I got tossed out of office in that famous meeting last night. Besides, my picture is in every newspaper in the world and I'm tagged as a dope fiend and a slut. Can you match that? But I'm not going to waste my time crying over my situation."

He sighed. "Good for you," he said cynically.

"But you're going to run off to South America and drink yourself to death. Do you think that's what father intended for you? He made us both rich, but I'm sure he didn't want us ruined by that."

"Death by drinking isn't such a bad fate. There's worse."

"I asked to see you for a reason," she said. "Even with all our troubles, we are extremely wealthy people."

"Yeah, but you have control of the stock and the power to vote it." He looked away from her. "Have you any idea how that made me feel? I was emasculated." He signaled for another drink. "In any event, you don't need me."

"Like it or not, we need each other," she said. "And you had better stop feeling sorry for yourself. I don't know much, but I've learned that if you don't fight you haven't a chance. The only person who can really defeat you is yourself."

He chuckled. "And I thought Knute Rockne was dead. Yea, team." He shook his head. "Look, why don't we just admit we're a couple of prize assholes and sneak offstage quietly. That's called reality, Vicky. There are no come-from-behind wins for assholes."

She studied him before replying. "Would you like to smash Chilton Vance?"

His expression didn't change, but sudden interest flashed in his eyes. "Of course."

"Rather than running away, suppose you combined with me, and we both went after that slick son of a bitch."

He smiled. "I don't think I've ever heard you speak quite so crudely. But I am interested. Go on."

"Between us we own an enormous block of stock. If we're united, Vance can't expect to survive the annual meeting."

Her brother nodded. "I was worried about that myself. I thought if I did become president you would have moved heaven and earth to throw me out at the annual meeting."

"And what were you going to do about that?"

He averted his eyes once more, as if ashamed. "I was planning to ruin you with that lawsuit, frankly. If I did, I thought I'd be able to wrest control of the stock away from you. That was the plan. As you've probably guessed, it was suggested to me by my wonderful friend, Chilton Vance."

"He's smart enough to know he's vulnerable. So what's the only way he can survive?"

"I don't understand."

Victoria frowned. "Even if I go to jail, Vance knows I'd use the stock proxy power to throw him out. So he has to have a plan."

"Go on."

"My guess is that he will sell off parts of the company, then allow the rest to be taken in a friendly merger. There'll be no Van Horn company left. Vance will make a fortune exercising stock options and end up in top management with whoever buys the company."

"Well, we'd make money too."

Victoria shook her head. "We have the largest block of stock, but Vance could drive the price down. We might not be completely ruined, but we could lose half of what we own, perhaps more."

Her brother suddenly sat up straight. "My God, he probably had that in mind all the time. But he's clever, Victoria. How can we possibly stop him?"

"We can fight," she replied. "We have the support of some of the board. We could try to line up others. I know a man in Hong Kong, Jon Krugar, who controls a board member. I could call him. It's a start."

"That doesn't sound very promising, frankly. Vance owns the majority. Going after control of the board isn't likely to work."

"That's only part of it. We can combine and take him on in court. Vance likes to see other people fight; it keeps him from getting his hands dirty. I think we should launch a deluge of lawsuits against him and the present company management. He may win, but he won't come out unbloodied."

"That would cost a fortune," her brother replied.

"Half of it's Cecelia's money anyway. What do you care?" She met her brother's eyes. "It would mean total effort. We would have to put all differences behind us. Either we do this as a united family, or it won't work."

He considered her words for a moment, then laughed. "I like that part about some of the money being Cecelia's."

"Then it's agreed? We'll combine to destroy Chilton Vance?"

His smile became a wide grin. "God, that does sound good, doesn't it? Okay, I'm in. You call the shots, Vicky. I'll do whatever you want."

"We'll work as a team. This is going to be a joint effort."

He stood up and awkwardly moved toward her, bending over and kissing her forehead. "All right, sister. Maybe I'm a little late, but I'm finally aboard. Let's see if we can kick a little ass. Maybe, with a little luck, we just might win."

"We will, Hunter. We will."

He was smiling as he looked at her, but he was close to tears. It was the first time anyone had called him Hunter in years. It sounded good.

━━━━━━━━━

Jon Krugar's granddaughter gently awakened him.

"Your visitor will be here in a few minutes, grandfather."

He had prepared for what could prove to be a very important meeting by taking a short nap. His mind was always resilient, but he had learned to pamper his aging body. His granddaughter helped him sit up. She knelt down and slipped on his shoes.

"This lady, Victoria Van Horn, is the one you met with in Hong Kong, yes?"

He half smiled. The girl was more than curious. She had a sharp and searching intellect. Hers was the kind of wisdom that the family could use in the future. She would have to be brought along very carefully if she was one day to rule the Krugar empire. Like Victoria Van Horn, she was extremely beautiful, which could prove to be both an asset and a curse. Time would tell. She helped Krugar to his feet.

"Miss Van Horn was our guest. I was merely helping the daughter of an old friend then. Now my kindness may be rewarded. We can never foresee the future, but we can do our best to prepare."

"Will you be taking tea?"

Krugar nodded. "Yes, my dear."

He walked from the bedroom into the main room of the large suite. He felt at home in the high-ceilinged luxury of the old-fashioned Sherry Netherland. It had the feel of a time when tradition and comfort had their own special meaning. He looked down at Central Park. The trees were budding and an eruption of fresh growing vegetation made the huge park look like a lush green rug. Spring was his favorite time of year.

It had been a stroke of fortune that Victoria had contacted him. His Hong Kong office had given her his hotel. He had planned to call her, but this way he had the upper hand. She was the one who apparently wanted a favor.

His granddaughter admitted Victoria, who was precisely on time. They did not speak of important matters until tea had been served.

"I hope this doesn't embarrass you, my dear," he said, "but I have been reading of your, ah, difficulties."

She looked at him and shrugged. "As you might imagine, I am quite beyond embarrassment. And it's those difficulties that have brought me here."

He sipped his tea. "Oh?"

"Mr. Krugar, you were the one who told me the true situation existing in my father's company. Everything you said was true. Since we talked, I've discovered that Chilton Vance is the one who was and is responsible."

"He's the new chief executive officer, is he not?"

Victoria nodded. "He engineered everything. I really don't know why. But I'm going to try to persuade the board to throw him out."

"He controls the board," Krugar said.

"Yes. For now. But if I can line up the right kind of help we can change that."

Krugar pursed his lips before replying. "As you know, I have a man on that board, and I strongly influence another. My help wouldn't be the key to ultimate victory, however. It would require much more effort."

"I'm prepared to make that effort. Can I count on your help?"

He arched an eyebrow. "Are you still a member of the Vault?"

She smiled wryly. "For the moment. I'm afraid I'm to be ousted there too."

He nodded. "But at least until now you haven't been?"

"No. And I'm going to try to fight that too."

Krugar pretended polite indifference. "And do you have any allies on the Vault?"

Victoria was puzzled by his apparent lack of real interest. "Yes," she replied. "Luke Shaw is a member, and he is helping me. Elias McKensie will be in my corner too."

"The former secretary of state?"

"Yes."

Krugar nodded slowly. "There are eight members, counting yourself, correct?"

"Yes. I think Sander Blake might help too, although I'm not sure." Victoria felt her confidence slipping away.

Krugar half smiled. "So you might have four votes. Do they need a majority to eject you?"

She felt herself coloring. Her world was falling apart and he seemed interested only in some abstract political considerations concerning seven men. "I don't know their rules. I'm too new."

Krugar put his cup down. He reached over and gently patted her hand. "Your father was a special friend of mine. I am favorably disposed toward you on that account alone. However, I've learned, having lived so many years, not to make rash promises. With your permission, I should like to talk to your Mr. Shaw, and perhaps even Elias McKensie. Then, after I've made other inquiries, I can judge if my help might be effective."

"You don't need my permission to talk with anyone, Mr. Krugar. I hope you know how grateful I am for anything you do."

He smiled. "Perhaps you could have Mr. Shaw call me? I don't know him. Elias McKensie is, however, an old acquaintance." He pushed himself out of the chair and escorted her to the door. "Don't look so forlorn, Victoria. I am just being prudent. I think all will be well."

She looked up at him, her eyes wet.

He walked her to the elevator. After she had gone he returned to the apartment and once again looked out at Central Park. It had a calming effect on him. He wished he could have assured her of his help; she would have it completely. But to give that assurance now would rob him of the bargaining lever he would need later. Jon Krugar had spent his life bargaining. He was very good at it.

Below his suite, the streets of New York teemed with life and commerce. He would miss Hong Kong, if he succeeded. But, fortunately, he liked New York. If he was clever and wise the ultimate prize would be his.

"Did your meeting go well, grandfather?"

He turned and smiled. He would hate to be parted from her, but it was time that she received an education, the very best. She would need that in the modern world if she was to lead. "So far," he said gently, "things seem to be progressing very nicely."

Once again Chilton Vance had taken possession of Hunter Van Horn's office and desk. But Vance had no opportunity to even celebrate his coup d'état. Time for triumph would come later. He had to move fast and he knew it.

Vance had set up a press conference for later in the day. He would announce the losses in the Entertainment Group first. Then he would publicly fire Adam Robins as chief of Prometheus Pictures. That would make headlines, and not just in the business sections. The firing of a major movie studio executive guaranteed front-page coverage. It would be an excellent way to begin.

Prometheus Pictures would be a nice little bauble to dangle before the rapacious eyes of greedy big businessmen. Everyone, no matter how rich, had Hollywood fever. The prospect of owning a major movie studio would be tasty bait to attract potential buyers.

Vance was quite pleased with himself. Everything was going splendidly. Soon his name would be etched in the mind of American business as the man who had saved the Van Horn giant from bankruptcy and managed to sell it.

Since Van Horn's death, Vance had seldom tortured himself with speculations about his wife's possible affair with Hunter Van Horn. Now, unexpectedly, his mind was full of painful imagined images.

Ruining the Van Horn children and destroying Van Horn's company would go a long way toward ending those torturing thoughts.

24

Pelegrine sat happily aboard the Alitalia flight scheduled to depart for Florence in twenty minutes. He had delivered the paintings, and, as promised, his share in the transactions had been paid to him in cash. Cecil Driker had made an enormous profit, but to Pelegrine that seemed fair enough; the little man was taking most of the risk.

It had all been a delightful adventure. His spectacular affair with Cecelia Van Horn had been so violently sexual and exhausting that Enrico Pelegrine, despite his passionate Italian blood, was secretly glad it was over. Cecelia had the big German now—God help him—and seemed quite content. The divorce would give her a generous slice of her husband's enormous fortune, but even money was no substitute for health. He hoped the German had a constitution equal to the task. He didn't envy him.

The money, most of it, was deposited safely in his Swiss bank account. He had converted the rest into bonds, which had been mailed to his home in Italy. He wasn't yet financially independent; he would have to continue as an art dealer, but at last he had breathing room. He found that a most comforting feeling.

Pelegrine sat back, relaxed and content, as the plane taxied down the runway in preparation for takeoff.

He knew they would catch Driker eventually. Cecil was such an arrogant, pompous little fool.

When they finally did catch up to Driker, Pelegrine realized they might try to extradite him, but he doubted it. The art world was civilized; no one liked such publicity, since it tended to depress an already suspicious market.

He considered it unlikely that anyone would even bother Enrico Pelegrine, the Italian art dealer.

He smiled.

"The almost rich Italian art dealer," he whispered to himself as the plane roared from the runway, climbing out toward the Atlantic.

"Did you have much difficulty finding this place?" Krugar's fleshy face creased into a wide smile.

Luke Shaw nodded. "I thought I knew Manhattan like the back of my hand, even Chinatown, but I didn't know this place even existed."

They sat in a small cramped restaurant on the second floor above a number of Chinese shops on Pell Street. It was a place of wooden tables and mismatched chairs.

Krugar chuckled. "This establishment is for the Chinese themselves, not the tourist. It is owned by an associate of mine, that one-armed man seated near the door. The food here is what one might find in the Orient." He looked around. "It serves no liquor, provides no frills, but the fare is quite authentic. I plan to order snake." Krugar watched Luke's reaction. "Unless, of course, that would offend you?"

Shaw shook his head. "It's not my choice, but I've seen it eaten before."

"Oh?"

"In Vietnam. Occasionally we would kill a snake over there or find one on our protective wire. The Vietnamese clamored to get the snake; they find it a rare delicacy."

Krugar nodded. "It is. Very healthy. I consider myself living proof of that. But enough of the exotic menu, I asked to meet you on a matter of business. You are, I'm informed, a member of the Vault."

Luke nodded. "Yes."

"Do you know who I am?"

Shaw smiled. "One of the world's richest men. Low profile, but you control an impressive number of businesses from your Hong Kong head-quarters. Frankly, I looked you up before I came over here."

Krugar signaled for another pot of tea. "Very prudent. You are a friend of Victoria Van Horn, correct?"

Shaw nodded guardedly. "Yes."

The one-armed man silently replaced one ancient pot with another, and poured fresh tea for both men.

Krugar took a sip of the steaming liquid.

"She has asked me to assist her in her troubles, at least in the ones concerning her father's company. I have some influence on that board."

"Are you going to help her?"

Krugar noted Luke's intensity. He shrugged. "That depends."

"On what?"

Krugar's eyes seemed fixed upon Luke. "On you," he replied.

"I don't understand."

Krugar sat back, his bulk making the old chair squeal in protest. "I will ask that what I say be kept in confidence. I too looked you up. You have an honorable reputation." He smiled. "For a number of reasons I feel I must move my operation from Hong Kong. As you can imagine, this is not an easy thing to do. Billions are involved. And, perhaps more important, the protection of that money and my family's business interests. I need influence and a measure of practical protection wherever I decide to move. I would like to come here to New York. But I need to become a member of your Vault. I belong to a similar organization in Hong Kong."

Luke shifted uncomfortably. "Mr. Krugar, if you've checked, you must know that the Vault is made up of . . ."

"Old, established New York families," Krugar interjected. "I know that. These are changing times, Mr. Shaw. I would hope that an exception might be made. I will be bringing much commerce with me when I come. It would benefit the city, I can assure you."

"What has all this to do with me? I'm only one member."

Krugar's expression became solemn. "I'm in a position to help Miss Van Horn. If you agree to help me become a member of the Vault, I shall undertake to help Victoria. One hand washing the other, as your politicians are so fond of saying."

Luke felt himself flushing. "You're using her like a hostage."

Krugar shrugged. "A bargaining chip, Mr. Shaw. I sincerely like the young lady. But I am a businessman. Circumstances are such that I can barter my help for something that I want. All quite legal, obviously. I feel no guilt, asking a favor in return."

"She deserves your help without any conditions. She's the victim of a . . ."

"Ah, Mr. Shaw, there is so much injustice in the world, isn't there? Years ago I discovered that I could have little effect beyond my own interests."

"Look, I can't guarantee anything. I can try, but I doubt if I can make any difference."

"And you would like me to help Miss Van Horn on that basis?"

"It's the only basis I can offer."

Krugar chuckled. "As I say, I checked you out rather carefully. You are a man of your word. If you say you will help me, that's good enough. I will use whatever resources I have to assist Miss Van Horn. Fair enough?"

Luke couldn't conceal his surprise. "Yes, quite fair. I'm grateful."

"I detect an interest in Miss Van Horn that exceeds mere concern for justice or a fellow member of the Vault. Are you and she . . ."

"No," Luke said quickly. "There's nothing between us. I like her and I think she deserves help, that's all."

Krugar nodded. It was too bad. It was obvious that Luke Shaw was in love with Victoria, whether he realized it or not. Shaw was young, vigorous, intelligent and a leader. He would have made an excellent husband for his granddaughter. The House of Krugar could use such a man, an infusion of new blood. He smiled at Shaw. But it was not to be.

"I've already contacted Elias McKensie," Krugar said. "He is favorably disposed to my membership. Also, I have talked with Franklin Trager."

"Trager would never go for it," Luke said.

Krugar smiled again. "Ah, but you see, Mr. Trager and I have been partners for years in his manufacturing operation. I own the plants and he leases from me. I think you may find him favorably disposed."

Luke was surprised. "If that's true, counting Victoria's vote and mine, you have half already."

"One more will do it, providing the Vault does not remove Victoria," Krugar said. "So, you can see your task may not be so difficult after all."

Luke studied the elderly man for a moment. "Tell me, honestly, Mr. Krugar, would you have helped Victoria if I hadn't agreed to your terms?"

"What difference does it make, Mr. Shaw? What's done is done." Krugar signaled to the one-armed man. "Are you sure you wouldn't like to try the snake? It is said to assist not only in long life, but in aiding good fortune."

Luke shook his head. "I think I'll stick with chicken or pork. Besides, I'm healthy, and reasonably prosperous."

Krugar chuckled. "It's even said to be valuable in finding true love."

Victoria strode into the offices of her development company, startling the handful of reporters and photographers staked out as sentries. She walked through them to her office door before they reacted. Cameras clicked as she turned to face them. Questions were lost in a shouted blend of voices.

She held up a hand to quiet them. Tape recorders were thrust toward her. "I have consulted with my advisors and with my brother, Hunter Van Horn. The false criminal charges leveled against me have been contrived to discredit me and are all part of an effort to dislodge my brother and myself from rightful control of our late father's company. As a lawyer, let me assure you, those despicable charges will be thrown out of court. And let me further assure you that the people who instigated them will be thrown out of Van Horn Enterprises. Thank you." She turned and sought the privacy of her inner office as Joyce Spitz acted as a rear guard.

Joyce managed to close and lock the door. "When did you think all that up?" she asked.

"Just now. Did it sound convincing?"

A rare smile played across Joyce's face. "You sure made a believer out of me."

Victoria looked around at her office. Nothing had been changed. Framed photographs of her East Port project, together with drawings of her plans for the Hudson River property, covered the walls.

Craig Hopkins came in through the side door. He looked at her as if she were an apparition. "Where have you been? All hell's been busting loose." He seemed harried and irritated.

Startled, Vicky snapped a biting reply. "If you've read the papers, Craig, you'll know I was a temporary guest of the police department until I made bond. Also, there's been a passing mention or two of the fact I was thrown out as head of my father's company. In other words, I've been busy."

His irritation turned to embarrassment. "I'm sorry," he said quietly. "That wasn't much of a greeting. Forgive me, but things really have been going to hell in a handbasket around here."

Victoria sat down at her desk. "Enos Peacock tells me the banks are calling in their loans."

He nodded. "Everyone is canceling: the contractors, the architects, everybody. I've been trying to buy some time, but I haven't had much success."

"We're not in too deep at this point," Victoria said. "If we scrub the Hudson River project I should be able to raise enough money to pay off the banks."

"Time is the problem," he said. "They really don't want the money back; they want to take the property you put up as collateral. They're after everything you've built. They stand to make one hell of a profit if they levy against your holdings."

"So they won't give me time to pay back?"

He slowly shook his head. "Not one of them. They smell blood. The bunch of them are like tigers moving in for the kill. I'm sorry, I wish I had better news for you."

"Couldn't we sue to stop them?" Joyce asked. "To gain time?"

Hopkins again shook his head. "I thought about that. If we did, they'd be able to demand a bond equal to the value of the property pledged. There's no banking firm in America that would put up that kind of money, not in these circumstances. A lawsuit wouldn't help."

"I could pledge my stock in Van Horn Enterprises to cover a bond," Vicky said.

Hopkins sighed. "After all that's happened, that stock is coming down like a dead rocket. At the moment, I'm afraid no one would touch it, at least not as collateral for such an enormous bond."

"Then I'll sell the stock and pledge the cash."

Hopkins tried to smile but couldn't. "I don't want to sound like the voice of doom, but even that's impossible."

"Why?"

"You'd have to get formal permission from the Securities and Exchange people to sell a block that size. That would take time, much more than you have. Besides, if you did that, you'd be risking every dime you own."

Victoria sat back in her chair. "We're both lawyers, Craig. Surely, between us we should be able to come up with something."

He avoided looking at her. "Give up, Vicky. Let them take East Port and the river property. At least you'll still have your stock. It's the only thing I can think of to do."

Victoria looked at Joyce Spitz. "What do you think, Joyce?"

Joyce was solemn. "This is out of my league," she said. "The risk is yours, the decision should be too."

Victoria got up and walked to the large framed photograph of her completed East Port project. She studied it for a few moments, then turned. "If they take East Port away it will have to be over my dead body."

She looked at Hopkins. "Get me a list of all cooperating banks that made the loans. I'm going to start calling them right now."

"I've done that," he replied. "They don't even return my telephone calls."

She thought for a moment. "Okay, then let's go at this from a different angle." She spoke to Joyce. "They've made this whole thing a media event. Now that's something I understand and which I'm good at. Joyce, set up a press conference at the Sheraton Centre for eight o'clock. Bankers may not answer their phones, but they do watch the news broadcasts."

Victoria turned to Craig. "Bond or no bond, we're going to use the courts. And if we get thrown out, we'll just think of another way to bring suit. Start thinking, Craig. We need something legal that might have a chance of sticking. There has to be some way we can force a delay. You do the book work and I'll handle the courtroom stuff. That will help our publicity attack."

Utter determination was reflected in her stern expression. "I'll send them a message they won't soon forget."

It was impossible.

Beth Haslett checked the figures once more, just to make sure. The museum's money, not only that set aside for acquisitions but also the operating funds, had been drained away, and all in the past few days. The museum's nervous bookkeeper had brought the printouts and canceled checks to her. He was one of the few museum employees who knew that the assistant curator was the niece of John Robertson, one of the museum's most important trustees.

The figures he presented were shocking. Cecil Driker was looting the museum. No other explanation seemed possible.

Driker was operating within a pattern historically familiar in the art world. Kickbacks were the traditional method of corruption in museum transactions. Driker was buying art objects for much more than they were worth, and Beth presumed he was getting the major share of the inflated price. Almost all the sales had been made through Enrico Pelegrine, a small-time art dealer who lurked in the far shadows of legitimate trade.

Beth Haslett had always disliked Driker, but she felt she owed him the opportunity to provide an explanation. His reputation was at stake, and, like him or not, that was a very serious matter. If his answer wasn't satisfactory, then she'd go to the trustees.

She climbed the marble stairs to his palatial office. Seated behind his huge antique desk, he did not get up when she entered.

"Well, what is it?" he snapped.

"Mr. Driker. Our accounting department may have made a mistake in totaling the money paid for recent acquisitions, but if the sums are correct, almost all of the museum's funds have been depleted."

He scowled. "I assume you've gone over the figures?"

She nodded. "Yes."

His expression became a smirking smile. "Miss Haslett, those were all legitimate acquisitions of wonderful pieces of art. They were bargains that couldn't be resisted, not at those prices. I snapped them up before some other buyer or museum got them." He paused and sat forward. "I'll admit the expenditures were a bit large, and I didn't have time to get board approval. But a bargain's a bargain. We'll come out ahead in the long run."

"But, Mr. Driker, what are we to do about meeting our operating costs, even our payroll?"

His smile became a sneer. "I'm afraid this museum will be closed very soon. If I were you, I'd think about seeking other employment. Keep all that to yourself, of course."

"Closed? I can't believe that. The Habermann is one of the best-financed museums in the world. It's supported by some of the nation's wealthiest people."

Annoyed, especially since he had just given the ungrateful girl a valuable tip, Driker glared at her. "Just take my word for it," he snapped. "This museum is going to close, perhaps not right away, but very soon."

"The trustees wouldn't allow such a thing to happen."

His sneer was even more pronounced. "The trustees are the very ones who are going to close this place up."

She was puzzled by his obvious confidence. "Mr. Driker, the trustees, at least some of them, are also members of the Vault. I know you're not familiar with that group, but the Vault is said to run New York . . ."

He chuckled. "Familiar? I'll show you just how familiar I am. Mr. Franklin Trager, the merchant prince himself, got them all to agree to leave New York. I presume that at this very minute they are all very busy selling off whatever New York holdings they still own. My dear young lady, your precious Vault is leaving New York City to the hooligans. They are all getting out before it's too late." He made a fluttering motion with his delicate hands, like a bird flying. "It's all over for this city, and for this museum."

She stared at him. "Where are you getting your information? A Vault member, I suppose?" Her incredulity was reflected in her voice.

He laughed. "Several, you might say." He sat back again in his large chair. "I have sources, very good sources, perhaps even perfect. Profit from it if you can, but keep it to yourself." His conspiratorial manner indicated he was following his own advice.

She walked calmly from his office, then left the museum. She made the telephone call from an outdoor phone on Park Avenue.

John Robertson, Beth's uncle, was both a trustee of the Habermann and a member of the Vault.

She went right to the heart of the matter. "Uncle John, did Franklin Trager propose that the Vault withdraw from New York City?"

Silence was her only answer.

"I said . . ."

"I heard the question," he said firmly. "Where did you pick up such a ridiculous idea?"

"Is it ridiculous? I'm serious. I really have to know. It concerns the Vault's security."

Again there was no immediate response. When he did speak, his voice was commanding. "This can go no further, you understand, Beth?"

"Of course."

"At our last meeting Trager made some wild-eyed proposal along those lines. There was, of course, no support. Now, how could you possibly know about that?"

She quickly told him of the situation at the museum and her conversation with Cecil Driker.

"I have no idea, Uncle John, of how he knew about that discussion. But he's convinced the Vault is pulling out of the city."

This time her uncle's voice was nearly a whisper. "If anyone had been present, our faces would have shown what we thought of Trager's nonsense." He paused. "But if someone were only listening in, they might have drawn the conclusion that since no one voted against it, it was adopted. I think your Mr. Driker has wired our conference room."

"My God, I don't see why he would . . ."

"Beth, this is a most serious matter, for a number of reasons. Say no more to anyone else. Take a few days off from the museum. Call in sick. I'll let you know when to go back."

"But I'm in the middle of a project. I can't . . ."

He chuckled. "Beth, you are so like your mother; a real pain in the ass. But this time, please do as I ask. Do you agree?"

"But Uncle John . . ."

"Beth, shut up!" he thundered.

After talking to his niece, John Robertson dialed Sander Blake's private number.

It was the second time they had talked that day. Blake had notified him of a special Vault meeting and the reasons for calling it. They had also discussed Jon Krugar. The meeting was scheduled for that night.

"What's up, John?"

"Sander, to be blunt, I have information that leads me to believe there might be a bug in the museum's conference room. I think we had better switch the place of the meeting."

"You have to be kidding! Who the hell would bug a goddamned art museum?"

"The director."

"That wimp, Driker? I hardly think so."

"I just received an almost verbatim report on what was said at our last little gathering. The information came from him. Unless he was hiding under the table, he's wired the place."

"Damn!"

"We could meet here at my offices." Robertson laughed. "This is off the record, Sander, seeing that you own half the newspapers in America, but I have my conference room checked regularly. As they say in mystery novels, it's clean."

"All right. I'll call the others and tell them of the change."

"Have all of them agreed to come?" Robertson asked.

"Yes, all of them," Blake replied.

Robertson nodded to himself. "It could turn out to be quite painful."

"It probably will."

"Has to be done though, unpleasant or not," Robertson said.

"I agree," Blake answered. "I'll see you tonight."

"I'm not looking forward to it," Robertson said.

"Nor I."

25

Victoria pushed past the reporters and cameras as she walked briskly away from the federal court building. Her request for an order prohibiting any action by the board of Van Horn Enterprises had failed. It had been a long time since she had been in a courtroom, and she felt out of place. The judge had openly sneered as she made her presentation. Chilton Vance's lawyer exhibited disdain and had hardly bothered to reply. The polished corporate lawyer treated her suit and request for an injunction as a joke. The judge had refused the temporary order and made it more than clear that if the other side brought the proper motion, he would dismiss her entire lawsuit against the board.

Victoria had to fight against crushing feelings of defeat. She had been humiliated in federal court. She was almost glad that the cameramen clustered around her. She had too much pride to let them record tears.

It was only a short walk to the state court. She wondered if the New York judge would treat her any differently. The army of newsmen trooped behind her like unruly schoolchildren following a teacher.

Judge Wilfred Hathaway of New York's Supreme Court had drawn the case. Victoria slipped into his courtroom and saw Craig Hopkins seated near the front.

"We're up next," he said. "Hathaway seems to be in an ugly mood, so be careful." Craig dropped his voice to a bare whisper. "How did you do in federal court?"

"We lost. The judge wouldn't even consider a temporary order. He intimated that if Vance's lawyer will just file a motion, the whole thing will be thrown out."

Craig's eyes met hers. "Was it tough going over there?"

"Very." The disapproving glance of the court clerk let her know any further conversation was at her peril.

The judge, a tall man, stood behind the bench. He used the leather chair like a lectern. Wilfred Hathaway was indeed in a testy mood. His hemorrhoids were acting up again, a condition that caused his usual state of perpetual irritation to increase in direct proportion to his discomfort.

He glared out at the media people who were noisily filling the spectator benches. The clerk called the case.

Victoria had lost all enthusiasm. She stood up slowly.

Hopkins noted her reluctance. "Do you want me to argue it?"

She shook her head. A gray-haired lawyer, whom she recognized as the head partner of one of New York's most powerful law firms, took a place at the counsel table next to her.

"Your Honor," Victoria began, "this is a request for an injunction to prevent the defendants, a group of banks, from bringing foreclosure proceedings under a certain contract . . ."

"I read the pleadings," the judge snapped. "Let's not turn this thing into a circus." He again glared out at the small army of media people. "I understand your position, Miss Van Horn. It seems clear enough. I'll hear what the other side has to say."

She was going to protest, but found she just wasn't up to the fight. Her right to speak was being unfairly denied, but she considered any argument to be fruitless, so she merely nodded and sat down.

The older lawyer stood up, a knowing smile on his features. "As Your

Honor indicates, this is basically a simple matter."

"I didn't indicate anything of the kind," the judge growled. "Get on with it, man."

"As you know, Your Honor, I represent a group of banks that arranged financing for this, ah, young woman. It was a questionable venture, so my clients, the banks, needed to be secured adequately."

"If it was questionable," the judge asked, "why did your people finance it?"

The lawyer stopped smiling. "It's their business to make loans. They were hoping to help develop the city."

"Banks," the judge snapped, "are in the business of making money. Let's try to make some small stab at credibility, okay?"

The lawyer colored slightly. "Miss Van Horn has brought this action and has asked for a temporary restraining order. She claims irreparable harm if foreclosure is begun. No such harm will result. We respectfully request . . ."

"Has she missed a payment?" Judge Hathaway asked, his voice suddenly mild.

"No. But the financing agreement . . ."

"Isn't it unusual to foreclose if the mortgage is up to date?"

"Your Honor, if you had taken the time to read those agreements, which are part of our answer, you would know . . ."

Hathaway's expression was half smile, half grimace. "I read the agreements. It's part of my job, counsel. I may not like taking the time to do it, but that's what the people who elected me expect."

"I was only . . ."

"You!" The judge scowled at Victoria. "You allege you'll be harmed irreparably if I don't stop the banks. Why?"

He frightened her, but she managed not to show it. She spoke quietly, feeling that nothing she might say would make any difference anyway. "If they foreclose—if I don't have the time to raise the money to pay them off—I will lose everything I have built, my business, my projects, everything."

"She agreed when she signed . . ."

"Who asked you?" the judge snapped. He frowned as he spoke to Victoria. "You did sign those documents, and you are a lawyer and an experienced businesswoman: are you trying to escape your responsibilities?"

Victoria sighed. She spoke without thought. "I'm not trying to escape anything. You've read about what happened to me. I'm innocent, but by the time I get through proving that, the banks will have taken everything. The clause they rely on is used for an entirely different purpose. It's not fair to use it this way."

She knew the lawyer for the banks was on his feet. She sat down.

"Your Honor," he began, "you've stated it precisely. She knew exactly what she was doing. We have a right to enforce . . ."

Judge Hathaway held up a warning hand. "Maybe you do, maybe you don't. I'll set this whole thing for additional hearing a week from Friday. In the meantime, I'll grant plaintiff's request for a temporary restraining order."

"You can't do that!" the lawyer said.

This time Hathaway's smile was genuine. "But I just did, counsel."

"In that case, we demand that you set a bond . . ."

Hathaway shook his head. "What for? Nothing is going to happen to that property by a week from Friday. Believe me, your banks won't go out of business. No bond."

"I will appeal," the lawyer shouted.

"Keep your voice at a reasonable level, counsel, or you're going to need a lawyer. Understand? I doubt that an appeal of this little order of mine will be entertained, but in case you don't know the way to the appellate court, my clerk will give you directions."

Victoria sat in disbelief.

"That's all," the judge growled. The clerk rapped a gavel as the judge gingerly walked off the bench.

Craig Hopkins got to her before the reporters. He squeezed her. "You've won, Victoria. It's a damned miracle."

She stood up and put her papers back in her briefcase. "It's only a skirmish, Craig, not the main battle. We've bought some time, that's all."

But her reply didn't dampen his enthusiasm. "It's a good omen, Vicky. Maybe we do have a chance after all."

Victoria again had to push through the mob of reporters. She didn't feel victorious, only tired. Nothing had really changed. She knew she should be grateful for even a small victory, but she had a sense of the enormity of the challenge that lay ahead. She wondered if she would have sufficient courage or energy to keep on.

"What will happen now, Miss Van Horn?" A woman television reporter thrust a microphone close to her face.

"I've never lost a fight in my life," she snapped with a conviction she did not really feel.

The members of the Vault sat in uncomfortable silence after Stewart Lytle left. What they had done was necessary but distasteful. Sander Blake stood up. "Luke, would you please bring Mr. Krugar in?"

Jon Krugar had been waiting in a side office, kept out of sight until the Vault had disposed of the Lytle matter. "I'll get him," Shaw said.

They had changed the meeting place to John Robertson's brokerage firm because of the suspicion that the Habermann might be bugged. Robertson's conference room was as large and posh as the Habermann's but no one except Robertson really felt at home there. Luke walked down the thickly carpeted hall and entered the office where Krugar waited.

The big man looked up. As usual he was accompanied by Mr. Yee. "Well, how is it going?" Krugar asked.

"There's a vacancy," Luke said. "Ambassador Lytle has resigned."

Krugar nodded. "Because of his son, I presume?"

Luke nodded. "Indirectly. Lytle knew of his son's problems, and despite that, he tried to use the Vault to further his son's career, even allowing a Vault member to be destroyed."

"Miss Van Horn."

"We insisted not only that he resign the Vault, but that he resign from his bank. The members thought it might be awkward doing business with Perry Stanley if he was still at the helm. Certain arrangements relative to his son were also proposed."

"He agreed?"

Luke smiled wryly. "Basically, he had no choice. He knows the power of the Vault."

Krugar struggled to his feet. "And, what may I ask, is to be the decision about me?"

"Do we still have our deal?" Luke asked.

Krugar chuckled. "Of course. If I'm accepted for Vault membership I will undertake to help Miss Van Horn. I am a man of my word, sir."

"I suppose I should let them tell you," Luke said, "but we have voted to accept you as a member."

Krugar smiled. "Don't worry, my young friend. When they inform me I shall register the appropriate surprise."

"Come with me."

Krugar lumbered behind Luke. "Are you going to propose that the Vault help Victoria?"

Luke nodded. "I am going to try. Some of them don't like having a woman as a member; they may not want to help."

"You will have my vote, and my enthusiastic support." Krugar placed a large hand on Luke's shoulder. "Between us, Mr. Shaw, we may have the makings of a very potent team. Let's see what we can do if we really set our minds to it."

Although Barry Lytle was ready, he thought it was a bit like being transported to one's own execution when Luke Shaw picked him up. It was the first time he had met Shaw, and Lytle was surprised to find him so young. Barry had presumed that all members of the Vault were ancient.

Neither man felt like talking as they headed out toward Lytle's home congressional district. Luke Shaw drove through the clutter and graffiti of upper Manhattan, crossed the desolation of the South Bronx, then moved beyond the city, passing through levels of economic strata; concentric rings of upward mobility. Soon they came to neighborhoods of rolling lawns and center-hall colonials, the homes of the voters who had elected Barry Lytle.

Lytle's district office was located in a pleasant modern shopping mall. He seldom visited his district office except during elections. He didn't need to. Experienced and politically tactful assistants handled everything competently for him. Shaw swung the car into the vast expanse of the mall's parking area. They could see television remote trucks clustered in front of the office. Attracted by the trucks, a crowd had gathered.

"Look at that. If I was to be hung it wouldn't draw more of a crowd." Lytle laughed. "Well, maybe a few more, but not many."

"You've been briefed," Shaw said quietly. "Do you remember everything you have to say?"

Lytle sighed, then glanced over at him. "I've heard all about you, Shaw. They say you were raised by your fucking uncle. Your father, the unofficial historian of the upper classes, I'm told, never had much to do with you."

"So?"

"You probably feel deprived. If you do, you're goddamned mistaken. My old man made me his puppet and it was pure hell. I wish he had neglected me, but I couldn't take a crap without getting his approval first."

"Feeling a bit sorry for yourself?"

Barry Lytle chuckled. "Quite the opposite. From what I understand, you people are forcing my father out of Perry Stanley. He'll still have buckets of money, of course, but no power. For him, that's the worst punishment possible."

"I take it you're happy about that?"

Lytle nodded. "To be candid, yes. I'm about to admit to being an addict. My career, such as it was, is over. Fortunately, I have money too, left by my mother, so I won't have to suck around the old man for handouts. He'll have no more control over me. Given the circumstances, and I admit they are peculiar, I still feel like a prisoner being set free."

"You have to go back to the hospital. That's part of the deal."

He nodded. "I'm a lawyer. I know about deals. The prosecutor hits me with the possession charge. I make my tearful little speech in court, and then the judge sends me to the hospital for rehabilitation. After a suitable time, they let me out." He sighed. "If I wasn't the son of wealth, they'd probably send me to a very different place. But I'm a rich repentant sinner, and everybody likes them. Most people will say I've been punished enough just by resigning from Congress and being confined in the hospital. Hell, I would too, except that's not the case."

"You don't sound repentant."

He laughed. "I'm not. As soon as I can, after they let me out, I'll pop down to Mexico for good. Hey, there're worse places. Nice supple señoritas, lots of margaritas, and a snort of the white stuff now and then just for old times' sake. It sure beats being a prisoner in the White House, which was exactly the fate my father had planned for me."

They pulled up next to the television trucks. Photographers moved toward the car. The air seemed charged with drama.

"You won't forget about Victoria Van Horn in your statement?" Luke reminded him.

Lytle looked over at him. "Appeals to you, does she?"

"She's a fellow member of the Vault," Shaw said defensively.

Lytle smiled and shook his head. "I'll tell you something, Shaw, if she doesn't appeal to you, something's very wrong. She's a real beauty. Nice girl too." He started to climb out of the car, then looked back at Luke. "Say, you're not like your uncle, are you?"

Shaw shook his head and laughed for the first time.

"Don't worry, I'll clear Victoria completely. That will be a refreshing change for me; usually I blame everyone but myself."

Luke followed Lytle into his headquarters. The place was jammed. Lytle was perspiring slightly as he stepped into the glare of the television lights. His expression was solemn and his voice quietly dignified as he began to make his statement.

Chilton Vance returned from his business meeting and hurried into the Van Horn Building. His heels clicked on the tile as he strode toward the executive elevator. People stared, even those who didn't know who he was. He exuded an air of command. He liked the attention. He enjoyed being respected.

His secretary looked up as he briskly walked past her.

"Oh, Mr. Vance," she called after him.

He turned. "Yes?"

"I just heard on the radio. Congressman Lytle has just resigned. He took full blame for those drugs, at least that's what the newsman said."

"What do you mean, full blame?" he snapped.

The sharpness of his words frightened her. "According to the radio report, he said Miss Van Horn had no knowledge of the drugs and had never used any to his knowledge. It turns out he's been, well, an addict for years."

Vance experienced the prickling sensation of vague danger. Victoria's criminal problems had been mere icing on the cake, but they had helped expedite his plans. Nothing would be changed, he would still be in complete control of Van Horn Enterprises; there was nothing she could do about that. Still, he found the unexpected turn of events strangely unsettling.

"I'm pleased for Miss Van Horn," he said, forcing a smile as he continued into his office. He closed the door, then turned the radio on, keeping its volume low. The next newscast was scheduled in twenty minutes and he desperately wanted to hear the details for himself.

He told himself again that it made no difference, but he really didn't believe it. He would have to do something. And it would have to be clever—and quick.

PART
FOUR

26

Jon Krugar beamed as Mr. Yee ushered Victoria into his suite. "I'm delighted you could come," he said. "I saw you on television. You sounded like a Wagnerian heroine. A very effective presentation, indeed." He indicated a chair. "Please sit down."

"I'm afraid I've been so busy, Mr. Krugar, that I haven't had an opportunity to do anything about helping you become a member of the Vault. I shall try, of course, but I don't think . . ."

Krugar sat opposite her in one of the high-backed tapestry-covered chairs. He chuckled. "I have become a member of that honorable body on my own."

She didn't even try to hide her surprise. "Congratulations. Is it my spot?"

"Why do you say that?"

She shrugged. "Considering all that has happened, I presume I have been removed as a Vault member."

"Presumptions are often wrong."

"Oh?"

"May I offer you some breakfast? Or at least some coffee?"

She nodded. "I could use some coffee. I came out on the run this morning."

"Mr. Yee," Krugar said, smiling, "please demonstrate your magic as a master brewer." He returned his gaze to Victoria. "You didn't listen to the news this morning?"

"No. Why?"

"Much has happened," Krugar replied. "Not the least of which was the business with Congressman Lytle this morning."

"I don't follow you."

He smiled. "It is happening almost as we speak. There was a press handout this morning that the radio people are using. By tonight the story will be all over the newspapers and the evening television news."

Victoria felt her heartbeat accelerate as if threatened with physical danger. "What's happened?"

Yee returned and set out steaming cups, together with a plate of rich pastry. Krugar took a cup and sipped eagerly. "To put it as kindly as possible, the congressman hasn't been entirely honest with the public, the police, and especially you. He has a long history of drug abuse, did you know that?"

"No, but it doesn't surprise me."

"I thought not," Krugar said, taking up a pastry with his other hand. "The congressman has made a deal with the prosecutor. He will plead guilty to the possession of those drugs he said belonged to you. At this moment, he is resigning from Congress."

Victoria suddenly felt as if the room were spinning.

"Do take some of this delicious coffee," Krugar said. "Barry Lytle has cleared you completely." He took time to finish off the pastry and then reached for another. "Odd business. His father, Ambassador Lytle, knew of his problem and had shielded him all his life. Obviously, Stewart Lytle was more than dishonest with his fellow members of the Vault, including nearly destroying you in the process. Disgraceful conduct. He has not only resigned from the Vault, but also as the head of Perry Stanley. The Vault members felt his continued presence as head of that bank might prove awkward. It is his spot on the Vault that I was so happily selected to fill." He laughed at her surprise. "So, my dear, you won't end up as the best-looking prisoner in the New York penal system after all."

For a moment she couldn't speak. Her sense of relief was almost overwhelming. "It's been like . . . 'Nightmare' is too weak a word."

He noticed her reaction. He put down his cup and reached across to pat her hand. "There, my girl, the worst is past. Would you like something a bit stronger, brandy perhaps?"

She shook her head. "Things haven't been going very well. This is really the first good news that I've had." She looked up at him. "I imagine the Vault still wishes my resignation."

He noted how pale she had become and nodded to Yee, who returned quickly with a brandy. She took the snifter and drank.

"The members of the Vault appreciate the difficulties you've experienced, Victoria. You've been publicly disgraced by unscrupulous men, thrown out of your father's company and had your own business placed in peril." He again patted her hand. "And your fighting spirit has been greatly admired too. I understand you've reconciled with your brother, despite what he tried to do to you."

"That's true."

Krugar chuckled. "I like that. That shows real class, Victoria."

"Class or not, we don't seem to be doing very well. Nothing seems to be working."

"Are you still interested in a bit of help?"

She slowly shook her head. "We had an agreement. If I helped you, you would help me. I didn't even have the chance to try. You have no obligation to me, Mr. Krugar."

He sighed. "Ah, but I do."

"I don't understand."

Krugar took up his cup again and sipped. "You have a very effective champion, Victoria. I was bargained into a corner, so to speak. My membership on the Vault depended upon my agreement to help you. As an honorable man, I have no other choice."

"Champion?"

"I don't completely understand his motivation. He claims no romantic interest, but he certainly acts as if there were." He laughed. "Luke Shaw has been frantically twisting arms in your behalf, my dear. One of the arms was mine. But the other members of the Vault have also agreed to help. Mr. Shaw is a hard man to refuse."

"Help me?" Color rose to her cheeks.

"Indeed. We are quite united, thanks to your champion. You are still a member of the Vault. You can sit back, Victoria, and relax. We'll take it from here."

"Even the Vault can't . . ."

Krugar signaled to Yee to refill his cup. "I think you may be surprised. Power, when used judiciously, can be truly awesome."

Victoria couldn't hold back the tears. At last there seemed to be a promise of hope. She sobbed with relief.

Krugar pulled out his huge white handkerchief and handed it to her. He chuckled. "I hope that if I'm ever in trouble, your Mr. Shaw will be on my side. He's quite the fellow."

The Thompson family ran the bank, a tradition as certain as the tides and moon. Ralph Thompson had replaced his father as head of the Wheaton International Bank, and he fully expected, in due time, to pass that office on to his son, who now served as an assistant vice-president in the trust department. The certainty of continuity was comforting to officers, employees and customers of the bank.

Ralph Thompson had listened carefully to his soft-spoken visitors. He knew and respected them, but more importantly, he feared them. It had been a pleasant meeting, at least on the surface; everyone was genial and polite. There were no threats as such. But his visitors had discussed the bad loans—given at the insistence of the government—to the Central American banks; loans now uncollectible unless Washington decided to step in and bail everyone out. Wheaton was only one of several banks that found themselves in this position. Thompson's visitors merely discussed the enormous trust deposits that formed much of the base of the Wheaton as a banking institution; trusts that they controlled. Without it being said, Thompson understood that if the trust money were withdrawn, that, together with the foreign loans, would destroy the Wheaton. Then they let him know what they wanted.

After they left, the irritating cramping began in his left shoulder. As usual, the sensation traveled down his left arm, ending in a small explosion of pain in the fingers of his left hand. It was the first time in months that it had happened. He took the small vial from his pocket and shook out one of the tablets, placing it beneath his tongue. He sat back in his leather chair and tried to relax. The nitroglycerin caused a throbbing headache, but the numbing pain in his shoulder and arm subsided quickly. He waited until the headache ebbed, then asked his secretary to step into his office.

He gave careful instructions. She was to set up a conference call with the chief officers of all the participating banks. Fortunately, he had some leverage with most—the Wheaton was an important part of their business—and expected no serious challenge to his proposal. But there would be embarrassing questions. He could anticipate what might be asked, though, and would be prepared.

There would be no quick killing, no profit from a well-timed foreclosure. The loan to Victoria Van Horn would be continued according to the provisions of the agreement.

There was no other way.

If he didn't arrange to withdraw the foreclosure, huge deposits would be taken out of the Wheaton and the bank would come crashing down. And no one, not even Washington, would dare help. The Wheaton would cease to exist, its assets taken over by a larger, sounder bank; that was the custom. There would be no more Wheaton, and no more Thompsons to run it.

It amounted to a simple question of survival.

He felt the beginning of the shoulder pain again and popped another pill. He wished he would never have to deal with the Vault again. They were dangerous people. But he knew that was foolish. They were too powerful. He would always have to do business with them.

Thompson closed his eyes and lay back in the chair. The pain, he knew, would eventually go away. But the Vault would not.

Luke Shaw was busily trying to make up for lost time. The others would do what still had to be done; he was no longer needed. Now his own business demanded urgent attention. His usually untidy office was even more cluttered with blueprints and plans of new assignments, jobs that needed his assessment and approval. Piles of papers and plans were stacked on his desk and on every other flat surface in his office, including the hardwood floor.

The telephone interrupted his study of a proposed construction in France. He snatched up the receiver, holding the French plans open with his other hand. "Yes?" he snapped irritably.

His secretary was used to such abrupt responses. "Miss Van Horn is here to see you," she said, a triumphant note in her voice. She sometimes took perverse pleasure in interrupting him. This time it was legitimate.

Luke was startled. "Miss Van Horn? You sure?"

"She's right here." She knew there was no graceful way he could decline to see his visitor. "Do you want me to send her in?"

The French blueprint rolled up as soon as he released it. "I suppose so," he replied.

He sat back in his old swivel chair. For a minute he was tempted to try to straighten up the place, then he abandoned that as hopeless.

He was always surprised at the effect she had on him. Each time she seemed more lovely than he remembered. He stood up as she walked in. "This mess is worse than usual." He shoved some architectural drawings off a chair. "Please sit down."

As he returned to his old chair behind the desk, Luke wondered at his own feelings about Victoria. He found himself delighted and excited, but also strangely afraid.

"I came to thank you," Victoria said simply.

"Nothing to thank me for." He knew he was blushing and it embarrassed him. "You needed a helping hand, and you're a fellow member of the Vault. It was merely an act of friendship."

"According to Jon Krugar, if it wasn't for you I would have been fed to the wolves. He said you were my champion. I consider what you did much more than just a friendly gesture."

He tried not to look at her. She distracted him. "Well, whatever, things seem to be getting back on the track."

"Thanks to you."

"Someday you can do me a favor," he said quietly. Despite himself he looked at her. Her extraordinary beauty was matched by her strength of character. There was nothing about her that he didn't like. For the first time he realized he had fallen in love with Victoria Van Horn. That sudden revelation was both frightening and discomforting. He had resolved long ago never to love again. It was too emotionally dangerous, and he had determined never to even get seriously involved.

"How are things coming along?" He managed to keep his voice from reflecting his turbulent feelings.

She seemed puzzled by his attitude. "I really don't know. Jon Krugar says that the Vault will help me. But the banks are still foreclosing on my property, although I managed to fight for some time in court. And Chilton Vance has firm control of my father's company. I appreciate the Vault's efforts, but I don't hold out much hope for success."

"You never know," he said. "I'm a new boy, as you know, but they seem pretty confident about their ability to help out."

She smiled. "Whether they do or don't, at least I don't have to go to jail, thanks to you, and at least some of my reputation has been regained. And that's the most precious thing I have, Luke, even if I lose everything else." She looked directly into his eyes. "Can I ask you something?"

He shrugged. "Sure."

"Why did you do it—help me, I mean? I deeply appreciate what you did, I just don't understand why."

He was suddenly even more flustered. "Like I said, you were a fellow member of the Vault . . ."

"No other reason?"

"Like what?"

This time she was the one who looked away. "I thought you might have done it because you liked me."

"Of course I like you, Vicky. But that's not the reason. It was a matter of simple justice. I resented what was being done to you. It seemed so unfair."

Her eyes sought his. "I've never known a man quite like you."

"Well, you haven't known many people then." He managed a quick laugh. "Nothing's changed, Vicky I'm the same working engineer you got so angry at out on that pier. You've just gone through one hell of an experience, that's all. Anyone who helped would look pretty good."

She shook her head. "No, that's not true and we both know it. You're very special, Luke, the kind of a man a woman looks for but never expects to find."

He was aware that her attraction for him was almost overpowering, and he fought to control his rising feelings. He was determined not to hurt her. "Can I be frank?"

She nodded.

Luke tried to select his words carefully. "I'd be a damned liar if I said I wasn't, well, drawn to you. You are a most unusual woman. I suppose I could easily fall in love with you, but that would be quite unfair."

"Oh?"

He shifted uncomfortably in his chair. "I've been married before, as you may know. I have a son. I didn't have time to devote to my marriage or my child. I failed as a husband and as a father, rather badly. My former wife is happily remarried and my son is being raised by someone who does take the time to make the effort."

"Everyone learns from the past, Luke."

He sighed. "That's just it, Vicky. I have learned. If I ever got involved again nothing would change. I don't run this business, it runs me. I'm wise enough to know it now, that's all." He looked away. "I wouldn't do that to anyone again, especially someone . . . I might, ah, care about deeply."

She was no longer smiling, her expression solemn. "I'm wedded to my work too, Luke. But life, fortunately, is expandable. People, even busy people, work around problems."

He shook his head. "We both probably feel a mutual attraction. We are somewhat alike."

"Is that all it is, just a mutual attraction?"

He shrugged. "Maybe more, but what difference does that make?"

"It could make all the difference in the world."

"No, not really. I've thought it all out long ago, Vicky. There'll be no more personal commitments from me. I could never keep them." He wanted to take her in his arms, almost desperately, but he was determined that he would not. "Believe me, I think too much of you to take advantage of your gratitude. I'm a loner, Vicky. Always will be."

She stood up, color highlighting her cheeks. "Well, I may be embarrassed, but I am appreciative. You've made your reasons clear, Luke, and I respect them." She tried to smile. "Still friends, though, I hope?"

Luke too stood up. "Of course." He felt sudden fear. He didn't want to be parted from her. "We'll always be friends."

She reached into her handbag and pulled out a pen. "Do you have a scrap of paper?" She wrote out an address and handed it to him. "This is my brother's address. He's having dinner for myself and Joyce Spitz tonight. I'd like you to come."

He took the note. "I really have so much work . . ."

"Promise that you'll at least try to come?"

He walked her to the door. "If I can make it, I'll drop by."

Suddenly she reached up and kissed him quickly on the cheek. Then she turned and was gone.

He was conscious only of her touch and perfume, and his own urgent hunger for her. He was in love, perhaps for the first time in his life, really in love. It frightened him. There was no place in his life for anything but his work. He had told her the truth, only she could never know what he was feeling.

He walked to his desk and looked at the jumble of plans. It was no use, he could think of nothing but Victoria Van Horn. He would have to do something about it or all would be lost. He would have to escape from her, and from his feelings about her.

He looked longingly at the address she had given him, and he knew he would have to do something immediately.

———————

Victoria, Joyce and Craig Hopkins had been invited to Junior's apartment for dinner. Victoria had hoped Luke Shaw would come too. But he did not, and she felt his failure to appear was his way of saying, for good, that nothing more could ever exist between them. She sadly accepted his decision.

They dined quietly, their mood subdued, neither joyous or depressed. They were very like a team that had played very well but had lost.

Junior was reserved but seemed more contented. Victoria noted that he had returned to drinking only tea. He seemed delighted to be free of Cecelia. With sobriety his slightly stuffy mannerisms had returned, but he exhibited occasional flashes of a keen sense of humor Victoria had never realized he possessed.

The dinner—chilled salmon with dill sauce—prepared by Junior's chef was excellent. They lingered over the expensive brandy Junior had provided.

Craig Hopkins raised his glass. "Here's to us. We made a hell of a run at it, no matter what the outcome." He downed his brandy. "As soon as everything is wound up I'm going back to the firm. As a businessman, I'm a pretty good lawyer."

Victoria looked at him. "You were a great help when I needed you."

He laughed. "My intentions were good, Vicky. I don't think I helped worth a damn, to be frank. But if you decide to start your own law firm, let me know. I think we did pretty well together. Otherwise, I'm going back to the same old stand."

She realized it was his way of saying their lives were parting once more.

"I called every member of the Van Horn board today," Junior said, taking a delicate sip of his tea. "I started with the ones who were loyal to father. Happily, they still seem loyal to our family, but I was advised, very diplomatically, that nothing could be done."

"And the others?" Victoria asked.

He smiled wryly. "With one exception, they wouldn't talk to me and they didn't return my calls. However, Bradford Lewis made it a point to express personal hostility. Delightful man, he was the one who advocated my taking over the company in the first place." Junior chuckled. "Well, at least he's predictable. I received a heated lecture on why no Van Horn would ever again serve the company in a position of trust. He was, even for him, extremely pompous about it."

"He's Chilton Vance's man on the board. One of several." Joyce Spitz studied her brandy glass. "He's like a weathervane. He'll always show the direction Vance will be coming from."

"I'd love to tie the can to that fellow." Junior sighed. "Oh well, there's a lot of things I'd like to do; some possible, some impossible. I suppose I'll have to put that on the impossible side of the ledger." He looked across the table at his sister. "I'm sorry, Vicky. I thought I might get a few of them to change their minds."

"Perhaps the Vault can do something."

Her brother shook his head. "Vance is too entrenched. No one could possibly get him out, at least not quickly."

"Maybe not," Joyce Spitz said, "But I wouldn't discount the Vault's power. I saw it when I worked for your father. They don't often use it, but when they do, it can be awesome."

Craig Hopkins helped himself to more of the brandy. "There's help, and there's help. It may be a matter of degree. We don't know what they're prepared to do."

"Have you talked to Luke Shaw?" Joyce asked.

Victoria nodded. "He's been a tremendous friend, as you all know, but he's leaving the rest to the others on the Vault. I had hoped he would come here tonight, but I guess he couldn't make it."

Her brother's laugh was without humor. "We don't seem to be overwhelmingly popular with anyone, do we?"

They fell into an awkward silence.

Finally Junior spoke. "I propose a parlor game of sorts. Joyce, you were closer to my father than any of us. If you were made head of Van Horn Enterprises, given all the circumstances, what would you do?"

"You mean what would your father do?"

He shook his head. "No, not at all. I think you know the business better than anyone. Just for fun, what would you do?"

As she talked, Joyce Spitz warmed to the subject. She knew every nook and cranny of the giant conglomerate, and she had specific ideas for curing the various ills of the company. The others listened in fascination until she finished.

"Well," Junior said, "it seems we've had the wrong person running the company right from the start. Didn't you ever tell my father what you thought?"

She blushed. "You know how your father was. He was in command at all times. I did make some subtle suggestions now and then. Remember, I was his secretary. Anything else wouldn't have been respectful."

"Respectful or not," Junior said, "he would have appreciated your ideas. I'm certainly impressed."

"So am I," Victoria added quietly.

———————

When the telephone rang, Vance was awake and answered it himself. His wife and the servants had all retired.

"Yes?"

"Chilton, is that you?" The unrecognized voice sounded strained, almost bleating.

"Pardon me?"

"Chilton, this is me, Bradford Lewis."

"Is something wrong, Brad? You sound strange."

"I've been fired."

"What?" Vance was genuinely surprised. Lewis was the chief executive of his brokerage firm. "I don't understand."

"Jesus, me too!" Lewis obviously had been drinking. "I've been with the firm since I got out of Harvard. They just told me to pack up my things."

"Who are 'they'?" Vance was alert, instinctively sensing danger.

"Murphy, the chairman of the board. Even old man Wellington, the founder, himself. They told me I was fucking up the firm, and let me go. Just like that! It was awful!"

"What did they say?"

He was greeted by a sound that was half laugh, half sob. "Do they need any reason? They do what they want to do. Oh, they did give me some baloney about making enemies of powerful people, but that's bullshit, Chilton. I've kissed so many asses my lips are chapped. I just don't understand what happened. The company is making money, the books are all straight. Jesus, there just wasn't any reason for them doing this to me."

"Are you going to fight it?" Vance asked.

There was a pause. "No. They were quite generous, actually. They let me keep my stock options. I can exercise them. That's quite a lot of money. And my pension is vested. They're going to pay me my salary for a year. I'll be a consultant with no duties. They did a shitty thing to me, but at least I won't starve."

Vance, like an animal, sensed the presence of an unseen enemy. "And what did they get in return for all this munificence?"

He heard ice cubes clink in a glass on the other end of the line. Then Lewis spoke again. "Not much, really. I had to resign, of course. And I had to resign all my other offices too."

"Such as?"

"Directorships, that sort of thing. I had to sign papers right there. It was humiliating."

"Did you resign as a director of Van Horn Enterprises?"

"Oh sure, that was one. I hated to do it, but I had no other course. I had to protect those stock options. You understand?" His last words were so slurred they were almost unintelligible.

Vance nodded. "Did they say who they might nominate to replace you on our board?"

"Yeah, as a matter of fact, they did. Murphy himself. He doesn't ordinarily do that sort of thing, but old man Wellington insisted."

"What about your other directorships?"

"Funny, they didn't seem to care about those. Look, Chilton, old boy, I need a favor."

"Anything I can do, of course."

The ice cubes clinked again. "In a year I'll need a job. You know me, I'm a pretty fair executive. I know how to play ball—you, of all people, know about that. Maybe you could find a spot for me in Van Horn, maybe one of the subsidiary companies?"

"That's a very good possibility, Brad," Vance replied, knowing that he didn't mean it. "Perhaps we can have lunch soon and discuss it. All right?"

"I knew I could count on you, Chilton. You are a true friend."

"It's been a hard day for you. By the way, when did all this happen?"

"About an hour or two ago. I was at home and they called me down to the office. Jesus, it was almost midnight. I still can't figure out why they had to do it so quick. It would have kept until morning. The whole damn business is strange." He hiccuped. "Well, at least I still got the stock, eh? I'll be starting a new life and all that, what?"

"Good night," Vance said, quickly hanging up the telephone.

He sat quietly for a moment, not really thinking, just allowing his mind to float, not focusing on anything specific.

Then he got up and poured himself a glass of whiskey. He consulted his personal telephone book for the private number, then dialed.

The phone rang a number of times before being answered. A polished but annoyed voice answered at last. "The Van Dyne residence."

"This is Chilton Vance," he said distinctly and with authority. "Do you know who I am?"

"Yes, sir." The annoyance was instantly gone.

"I realize it's late, but I would like to speak to Mr. Van Dyne. It's important."

"Just a moment, sir. I shall have to get dressed."

"I understand."

Vance sipped at the whiskey as he waited. Sinclair Van Dyne was an independent on the board of directors, not pledged to either side. The telephone call was Vance's way of testing the water.

It seemed to Vance that an unusually long time passed before the man came back on the line. "I'm awfully sorry, Mr. Vance. I'm the butler and I was asleep. Mr. Van Dyne seems to have stepped out this evening. I'll leave a message to call, if you like?"

Vance slowly shook his head. "No. Thank you. I'll call him in the morning, at the office."

"As you wish, sir. Good night."

Vance replaced the receiver. The butler had been just a touch too cheerful. He had lied. Van Dyne didn't wish to take the call. Vance had stuck his toe in the water and found it very hot, perhaps even scalding.

He turned off the lights and opened the drapes. He knew he would not be able to sleep. Chilton Vance sat quietly and looked out on the lights of New York City. Tomorrow would tell the tale.

27

Cecil Driker always walked from his apartment to the museum, unless the weather was bad. His morning walk was his main source of daily exercise. He would have to find some other way to keep fit when the Habermann closed.

It was a beautiful warm spring morning and he felt relaxed and happy. Driker whistled softly as he climbed the front steps of the museum. The guard, as usual, touched his uniform cap as Driker passed. Driker decided against using the small elevator and took the marble stairs, again for the purpose of exercise.

His secretary was not at her desk. He found that annoying. He was the museum director; he could be late, but not she.

He was surprised to see John Robertson seated behind his desk. A stern-looking man in an ill-fitting suit sat on Driker's leather couch. Driker did not recognize him. He found the invasion of his private office offensive but concealed his feelings. "What a pleasant surprise." Driker forced a quick smile.

Robertson looked up; there was no smile on his fleshy features. "This is Mr. Anthony Griswak." He nodded toward the man on the couch. "He's an investigator hired by the trustees."

"Oh?"

"Our accountants have been examining recent acquisitions," Robertson continued. "They seem quite irregular."

Driker was painfully aware that he hadn't been invited to sit down in his own office. Nevertheless, he primly took a chair in front of the desk. "We have been most fortunate in finding some very unusual opportunities lately," he said. Driker had practiced what he might say in case of discovery. But he hadn't thought it would happen quite so fast. "I would have sought authority from the trustees, but everything happened so fast. I had to make the buys or lose out. There just wasn't any time."

"The invoices show you purchased the paintings from Enrico Pelegrine, an Italian art dealer."

"That's correct," Driker answered, feeling more confident. "Pelegrine sometimes comes across spectacular buys. This time he really outdid himself."

Robinson's face was expressionless. "Did you receive any money or any other consideration from the sales?"

Driker drew himself up in indignation, or what he hoped passed for indignation. "Of course not! What do you think I am? I have an international reputation. I would never accept a kickback under any circumstances."

The man on the couch took a cheap notepad from his inside pocket and flipped it open. "We had some people talk to Mr. Enrico Pelegrine in Florence," he said. "As soon as he was assured he wouldn't be prosecuted, or have to give any money back, he agreed to cooperate. He admitted that he kicked back most of the purchase price for the pictures to Cecil Driker." Griswak looked at Driker. "He made a positive identification, and gave a signed statement."

"Absolute rubbish!" Driker shrieked. "He's lying!"

"Mr. Pelegrine says the prices were greatly inflated on your orders." Griswak flipped another page. "According to our figures, although they are rough estimates, you made almost two million dollars from the kickbacks."

"I demand a lawyer." Driker was suddenly afraid for the first time. The money figure was surprisingly accurate. Pelegrine had obviously talked.

"This isn't a criminal matter," Robertson said quietly. "At least, not yet."

"None of this is true," Driker said quickly. "But you say 'not yet,' and that means it could become a criminal charge. I demand a lawyer. That's my right."

Robertson shifted his huge bulk. The chair creaked in protest. "Driker, we also discovered the bugs you planted in the conference room."

"What bugs? I know nothing about any bugs!"

Robertson half smiled. "The little listening devices you had installed downstairs; the ones that broadcast to the nifty little receiver you have hidden in that cabinet over there."

Driker's heart was pounding. "I want an attorney."

Robertson ignored him. "We want the money, Driker; every last cent you received from your little scheme. And don't try to lie about the amount. We'll have an exact tally from our accountants by day's end."

"None of this would even stand up in a court of law." Driker tried to keep his voice from shaking.

Robertson suddenly grinned. "On the basis of Pelegrine's testimony alone I should think you could look forward to a number of years as the guest of the New York penal system. Perhaps there you might even start a collection of prison art."

Driker's stomach churned. "What do you want of me?"

"We want the money back, obviously. And we want your resignation." Robertson again shifted in the protesting chair. "If you have made any recordings of the Vault meetings, we want those too."

Driker knew there was no way out. He nodded meekly.

"Based on what you heard, you presumed we were going to abandon our interests in New York City, right?"

Driker again nodded silently.

"Mr. Trager's suggestion was so foolish it wasn't even considered. But your little bugging devices, having no eyes, failed you there. You acted on the basis of completely incorrect information." Robertson shook his head. "You're a stupid man, Driker. Oh, there is one more thing."

"And that is?"

"Our lawyers will draft a document in which you agree not to serve any museum in the world in any capacity for five years. We wouldn't want you trying the same thing with anyone else, would we?"

"That's unfair. Museum work is the only thing I know. I'll starve!"

"You know the art world as well as I. Word of your little adventure here will spread all over the world. No one in their right mind would ever take the chance of dealing with you. You will have to find some other kind of occupation." Robertson's face grew stern. "It's up to you, Driker. Either agree to our terms or go to prison."

Driker's face was jerking involuntarily. His wonderful future had suddenly become no future at all. But prison was unthinkable. "All right," he said, his voice a whisper.

"Good. Go with Mr. Griswak. He'll take down the necessary information and make the arrangements." Robertson looked up at Driker as the little man stood. "Your personal belongings here will be packed and sent to you." Robertson's expression was disdainful.

"You've ruined me," Driker shrieked. "You and the damned Vault!"

Robertson shook his head. "No, Driker, you ruined yourself. And I must say, you seem to have done a splendid job of it."

Chilton Vance had spent most of the day on the telephone, until the true picture of the situation emerged. Then he knew there was nothing more he could do.

He hadn't told his wife of his suspicions after Bradford Lewis's drunken call. He wanted to find out what was really happening. Now that he knew, it was time to let her know. He called her at her office.

"Hi," she answered. "Listen, I don't want to be rude, Chilton, but I'm just between meetings. I don't have much time."

He had only wanted control of the company, but she had seemed determined to have revenge for something unnamed. Breaking the Van Horns seemed so important to her. He wondered now how he could tell her.

"There's been some rather startling developments here," he said.

"Oh?"

"An emergency meeting of the board of directors has been called for tonight."

"Again? Good God, those people will quit if you keep this up." She sounded amused. "You have some very successful and busy people serving on that board, Chilton. I wouldn't burden them with unnecessary meetings. Especially at night, and without decent prior notice."

He paused, trying to think of the right words. "This meeting wasn't my idea."

"What do you mean? You're president and chairman of the board. Who else can call a meeting, if not you?"

"The majority of the board."

"What on earth for?"

Suddenly he had a mental picture of her in bed, nakedly wanton, casually creating desire. He would miss that.

"Roberta," he said quietly. "I believe they plan another change at the top."

"What the hell are you talking about?"

There was no use in delaying the news. Time wouldn't make it any more palliative. "It seems each member of the board has been approached and asked to vote me out. Several wished to resist, but they could not."

"Why couldn't they? Chilton, have you been drinking?" Her last statement sounded more like a hope than a question.

"Not yet," he answered truthfully. "I'm afraid I have run afoul of the Vault."

He heard her intake of breath.

"Victoria took her father's place on the Vault, just as she did here at the company. I didn't think it would matter to them. But they feel, apparently, that I haven't dealt fairly with her."

"What difference does that make? That's business. If they put that bitch back in, it will make a mockery of the company."

He felt weary. It had been a long day, and he had had no sleep. "Have you seen the newspapers?"

"I've been busy."

"Well, they are doing something of a magical reconstruction on our Victoria. Lytle, the congressman she was seeing, as you know, took full responsibility for the drugs, admitting he lured her up to that hotel room and tried to attack her. It's the sort of thing the public loves. Victoria will soon look like a local Joan of Arc. It's an inspired public relations campaign, and very effective."

"I don't give a damn about that bitch, or her publicity. You can beat the Vault. How many votes can you count on? You must have found out by now."

"None."

"None?" she shrieked. "How can that be?"

"I told you. The Vault has decided to take a hand."

"So fight them, Chilton. Show them what you're made of. Don't let those goddamned Van Horns back in."

"That's what really matters with you, isn't it, whether the Van Horns are made to suffer?"

She paused. "That's part of it, yes."

"Well, there's no hope, my dear. I have just dictated my letter of resignation. There's no point in even staying for the meeting. I'm in the process of packing up right now."

"You're gutless, Chilton. A real man would show fight."

"You'll have to seek your revenge in another arena, Roberta. It seems we've lost in this one." He paused. He was compelled to ask the question, although he dreaded the answer. "Now tell me the truth. Hunter Van Horn was one of your lovers, wasn't he?"

For a moment he wondered if she might have hung up, then he realized that her silence was her answer.

"I always thought so," he said quietly.

"And now you know." Her tone was suddenly formal, cold. "I'm sorry, Chilton, but I must go."

"You must really have hated Hunter. What did he do to you?"

Again there was a delay before she finally answered. "That doesn't matter anymore, does it?"

"I'll see you at home?"

"I think not," she said. "I don't think we have much to offer each other anymore."

"Roberta . . ."

"Good-bye, Chilton," she said coolly. "As they say, my lawyers will contact yours."

She hung up.

He replaced the receiver. He would miss her, but he was surprised at his feeling of relief. He slowly shook his head. He was getting old. Everything lately was becoming something of a chore, even love.

His tearful secretary brought in the finished letter. He read it again. It was good, there was no bitterness in it. At least he would go out on a decent note.

He signed it with a flourish.

Victoria entered the boardroom accompanied by her brother, Joyce Spitz and Jon Krugar, who had asked to come along. All of the board members were present except Bradford Lewis. His proposed replacement waited outside. A formal vote admitting him to the board would be taken later. There was much more pressing business to attend to first. The atmosphere in the room seemed charged with nervous anticipation, strongly tinged with the shadow of real fear.

Victoria walked to the empty chair at the head of the long table but remained standing. "Each of you has been provided with a copy of Mr. Vance's letter of resignation." As she spoke, Victoria vividly recalled Joyce's notes of what had been said about her at the last board meeting. She made it a point to make eye contact with the men who had made the unkind remarks. Some looked away, whether in shame or in anger, she couldn't determine. "Unless there is an objection, I will serve as temporary chairperson."

"So moved," said one of the Van Horn loyalists. His motion was immediately seconded. They quickly went through the parliamentary formalities without incident.

"The reason for this meeting is obvious," she said. "We are here to name a successor to the posts held by Mr. Vance."

"I nominate Victoria Van Horn." There was a note of triumph in the voice of the loyal board member as he grinned at her.

She shook her head. "I'm sorry, I'm not a candidate. As you know, I have my own development company and a major new project under way. That will take all of my time. I do appreciate the thought, however."

She noted the shocked surprise in their faces. She had been thinking about the company and its future; now she spoke those thoughts. "There are two offices to be filled: chairman of the board and president. Mr. Vance served in both capacities, but I don't think we should continue that precedent. The chairman, with the board, has the responsibility of setting the general goals of the company. The president's job is to see that those directions are carried out. I would like to place in nomination two names, one for each office."

She looked over at her brother, Joyce and Jon Krugar. They sat in chairs placed against one wall, well back from the board table. "A Van Horn founded this company, and a Van Horn has always served, with one recent exception, at the top. For chairman of the board, not only because of his experience, but also to maintain that tradition, I nominate my brother, Hunter Van Horn." She purposely left off the "junior."

For a moment it seemed as if her brother hadn't understood what she had said. Then, when he realized her meaning, he quickly put his hand over his eyes. Suddenly Victoria too had to fight back tears.

She continued. "The president should know everything about the company, every manager, every problem, every function. As far as I can determine, there is only one person who qualifies. My father recognized her abilities, and I recognize her instincts. I nominate Miss Joyce Spitz to be president."

Joyce, shocked, sat rigidly. For the first time in Victoria's memory Joyce Spitz looked frightened, even confused.

"I second Miss Van Horn's motion."

"I move we make the appointments unanimous."

The formal vote was taken quickly.

"That's settled," Victoria said. "We have many problems in this company. We must all put the past behind us and devote all our efforts to turning this company around."

She stepped back from the table. "But I'm just a visitor now. My brother will continue this meeting. Hunter?"

He had composed himself. To her surprise he gently embraced her and kissed her cheek. "Thank you, Vicky," he whispered. "You can't know what this means to me."

Victoria was on her way out when Joyce Spitz stopped her at the door. "I'm only your secretary, for God's sake," she whispered, trembling. "This will never work."

"You were my father's unofficial vice-president, and you know it. It will work out quite splendidly."

Joyce still looked frightened. "This is a dirty trick. What if I can't do the job?"

"Then they'll throw you out. But you'll do just fine, Joyce." She patted her arm. "You better get back in there. Good luck."

Jon Krugar lumbered after Victoria as she left the boardroom. His ancient fleshy face gave no indication of his opinion.

"Do you approve of my actions?" she asked.

His expression didn't change, but his surprisingly youthful eyes seemed to twinkle. "You are your father's daughter," he said, his voice deep but reedy. "As a matter of fact, although you didn't consult me first, I do approve. Your brother may not have the flair of you and your father, but he's probably basically sound, particularly since he's divested himself of that floozy wife of his. As to the Spitz girl, I'll trust your instincts. I approve, but I would like to know why you did it."

"Van Horn Enterprises is father's company, not mine. I have my own. And, very important to me, I have proved myself on my own. I intend to keep doing just that. When my new Hudson River project is done, I'll build another, and another after that. That's what I do best, and that's what I like."

A small smile ghosted across his lips. "And the Vault?"

She smiled. "They saved me, thanks to you and Luke Shaw, and I will never forget that. I'll try to make my contribution in the future. The Vault will have my complete loyalty. Remember, as I told you, I have always believed in New York."

He nodded. "The Chinese say the hunter is most successful in his own fields. It is important to know where you are and for what you hunt. I hope you do." Jon Krugar's face became solemn. "Should you ever need my help, you know you have it."

She took his hand. "There's no way I can adequately thank you for all you've done." She reached up and kissed his cheek.

When they reached the street Victoria turned and looked up at the soaring skyscraper. It could all have been hers, but she felt she had made the right choice.

The Van Horn Building: her father had built it to last, and it had.

She was her father's daughter, but she would build her own monuments.

28

Lunch at the Ritz had been superb by any standard; some said its food was the best in the world. If not, it certainly came close. But Luke had been inattentive. His potential clients pretended not to be impressed, acting with the indifferent aplomb that marked a true Parisian, but Luke knew even they were caught up by the famed elegance. Despite his lack of enthusiasm, or perhaps because of it, the deal was quickly sealed over the famed Ritz martinis.

He waited until his luncheon companions were gone. He had nothing planned for the afternoon, but he did not feel like returning to his sumptuous suite. He walked out the red-carpeted main entrance of the Ritz and stood a moment to look at the beauty of the Place Vendôme. The imperial splendor of the seventeenth-century architecture was awe-inspiring, the eye drawn toward its centerpiece, Napoleon's towering bronze and stone column.

Paris was a busy city, but the bustle was so different from New York, more rhythmic, more harmonious. There was an indefinable gentleness to the pace of the city and its people. He began to walk in the direction of Tuileries Gardens, passing by the elegant high-fashion shops.

The air was fragrant with the wonderful aroma of Paris. Flowers seemed to be everywhere.

He experienced an almost painful loneliness. This was all meant to be shared. Alone, it was only a reminder of an empty, pleasureless existence. Despite himself, once again he thought of Victoria Van Horn.

Luke wished she was there with him. In trying to escape his feelings, he had managed to pick the one spot in the world where everything served to remind him, and even taunt him.

He was tempted to return to the Ritz and call her; it seemed almost like an obsession. But he kept walking, strolling along, envious of the couples he saw.

Luke continued in the direction of the Seine. It was a beautiful day. He would find somewhere quiet where he could sit and watch the ever-present river fishermen, perhaps near the Pont Neuf. It was always peaceful there. Perhaps in that magic tranquillity he could think of something besides Victoria.

But he doubted it.

The flow of publicity had become a tidal wave. Her story held a basic appeal and fascination for the American press and public. Victoria was again besieged by newsmen, magazine writers and television people, but this time she didn't hide. Instinctively she realized she had to capitalize on this brief opportunity before the parade passed by. She would never again have such a golden chance to repair the damage done her by the Lytle affair.

Craig Hopkins postponed his return to law practice to work with bankers and contractors for her Hudson River project, freeing her to keep the hectic schedule of interviews and talk-show appearances. Although the pace was frantic, everything seemed to be falling into place.

Vicky had tried again to contact Luke Shaw to thank him. First he was unavailable, then his secretary said he had gone to Europe on business. It was clear enough that he didn't wish to see her. That bothered her more than she cared to admit even to herself.

But she had little time to reflect on anything as she raced from interview to interview. *Time* put her on its cover. She came out very well in the in-depth article. The magazine called her the female Iacocca of American business.

Her new popularity was even reflected in the tentative offers, for enormous sums, by magazines for rights to her "own" story. Victoria was amused but politely turned them down. She was building a new image, one that would be important to her credibility and business reputation. She was being careful to do nothing that might jeopardize that.

And it all seemed to be just the beginning.

Joyce Spitz had taken firm command at Van Horn Enterprises, and had already begun the major pruning she said would save the company. Victoria's brother seemed content to let Joyce have her head. Surprisingly, according to Joyce, he was proving to be a wise counselor. From Vicky's brief telephone conversations with him, telling of the long hours he and Joyce were putting in together to rebuild the company, she began to suspect that her brother's interest in Joyce might be becoming more than just business.

Despite her fierce schedule, and obvious success, sometimes it all seemed insignificant to her. Victoria Van Horn was once more at the top, but, as before, something seemed to be missing.

Vicky finished the taping of a national television show. She had appeared with the secretary of commerce and several leading economists. The show, to be shown on Sunday morning, had a very small but very select audience, consisting of the nation's business and banking leaders. It was a mark of respect and also recognition of her regained honor that she had been invited to sit on the panel.

She now used a limousine service to help her meet her tight schedule, since getting a cab in New York was always a problem and she couldn't afford even a few wasted moments. Time had become priceless.

She had a half hour before being interviewed by a writer from a leading Canadian magazine. She hurried back to her office, hoping to have a few minutes to talk to Craig Hopkins. Things seemed to be going splendidly with her new project, but she wanted an updated report.

Victoria noticed the elderly man in her waiting room as she walked through. Her secretary followed her into her private office.

"I know he's not on your schedule, but there's a very nice old gentleman out there who would like to talk to you."

"I saw him. Find out what he wants. I really don't have the time."

Her secretary smiled. "I tried, but he insists on talking to you. He's been here for hours."

Vicky sighed. "Probably wants me to invest in some harebrained scheme. Get rid of him." She looked up at her secretary. "Nicely, of course."

"Sure. His name is Preston Shaw. I thought you might know him."

"Shaw?"

"Yes."

Victoria thought for a moment. It was probably only a coincidence. Still, there was always the possibility that it wasn't. "Send him in," she said. "But tell him I can only spare him a few minutes."

Her secretary escorted the man into the office. He looked around, as if trying to discover some clue to the character of the occupant by carefully examining her surroundings.

"Please sit down, Mr. Shaw," Victoria said. "I have only a few minutes. I'm terribly busy today."

He eased himself into the leather chair with laborious effort. "The legs are going," he said in explanation. Finally settled, he sighed softly, then smiled. "You're even more lovely than your photographs."

"Thank you." Her tone was friendly but crisp. "Now, what can I do for you?"

"I'm not sure, really. My full name is Preston Shaw." His smile was disarming. "I suppose I must sound a bit like those television commercials; the ones where someone holds up a credit card while his name is typed across the screen. My sole claim to fame, it seems, is that I am the father of Lucas Shaw."

"You're Luke's father?"

His smile widened at her reaction. "The very same." He looked again at her office. "I like this place of yours. No nonsense, a place of business. Very direct. I suspect it reflects your basic attitude." He sighed. "May I call you Victoria?"

"Of course."

He nodded. "Victoria, I have had very little input into my son's life. Luke was raised, primarily, by his famous uncle. I never concerned myself with his education, I'm afraid, or very much else."

He chuckled. "All this is preamble to what I'm about to say. Although I never interfered in Luke's life before, and therefore have little practice at it, I feel I must now."

Preston Shaw didn't physically resemble his son, but there was something about his eyes that reminded her of Luke and tugged at her feelings.

"My son came to see me just before he left for Europe," he continued. "Our relationship over the past years has been restricted to weekly dinners." He chuckled again. "Usually confined to lectures by me about my profound theories. But this time our meeting was a bit different."

"Oh?"

He nodded. "Luke has been married. He has a son, now being raised by his ex-wife and her new husband. Luke's marriage wasn't a disaster, but there never seemed to be any real passion on either side in that relationship. Their divorce was matter-of-fact, even friendly. Despite all that, perhaps because of it, my son has carefully avoided committing himself to any kind of meaningful relationship." His smile became almost wistful. "I have an opinion on everything, and I believe he's frightened of real passion. It's too risky for him. He likes to be in control at all times."

"Why are you telling me all this?"

His clear blue eyes seemed to be making a careful appraisal. "Luke has fled to Europe. He has business there, but it could have been done easily by any number of subordinates in his company. He never said it in so many words, but he's afraid he has fallen in love with you. So, rather than risk involvement, he has absented himself. Passion, my dear, can be very frightening to someone who has never known it. I'm afraid that's the case with my son."

"He's never said anything to me, Mr. Shaw, never once. And his actions have always been, well, gentlemanly. We were never lovers."

He sighed. "New York has become foreign to me, although I've lived here all my life. I seldom venture out from my club. But I did come out today, perhaps foolishly, because I would like my son to have the opportunity to know the richness of life. I too have avoided commitment, perhaps; in a way, even life itself. I wouldn't want my son to end up an ancient, archaic creature whose only world is books and a history not his own."

Vicky felt stunned, suddenly aware that her heart was pounding at a frantic rate.

"I've taken too much of your time, Victoria. I feel embarrassed. It's a bit late in life for me to become a father." He sighed. "I suppose I should have taken lessons."

She felt suddenly giddy, almost reckless. "There's no need to apologize, Mr. Shaw. Do you know where Luke is now?"

He pushed himself up awkwardly from the chair. "He's in Paris. He's staying at the Ritz. That's a bit upscale for my son, but he's trying to impress some French officials in the hope they'll award some contracts to his company."

His smile became impish. "By the way, I knew your grandmother. She was quite a gal, at least in the terms of those days." He turned to go. "Good luck to you, my dear."

"Do you think that I should go to Paris?" She asked the question as he reached the door.

His smile became quite gentle. "That's really up to you, isn't it?" He closed the door after him.

She sat quietly, her mind filled with images of Luke Shaw. Strong and rugged, he was also gentle and caring; he had more than proved that. His father seemed perceptive. Perhaps Luke Shaw was afraid of commitment. Perhaps she was, too. She wondered if what she felt might really be love.

There had been other men in her life, but she had never taken that final step, had never given herself totally. Some, like Craig Hopkins, had been fine and honorable, but they had lacked that something she could never quite define. Others, like Barry Lytle, possessed a compelling magic, but there was nothing of substance beneath their temporary spell. Luke Shaw was different from anyone she had ever known.

Her secretary announced the Canadian magazine writer, who proved to be young, pleasant enough, but insistent upon answers that conformed to pre-existing theories she had formed. Victoria found it difficult to concentrate during the interview, her thoughts returning to Luke Shaw.

Finally it was over. The writer left and Vicky was once more alone.

She sat back and idly studied the artist's rendering of her new project. It covered half the wall. She could almost imagine how it would be when completed. It would be her crowning achievement. It would be beautiful, but it was still a dream. There was so much left to do.

She tried to concentrate on the picture, tried to call up the iron determination that nothing could be more important to her than the Hudson River project, but she failed. Memories of Paris filled her thoughts. Each large city—London, New York, even Hong Kong—had its own personality, its own distinctive rhythm. But Paris was different from all the others. It was romantic and magical, a place conjured up for lovers.

It was spring. Poets had long celebrated the charm of Paris and its tree-lined streets in that special time of the year when everything came so wonderfully alive. It was the city of the ultimate passion, the passion for living.

She thought about Jon Krugar. He had said that the important thing in life was to know what you really wanted and then to go after it. Victoria buzzed her secretary. "Book me on the next flight to Paris. I don't care what airlines. And make reservations for me at the Ritz, if possible. If not, then at any good hotel near there."

"Now?"

"Yes."

"But you have so much scheduled: the newspapers, then the . . ."

"Cancel everything."

"Everything?"

"Tell Mr. Hopkins he is in charge. I don't know when I'll be back. It could be in a few days, or it could be longer."

She would have to hurry and throw some things into a bag. She could shop in Paris for anything she might forget. She grabbed her purse and walked past her startled secretary.

The girl looked at her as if she had suddenly gone mad. "Miss Van Horn, it's none of my business, but what will you be doing in Paris?"

She smiled. "I'm going hunting."